THE BARILLA CHRONICLES

THE
JOSEPH CAMPANELLA
JOURNEY

BY

DANIEL ROBINSON

Some long-standing institutions, agencies, and public offices are real, but this novel's story is fictitious as are most characters. The views expressed in this work are solely those of the author and do not necessarily reflect the views of the publisher, and the publisher hereby disclaims any responsibility for them.

No part of this book may be reproduced, stored in a retrieval system, or transmitted by any means without the written permission of the author.

ISBN/SKU:979-8-218-73425-1

This book is dedicated to my father, Donald E Robinson. His enthusiasm and encouragement throughout my life was an inspiration for me to succeed at all things I do.

Love you Dad,

A special thanks to my editor and audio narrator, Adam Picot. He jumped in and became an integral part of the final edition of this novel. His ideas and suggestions on improving the manuscript were awesome!

Thanks, Adam.

The Barilla Chronicles

Table of Contents

If Time is really only a fourth dimension of Space, why is it, and why has it always been, regarded as something different. And cannot we move in Time as we move about in the other dimensions of Space?

H. G. Wells – The Time Machine

PROLOGUE

"Suicide Hill"

US Army Training Facility, New Mexico

The United States military had used the secluded mountain course, deep within the Gila National Forest in southwest New Mexico, for more than thirty years. Though it did not feature the longest endurance test of the military's training courses, at eleven and a half miles, it was, nevertheless, the most grueling. The first eight-mile segment tested the average cadet's limits, but the balance of the arduous route stood millennia in the making and remained achievable for only a select few.

The upper mountain run totaled three-point-one vertical miles of zigzagging, treacherous, and often man-eating trails. Winding through handsome stands of soaring Lodgepole Pines at the lower level, the course soon gave way to tangled brushy patches of cacti and sage as you climbed.

Although the towering peak remained majestic, this appeal to beauty and grandeur soon crumbled as the mountain's perils hastily vanquished the contenders. This was especially true as weather conditions often declined from bad to worse in the blink of an eye.

In the winter, prolonged subfreezing temperatures near the summit could freeze the unprepared into stupefied blocks of frozen flesh. Conversely, during the summer months, when the climate frequently averaged ninety-five degrees on the lower section of the run, individuals often dropped, weak from dehydration and soaked in sweat. The terrain swarmed with stinging bugs, venomous snakes, biting insects, and scrubs whose thorns sliced through uniforms and exposed flesh like a knife through soft butter.

Most cadets would complete the lower section with little difficulty. However, getting to the halfway point of the mountain's higher portion was often considered a victory. Those who somehow advanced farther rarely made it to the actual summit. If they did, they did so with grave physical consequences.

In essence, the mountain course, recognized by the overwhelmed trainees as "Suicide Mountain," came as close to Dante's Inferno as any training facility in the U.S. military. These facts were well documented, which made the events of March 1, 1999, even more extraordinary. And yet, the efforts recognized this day became mere glimpses of what would occur many, many years in the past...

PART 1

CHAPTER 1

SUPERMAN?

March 1, 1999

"What's his time?" the gravel-voiced Major asked as he scanned his sightline of the trail below.

"Remarkable," the man with the stopwatch muttered. "If he arrives as expected, he'll record his best run to date. A run, I might add, which will destroy the record for finishing that any man has ever managed on this godforsaken mountain."

The Major, his aviator sunglasses positioned low on his aquiline nose, grunted a skeptical "humph."

"So, is your Superman going to show or not?"

Glancing with disdain at the stiff-backed officer, the timer couldn't hold back a hint of frustration, "I'm fully aware of this soldier's capabilities, and I am confident he'll be here soon. In fact," the timer added while scanning his notes and stopwatch, "based on checkpoint updates, he should arrive within the next, oh, forty-five seconds or so."

Unseen by these two men at a location no more than fifty yards away, Sergeant Brant Montgomery made an unscheduled change of course to his right. This lengthened the already backbreaking route, but the detour was created for a purpose.

The soldier knew that he'd reach his ultimate destination on time, as a check on his ops watch attested, but his mind was focused on two potential complications. Along this new route, scouted during the previous day's training, he had discovered a twenty-foot-wide, fifty-foot-deep ravine filled with jagged, bone-breaking boulders. But even this wasn't his biggest worry. His fear was that as he soared over the span, the observers above might spot him.

Though big and powerfully built, the six-foot-three-inch, 225-pound Marine executed a catlike maneuver over a large rock before scooting under a low-hanging branch of a stumpy Pinyon Pine. He moved with a ballet dancer's finesse yet at a pace that was seemingly unmanageable for a man his size.

The trainee hurdled several more obstructions before spotting the ravine a dozen or so paces ahead. His mind worked automatically, calculating the number of steps needed for the ensuing vault. Like a long jumper timing his last step to absolute perfection, the Marine's jump began mere inches from the chasm's threshold. Gliding gazelle-like, he cleared the span with ease. A victorious hurdle and one he hoped had gone off undetected.

Once on the other side, the soldier took two additional strides and then dug his right heel into the earth, readying his body for a hard left turn. Though he was now confronted by a fifteen-foot, forty-five-degree ridge, he easily scaled the slope in three huge bounds. Coming to rest at the ridge's crest, he hid behind a thick stand of scrub brush located between him and his unsuspecting victims.

He checked his watch again. Ten seconds remained until his assessors expected him to arrive. Montgomery slid silently down a small embankment, then crept toward the finish line with an assassin's stealth.

As he approached the two men, less than five paces away, their polar opposite personalities were starkly revealed by their proximity. On the left, peering at his stopwatch in anxious anticipation, stood the world-renowned surgeon and Nobel Prize-winning scientist, Dr. Dylan Blackwell. All of five feet two, balding, and wiry thin, the fifty-nine-year-old Peter Lorre clone was spoken of in the same breath as Lister, Pasteur, and Archimedes.

Over a tireless span of ten years, Blackwell had toiled on a ground-breaking drug called NM 19-57. Injected at the time of surgery, the radical formula triggered a micro-molecular healing process that far exceeded the body's standard regenerative capabilities. In essence, patients recovered exponentially faster with the injection than those who did not. Yet, the most remarkable effect was revealed once the procedure's curative properties fully developed within the host. At this point, the injured party's bodies became significantly stronger and more disease-resistant than before their injuries.

Sergeant Brant Montgomery, the soldier currently clambering Suicide Hill, was among the first human test cases for NM 19-57's unique involvement. He had suffered devastating wounds while deployed in Kuwait during Operation Desert Thunder. As fate would have it, a series of felicitous events brought him squarely onto the doctor's radar. Now, close to a year later, Montgomery's physical and sensory attributes provided real-life proof of the astonishing effects of the doctor's miracle serum. Blackwell hoped that those results were now going to be displayed in magnificent fashion to the man standing next to him — the stone-faced, rod-up-his-ass, Major James "Scarface" Pittman.

Nicknamed Scarface early in his military career, the moniker referenced, along with his demeanor, the jagged lightning-shaped scar that danced a zigzagging, three-inch slash down the right side of his face. Starting from just below his right eye and ending a tick above his jawline, it was the first thing you saw and the last thing you remembered about the man.

The startling wound was the result of an unfortunate parachuting mishap. Dropped from 3,500 feet during a routine training exercise, the then-youthful Corporal Pittman had been blown off course by unexpected gale-force winds. Gusts of up to forty miles per hour had forced him into a vast stand of trees instead of the intended landing location.

As he plunged through the top of a massive seventy-five-foot-tall oak tree, a pointed branch, hardened by wind and rain, shot through his open mouth. The unforgiving limb ripped a gaping hole in his cheek, resulting in thirty-seven stitches and agonizing weeks of sucking liquified slop through a straw.

Already a formidable-looking man with foreboding eyes and severe, angular cheekbones, this violent feature gave the soldier an uncompromisingly fierce grimace. To add to the oddity of the scar, the blemish transformed from a slight pink hue to a deep, pulsating red whenever the man was irritated, which was often.

"Your caped crusader's not going to show. We would have seen him by now if he was," Pittman gloated. "I knew this whole thing would turn out to be a bunch of comic-book superhero horseshit." He glowered at the doctor with derision and annoyance. "What a goddamn waste of time and government resources."

The Major had never believed the hype he'd heard about Montgomery, not for a minute. He was sure the man's accomplishments were big-fish embellishments at best. After all, a man so horribly injured only months before couldn't possibly beat the record of every soldier who had ever struggled to scale Suicide Hill, and certainly not by the enormous margins claimed. He should know; he'd trained nearly a quarter of the men who'd traversed the lower and upper mountain routes.

Before the start of this latest exercise, and with Pittman scrutinizing them within earshot, Blackwell had offered his last words of encouragement to Montgomery. The two discussed in detail the progress in Brant's general health, as well as in his increased abilities and efficiencies. Montgomery had listened earnestly despite being told nothing he didn't already know.

Once he was sure Pittman could not hear, Blackwell stressed, "Brant, this last run is *vital* for the future of this project. Do you understand? There can be no doubt about your capabilities. Major Pittman needs irrefutable evidence that you're not only fit but in an elite realm of physical health that he cannot yet imagine." At these words a devilish smile had crossed Montgomery's face, and he shot up the mountain.

"Time?" Pittman barked.

The doctor studied his stopwatch and commenced a countdown of his self-projected deadline, "five, four, three, two …"

CHAPTER 2

Montgomery, now no more than a breath away from the two observers, brazenly chimed in – "ONE!" The startled men whirled around, almost jumping out of their shoes as they did.

"God damn it, Brant, why do you always do shit like that? Are you trying to give me a myocardial infarction?" the surgeon exclaimed in his typical doctor talk.

Pittman reacted in an equally alarmed way, except no actual words escaped his lips. To Montgomery's amusement, only a loud guttural gasp emerged as the soldier spun toward the sergeant's surprising arrival. Unfortunately, this whirling reaction also triggered an unexpected result. As the major's left boot flew backward, loose gravel initiated a slide. Pittman's arms began windmilling as he teetered on the edge.

When a tumble down the steep slope became inevitable, Montgomery's lightning reflexes took over. He shot out a hand and grabbed the bulging-eyed 240-pound officer by the top of his shoulders. Half picked up, half dragged, Montgomery hauled the man from the brink of disaster as if plucking a small child up from the ground.

"So Sorry," Montgomery said with dripping sarcasm as he used his hands to straighten out the Major's now crumpled and disjointed uniform. "I was hoping to put a different spin on the day's training routine. Keep you on your toes, so to speak."

Pittman swiped Montgomery's hands away while glaring at the sergeant with cynical, disbelieving eyes. He held his gaze for several tense seconds before turning his stare toward Blackwell. Out of pure frustration, the shaken officer snatched the stopwatch from the doctor's grasp. As his infamous scar deepened in color to a now pulsating purplish red, he yanked his sunglasses off and studied the timer with blazing eyes before glowering back at Montgomery.

"I don't give a rat's ass what this thing reads. This time is not possible," Pittman said, appearing dumbfounded and thoroughly agitated. "No amount of training could allow you to run the course this fast. Not by…" he glanced down at the timer again, "FORTY GOD DAMN MINUTES!"

"Forty-nine minutes," Blackwell chimed in.

"Horseshit!" Pittman blustered as he took a somewhat aggressive step toward Montgomery. "What kind of crap are you two trying to feed me? I'm not sure why anyone thinks they can pull one over on me of all people," the irate Major said, anger-induced spittle flying from his lips. "But I can assure you of this: I will get to the bottom of it right now!"

Though the enraged Pittman had moved within inches of the sergeant's face, Montgomery gave no ground. After a second or two more of this macho posturing, with neither man speaking nor giving up their personal space, a transformation began to occur in one of the combatants. A slight yet noticeable smirk formed on Montgomery's face while his body tensed with a rigidity that appeared unnatural in appearance. The man's shirt appeared to ruffle as his muscles bulged even more than they did normally.

Sensing nothing good coming from the standoff, Blackwell strode over and wedged himself between the much larger men. As he did, Montgomery took a few respectful steps backward. The scientist, all 145 stiffened pounds of him, raised his scowl at the taller Pittman. His eyes narrowed, and in a voice that sounded bigger and more forceful than his body should be able to justify, he declared, "Major, now that you have personally witnessed the sergeant's efforts, all questions will be answered during tonight's briefing."

The doctor stepped back slightly before continuing. "Just to be clear, we purposely left out details of plans for this man so that you wouldn't be influenced by anything other than his performance. And I think you'll have to agree that Sergeant Montgomery has accomplished every possible physical goal we've asked of him. Therefore, I suggest we go to base camp and hold off on any questions or conclusions until the briefing tonight."

Blackwell didn't wait for Pittman to answer. He simply spun toward Montgomery. Peering up at the sergeant through twinkling eyes, he winked in satisfaction and ushered the soldier to a waiting Jeep some thirty feet away. Pittman stared in disbelief at the two departing men. He was incensed, but somehow, the doctor had stolen his ability to continue the argument.

The Jeep's driver dropped Montgomery off at his quarters ten minutes later. Blackwell left him with instructions to clean up and be back in the Major's temporary office at 1730 hours. Once inside, Montgomery undressed and walked from his room toward his shower. On his way, he caught an appearance of his body as he passed a full-length mirror. He'd seen his image in this mirror countless times over the previous few months; however, this time, he involuntarily paused and reflected.

****

Though Desert Storm had long since ended, Iraq had returned to the world's critical eye as the country refused to obey the mandatory weapons inspections imposed on them from that conflict. In time, this rejection by the Iraqis would prompt fresh infusions of U.S. and NATO military personnel into the area. Montgomery, by then a Senior Explosive Ordnance Disposal technician, became a member of the corps stationed in Kuwait at Camp Doha. In addition to being one of the best EODs in the military, Montgomery proved to be a fierce fighting machine.

The U.S. Armed Services understood the dangers of EODs working in such proximity to hot combat zones. Due to this they mandated training inspired by the Special Forces. This preparation gave Montgomery a distinct advantage over any foe he might encounter while performing his ordinance disposal duties. On several occasions, the Sergeant more than held his own in lethal confrontations.

During Montgomery's last tour in Iraq, a local informant apprised the company's Intel Officer of a significant cache of hidden explosives. These weapons had been concealed in an abandoned building some twenty clicks outside of the camp's boundaries. The informer provided a precise position, even going so far as to pinpoint the exact dilapidated floorboards under which the weapons lay.

Sergeant Brant Montgomery, the Senior-Badge EOD tech on base, was assigned to the disposal task of the derelict armaments. At 0545 on the day of the operation, Montgomery, with four men to a vehicle, loaded two military-equipped Humvees with their gear and headed out.

The pre-dawn air was unusually cold, which caused low blanketing clouds to cover the already bleak terrain. This atmospheric condition gave the sky over the tiny Middle Eastern country a painted black appearance, making traveling the desert roads problematic. With the Humvee's lights partially obscured, a standard precaution during armed conflicts, the pair of armored vehicles settled on a speed of thirty miles an hour, as fast as the pockmarked dirt road allowed.

The G.I.s in his task force consisted of veterans in the art of weapons removal and demolition. Hard-edged, experienced individuals with honed skills and stout nerves. However, no pre-education or training could have prevented what happened that ill-fated morning. With the sun still yet to rise, the Humvees had traveled a tad shy of ten clicks from their compound when they came to a slight bend in the narrow lane. As the lead vehicle navigated the dimly lit pathway, its right front tire rolled over an IED buried just below the rocky surface.

The ebony-blanketed night erupted in a giant orange and yellow ball of fire that sent the 5,600-pound Humvee soaring twenty feet above the road, fuel tank ablaze.

Private Herbert Anderson, the driver of the second Humvee, made an instantaneous evasive maneuver, swerving away from the carnage and piloting his vehicle around a massive crater formed by the blast. The rest of the crew sat in stunned horror as the mangling Humvee tumbled through the air, vomiting out a conglomeration of metal chunks, glass, and automotive fluids. But that wasn't all. Mid-air, the right passenger door flew open, and a human figure jettisoned out.

In a moment the surviving G.I.s later described as horrifically surreal, the body cartwheeled like a rag doll, arms and legs flopping and flailing wildly. The limp form arced away from the Humvee some forty feet before skidding and tumbling into a heap. Once the body had come to a merciful halt, it didn't move. The injured soldier lay on the road in a crumpled mass of bleeding and charred flesh.

As the second Humvee came to a screeching halt, the surviving men's training kicked in. Anderson called in the accident. Specialist Phillip Ryan Johnson and Corporal Donny Evans grabbed two fire extinguishers. Specialist James Ogden, the last soldier spilling out, seized the First-Aid bag and ran at breakneck speed to the inert body on the ground.

Ogden fully expected the man lying there to be dead. When he arrived at the injured man's side, he knew he must be right. What remained of the soldier was a blood-soaked mess, with arms and legs bent at grossly abnormal angles.

Even the most seasoned veteran might be stunned into inaction by this grotesque sight, but Ogden didn't hesitate. He initiated a quick check of his comrade's vitals, made difficult by the vast areas of torn and mangled flesh.

Ogden detected a faint yet definitive pulse.

Private Anderson yelled out from the idling vehicle for the man's name and condition as their base commander requested a radioed update. Retrieving a small flashlight from a pack on his belt, Ogden switched on the beam and gently pulled the man's shoulder enough to see the face. He gasped and swallowed back a heaving gag. He couldn't stop himself from turning away and closing his eyes to try to erase the dreadful image.

The soldier stayed like this for a dozen or more pounding heartbeats until another shout from Anderson jerked the young soldier back to the job. His eyes bolted open as he willed himself to continue. Jumping to the other side of the injured man, he shined the light on the battered soldier's nametag. Ogden stared at the cloth identifier, but the tag was smeared with the same soiled mixture covering the body. He wiped the label several times with his thumb to get a clear view…it was Montgomery.

Later, when asked to describe the scene, Specialist Johnson, the twenty-six-year-old son of a catfish farmer from southern Mississippi, said, "The Sarge shot out of the Hummer like someone spat out a spent wad of chewin' tobacca. By far the God-awfulest thing I ever seen. You wouldna believed the way his arms and legs were flying ever which-a-way. And then – SPLAT," he said as he whacked his fist into the palm of his hand. "He smacked the ground like a wet bag of manure dropped from the top of a two-story barn! - SPLAT!" He added again for effect, "Sure thought he was a goner…"

In short order, Montgomery was airlifted in a UH-60Q Medevac Helicopter to the base's field hospital. Once in the trauma unit, the medical team went to work with expert efficiency.

The list of injuries was extensive. Montgomery had suffered multiple broken bones, a ruptured spleen, and a collapsed lung. His left shoulder was dislocated, and he had tendon and ligament damage. Large chunks of flesh hung from gaping wounds, and over twenty percent of his body received second and third-degree burns. However, the severe head injury suffered by one or more roadway impacts during his somersaulting was the most concerning issue. In the early stages of this diagnosis, it was considered that he might be permanently brain-impaired.

The Camp Doha doctors worked with relentless fervor through surgeries and procedures lasting well into the following day. They set the damaged bones. A tube was inserted below the sergeant's left armpit to address his collapsed lung. The staff's burn unit treated the singed flesh and the remaining superficial wounds. However, the ligament and tendon damage to the knees, ankles, and shoulders all needed specialized attention, as did the critical head trauma.

Captain Neal O'Hearn, an Army neurosurgeon stationed in Germany at the Landstuhl Regional Medical Center, was flown in to evaluate the cranial issue. Once at the hospital, he quickly determined the base facility did not possess the needed equipment to undertake the intense surgery this injury required. A flight back to Landstuhl was ordered for Montgomery's survival.

To make the long trip with his injuries in their current condition, the doctor put Montgomery into a medically induced coma to limit any additional debilitating distress. O'Hearn knew that there was a chance, a significant one, in fact, that Montgomery wouldn't make it through the long flight. However, without the specialized attention, he would surely die, or, at the very least, be brain-damaged beyond repair.

While final preparations were made for the journey, O'Hearn forwarded Montgomery's medical reports to the Medical Center. Without the doctor's knowledge, the information sent was intercepted, secretly siphoned, and encrypted. The patient's data ended its journey in a secret clinic near Los Alamos, New Mexico, setting off a facility-wide alert. A mere handful of people in the entire world knew of the Los Alamos clinic, and those who worked there began to ready themselves with eager anticipation after a wait of nearly five years.

CHAPTER 3

Upon receipt, Montgomery's data sparked immediate action. Commands raced electronically through international digital channels, prompting an immediate diversion of Montgomery's travel destination. After a mid-air refueling over England, his plane was vectored to the United States for a landing in eastern Pennsylvania. Once on the ground, a new flight crew was added, the fuel tanks were topped off, and the plane took off to a desolate airfield in New Mexico.

Five hours later, the jet completed its final approach toward the 2500-foot runway, at the end of which an ambulance sat waiting. The unmarked vehicle would carry the patient to the secret Los Alamos complex, where a large staff of doctors were expecting his arrival. Included in the arranged team of specialists was Dr. Dylan Blackwell, who had arrived that day to prepare for the surgeries he knew would be required.

The initial eleven-hour surgery to mend Montgomery's head injury was led by Dr. Phillip Bronson of Johns Hopkins, with the pioneering NM–1957 already at work within his system. Thanks to meticulous planning and execution, the team faced no complications.

Subsequent surgeries by the acclaimed Dr. Herbert Mason from Mt. Sinai tackled the intricate ligament and tendon repairs. Recovery proceeded impressively under the careful watch of the attending neurosurgeons.

Within days, Montgomery started speaking. Three weeks later, he was walking. Soon after that, an intense total physical therapy regimen began. The team presumed that these events couldn't have occurred as quickly or with the subsequent results without Blackwell's serum.

Prior to Montgomery, only three individuals had received Blackwell's experimental drug, and none of these had produced similar results. When developing the serum, Blackwell discovered that A.B. Rh-negative blood types were required for the serum to perform at its greatest effectiveness. Other blood types produced far less intrinsic healing advantages. Unfortunately, AB Rh-negative is the rarest blood type on the planet, with fewer than one percent of the population possessing it.

In 1991, a construction worker in Sweden suffered a dozen severe injuries after falling three stories while working on a new apartment building. The injured man, Karl Johansson, was patient number one for Blackwell's latest iteration of the drug. A large man, not quite twenty-four years old, Johansson, broke his legs, left arm, and wrist. He experienced a fractured skull, although no brain damage, and lost five teeth. In ordinary situations, issues of this kind would require painstaking surgeries with long recuperation and recovery times.

Many of life's experiences revolve around a combination of luck and fate. In Johansson's case, both would play a significant role in allowing him to receive the serum. Blackwell had lectured on his new technology at the University of Sweden just weeks before Johanson's accident. Dr. Olaf Ahlberg, the chief surgeon at the Danderyd Hospital in Stockholm, attended the speech and spoke at length with Blackwell about his project.

Dr. Ahlberg was called in when the ambulance rushed the muscular construction worker into the Emergency Room. During his initial review of the medical charts, he immediately noted the A.B. Rh-negative blood type and called Blackwell.

"Dr. Blackwell, I've found your first test subject. Multiple injuries and A.B. Rh-negative blood," Ahlberg gushed through the receiver.

With great excitement, Blackwell chartered a flight back to Stockholm. Hours later, the Swedish surgeon initiated the surgery, assisted by Blackwell and his serum. Typical recuperation periods for this type of injury and the ensuing follow-up procedures would be counted in months and sometimes more than a year. Johansson recovered in weeks, healing in miraculous fashion and becoming stronger and healthier than before his accident.

Patients two and three were Americans Paul Jeffries, a firefighter from Pennsylvania, and Harry Morton, a food service salesperson in South Florida. Jefferies was injured while fighting a house fire when a weakened rafter collapsed on him. Morton had been involved in a five-car pile-up on I-95 in Miami.

Each of these men possessed A.B. Rh-negative blood and significant physical impairments. And both received Blackwell's therapy with astounding results. However, despite these successes under the doctor's belt, there were still individuals unsure if the achievements of NM-1957 would be replicated with the most seriously injured of the patients so far, Sergeant Montgomery.

For several anxiety-filled days, the assemblage of surgeons and support teams waited for signs of improvement with their patient – but they didn't have to wait long. In an astoundingly short period of time, Montgomery's recovery and developed abilities would far exceed the previous test subjects.

Later, when pressed to explain his patient's incredible, almost superhuman qualities, Blackwell would posit the theory that the man's cranial trauma triggered it. As the other patients had not experienced similar head injuries, Blackwell determined the interaction of Montgomery's rare blood type with his formula's unique properties may have provoked a hyperactive rebuilding progression as his brain healed.

Though not Superman, Montgomery was undoubtedly the closest any human had gotten to being a superhero.

CHAPTER 4

Montgomery scoffed at his image and turned away from the mirror. After showering, he dressed in a pressed uniform and headed toward the Major's office.

The night air was cold, and the sky was clear except for the occasional passing cloud that caused the almost full moonlight to flicker. Montgomery breathed deeply through his nostrils, fully inhaling the fresh spring aromas of Honeysuckle and wild peppermint surrounding the military base. He was reminded of the scents from the day's run on the mountain, and a low and full laugh bubbled in his belly and up through his throat at the memory of Pittman's bulging eyes and flailing arms – a scene right out of a Looney Tunes cartoon.

Suddenly, without an apparent cause, an unusual and unexpected apprehension snaked through his body. The sensation crept up his spine, and the hair on his neck bristled. An internal siren was wailing as his hyperactive nervous system sensed something out of place.

He and Doctor Blackwell often discussed the serum's results on his body and abilities. His muscle and bone strength were now off the charts, and he could best any other human in any physical feat. But they still didn't fully grasp how the drug had affected his sensory faculties.

They did know, though, that the results were incredible. Montgomery could read the smallest letters on the most challenging eye exams – dozens of paces away. His sense of smell and taste was also enhanced, which took some time to get used to, as certain smells were exacerbated to uncomfortable levels. His auditory perception had also vastly exceeded normal ranges. In fact, he found he needed to train himself on ways to tune out nearby sounds and conversations so that they didn't overwhelm him.

At times, these curious situations of cognizance caused inexplicable moments of hyperreality. Those occurrences included sensing when someone or something would soon enter the room or round a blind corner – many seconds before they did. Or a knowledge of being observed, which is precisely what he felt now.

Dropping into a defensive crouch, Montgomery allowed his formidable perceptions to take in the surrounding area. He'd always possessed decent night vision. Yet his newly enhanced eyesight permitted him to peer through the darkness with high-definition results. He scanned every inch of the base but realized no irregularities.

Taking a deep, mind-cleansing breath, he focused on a single light at the far side of the compound. Staring at the glowing object with incredible intensity, he listened for the slightest of noises. It was like being in a self-induced vacuum as he culled out the night's natural hums until he could only perceive uncommon sounds.

Nothing.

Though the hairs on his neck remained danger-stiffened and alert, Montgomery rose to his full height. He did a final 360-degree scan and still perceived nothing. Yet, the feeling someone or something had been there persisted. Pursing his lips in irritation, he let out a frustrated breath and continued toward his destination.

Arriving at the Major's building at 1728 hours, Montgomery walked in after knocking sharply to announce his arrival. Corporal Willard Stone, one of the few soldiers not involved in his training, sat at a desk just to the right of the Major's door. He acknowledged the Sergeant's entry with a nod.

"Go right in, Sergeant. They've been waiting twenty minutes already," he urged.

Montgomery passed through the Major's entryway and completed an automatic appraisal of his environment in barely the time needed to take an inward breath. The rectangular office, which Montgomery estimated to be twenty feet by twenty-five feet, was bleak and virtually unadorned.

Located along the back wall were four double-hung windows with shades fully closed on three and pulled halfway down on the fourth.

Florescent ceiling lights lit the room. There were four, but one was dark. This gave the drab gray walls an even more depressing shade of dull. The only adornment was a single picture of the current President, Bill Clinton, hanging on the north-facing wall. The portrait was positioned above a metal desk that had seen better times.

On the desk sat a calendar pad with no calendar. To the right of the pad was a black push-button phone, and next to the phone a round cup stuffed with pens and pencils of various sorts. The last object in the room was a weathered leather armchair pushed in behind the desk. With a stiffened grin, Montgomery considered how the office perfectly reflected the no-nonsense and bland Major Pittman.

Inanimate objects now fully cataloged; Montgomery focused on the ten men occupying the room. Six of these wore military uniforms, and four were in civilian clothes. Scanning their faces, he recognized Blackwell, Major Pittman, Sergeant Major Artie Johnson, and Sergeant Major Reginald Bates. Johnson and Bates were senior training team members, but the rest of the individuals in the room were strangers.

"Ah, Brant, punctual as always," Dr. Blackwell said as he observed the Sergeant enter. "Gentlemen, this is our man, Sergeant Brant Montgomery."

An officer with two silver stars on each shoulder wasted no time, covering the ten meters between them in rapid strides. Five foot ten with a stocky, squarish build, the man sported a graying crew cut and a thin salt and pepper mustache. The soldier introduced himself as Major General Samuel S. Dunston and produced his hand in welcome as he did.

Two colonels came next: Colonel Michael Bratton and Colonel Omar Sullivan. Both men bore U.S. Army Intelligence insignia on their uniforms. Neither had any unique facial characteristics, though Sullivan appeared older, and Bratton walked with a slight limp.

After these came Lieutenant Colonel Aldo Rosselli, whom Montgomery quickly discovered was a specialist in linguistics, or more to the point, phonetics – the science of the sounds of language.

"Delighted to make your acquaintance, Sergeant Montgomery," Rosselli said with a crisp, British accent you might hear in a 1950s BBC news broadcast. Though Italian, he had been Eton and Oxford educated and seemed to revel in his mastery of affected accents of the British upper class. "I am Lieutenant Colonel Rosselli," pronouncing his rank with a 'left' rather than a 'loo.' As he spoke, his mouth moved in cartoonishly exaggerated movements, and Montgomery had to greatly resist releasing the laughter roiling inside his chest.

Colonel Anthony Palermo, the last attendee in uniform, mercifully pushed past the still-speaking Rosselli. A wisp of a man, Palermo stood no more than five-foot-tall and 135 pounds – soaking wet. His hair was jet black and was parted with razor-sharp precision on the left side of his scalp. Its growth was exuberant, flopping over in a pronounced outcropping before cascading down the other side of his head. Palermo's eyes sparkled crystal blue, and his broad, confident smile was accented by a disarmingly large gap between the middle of his top two front teeth.

When he reached Montgomery, he bypassed the Sergeant's outstretched hand and instead bearhugged the surprised man as if reuniting with a long-lost family member. After several amusing, if not slightly awkward, moments for Montgomery, Palermo finally moved back and grabbed his hand. He shook the appendage with vigorous enthusiasm while repeating over and over, "Buon Giorno, Buon Giorno, Buon Giorno…"

The two chatted briefly, though Palermo did most of the talking. Then Major Pittman pushed his way brusquely into the group. Once he got near Montgomery, his hand extended in an almost robotic, choppy movement. The Sergeant hesitated a second before reciprocating with his own.

"Sergeant Montgomery, this isn't easy for me, but I apologize for my earlier behavior. You gotta understand my reluctance to accept the results the training crew provided. You see, I personally trained hundreds of young men on Suicide Hill, and your timings were…well, unbelievable – until tonight. I guess I'm a stubborn son of a gun," he said while eyeing the others around him in an apparent effort to gain some sympathy.

Montgomery did not verbally respond, only nodding slightly in agreement.

"Yeah, um," Pittman stammered, "Anyway, I spent the last two hours reviewing your training data with the instructors, and…well, I'm impressed. Christ, to be honest, I'm flabbergasted. You're an amazing soldier, goddammit, and I am sorry to have ever doubted you," Pittman said.

Again, Montgomery nodded in answer, this time with the hint of a smile on his lips in acknowledgment of the compliment.

The room went silent for an uneasy moment or two as everyone in the circle stared at the Sergeant without speaking. Their gaping grins and goofy smirks made him uncomfortable, causing an involuntary grimace to creep into his previously expressionless face. He felt like a prized stallion up for auction. At any minute, he expected one of them to reach over to inspect his teeth, feed him a carrot, and then pat him on the head.

An individual behind the desk moved around the high-backed chair and strode toward Montgomery. Quite tall and with a slight paunch at the waist, he wore a conservative yet expensive black suit with thin gray pinstripes, a starched white shirt, and a bold yellow tie.

The tie was narrow and looked to be silk. A silver clasp in the shape of the U.S. Capitol was set three-quarters of the way down its length. Wingtip shoes, polished to a mirror-like finish, completed the look. From head to toe, the man was immaculate in every detail.

"Has to be a politician," Montgomery thought.

The most memorable thing about this dapper gentleman was the peculiar silver-gray streak sprouting from his scalp. The odd coloration began beside a widow's peak at the top of his forehead. From here, it ran back along the upper part of his scalp for about three inches before fading out. It looked a little like a skunk's shock of white.

The ornately dressed man strode purposefully toward Montgomery. Though he expected a handshake, Montgomery received a bizarre Cheshire grin. The smile appeared to consume the entire bottom half of the man's face. It was terrifying, and he felt the sharp pang of alarm in the pit of his stomach.

"Sergeant, I am Congressmen Jeffery P. Samuels, representative of the fourteenth District of New York. In my life of public service, I've met many incredible people. Dignitaries from around the globe, sports figures, movie stars, you get the idea. But this is an honor like no other. The accomplishments reported about you are nothing short of amazing, son. I'd even go so far as to say profound. And, if truth be told, and I was the one standing in those rather large shoes of yours," the congressman chuckled as he glanced down at Montgomery's size fifteen shoes, "I am not sure I could commit to doing what we're here to ask of you today."

All the men in attendance appeared to stiffen. Some glared at Samuels, and others widened their eyes in surprise. Clearly, Samuels had let slip too much information. The congressman noticed the attention and seemed to revel in it, smiling even more widely.

To break the silence, Doctor Blackwell opened a pathway to the last individual to meet Brant. He had been separated from the others the entire time. Now, as a channel opened at Blackwell's insistence, the man turned so that Montgomery saw him in profile talking on the phone. His ebony black hair was graying slightly at the temples, and he stood six feet above the ground with broad shoulders and a lean, muscular frame.

Though his voice was barely above a whisper, the Sergeant still heard much of what this new man said. Most of the conversation meant little to him except when the man declared his nervousness about meeting Montgomery after waiting *"all these years."*

"Now, Brant..." Blackwell said while smiling from ear to ear, "... I'd like to introduce you to the benefactor responsible for this whole project. Everything that we've been able to do so far, including your medical procedures and rehabilitation, are owed to him," Blackwell finished as he waved his arm toward the last person Brant had yet to meet.

Montgomery scrutinized the figure as he ended the call and approached. Unlike Cheshire Cat man, this gentleman exuded confidence untinged by arrogance, something Montgomery instantly admired. His face was set, strong, and focused, and finely webbed wrinkles sprouted from the corner of each eye. With his thick curly hair and dark brown eyes, the olive-skinned stranger had movie star good looks.

If you could describe the mark as such, the man's lone blemish was a small but impressive scar below and to the left of the center on his chin. About three-quarters of an inch long and fishhook-shaped, the wound, though faint, was still clearly visible.

A warm, sincere smile developed as the approaching man held out his hand. Then, in a calm, soothing, and somewhat humbled voice that carried an Italian accent, he said, "Sergeant Montgomery, I have been waiting quite a while to meet you."

Though he couldn't understand how or why this man might have waited *"quite a while"* to meet him, Montgomery took his hand, and the two men greeted each other earnestly. For Montgomery's part, his welcome was a sincere appreciation for apparent reasons. But oddly, and though he had never met this man, the Sergeant sensed genuine affection and sincerity in this person's words and handshake.

"My name is Antonio Barilla," he declared, "and I can't tell you how pleased I am that you've fully recovered from your injuries. And..." he hesitated for a moment before completing his thought, "...No matter what you decide to do today, and beyond, please understand this, being able to help you recuperate from your accident has been an honor."

"I gather from Dr. Blackwell that you're responsible for my recovery. I'm forever in your debt," Montgomery said with heartfelt gratitude.

"Well, don't be so sure, especially when you hear what we are about to ask of you,"

That was the second reference to a significant request. But unlike the humor that the politician tried to interject, Barilla said it with the grim smile of someone with bad news to tell. He took Montgomery by the arm and walked to a door leading to a conference room adjacent to Pittman's office.

The room was larger than the Major's, with a computer, projector, and metal-backed chairs lined up in six rows. Barilla motioned for Montgomery to sit in a seat positioned in the center of the room.

"Brant, may I call you Brant?" Barilla asked.

"By all means," Montgomery said, nodding in approval.

"Great, thanks. Brant, for the last five years, I have exhausted almost every waking moment on a project so secret not even the woman I share my bed with each night has had any knowledge of its goal.

"You see, I am Italian, and Italians, like many European nationalities, are fiercely protective and proud of their heritage. Generations dating back thousands of years make this a reality no one can deny. So, when a man walked into my office on my birthday five years ago and handed me an old leather-bound book authored by my grandfather, well, you can imagine that I became instantly intrigued.

"This mysterious man appeared to be in his early fifties. He was tall, maybe six feet four inches, and quite muscular. He looked fit for anyone of any age. The gentleman had brilliant blue eyes, a strong nose, and a solid square chin. And while he spoke softly, what he said stopped me like a punch in the stomach.

"With his hypnotic soft monotone that revealed little emotion, he stated how the book, and its world-altering contents were intended for me, and me alone. And though I would have difficulty believing what I read, I would soon embrace every word as fact, leading me to embark on one of the world's most meaningful and essential journeys.

"I was baffled by his words and cynical of these claims, but I was also very anxious to plunge into what my grandfather had written for me. But before he would even allow me to open the manuscript, he explained that a vital part of this thousand-piece puzzle needed to be addressed immediately.

"Reaching into a pouch, he pulled out a Polaroid camera. He then told me to call my secretary and ask her to take a picture of us. After she did and the image developed, he wrote a note on the back and gave it to me. I was perplexed by his written message and asked what it implied. He just nodded at the book.

"I couldn't fathom what any of this meant, and I begged the man to stay as my mind swirled. He declined and assured me all would be answered once I finished the Journal. He shook my hand and hugged me, which seemed incongruous next to his passionless speech and stiff posture. After he left, I canceled my morning appointments and began reading fervently.

"Brant, this was the first line on the page:

To my beloved grandson, the man who saved the world.

At first, I was curious as to what the reference could mean. How was I to save the world? When? And probably the biggest question, why would I have to? Then I turned the page and started reading something straight out of an H.G. Wells novel.

"My grandfather began the diary the day I turned five: the first entry was dated July 22, 1939. If you recall your history, this date was at the beginning of the war in Europe. Almost one hundred and twenty-five pages later, his last recorded notation occurred as the conflict in Japan was ending. I assume he intended to keep the journal for the rest of his life, but regrettably, he was killed one month before the Japanese surrender."

Montgomery offered his condolences.

"Thank you, Brant," Barilla said. He took a moment here, closed his eyes, and then made the cross sign on his chest before continuing.

"Our families have resided in the Barolo region of Italy for many generations. Our homes and the surrounding vineyards are a mere stone's throw away from the foothills of the Alps. The area is breathtaking. You may know it from the fantastic wine we produce from the extraordinary Nebbiolo grape. Are you familiar with our wines?"

"I'm sorry, no," Montgomery said.

"Well, with no little pride, I confess that these wines today, by all accounts, are world-renowned and coveted by countless wine connoisseurs," he paused a moment and held up his hand with thumb and forefinger touching, adding, "Barolo is recognized, in historical terms, as the wine of the kings.

"In the ancient times of the monarchs, royal families from Europe imported so much Barolo that they almost monopolized the supply. This fact, I might add, merely enhanced the legend of our efforts. Anyway, suffice it to say that we are quite proud of our wines, and for dozens of generations, our nectar and that of our neighbors have graced the tables of the world's most influential decision-makers. An honor, to be sure."

Antonio's features were lit with passion, and Montgomery could sense intense pride emanating from his lips as he expounded upon his heritage.

"Our wines and their reputation for quality gave our ancestors great satisfaction over the generations. They were a product of the Barilla family's values and hard work. I understood all of this but didn't grasp in its entirety. Not until I read my grandfather's writings. Once I did, I experienced a connection to my lineage unlike anything else I'd ever known.

"As I read, my emotions bounced from uproarious humor to deep heartfelt sadness. From immense admiration to insightful compassion. I laughed at the crazy things my relations did before the war, and I cried when I learned of the fates of those members who fought and did not survive." Barilla stopped mid-thought and swallowed hard.

When Antonio began again, his voice was a little raspy though steady. "Along with my grandfather, I lost a sister, older brother, and two uncles during the Great War. As you can imagine, those losses were excruciating, especially since I was so young that my memories were sketchy. So, imagine my delight in receiving this magnificent manuscript and how the stories brought each family member alive. His words filled a void I'd had since childhood."

Barilla stopped his pacing and walked over to sit down next to Montgomery. Putting a hand on the sergeant's arm, he stared straight into his eyes. "Up to this point, the entries in the journal mainly pertained to my relatives' and our neighbors' everyday lives. But then, the contents changed dramatically from one page to the next!

"Brant, it was here that he wrote of a mysterious individual showing up at our home. The date was in May of 1943. His name was Joseph Campanella…" Barilla hesitated here. It was as if he half expected Montgomery to recognize the name, which, up to this moment, would be logically impossible since he'd never been made aware of it. When he didn't notice any sign of recognition, Barilla went on.

"My grandfather wrote of Joseph with deep reverence and, at times, awe. Through his writings, he painted a vivid mosaic depicting his arrival and incredible undertakings. The balance of the journal revolved around this man, his contact with our family, and…well…a grand and epic journey, I would say."

Barilla clasped his hands together before raising his thumbs and pointing his index fingers at Montgomery. With profound seriousness, he said, "The last eighty pages of the book contained detailed documentation about this new visitor and his interaction with the Barillas.

"The entries included precise explanations regarding the events leading up to his appearance at our home and everything that occurred after he arrived. My grandfather wrote meticulous descriptions of subsequent incidents and the people and places involved. And, for reasons I understood much later, he maintained strict timelines throughout."

Sitting back in his chair, he chuckled as he added, "At first, I was incredulous – at best. But..." he said as he raised a hand and extended a pointed finger for emphasis, "... I'd become a total believer by the time I turned the last page. And boy was that last page a doozy. On that page, along with some astonishing notations, were taped two peculiar photographs that sent shock waves through every fiber of my being. I sat motionless in a numbed state as I stared at these glossy reflections and recalled all I had read.

"The rational part of my brain, which we Italians seem to have less of than others," he joked, lightening the mood temporarily and causing Montgomery to smile, "told me that the story had to be an implausible hoax. However, I started contemplating the possible ramifications of what could happen if the events the journal explained were based on fact.

"Now, it is here that I must reveal the next segment of the story." Barilla inhaled deeply and slowly before expressing his following thoughts. "What I will tell you and show you will be hard to accept. Yet, I assure you..." he stopped here and glanced at everyone else in the room, "...we believe the narrative to be honest and factual."

Before Montgomery could say anything in response, Barilla nodded toward the projectionist. At this prodding, the operator switched on the power and signaled to another in the back of the room to dim the lights. The projector's light flashed in Montgomery's eyes, causing him to raise his hand against the glare. He changed his line of sight and then focused on the images projected on the hanging screen at the front of the room.

The image began out-of-focus, grainy, and unrecognizable. The projectionist soon adjusted the large lens, and three figures transformed from blurred shapes to vivid individuals. As they did, Montgomery's heart began to quicken.

He was staring at himself in the photo on the far left. The date of the color photo, written in neat block letters, read March 3, 1995. This picture pre-dated the roadside accident of the Humvee, and Montgomery remembered when the photograph was taken. Next to this photo was a black-and-white image of him. However, unlike the color shot, this image showed the small scar on his neck situated an inch below his right ear. This visible flaw was a direct result of the almost fatal bombing.

Montgomery stared at the picture, trying to recall when it might have been taken. The facts about its origin were unclear to him, and the clothes worn in this print seemed odd. It gave the impression of being many years old. Or, better described, outdated. The apparel reminded him of something worn by a farmer from the forties or fifties.

Finally, moving to the last photograph on the far right, he realized this picture was also of him, except his appearance was somehow aged. He looked to be in his fifties. Perhaps someone had doctored a younger photo of himself.

"Examine each of the individuals carefully. Do you notice the similarities?" Barilla asked.

"Yes. The one on the left is a photo of me before the accident. The black and white photograph was taken after my accident. I assume this because I can clearly make out the scar on my neck from the IED incident in Kuwait. However, the picture on the right is a modified print of me in clothes and styles from around the nineteen forties or fifties. But I've never posed in apparel like this, so I know the shot must be a fabrication," he said. "The last image may also be of me, but you've aged me thirty years. I assume this is also an altered photo."

Barilla smiled before asking for the lights to be turned back on. Once their eyes adjusted to the brightness, he said, "I mentioned that you'd find some of the things I planned on telling you hard to accept. Well, hold on to your hat, my friend; here comes a curveball, as they say." Then he stopped smiling and stared straight into Brant's eyes. "No alteration of these pictures has occurred in any way."

Montgomery laughed. "Okay. Sure," he said as he laid a hand on

Barilla's shoulder, letting him know he took the joke in good humor. "I think I'd remember having my picture taken in those clothes. And I'm certainly not as old as I look there."

"Brant, I know, this is beyond strange. Believe me, I do. None of what I read made any sense to me, either. But I assure you, the photograph on the far right portraying the older man, is you. It was obtained on July 22, 1993. The day happened to be my birthday, so the date is engrained in my mind. Though you didn't admit how old you were, I thought you to be at least in your early to mid-fifties. Remarkably, I would later find out you were over seventy. But we will discuss that oddity at another time.

"And the black and white photo? I had our technicians analyze the type of paper used and the image's chemical composition. We've confirmed the photo date as sometime in the early 1940s.

And, of course, as you said, you remember the last one from your time in Kuwait," Barilla said confidently. "These pictures of you, the one pre-incident and the black-and-white photo from the 1940s were taped to the book's last page. And you know who gave me the book?" Barilla said with a voice rising in intensity. His eyes took on the almost fervent, fever glint of the converted. "Mio Dio Brant, it was you. The older you in this photo here," he almost whispered, pointing at the photo as he spoke.

Montgomery studied Barilla's face, waiting for any hint of a smile or a telltale sign exposing this implausible story for what it must be – a preposterous joke.

However, no smile or laughter came forth. Eventually, with a somber slowness, Montgomery said, "You're not joking, are you?"

"No," Barilla stated without hesitation.

"Well, I guess my next question would be, how? How the *hell* is this whole thing possible?"

"Several elements made this conceivable, not least of which are you. Simply put, due to your unique blood type, a particular transformation has occurred since and because of the surgeries performed on you. You see, your blood is A.B. Rh-negative, and as you know, this is the rarest of all blood types on the planet.

"Only about one percent of the world's nearly seven billion people are born with this blood. For reasons we still don't fully understand, having this rare blood type combined with Dr. Blackwell's quantum leap in biomolecular nanotechnology has triggered undeniable alterations in your physical composition."

Dr. Blackwell chimed in. "Brant, a few years ago, nanomedicine was considered science fiction. Today, with the incredible participation and effort of an extraordinarily talented team of doctors, scientists, and a few billion dollars, this area of medicine is now science fact."

Montgomery's right eyebrow rose, "A few billion dollars? Yes, that's some incentive!"

"Yes, indeed..." Blackwell said. "What we can now do is take a genetically modified blend of nano-molecular elements, along with enhanced protein particulates from the host, and inject this infused serum into the body. These pre-programmed microscopic components seek injured areas and repair damaged bone and muscle faster and stronger than considered possible."

Blackwell stopped here, walked up to the front of the room, and began addressing the entire group. "Each stage of Sergeant Montgomery's surgery and corresponding injections went like clockwork. His recuperation progressed like any other patient until about three days after the last procedure. Gentlemen, this is when things changed and changed in quite a dramatic fashion.

"Subsequent tests we did on the Sergeant's blood showed a rapid mutation, or "morphing" as we termed it, to the extent that almost every inch of his body, inside and out, transformed. Even his toenails, fingernails, and hair follicles altered."

Congressman Samuels stepped forward to speak. "Dr. Blackwell, we all know why we are here and realize that Sergeant Montgomery is our guy. But why him, specifically? I've been told other injured individuals with the same blood type underwent comparable procedures, except no one responded with a similar reaction. Can you explain the reason for this?"

"Not entirely," Blackwell replied apologetically. "All I can do is theorize. The data falls well short of providing enough data for an accurate conclusion." The doctor paused here and removed his wirerimmed glasses. He reached back, pulled a handkerchief from his back pocket, and cleaned the lenses. He went on. "Brant's situation has been something of an enigma. And though we continue to evaluate him, the effects he has experienced are…well, inconclusive.

"However, I will say this. The entire team has given significant deliberation to the massive brain damage Brant received. It is not uncommon for our minds to send out biological altering signals to the body's various organs after a significant injury such as his. This natural process occurs to help the brain's restorative progression. It's possible this chemical phenomenon, in combination with our serum injections, caused the differing mutations that our other test subjects didn't experience. But to be frank, we've discovered no definitive reasons for things to have happened the way they did."

With an expression of exasperation, Montgomery blurted out, "Okay, I'm different, a mutant – I get it. But what does any of this have to do with me."

Barilla retook the lead. "Well, I guess this is as good a time as any to tell you why you are here and what we must ask of you. And you will also find this hard to accept. But here it is in black and white. Because of what the journal said would need to happen, I have spent the last five years working with an international group of scientists and technicians with a single purpose – to portal you back to 1943 for a mission of the greatest importance. An undertaking, in fact, with history-altering ramifications if the operation is not successful."

"You've got to be kidding," Montgomery said with a tinge of fear and a dollop of incredulity. A slight chuckle of disbelief escaped his mouth as he scanned each person in the conference room. "Come on, time travel – a joke, right?"

"No, we are not joking. Honestly, I wish we were." Barilla said with a sigh. "Trust me when I say this: each of us in this room has questioned almost every phase of this historic project. Yet the story and all the details that bring it to life are accurate down to the last detail.

"Brant, this is what we know. Due to your accident and the ensuing surgeries, your body has altered to the point where your physical being is unlike anyone else's on Earth. Through some unknown but miraculous transformation, ninety percent of your cell structure has taken on an almost android-like composition. A composition made up of a unique blend of organic and inorganic molecules that allow you to, well, literally survive the test of time."

Barilla raised his hands and balled them under his chin as he pondered his next utterance. He realized that from this moment forward, he needed to paint a persuasive and credible verbal picture for Montgomery, enabling him to comprehend and believe the unbelievable.

In a reasoned tone, he straightened up and said, "Think about what has transpired to this point. Consider your incredible recovery in quickness and physical reclamation and the incredible results you've accomplished since then. Your physical achievements outcompete even the grandest of any other human. Because of these anomalous bodily alterations and triumphs, you are the lone individual capable of doing what must be done."

"Which is...?" Montgomery said, exasperation creeping into his voice.

"Well, Sergeant Montgomery, here comes another one of those curveballs...After you arrive in 1943, your mission will be to prevent an event that will surely bring dire consequences if not stopped. These consequences will forever change the time we live in now."

Montgomery blinked multiple times while staring at Barilla. "Guys, this is ridiculous, it's insane – I mean, you can't be serious. Look, I've heard all the sci-fi crap regarding changing moments in past times and the unspeakable things that happen when you do. There's supposed to be some type of time continuum thing that gets disrupted and causes chaos, right? Because of this, no one can time travel. I…"

Barilla raised a hand, stopping Montgomery mid-sentence, and beckoned Blackwell. He walked straight up to the sergeant and offered him two snapshots. Montgomery, whose mouth still hung open from his last words, closed it like a trapdoor swinging back shut. He scrutinized the photos before turning his attention back to Barilla.

"These are two photos you displayed on the screen earlier," Montgomery said.

"Yes. We purposely didn't show the back of the shots as we wanted you to see that what you read has not been altered or recently added. Go ahead, turn them over," Barilla said.

Montgomery turned over the photos. He scanned the notes on the back of the black-and-white shot first. The names Joseph Campanella and Brant Montgomery were written side by side in block letters. Printed below these notations was the date of 1943. This information meant nothing to him. But the handwritten lines inscribed beneath the date struck a nerve: "Believe in Barilla and Blackwell. Time travel is real."

Montgomery blinked back in disbelief before numbly shifting the prints in his hand and reading the back of the next glossy. This shot depicted him as the older man. And once again, three lines of notes were written below the picture. The same two names in block letters as before, and then the date, July 22, 1993. He then focused on the last line, and the handwritten note triggered a reflexive gulp: "We stopped the assassination. You made it!"

The photographs, names, and dates were thought-provoking, to be sure. The notations themselves caused Montgomery a shock, like sticking his finger into a live socket. However, what staggered the man and caused him to sit upright and rigid in his seat was when he recognized that the handwriting – was his own!

CHAPTER 5

Montgomery closed the door to Pittman's office and stood on the step of the building's front landing for several moments. The area was well-lit by an overhead lamp that allowed him one more opportunity to study the two pictures and writings on the back of each.

"Can this be me? Can this crazy story be real?" Montgomery muttered to himself while shaking his head in disbelief. He unbuttoned his shirt pocket a minute later and placed the photos inside. He re-buttoned the pocket and then checked the time. It was 2250 hours.

As he descended the steps, he glanced up toward the night sky. In an instant of wonder, Montgomery realized he was witnessing one of the fullest moons he could ever recall. The oxygen-deprived sphere was huge, and he felt he could make out each crater mark and mountainous peak. He couldn't remember the moon ever being this radiant.

And then it hit him, and it was like an epiphany. "I'll be damned!" he exhaled. At that moment, he consciously bridged the gap between his surgeries, remarkable recovery, the base, his training, and, ultimately, why he was brought to the facility. Montgomery now believed they truly intended to catapult him back to 1943 and World War Two. He didn't know how it was possible, but he was sure they were going to do it.

Even during these swirls of thoughts, Montgomery's intensified and enhanced perceptions suddenly kicked in, and they were buzzing with ferocity. Instinctively, he went into a combatant's crouch. After a few feet more, he froze as the hair on the back of his neck bristled, and his skin tingled from head to toe. An odd stillness settled over the camp as if to say *all was well*. Montgomery sensed otherwise.

He scanned the area grid-wise, moving his search from the left side of the camp to the far right, scrutinizing every possible hiding spot. He kept this vigil for several minutes, trying to find any reason for his synaptic overload. But he couldn't visually perceive anything out of place.

Though still sensitive to his internal alarm, Montgomery rose from his crouch and moved a few more paces toward his barracks. He received the first physical confirmation of his subconscious apprehension twenty yards out. The light over his door, which had been on when he'd left earlier that evening, was now smashed, and lying in fragments on the ground.

Now, on full alert, he leaned forward on the balls of his feet and used the moon's glow to focus on the front stoop of his quarters. Scanning down from where the light once shone on the ground, he picked up the outline of broken glass scattered on the cement landing. He also saw a round brass object. His eyes shifted up and ran along the door frame to where the door handle would typically be. The internal mechanism was still in place, but the handle was gone, and the surrounding wooden frame shattered.

Montgomery decided to return to the Major's office to alert the staff to the incident. But before he took the first step, he saw a shadow of movement behind the right side of his building. Without conscious thought, he exploded toward the unknown threat like a shot from a cannon.

An eight-foot fence separated the front of his barracks from the back, with no gate or entryway nearby. As Montgomery approached the chain-linked obstacle, his mind instantly formulated a plan to solve the problem. He zeroed in on a large air conditioning unit next to the fence and a few feet to the right of his building. When about ten feet away, he sprang up and soared toward the unit.

As soon as his boot touched the solid edging of the square metal box, the finely-honed man utilized his momentum and the potent strength in his legs to catapult himself up to the top of the fence. He then used the cross-railing to springboard up and over the galvanized barrier to his building's roofline. He made minimal noise during these maneuvers except for a slight jangling sound as he pushed off the railing.

Once on the ridge of his building, Montgomery inched along, moving low and snakelike, his chest almost touching the shingles. After he'd reached the jutting righthand corner, he froze in position. He hovered there for a moment, surveying the area behind the structure. As before, the sergeant saw no tail-tell signs of a trespasser. He shifted his location by pivoting on his right foot to study the structures to either side of his billet. Again nothing.

Changing sensory functions, he concentrated on listening for footfalls. Other than the standard nocturnal reverberations of insects, frogs, and the occasional whippoorwill, Montgomery heard nothing. In a cat-like movement, he slipped over the eave and dropped the twelve feet to the ground. With refined stealth, he sidled up to the wooden skin of his building and edged toward the back entrance. As Montgomery neared the door, he realized this, too, had been disturbed. Although he had checked the lock and remembered the mechanism to be secure when he left for the meeting, the door now stood open three inches.

Montgomery eased up to the left-hand side of the entry, stopped, and then waited a few moments for any signs of movement or any sounds from within.

Nothing.

Reaching over, he pushed the door inwards. The rust-coated hinges creaked like a cackling witch as the door slowly opened. The sound made him grimace, and he reflexively snatched his hand back. After an excruciating couple of seconds, Montgomery peered into the building, exposing the slimmest portion of his right eye. But this angle only gave him a limited line of sight into the inner room.

In a deliberate motion, he took one gaping step to the other side of the door. With his back pressed tight to this side of the entrance, he slid his hand inside the door and up along the wall, feeling for the light switch. After his fingers rested upon the toggle, he counted to three in his mind and flipped the button.

As the room exploded in glaring illumination, Montgomery prepared for the worst. Once again, agonizingly – he discovered nothing. No sound, no movement, nothing. He opened the door open enough for him to enter. Making no noise, he slid in and then stooped into a slight crouch. At first glance, his billet appeared empty and undisturbed. It wasn't until he entered his sleeping quarters that he saw incontrovertible evidence an intruder had been inside.

The closet door, which he closed earlier, was now open…

CHAPTER 6

"So, Sergeant," Major Pittman started for the third time, "you saw nothing in the back, only heard what you believed might be an intruder?"

Montgomery's teeth clenched. "No sir," he said firmly, "I reported that I observed movement to the rear of the building. I moved to the location and searched as much of the grounds as I felt was prudent. Whatever or whoever may have been lurking around was gone."

"This is when you came in and realized someone went through your belongings?"

"Yes, sir. Everything I placed on the top shelf of the closet was now on the floor. A few boxes stacked on the floor were emptied and rummaged through. How you see things now is how I found them," Montgomery said while nodding at the closet.

"What do you think they were searching for?"

"As I've recounted, I own nothing not given to me by the military since my surgeries and recovery. I can't think of anything anyone might want or consider valuable to me or the mission. I've retained no memos or briefings. I possess no laptop, PC, or other computing equipment containing sensitive information," Montgomery said.

Congressman Samuels rushed into the room, hair mussed and dressed in striped pajamas. With his hand on his head, as if trying to keep it from floating away, he said, "I heard you had some trouble. Is everything okay?" He turned to Montgomery. "Are you hurt?"

"I've received no injuries," Montgomery stated bluntly.

Pittman instructed the Sergeant to explain, one more time, what had happened. Montgomery obeyed but sensed a hidden agenda from the men in the room. While detailing his actions during the time in question, he spotted Pittman turning to a young Corporal standing at the barracks door. The officer nodded, almost imperceptibly, in the enlisted man's direction. This non-verbal action elicited a return nod from the Corporal, who then sidled from the room.

Montgomery's patience evaporated. He spun toward his superior. "What the hell is going on here? I have thoroughly described the encounter three times. I'm getting the impression you're accusing me of something, and I have to say that it's beginning to piss me off."

Listening intently to the Sergeant's recollections, Samuels took a startled step backward. Major Pittman, on the other hand, reacted quite differently. He stepped before Montgomery and barked, "Sergeant, you are still a United States Marine, and you will respect my rank."

Montgomery stiffened and, through pursed lips, answered, "Yes, sir. My apologies." He was angry, not from retelling the story, but because something else was happening, and he wanted to know what it was. There was an outside element of some kind at the base; he could feel it. Montgomery bit his lip and stepped away from the closet to allow Pittman to continue his inspection.

Silence prevailed for ten minutes as the men conducted a methodical examination. During the process, Montgomery caught another non-verbal exchange. This time between Pittman and the Congressman. A glance from one, a nod from the other, and then Samuels walked out. And though he was rightfully reprimanded for his insubordination moments before, his mind was screaming for answers. Before he could say anything, Pittman turned to him.

"Sergeant, I know you have many questions, but I'm afraid they must wait until you decide whether to accept the mission. Once your decision is made, everything will be explained in detail. In the meantime, we'd like you to move to other quarters for the night. I've sent Corporal Jenkins to an alternative barracks to ready it for you. Grab what you need and head across the compound to billet number eight. Get some rest and then be in my office at 0830."

Before waiting for any response, Pittman nodded curtly and strode from the room, leaving Montgomery staring after him with some frustration.

****

The following morning, prompt as ever, Montgomery walked into Pittman's office, finding the same attending Corporal from the previous evening. "Good morning, Sergeant. They're expecting you in the conference area," he said. Montgomery nodded and went toward the meeting room door. Dr. Blackwell saw the door open from the corner of his eye as he reviewed the mission notes. He nodded and smiled at his patient as he entered the room.

"Brant, good morning. I understand you experienced some excitement on your way back to your quarters last night. I hope you eventually got some much-earned sleep," Blackwell said.

"Yes, I'd like to talk to you about…"

The sleazy politician from New York held up a hand and rudely stopped him. "Sergeant, I apologize for interrupting you, as I'm sure you have many concerns going through your mind right now. I know I would. We realize we're asking you to volunteer for an assignment without a thorough briefing. But for your safety, we need a commitment from you before we can continue. Can you understand that?" Samuels asked.

Montgomery nodded, though a bit hesitantly.

"Well then, shall we begin?" Blackwell asked. With an apparent signal of approval from Barilla, the little man took Montgomery by the arm and led him to the same chair he'd sat in the previous night. Once Montgomery was settled and comfortable, the doctor walked to the front of the room.

Montgomery studied Blackwell with heartfelt admiration. This man saved his life. He was undeniably trustworthy and dependable, with a genuine passion for his work and an interest in Montgomery's health and safety. They'd laughed together and cried together. In fact, Blackwell had participated in every step of his recovery. He had held his hand, literally and figuratively, and infused the constant breath of hope into Montgomery when all seemed hopeless.

A sense of sudden relief and calm washed over Montgomery. It was a twinkling instant of enlightenment accompanied by an unexpected and overwhelming feeling of liberation and clarity. His decision became definitive and lucid. Montgomery stood and said, "Doctor Blackwell, before you start, may I have a minute?"

"Yes, of course," Blackwell said as he peered over his wire-rimmed glasses.

Not taking his eyes from the doctor, Montgomery spoke with a sincere and honest tone. "I'm confused about much of this project, especially last night's break-in. But what I am certain of, and maintain complete confidence in, is your apparent dedication to this mission and your trust in me to fulfill it. So, if you believe I should do this, I will. No questions asked."

With this simple declaration, each man in the room visibly relaxed.

"Excellent, Brant. Excellent indeed!" Blackwell said, grinning from ear to ear. "We all know this was not an easy decision for you, but it is one we're confident you will not regret. So, rather than reviewing my materials, I think it would be best to turn the floor over to Mr. Barilla."

Antonio Barilla, antsy and unable to sit, had been leaning against the wall to the right of Montgomery. As soon as he agreed to the undertaking, the Italian sprung away, briskly walked up, and took the spot where Blackwell had vacated.

"Thank you, Doctor," Barilla said. "Sergeant, first, from each of us here in this room, thank you for agreeing. Your no-questions-asked commitment is just another corroboration in the grand scheme of this critically important undertaking. We are exceedingly grateful and will forever be in your debt." As he finished speaking, he began clapping his hands. Within seconds, every man in the room was standing and clapping.

"Really?" Montgomery said. "Is this necessary?"

After a few minutes, Barilla held up both hands to quiet the room. "Now, so we don't waste another moment, here is the no-bullshit version of what we will do. Based on what we reviewed last night, we intend to transport you back to 1943 to participate in a historic military mission of the utmost importance.

"Though I do not want to put more undue pressure on you than you must already feel, I would be remiss if I didn't emphasize the significance of this mission. There has never been an undertaking of this magnitude and consequence in any history we have experienced up to this point."

"Understood," Montgomery replied without hesitation.

Barilla took a deep breath, smiled, and then released the breath in an extended cleansing release. "Okay. Here we go. Please bring the first slide up on the screen?" With this request, a map of 1943 Italy appeared.

"You will be sent to an area in Italy, a little south of the Swiss Alps," Barilla said as he indicated a circled spot in the northwestern part of the map. "The exact location of your arrival will be one mile south of a town called Diana d'Alba. After you arrive, you will review the charts in your possession and get your bearings.

"Once set, you will walk to my family's farm…" Barilla pointed to a spot just north of the insertion site, "…and find a way to seek out my grandfather when he is alone. Once you and he are isolated, you will recite a predetermined script to convince him and, eventually, nine others to help you conduct your mission."

"Which is?" Montgomery said with arms crossed.

Barilla hesitated before reacting to the question. He took a moment to glance at the two new men in the group and then returned his attention to Montgomery. "Brant, on the evening of November twenty-sixth, 1943, Winston Churchill will make an unscheduled stop in Naples, Italy.

"Though his ultimate destination will be the Tehran Conference in Iran, he will stay at the Villa Rivalta for a few days of rest. While the Prime Minister is there, an assassination has been planned."

"Well, apparently, things didn't go as intended since we know Churchill lived well past the war's end," Montgomery said drily.

"Now you're catching on," Congressman Samuels said.

"Hold on, let's not get ahead of ourselves," Barilla cautioned. "Brant, you'll soon understand why Churchill survives and how your arrival in 1943 matters," Barilla said, holding his hands up to stave off any divergent discussions regarding Montgomery's role in Churchill's survival.

"First, let me present you with the necessary materials and background of the mission, starting with the man at the head of the scheme.

"The plot to kill the Prime Minister was the brainchild of fellow Briton, Paul Bedford Jones. He was the son of Gerald Preston Jones, a longtime member of the English government. Jones was an Eton graduate with ambitions to follow in his father's diplomatic footsteps. Unfortunately, this strategy didn't work as planned, as it became evident the prodigal son did not inherit the honor and dignity of his illustrious father.

"Working in a low-level position at the Home Secretary's office, a title akin to our Secretary of State, Jones soon became discouraged by *Britain's bureaucratic cronyism*. We discovered that Jones' father and the Home Secretary at the time, Sir Samuel Hoare, did not get along. They were constant sparring partners in the English political world, and this caused Hoare to cast a punitive spotlight on the younger Jones.

"Hoare didn't want him on his staff, even in a minor role. But the young man was forced into his office because of favors asked and granted. Hoare believed that Jones' father wanted a mole in his midst, making the young man's life at the Ministry miserable.

"Discouraged and searching for ways to prove himself outside Britain's typical governmental arenas, Jones found sympathetic ears in a sect of the British Union of Fascists. This group was founded by Oswald Mosley, a member of Parliament and a 6th Baronet. Though Mosley would be jailed in 1940 and the assembly disbanded shortly after, a few stragglers who believed in his cause remained in the country. Jones would stay in contact with these men and continue meeting while recruiting others to join.

"In time, and unbeknownst to most of the remaining supporters of the movement, spies from Germany slipped their way into the clan. These well-trained infiltrators soon realized that the impressionable young Englishman was a ripe target for their influence.

"Initially, we found no public documents linking Jones to the covert cartel. Influential family members likely removed any such information sometime after the war. It wasn't until we uncovered a cache of Jones' private letters hidden in the London Archives that we understood how severe his issues were with the British leadership. The handwritten papers prove his intentions beyond a reasonable doubt.

"While sifting through the timelines of documents, we discovered Jones was deep in the grasp of the Nazi spies months before the global conflict even started. Beginning with letters Jones had written dating from 1938 to 1942, he wrote how the country's political machine was leading the English people to ruin. Each letter expressed a more profound resentment toward the villain Churchill, who had taken over for Neville Chamberlin as leader of the country in May 1940.

"Like a puppet on a string, the clandestine group deftly maneuvered Jones into using his name to gain a position with direct access to the ruling party. Still held in esteem by those close to his father, Jones requested and received a transfer from the Home Secretary's office to Churchill's staff. It was the faction's hope that he could feed them valuable intelligence. This information, they believed, could aid in the downfall of the British and Allied war machines.

"A little more than two years into the conflict, with many thousands of English soldiers used as cannon fodder, Jones was ready and eager to help stop Churchill. So, when the trip to Naples came to his attention, he was the one to present an assassination plan. One he volunteered to lead, no less.

"When you arrive on the scene," Barilla said, with gravity, "Jones will already be on his way to Naples, along with an organization of unknown accomplices. They will use aliases and forged documents to allow them to be in the city to kill the Prime Minister when he arrives. These men are ruthless, cunning, and unafraid of death. They will do everything they can to slay Mr. Churchill and do not care who they must eliminate to accomplish their goal. You and your group must find and stop them before they can carry out their plan."

Montgomery gawked at the man. He was truly in shock as he rotated his head to examine the rest of the men in the room, all of whom were looking at Barilla and Montgomery with serious expressions. Turning back to Barilla, he exclaimed, "Hold on a second. Something isn't making sense here.

"For one thing, you don't know if I will survive this crazy trip back to 1943. You also don't know if your grandfather and the other people you want me to befriend will accept me. And you don't know if I will successfully convince those relations to follow me on this obvious suicide mission." Montgomery stopped here, eyebrows raised high on his forehead, challenging for a response.

"To be sure, there are a lot of variables we can't guarantee here," Barilla admitted. "But Brant, our hopes are raised significantly by what we know for certain. For example, as soon as I read about Paul Jones being a principal figure in the conspiracy to kill Churchill, we initiated an all-out investigation on him as a primary suspect.

"We researched any record of him from when his name became available until the last known records of his involvement in the scheme and all the components in between. And though it took a significant amount of digging, we ultimately uncovered the letters proving Paul Jones had indeed been complicit in the assassination plot.

"In the same data cache, we also discovered notations of how Barilla family members, along with an undocumented man, participated in the operation to foil Jones and his thugs. And don't forget this point: history, as written today, says Winston Churchill survives well past the war years."

"Maybe someone else stops these killers?" Montgomery offered.

"Based on our information, we don't think so."

Montgomery raised his hands to his face and vigorously rubbed his eyes to eradicate the developing fog in his brain. After a few seconds, he slammed his hands on his knees and stared brazenly at Barilla.

"This may be the single craziest story ever told. I must confess; I can consider no conceptual way of anything, anyone, or any way to send me back in time fifty-plus years. The whole idea seems preposterous. Not only that," Montgomery contemplated further, "if the journey to the past doesn't kill me, you expect me to not only survive in Italy during World War Two but to plan and execute a mission with untrained, ill-equipped, and unprepared people. Individuals, I might add, with no idea who I am or why I've come? It's just too much!"

"A fair assessment. But first things first," Barilla said in a calming voice. "Let's discuss the how – the condensed version, anyway. Brant, feeling as you do right now, imagine how hesitant we were. From the start, it would have been easy to ignore this entire project. It seemed too fantastic. However, the more I thought about it, the more I realized I couldn't let it go as some children's fairy tale.

"You see, there were things I did not know about events my family was involved in during the war. Stories handed down that referenced their activities. But until I read the Journal, I had no idea of the true magnitude. It was then that I felt an obligation to verify what I could. I began by hand-selecting a few trusted and essential personnel from my staff to help me investigate. We immersed ourselves in the task and spent countless hours researching vital sections of the Journal. Each part of my grandfather's account was examined as thoroughly as possible. And to our amazement, every detail that could be verified from the historical records was authentic.

"We went to Italy to follow the trail of those involved in the mission. We started in Diana d'Alba and finished in Naples. The trip took less than three weeks by car instead of the several months the partisans required. We found that all the players existed by the time we left the Villa Rivalta, the final stop of this courageous group's journey. The time frames discussed were one hundred percent accurate. The locations, sites, and written material matched without the slightest variation. It all checked out.

"To be honest, when we stood at the bottom of the hill in front of the Villa, we were all amazed. More to the point, each of us in our small circle had finally become convinced of the veracity of the diary's account! And yet, we knew how hard it would be to convince the dozens of others we needed to bring on board. Frankly, many of our group considered this the most challenging and daunting part of this process."

"I have no doubt," Montgomery said dryly.

Barilla winked and smiled before continuing. "Well, we devised a strategy, made sure we had our information documented and cataloged, and then went on a worldwide barn-storming mission. We visited multiple dignitaries from each country, starting with the U.S. agencies. We were confident that without this group's involvement. Without them," he said with a laugh of his own, "our efforts would have ended before we could get started."

"We spent hours upon hours explaining all the material we found. We didn't leave out a single detail or explanation. Like us, we were hoping they would draw the same conclusions. No offense to the Congressman," Barilla said as he glanced at Samuels, "but our first obstacle to deal with was our U.S. politicians. Some claimed to be intrigued by our story, but none were persuaded. And, as many legislators tend to be when allocating funding, skepticism reigned supreme.

"For quite some time, we were brandished as crackpots and, for the most part, were unceremoniously swept aside by almost everybody we met. But two critical things happened, and these events changed the entire complexion of what we presented.

"First, we convinced London to let us open their files. Getting to this point had been a long and infuriating process; I understand Jones' frustrations with his government a little better now," he laughed. "We may never have uncovered the documents if not for a little-known British official who found our narrative worth investigating.

"And Brant, many of those in the English government who had

previously stonewalled us, calling us insane and foolhardy, had no idea this plot to kill the prime minister had existed. So, after we reviewed the archives and the documentation about Paul Jones and were able to substantiate this conspiracy, people began to amend their thoughts on the subject."

"Hold on a minute," Montgomery interjected.

"Yes?"

"I have a stupid question," Montgomery said with an edge of sarcasm. "If you knew about Jones, why not go back, and erase him from history and make everything easier? You wouldn't need to solicit any of your family or go cross-country to accomplish the goal."

"That is a very legitimate question and, frankly, one we discussed on many occasions. However, without knowing the other accomplices, we risked destroying a singular piece of the conspiracy puzzle, not a finished picture. Do you understand? We needed all the assassins together at one time. If we didn't accomplish this, how could we know if the entire group of plotters was eliminated?"

"Damn," Montgomery said as he realized Barilla was right.

"Yes, indeed. Now to the second critical resolution. While researching at the National Archives building in London, the bank President of Lombard, Odier, Darier, Hentsch, and Cie of Geneva called my New York headquarters. He advised John Snyder, the CFO of my company, that a sizeable amount of money was due to be transferred to us on September 1st, 1993, and wanted to know which account we wanted it wired to.

"Brant, we couldn't fathom why we would be getting a financial transfer. We asked the usual questions anyone would ask. Who did the money come from, why were we receiving the cash, and how much was being deposited." With a look of incredulity, Barilla stopped here and began to smile and laugh while shaking his head.

"Okay, you grabbed my attention," Montgomery said.

"The answer to our first question of who bequeathed us the endowment – was you. The officials of the Geneva bank told us you supplied the capital."

"Wait, what…me?"

"Yes, they said the money arrived from an account owned by Joseph Campanella."

"Well, there's the first issue. Campanella is not my name."

"No, not yet, it isn't," Barilla said. "But please, before we discuss the matter of the name, bear with me a little while longer as I explain the money. The who in the equation was solved. The reason as to why came in the form of a handwritten dispatch to be delivered at the same time as the transfer. The simple note read: 'Use these funds for travel – back in time.'

"The message might have seemed strange to anyone else, but, well, obviously not to us." Barilla paused here before saying with eyebrows raised, "The total value to be wired to us exceeded two point one billion dollars in cash and stocks!"

Montgomery's mouth flopped open, and his eyes bulged. He swallowed back a disbelieving nervous laugh and said, "Excuse me, how much?"

"You heard right – over two billion dollars. Apparently, some rather sage investments had been made in a few U.S. companies. Coca-Cola, McDonald's, IBM, and Microsoft are just four of the several businesses our savvy donor invested in. Impressive foresight, or maybe you were somewhat aware of opportunities before anybody else," Barilla said with a wink.

"This keeps getting harder and harder for me to wrap my mind around," Montgomery said.

"I know how you feel. I was baffled and amazed just as much as you are now. But with the message and the money soon in the Barilla bank accounts, the people we desired to buy into our story and climb on board

– did. They began to take the situation much more seriously, and shortly after, we had real partners in this venture.

"Once we had achieved the backing from the financial and political worlds, we reached out to those who would participate in the initial stages of the undertaking. We contacted everyone from the builders of the facility to the scientists, academics, theorists, and the training personnel for you.

"Even the scientists, who tend to want lots of information about what they are being asked to work on, didn't balk. To the last person on our list, each readily agreed to be here. In fact, all were anxious to be involved." Here, Barilla nodded toward the doctor.

"Dr. Blackwell was the most critical and distinct component. We weren't sure if he would leave his facility to work with us. However, he couldn't get to us fast enough when he found out we intended to support his new nano-molecular research and had more than enough money to fund him."

"It's true," Blackwell said with a laugh.

Barilla's face brimmed with excitement, and Montgomery sensed the energy flow throughout the room as he continued.

"And then, after weeks and weeks of effort, we assembled all the necessary players in one room. The chatter and posturing, both positive and negative, ebbed and flowed and, at times, became unnerving. And yet, in the end, we received a green light on the project. This verification was a miraculous conclusion to the first leg of what was initially deemed an impossible journey.

"Within days of this meeting, we obtained a further pledge from the United States government. They arranged to supply us with any additional funding we might need beyond the Campanella donation. Brant, this was huge." He said with great emphasis. "This vote of financial confidence became one more major piece of the puzzle. We knew the expenditure would be high, but no one involved had any real inkling about the total cost. This additional monetary endowment ended up being vital."

"Things got a little pricey, did they?" Montgomery offered.

"Slightly," Barilla said – tongue firmly planted in cheek. "Brant, the various technologies we needed were in their infancy. I mean, mio Dio, some of the processes hadn't even been envisioned yet on any level. Plus, many integral players resided in other parts of the world, working on their own diverse theories.

"We realized if we were going to pull off this improbable project, we had to get all the contributors under one roof, with one primary goal, and with the money to make all the pieces come together. Once again, we couldn't be sure these participants existed without my grandfather's account.

"Finally, timing became our chief concern. Construction of the structure and all the interior machinery had to be planned and completed. After the facility was built, the entire system needed to be thoroughly tested. And all of this had to be finished in less than five years. Now, you might think this is a long time, but it was a mere blink of an eye for these endeavors.

"Of course, there were struggles throughout; in fact, during the construction phase, we made many mistakes. And…well, putting it bluntly, the thing didn't work at first."

"Sorry?" Montgomery said.

"Yes, let's just say the initial transporting procedure didn't go very well," Barilla said tentatively. "After a few tries, we learned and identified that our original test subjects didn't enjoy the same physical or chemical makeup your body does."

A voice called out from the back of the room, "After fine-tuning circuitry inputs and making other minor alterations, we resolved the issue and are on track now. So, no worries, Sergeant."

With a slight frown and raised eyebrows, Montgomery asked, "Really?"

Barilla nodded confidently and then continued his story. "And then there was you, or more precisely, the 1998 version of you. We knew your name, of course, as we studied information about your achievements and involvement in the Journal. But most of those things happened after you came to us. The mission was well documented, yet technically, you weren't supposed to exist to us until after your injury."

Barilla stopped here and searched Montgomery's eyes. The accident and the devastation the soldier had endured, both physically and mentally, caused Barilla many sleepless nights. However, Montgomery didn't flinch; he remained stoic and unmoving. Barilla took a small breath and began again, though his voice was less enthusiastic now.

"Brant, we were aware of your combat injuries and argued how that we should bring you in based on altruistic reasons before the roadside bombing incident occurred. At this point, Dr. Blackwell informed us of a potential obstacle to this thinking. If we simply brought you in and injected you with his serum without the effects of the injuries you sustained, he wasn't confident it would produce the necessary results. And no amount of research contributed any definitive answers for an accurate assessment of this concern.

"Believe me; we considered long and hard what to do. Ultimately, we knew events concerning your well-being needed to occur naturally and in their respective timeframe. So, though we understood the terrible consequences of what would transpire, we realized it was vital for us to wait and be patient.

"To be sure we would be ready for you, we developed a national data system to alert us to the exact moment you arrived at the field hospital after the accident. Our staff would receive an instantaneous notification, and you would be redirected to our facility." Barilla smiled widely and spread his arms wide before clapping them expressively against his sides. "And, well, here you are."

Montgomery stared in disbelief. Though now more digestible, the story still raged as a fabulous fairytale. He couldn't fathom how any of what he was hearing could be real. Barilla saw the hesitancy in the man's eyes and grasped what must be done. Rising from his seat, he went to the front of the room and picked up a leather-clad book lying on a table.

"Now, imagine the first time I read the passages I'm about to recite to you. I can assure you that skepticism is a massive understatement of the reaction I was experiencing. In time, though, I became a believer. Listen to my grandfather's words, and I am sure you will fathom and appreciate what we are doing here."

Barilla opened the book to a pre-marked section and began reading the words, translating them into English with effortless fluency:

Antonio, what you're about to read will be difficult to comprehend and even harder to admit as the truth. And yet, everything I have written is honest and real, and you must, MUST believe. I know it will be much of me to ask as your mind will hesitate to trust what you initially examine in these passages.

During your perusal, you might decide not to finish the manuscript because it will be too much to accept. But grandson, I must emphasize how many people depend on you to finish reading the Journal and trusting in it. You have a harsh destiny to grasp, but you must embrace it. This is imperative.

If events go as conveyed to me, you will have received this memoir from a close and loyal friend of our family. His name is Joseph Campanella. Joseph has done more for the Barillas than you can ever imagine and has accomplished things the world's population will never know or comprehend.

You already know that several of your relations participated in the war. However, the only facts documented were how we worked with the partisans, and some of us did not survive. Now, more than fifty years later, you will grasp the rest of our history.

Please believe me when I tell you this. With this man's guidance and unique abilities, Joseph led a group of our family and friends on a mission of critical importance to the world. By May 1943, the Great War raged throughout Europe for over three years. During this time, we managed to avoid the fighting, hoping the conflict would end before being forced to participate. But, due to fascist brutality and a total disregard for human decency, some of us were compelled to get involved.

There were close to 600,000 German troops in Italy at different stages of the war. These soldiers bullied us, stole our crops and livestock, and did unspeakable things to our women. Our decision to fight as partisans soon became an easy one.

Though the documented establishment of the Italian Resistance didn't occur until later in the year, small pockets of defiance had already sprung up. We joined in…and then Joseph arrived at our door, and the reasons for our involvement took a radical turn. This odd visitor explained how he appeared with a single purpose – to fulfill an undertaking of the most significant importance.

He told us he would go to Napoli to stop the assassination of England's Prime Minister, Sir Winston Churchill. This statement alone stunned me, but when he said Barilla family members would be going too, as you can imagine, I considered him mad. We were simple farmers and winemakers, and though we fought with the local partisans, we did this to keep our homes and families safe.

To participate in a mission to protect the Prime Minister from being assassinated seemed too far-fetched. We had not been trained for such a thing. And yet, our peculiar friend was quite persuasive and repeatedly insisted that recorded history would prove our involvement.

Antonio, I know this story is too outrageous to contemplate. Just as you must think now, I thought our visitor had consumed too much of our beautiful wine. But in a short time, I realized a complete honesty in him I rarely detected in anyone. His personality, gentleness, and compassion for all the Barillas made me want to trust him. Finally, I felt obliged to allow him to prove his claims to us.

He told me that he needed to make a confession to prove all he related to me. He professed to be a time traveler from 1998! The look on my face after this comment surely was comical, but when he said YOU were the one who sent him here? I must have looked like someone had just thrown a glass of wine in my face.

He allowed me some time to regain composure before he resumed talking. At first, he spoke of the war and about battles soon to be fought. The stories were intriguing, though not nearly convincing enough to sway us. After all, we weren't getting global information very often in those days, so I was hesitant to believe that the events he described just hadn't happened and that we were yet to receive the news.

However, when he made predictions regarding incidents that were about to happen to our family – and then they occurred – precisely as he predicted, I had no choice but to acknowledge that the story he was relating must contain some authenticity.

To give you one incredible example, let me relate to how Joseph predicted a visit from Paulo Gianelli's father to our home. He detailed the man's physical appearance, the day, the time, and why the elder Gianelli was there. He went so far as to recite what the man would say – exactly what he would say.

Of course, doubts crowded my mind; who wouldn't question this ridiculousness? But when a loud knock at our door during breakfast occurred on the day and time he prophesized, I practically fell out of my chair. I gathered my senses as best as I could and hesitantly shuffled to the door. When I swung it open, there stood Daniel Gianelli!

Grandson, I must admit the moment almost scared the life out of me. Even if this foretelling wasn't enough to influence me, his following example floored me. Take a second to examine your image in the mirror, and you will appreciate what I mean.

You see, Joseph precisely predicted when and how you would get the small scar on your chin. He told me specifically on your face where you would be injured. He also described the exact shape of the blemish. Although you were only five, think back, and you will remember.

My boy, I soon comprehended how no one could know about the things he did before they happened. The lone explanation was that he came from a time when these events had already occurred.

As a final testimony, so you believe in what is written, here is one prediction this man made involving something that will happen after you receive this Journal. You will be given a rather generous financial contribution to be used solely for this mission. The actual figure seems larger than I can understand, yet he says you will comprehend the amount. Along with the funding, you will be provided with a simple but significant note. According to Joseph, the message will be short, to the point, and with little room for misinterpretation.

Now, I have one more thing to say. But, before I do, please understand this. With all my heart and soul, I know what I write next is the absolute truth. Joseph M. Campanella's real name is Brant Daniel Montgomery. He is a sergeant in the United States Marine Corps in your era. At the right time, he will come to you. When he does, you must show him the book and pictures and MAKE HIM BELIEVE…

Montgomery sat stunned as Barilla finished reading. He did not speak as he digested the Journal's contents. Finally, he inhaled deeply, let the air out in one deep, mind-cleansing exhale, and said, "Okay, back up a minute. Let's just say I somehow miraculously do succeed in completing the mission. How do you bring me back?"

Complete silence devoured the room.

"Oh," Montgomery said. "So, there is no plan to bring me back?"

"There is good news and bad news on this subject," Barilla said, trying to sound reassuring. ""The good news is we know you survived because, as Joseph Campanella, you brought me my grandfather's Journal in 1993. During the same visit, a picture of you and me was taken, and you wrote a message on the back of the photograph. So, we know you live a full life. But…"

"And now the bad news…" Montgomery interjected.

"Uh, yes. Well, here's the thing. I'm afraid we cannot bring you back without a sending unit like the one here at this facility."

"Holy shit," Montgomery said under his breath. He spent several long moments reflecting. Finally, he said, "So, when am I supposed to become Joseph Campanella?"

"Now," a hoarse-voiced man from the back of the room said with unbridled eagerness. The booming voice belonged to Major General Dunston. Dunston had been sitting in the back with the rest of the group, but he now jumped up and moved toward Montgomery without provocation.

"The entire staff had previously decided it would be prudent to refer to you by your new name immediately after you had agreed to participate. So, as of today, you will answer only to and respond only as – Joseph Campanella. Getting used to the new moniker will be hard at first, but in a short time, you will embrace the name as your own. Think of it as a forever nickname."

"Right…" Montgomery said, stretching out the word.

Ignoring the sergeant's lack of enthusiasm, Dunston said, "I've reviewed your records and believe you were already an excellent soldier. Now, after your surgery, your physical abilities are beyond anything we could imagine. That's the good news."

"And once again, there is bad news?" Montgomery asked, his left eyebrow rising in question.

"The *not-so-good news* is that the mission has a strict and imminent timeframe which must be adhered to. This means we cannot enjoy the luxury of a gradual training process. We will need to start immediately, Joseph Campanella.

CHAPTER 7

"I wanted to ask you about a tidbit I saw in your file. It says you speak a little German. Is that correct?" Dunston asked.

"*Very* little," Campanella replied, emphasizing *very*.

"Excellent!" Dunston exclaimed as he clenched his fist and shook it for emphasis. "Your *very* little German, with additional tutoring, will come in quite handy. Colonel Rosselli, can you come forward," Dunston asked as he motioned toward the back of the room.

As the officer approached, Dunston continued, "Joseph, for every waking minute right up to the moment you leave, you will be learning to speak fluent Italian with a flawless Milanese accent. To enable this to happen, Colonel Rosselli here will be a constant shadow, training your ear and tongue. As a linguist, he'll also be helping you brush up on your German."

Rosselli stood next to Campanella. Wasting no time, he said, "I will be utilizing some unique teaching tools I've recently developed. There are some intriguing subliminal programs I will be applying while you're sleeping, so most of the time, you won't even know you're absorbing the information. We'll have you speaking like a native in no time."

"Great," Campanella said, forcing a slight smile.

"As I was saying," Dunston added, "Colonel Rosselli will be on one side of you, and on the other will be our topography specialist, Colonel Palermo."

Palermo made his way through the group until he reached Dunston, who put a hand on his shoulder and said, "As Rosselli saturates your brain with the language, Colonel Palermo here will do the same regarding the topography of the region in which you'll be operating. You'll undoubtedly be sick of these two after their constant lectures…" Dunston paused as a knowing smile crossed his face, "…but rest assured, once you cross into

1943, you will appreciate their efforts."

As the Major General finished speaking, the two newest arrivals marched forward and stood on either side of the officer. "Now, here are two absolute geniuses," he gushed, grinning widely as he said so. "Let me introduce you to Jesse Robbins and his brother Cody – two brilliant physicists," Dunston said as he put his arms around both men. "They are the ones who designed and developed the teleportation unit with Dr. Blackwell, and they will provide you with the necessary preparations for your leap through the time portal. Any questions whatsoever about this procedure should be directed toward them."

The two physicists began speaking at once, words rushing excitedly from their mouths. Like a Ping-Pong ball, Campanella's head went back and forth as they tried to fill him in on their area of expertise. They overwhelmed him with pointed data regarding a whole litany of esoteric and confusing science: closed timeline curves, gravitational fields, and Thornian theory. None of it made any sense.

"Okay, guys, I think that's enough for now. Let's show Mr. Campanella where he will be spending most of the next three months," Congressman Samuels said.

The change in the group was instantaneous. Like a herd of prodded animals, the collection of men turned and made a beeline toward the back door of the meeting room. This exit led to a garage with three black SUVs parked and running. Campanella got into one of the cars with Dr. Blackwell, Barilla, the Congressman, and Major General Dunston.

As the vehicles pulled away, Congressman Samuels turned and asked, "So Joseph, what's going through your mind right now?"

Campanella didn't answer, staring blankly out of the tinted window with his chin rested on a cupped and pensive hand. "Joseph?" repeated Samuels, a little louder this time.

"Sorry…what?" the anointed world rescuer mumbled while shaking his head. "Oh, yeah. Joseph, that's me. That will take some getting used to…what did you ask?"

"What's going through your mind right now?" Samuels repeated with a gentle smile.

"To be honest, I'm in disbelief or shock. I'm not quite sure which. I feel like I'm in one of those movies where I'm in a coma, living another life. At any moment, I'm going to wake up in that hospital in Doha, paralyzed from head to toe."

"Well, I assure you, this is no movie. I know it's a lot to grasp, but when you see the facility, I think your doubts will disappear," Samuels replied. Campanella sighed in response and took up his previous position, chin cupped in hand, staring distractedly through the window.

Twenty minutes later, the group boarded a nonmilitary, fourteen-passenger Gulfstream G550 jet. Their destination was a secret site in the middle of the Mojave Desert, one hundred miles north of Las Vegas. During the flight, Blackwell spent most of his time sitting beside Campanella with the Robbins brothers across the aisle. The two Italians, Palermo, and Rosselli, plopped down in the seats behind him. The men chatted about all manner of things until the talk made a full circle back to the mission and the people who were instrumental to its success.

Blackwell explained that Jesse Robbins, better known as JT, was a quantum physics mastermind and that his brother Cody was a molecular physics genius. Together, they developed a new theory of quantum time alteration, allowing them to bend time and then stop it entirely for a determined period.

"You see," Blackwell said, "The procedure was accomplished by utilizing conceptual formulas the boys developed in conjunction with colliders used to smash atoms, like those in Geneva, Switzerland. After the influx of financial aid you provided, they were able to design and construct a facility to house the mechanisms needed to harness the time travel process."

JT stepped in here to detail the machine's ability to create a gateway in time. "Joseph, think about how a GPS system works and how it gets you to a destination. However, instead of picking a point on earth and being told how to navigate to that location, we can choose a place and time, open the gateway portal, and send someone through."

Blackwell anticipated Campanella's next question. "Why you and not someone else? The simple answer? As mentioned yesterday, the tests failed because an ordinary human being's molecular structure could not withstand the crossover between our time and any other time."

Once again, JT interjected. "The machine, and the process it developed, causes a high-frequency stress level, which is a bit…excessive. In other words, when the portal transfer occurs, the magnetic and electronic outputs would scramble molecules and cause them to…well…explode."

"Yes, the result would be quite messy, I'm afraid," JT's brother interjected.

"Joseph, because your molecular structure has been so dramatically altered from your accident and the resulting surgeries, we are confident you will survive the time jump – whole and unharmed," Blackwell continued. "I also want to reiterate this important, if not vital, detail. The Journal explained how you made it through the process and how you, as Joseph Campanella, showed up in New York over fifty years later. This fact makes the entire narrative more than a vague theory."

The conversation continued as JT described the actual time travel apparatus. He detailed how the complex ultra-high-powered particle refraction mechanism utilized a portal unit fueled by an atomic reactor. As he began to go into detail regarding how this worked, Campanella's skull started to pound. He'd had enough and wanted the man to stop talking. JT might as well be speaking Latin as far as he was concerned. Besides, all he could think of was the movie The Fly. And that didn't turn out so well.

"Joseph, when we arrive at the facility," Cody said, "I will walk you through the entire process. Although the systems and functionalities are as complex as anything ever developed, I believe a visual explanation will help you understand." With that, Campanella smiled, nodded, and closed his heavy eyes.

The Robbins boys had accomplished something Suicide Hill could not. They had exhausted Campanella and put him to sleep.

****

Less than two hours after takeoff, the Gulfstream initiated its final approach to what looked to be a dilapidated airbase. Campanella had awakened as the plane descended, gazing out his window to see where the aircraft was headed. Except for a few buildings and the long runway, the inhospitable countryside looked as barren and lifeless as the moon's cratered surface. There were no other planes or vehicles, and the only moving objects to be seen consisted of a dozen or so tumbleweeds scurrying about like frightened rats.

The pilot landed the plane and taxied the jet toward two large hangers. The buildings sat fifty feet apart, with a small office between them. An aged air traffic control tower straddled the office, rising some hundred feet into the sky. Campanella could also make out six other building foundations, though the structures no longer existed. The entire place had an eerie graveyard look to it.

As the aircraft approached the structures, it became clear that the remote airbase had been out of commission to any regular usage for years. Grass sprigs littered the concrete surfaces, and angry cracks ran through the cement. It had been years since anyone had used this airfield. It seemed a fitting starting point for this crazy venture, Campanella mused.

Three Chevy Tahoes inside one of the hangers waited for the passengers as they disembarked onto the tarmac. The SUVs were lined up in a single file with drivers stationed at the ready. Those passengers who rode together earlier boarded their respective cars. As the doors thudded closed in a syncopated cascade of satisfying wumps, the procession of vehicles left the hanger with Campanella's group in the lead.

The caravan exited the airfield and headed north on a two-lane road as derelict as the airfield they'd departed seconds before. A chain-link fence, which started at the airport, ran along the road the entire length of their journey. No trespassing signs were attached to the fence every hundred feet, alerting intruders that the land contained radioactive fallout. Campanella hoped the warnings were meant as a deterrent rather than a

72

reality.

After thirty minutes, the group came to a side exit. This new track was a single-lane dirt path dotted with potholes that were impossible to avoid. The roads in Iraq were superhighways compared to this. The vehicles bounced down this route for another half-mile until they approached a gate with a guard shack. Campanella studied the horizon in all directions, and except for the endless line of fencing, he observed nothing. He looked at the young Private walking up to the cars and wondered what the sentry had done to deserve being placed on such shitty duty.

The sentry collected the lead Tahoe's paperwork and photo identification of every person in the cavalcade. After scrutinizing the documents, he went inside the small wooden structure and made a call. Within seconds, the large steel bar blocking the roadway rose out of the way. The soldier handed the IDs back and saluted the three cars on.

Campanella continued to scan the barren countryside as the vehicles headed toward their destination, wherever that might be. Nothing out of the ordinary occurred for the first half-mile or so, but then the same sensation from the night before on the base crept up his spine. The hairs on the back of his neck stiffened, and his muscles tensed.

As the black Tahoes rounded a bend in the road, Campanella caught a brief glint of light in the hills ahead. At first, the glimmering only made him sit up straighter, but the flash occurred again seconds later. He was about to alert the driver to take evasive action, but it was too late. A sound like two champagne glasses being tapped together accompanied a bullet hole that appeared in the windshield.

The bullet whizzed by the driver's ear and passed through his seat's headrest and the rear window. No one in the car had enough time to comprehend or react before another hole materialized in the windshield. Though the first shot failed to hit a target, this one rang true. The unbuckled congressman's body in front of Campanella slammed back into his seat before lurching toward the dash. His face whacked the console, and then his body and head slumped sideways against the door.

The SUV driver jammed on the brakes, and as the vehicle came to a grinding halt, another hole sliced through the glass. The right half of the driver's face vanished in a red mist of skull and brain matter. Campanella reacted without thought. He reached across Blackwell and opened his door. "Get out!" he ordered the terrified doctor. "Get out and move behind the vehicle's rear wheel."

The doctor scrambled out of the car with Campanella shadowing him. As the sergeant exited the Tahoe, the window next to where he had been sitting shattered, and glass rained down on the seat, some of the shards resting in Campanella's hair.

By now, Barilla was over the rear seat and scrambling out the back door. The other two SUVs came rushing up alongside the ambushed vehicle, with the nearest car's back door flying open. Campanella pushed both Blackwell and Barilla toward the back seat. Once they were in, he slammed the door shut and gestured to the drivers to turn back and get out.

The men in the two unscathed vehicles screamed for Campanella to join them. Instead, he opened the door of the attacked SUV and yanked the dead driver's body out. Determined and angry, the single-minded soldier leaped into the vehicle and jammed the gear shift into drive. He pounded the accelerator and whirled the car around just as another bullet thumped into the hood, no more than two feet in front of where he sat.

With wheels spinning and rocks and sand spraying, he steered the car in the opposite direction. He snuck a quick glance in his rear-view mirror and observed the other two vehicles no more than twenty yards behind. About a half mile later and out of sight from the attack, Campanella pulled over and motioned the two other cars to pull up.

Major Pittman lowered the window and yelled, "I've radioed security at the facility, and they're sending help. We're to stay here until they get to us!"

"That'll be too late," Campanella roared back. "Stay here!" He punched down on the throttle and spun the steering wheel to the left, propelling the SUV straight into the desert. He piloted the careening vehicle toward the position the shots came from, determined not to let the sniper escape. Driving with reckless aggression, Campanella maneuvered the Tahoe around the base of a small hill before turning and racing up the incline.

Once he reached the crest, he slowed the vehicle and scanned the horizon. A flicker of movement caught his eye, and he had them. Two men were running down a larger mound about a quarter of a mile away. He jammed the gas pedal to the floor, igniting the 450-horsepower motor. The powerful thrust shot the car across the harsh terrain and directly at the attacker's position.

Campanella then veered on a diagonal path to be level with his targets. With the car on flat ground, he made a hard left, and the bulky vehicle fishtailed back and forth several times. He was about seventy-five yards away from the fleeing men when the right front wheel of his SUV dove into an unseen washout running across his route. The Tahoe crashed into the cavity, sending the five-thousand-pound car bouncing ferociously off the other side and high into the air. When the front end came down, it slammed onto a large rock, obliterating the right wheel assemblage.

Though the terrain's featureless horizons made the deep crevice hard to see, Campanella had caught sight of the impression an instant before the SUV rammed it and had braced himself for the inevitable collision. Any other human not wearing a seatbelt would have lost their grip and collided face-first into the windshield with catastrophic results. But the nano-molecular enhanced man held fast, and the steering wheel bore the brunt of the damage.

Just as Campanella's vehicle came to a bone-jarring stop, the two assassins reached their Jeep Wrangler and jumped into the front seats.

Realizing he hadn't been injured, an even more furious Campanella leaped from his SUV and ran full speed toward the snipers.

Assuming the attacking man to be insane, the driver of the Wrangler snapped on the ignition, threw it in first gear, and stomped on the gas. The men drove directly at Campanella, and he ran straight at them, a bizarre game of chicken that would seem absurd to an onlooker not involved in the deadly pursuit. It was a 200-pound plus rampaging man against a 4,000-pound four-wheel drive vehicle.

Campanella liked the odds.

When the vehicle was no more than thirty feet away, the U.S. Marine sprang into the air. A two-foot-high rock protruded from the soil just to the right of where the Jeep was approaching. He hit the stone in stride and catapulted at the gravel-spewing Wrangler.

The two assassins gaped in wide-eyed amazement. Reacting to this insane feat, the driver let off the accelerator as Campanella passed over the windshield. Both men's heads rotated up in slow motion unison to watch. As they did, Campanella shot out his right leg and slammed the heel of his boot into the driver's face. It was a lightning-quick action with deadly accuracy.

Like a rag doll, the man toppled out of the open space of the Wrangler's door. His limp form crashed onto the gravelly terrain in a face-first impact. The body bounced and rolled along the surface of the desert before stopping some twenty-five feet later. The one-time paid killer now lay face up, unmoving, and with wide, unseeing eyes.

Campanella did a tuck and roll as he hit the ground, allowing him to pop back up into a defensive stance. He spun around toward his previous point of attack and dashed over to the driver. As he arrived at the fallen man's side, he saw a large protrusion at the base of his skull. Broken.

Campanella focused on his next objective, the Jeep's remaining passenger. Now, without its driver, the vehicle was traveling up the same hill the two snipers had run down minutes earlier. The second assassin did his best to move into the driver's seat, but the incline and gravity resisted his efforts. At about forty feet up, the vehicle had turned slightly and was sitting at a precarious angle to the ground. As he was about to slide into his fallen comrade's seat, the front right wheel of the Jeep began to rise.

The time to abandon ship had arrived.

The would-be killer bailed out a split second before the jeep started its first revolution down the mound. He catapulted out of the open rooftop, traveling twenty feet through the air. The sailing man tried to start running the moment his feet hit the sandy soil, but he could not keep up with his body's momentum and began stumbling. Soon, the assassin was out of control and somersaulting head-over-heels in a cloud of dirt, dust, and flailing body parts.

Campanella watched the whole event in amazement as the tumbling human mass came to a crash landing at the bottom of the dune. Initially, he thought the man was unconscious. But after a few sunbaked seconds, he perceived movement. He didn't hesitate and bolted toward the stirring form at blistering speed.

The sniper, sensing the approach, somehow unwound his body and elevated himself into a kneeling position. As he did so, he jerked his arm from his side, revealing a revolver. Campanella came to a sliding stop no more than fifteen feet away with the assassin's pistol aimed dead at his chest. With victory at hand, the disheveled man smiled a gold-toothed grin. A trained marksman, he could not miss at this distance, of that he was sure.

He put his finger on the trigger and aimed.

CHAPTER 8

As the hammer cocked back, Campanella did something that made the sniper pause. He held his ground and smiled.

After an endless moment frozen in this strange tableau, a loud crashing noise restarted time. The gunman spun around, weapon leveled in anticipation of another foe, only to see the out-of-control Jeep bearing down on him. The terror-stricken and astonished man raised his arms in a futile gesture of self-preservation. To Campanella, he couldn't help but think of the attorney who cowered in the toilet in Jurassic Park as the storm ripped away the structure. Like the massive T-Rex in the film, the Jeep appeared to swallow the man whole as it collapsed down upon him.

****

"I wouldn't have believed the whole thing if I hadn't witnessed it with my own eyes," Barilla said as he jumped out of the SUV. Blackwell also sprang from the vehicle, his face still covered in splattered blood from the assassin's previous kill.

The doctor made his way over to the scene of destruction. First, he began waving at the rock where Campanella launched himself at the Jeep. Then he swung around and pointed at the first body crumpled some twenty feet away. Blackwell then turned and rushed toward the overturned automobile. He tried to talk the entire time he was darting about, but no speech emerged.

"Are you alright?" Pittman asked Campanella.

"Yes, much better than our two friends here. Do you know who they were?"

Shaking his head, Pittman said vaguely, "To be honest, we're not sure."

Three black jeeps arrived with four soldiers in each. Over the next fifteen minutes, the group scurried around the hot desert ground, investigating the incident. As they talked in muted tones, pointed, and gestured in all directions, Campanella ambled over to a large rock some sixty feet from where the Jeep Wrangler lay. Leaning against the stone, he put on his sunglasses, folded his arms, and watched.

When the men finished, the original group made their way back to where Campanella stood. As Barilla approached, he could tell the victorious combatant was unhappy and realized why. Campanella expected an explanation.

"Joseph, I know dozens of questions are running through your mind right now but let me save you the time to ask them by giving you the answers we know. Let's head to the base, and I'll bring you up to speed," Barilla said, gesturing for the Sergeant to get back into the SUV.

Once in, the driver made a U-turn and headed back the way they'd come. Barilla got on a government-issue walkie-talkie and furnished someone on the other end instructions for their arrival. Within minutes of the call, the vehicle neared the spot where the snipers had slain two of their companions. Several military vehicles had arrived, and their crews were already busy recovering the dead and cleaning up the debris.

Though Campanella had witnessed his share of death, viewing these men being loaded into the ambulance unsettled him. As the black Tahoe passed the scene, he turned his attention to the area where he'd previously spotted the glare. He now understood the flash of light had come from the sniper's scope. A sense of regret came over him. *If only I'd reacted sooner.*

Barilla saw the look and sensed the Sergeant's remorse. Trying to pull the man out of self-recrimination, he asked, "Joseph, what do you think will happen if we don't stop the slaying of Churchill at the Villa Rivalta?"

Campanella gazed at the Italian and thought momentarily before responding. "I can't imagine it would be good." After a short reflective pause, he added, "I assume it would change history in a terrible way."

"Yes, in ways we couldn't possibly predict. In fact, sane conventional-thinking people would say the changes could, and most certainly would, be catastrophic," Barilla said. He held his hand up, index finger pointing upward in a pausing gesture, and said, "And yet, some individuals feel that eliminating Churchill would alter things positively for their cause.

"The assassination, based on their theories, would start a chain reaction of world-altering historical events. Even though the Germans were on the ropes by this point of the war, the loss of Churchill might alter the war's ending in Germany's favor. To that end, they are trying to prevent us from completing our mission; your mission," Barilla said, staring the Sergeant straight in the eyes.

"Okay, I get that. But for this to be a reality, someone knows what you're doing here. There must be an insider helping them," Campanella stated with certainty.

"Yes, you're right, Joseph. But we don't have any suspects. Each person involved in this project has been checked and double-checked."

Barilla raised his hand, halting the conversation. He indicated ahead of the SUV, nodding in the same direction while beckoning the Sergeant to look. They were observing a rise in the terrain in front of them about an eighth of a mile away. The mound looked around seventy-five feet high and about three hundred yards wide. And though numerous typical desert groundcovers blanketed the formation, something seemed too symmetrical about the form to be a natural occurrence.

"We're here?" Campanella asked.

"Yes, we are. We can continue this chat later," Barilla said as the vehicles slowed.

"Landscaping is lovely," Campanella said, as drily as the desert air. "It's clear you've put some money into it."

Barilla gave a full-throated hearty laugh. "Thanks, Joseph. "We applied a nouveau barren style." He winked and said, "We even have a crew keeping it looking its best."

Both men were smiling at each other's lame attempt at humor as they watched the driver of the lead SUV make his way around the left side of the mound. As they followed, Campanella detected additional characteristics of the knoll. The top of the configuration was flat from front to back and side to side for about two hundred yards. It then tapered off until reaching the surrounding ground another hundred yards down the slopes.

From what he could ascertain, the form appeared to have equal dimensions in all directions. While he continued to look on, Barilla picked up the walkie-talkie again and announced, "Team Campanella has arrived. Barilla ID 1957 - Yellow, Tango, Tango, 1943," and clicked off.

"Yellow, Tango, Tango 1943?" Campanella asked with humorful disbelief.

"Simple, I know, but we have an extremely sensitive voice activation system. Had I not said the phrase in the exact order I did and the way I did, well, let's just say we wouldn't be able to observe *this*," Barilla gestured ahead of them with a nod.

Campanella stared intently in the direction Barilla indicated, unsure what to expect. His eyes, though, were not the first to register the incredible event that was about to happen. He began to feel a slight shudder in his seat. This soon became a shake that gyrated into a sway. At one point, Campanella thought the SUV might start bouncing down the road like a rubber ball.

He glanced down at the ground to his left and watched sand and small pieces of gravel bounce around like Mexican jumping beans. Barilla interrupted his fascination by grabbing his arm and motioning ahead. As Campanella stared at the enormous hill, a large section of the mound began to rise upward and back before folding into the upper portion of the formation.

When the ponderous movements were finished, a gaping hole appeared, tall and broad enough to allow massive earth-moving equipment to enter. The vehicles entered the opening, and as the last car cleared the entrance, a series of horn blasts rang out, and the door began to close.

Inside the underground structure, the noise of the sliding door apparatus was deafening, as an overwhelming echoing of machinery and powerful gearing vibrated throughout the interior of the vast yawning area. The whole thing had been incredible, and Campanella couldn't imagine the power needed to operate the machinery. He would soon discover that what he'd seen was an amuse-bouche compared to what lay ahead.

****

The closing process was much quicker, and the enormous aperture sealed shut just as the cars stopped on the far side of where they entered.

The vacuous garage became pitch-black, with the area sealed off from all external lighting. Campanella wondered why the cars' headlights were off, as no internal lighting had been on when they entered. Just then, dozens of banks of lights in the ceiling came clanging on, and the vast expanse erupted in brilliant and dazzling illumination.

"Whoa…and I thought the landscaping outside was impressive," Campanella said, eyes shielded with his forearm and nearly shut against the glare.

"Yes, but if you think this is something, wait till you see what's below," Barilla responded while exiting the SUV.

The facility's interior was smaller than the overall exterior of the formation. Enormous steel girders spanned the roof and along the sloping walls. The ceiling, walls, and floor were all constructed of poured concrete. High-gloss gray paint covered the floor with a just-polished look. Many vehicles of multiple shapes and sizes filled the parking area, yet the floor was spotless. No tire marks or oil stains of any kind.

"This is highly impressive," Campanella reiterated to Blackwell as the scientist strode beside him.

"Yes, I suppose it is. But as Mr. Barilla said, it's what's about sixteen hundred feet that will blow your mind," Blackwell offered sincerely.

"Wow. Sixteen hundred feet down, huh? Well then, let's get to it," Campanella said, excitement now creeping into his voice for the first time.

The group moved to an elevator where Major Pittman rapidly punched a nine-digit security code into an electronic keypad beside the door. He leaned over and put his right eye over a retina-scanning sensor.

When a green light appeared above the pad, he pushed the lone button alongside the eye sensor. A red domed light flashed above the door, and the double sliding elevator door swooshed open.

As he walked onto the lift, Campanella realized the spacious interior could easily accommodate as many as two dozen men. The walls, floor, and ceiling were stainless steel. Every joint was welded with precision. A replica of the outside red alert light sat in a similar position over the doors inside the elevator. Glancing around, Campanella considered the distinct similarities between where he stood and the interior of a massive steel bank vault.

Once the rest of the men had entered and the doors closed, Barilla eyed Campanella. He smiled as he pressed the down button on the panel. "Just to warn you, this ride is intense. Hold on to the railing."

A slight tremor jostled the elevator as the car initiated its long descent. At first, the lift lowered at a moderate pace. As the descent continued, the vehicle picked up momentum until it plummeted downward at a terrifying velocity. At one point, Campanella felt the weight of his body evaporate and realized his feet were about to lift from the floor.

And then, just as fast as it had accelerated, the elevator slowed. This change was followed by an annoying clanging alarm, presumably to announce they were nearing the end of the ride. Once the lift had come to a surprisingly smooth stop, the red domed light inside the car began to flash, and the doors opened.

The group exited, feeling heavier than before the descent, with Barilla emerging first. He led the gathering across a threshold to a stainless-steel footbridge opposite the elevator opening. The ten-foot-wide structure spanned a cavernous gap from the landing area to a similar site in front of another set of elevator doors on the opposite side of the span. Once on the bridge, Barilla stopped and turned toward Campanella.

When the Sergeant exited the elevator, he was having an animated conversation with the Robbins boys about the ride. As he turned toward the now waiting group, he was immediately accosted by a visual spectacle that stopped him dead in his tracks.

Stunned, he no longer walked with conscious thought as his feet shuffled toward the Barilla. Inching along, his head rotated in every direction as he marveled at the enormity of it all. Once he made his way onto the bridge, Barilla moved past the others until he stood beside the gaping Campanella. "Joseph, what you see all around you is a compilation of blood, sweat, and five years of night and day toiling."

"And a lot of money, I'd guess," Campanella said absently.

"That would be a somewhat colossal understatement," Barilla replied, nodding, and smiling.

Campanella guessed the inside of the structure to be twenty stories or so from floor to ceiling and at least two acres in circumference. There were machines of every size, throbbing and generating God knew what. This would have been an awe-inspiring sight anywhere on the planet, but it staggered his imagination, considering they were sixteen hundred feet below ground.

In the center of the cavern was a vast, glowing, floor-to-ceiling silo that had drawn the air from Campanella's lungs. The mass of pulsating equipment was easily forty feet in circumference. Campanella's bug-eyed scrutiny rose to the tower's top, where it emerged from the concrete ceiling. Here was a round enclosed chamber about twice as large in diameter as the column. This section looked about a story tall, with thick, opaque, grainy blue glass covering the entire exterior. It radiated with a mesmerizing heartthrob rhythm.

At least a dozen stainless-steel pipes sprouted from the bottom of the glass unit and wound their way around and down the silo. Thousands of slender fiber optic cables were wrapped around the outside of these pipes. These strands throbbed with the same intensity and rhythm as the unit above. The overall conglomerate of elements gave the structure an unearthly alien feel as it bathed the facility with its glowing force.

As Campanella further examined the machinery, he saw where the piping disappeared into the top of a broad collection collar, which ringed the circumference of the lower part of the tower. At the base, massive steel "feet" emerged, each secured to three points around the bottom of the silo.

Sitting below this collar sat another extensive accumulation unit. This stainless-steel section possessed another set of pipes emanating from it. These ran in pairs: one stainless steel and one clear glass.

The metal pipes looked about a foot in diameter, and the clear tubes about half that. The tubes shot out in all directions, ending almost two hundred feet later as they injected themselves into massive futuristic-looking generators. The motorhome-sized units reminded Campanella of the laser pulse cannons from Star Wars movies.

While marveling at these mechanical behemoths, a globed red light attached to the top of each unit began flashing. At the same time, a siren started blaring, filling the cavernous facility with an ear-piercing wail. When these overt warning alarms went off, Barilla touched Campanella's arm and leaned close to the Sergeant's ear, "Watch this."

The generators made a thunderous clunking sound as they engaged, and seconds later, an earth-shaking rhythmic hum filled the room. After a few moments, the low pulsing sounds increased dramatically until the units growled with a deep-throated roar. When Campanella thought the entire mass of machinery might explode, pulses of brilliant blue energy shot out from each generator unit. The blue flashes raced through the clear pipes in blinding speed toward the stainless-steel assemblage component below the silo.

Within a few moments, the bursts were shooting out so frequently that only a continuous blue flow of light could be seen.

A glass collection unit sat under the area where the clear pulse cylinders gathered. The mechanism looked to Campanella like revolving doors in a hotel lobby. Around eight feet in diameter, the apparatus contained a wing-shaped mechanism in the center of the device. He guessed the pulses entering from above drove the rotation of the wing. However, unlike a hotel's revolving door, no perceptible entry or exit was apparent.

The glass cylinder was erected on a floor Campanella surmised to be granite or marble. Ten feet thick or more, the round surface matched the unit above, though it was at least twenty feet wider.

Barilla touched the Sergeant's shoulder and yelled, "Joseph, let's head down to the brain of the facility. Come, follow me."

As they got to the other side of the bridge, Campanella glanced down and saw the span was equipped with a quick disconnect mechanism. This system would allow an operator to initiate a hydraulic function to draw the span back and down. Once retrieved, getting from the main elevator area to this elevator would only be possible with grappling gear. Even then, the distance was such that a safe crossing would be difficult.

Situated in a concrete shaft about twice the size of the elevator car it supported, the column rose like an obelisk from the ground floor below some five or so stories high. Once these elevator doors opened, the men got on. Barilla reached over and pushed a button marked "MC", one of six buttons on the panel.

After the car stopped, the doors parted to reveal a holding room for level MC, or the Mission Control Level, as Campanella would be informed. This area measured about thirty feet square and easily twenty feet from floor to ceiling. Several sets of cushioned chairs were positioned around the room, as well as a few end tables. Three large steel doors stood before him. One was in the center of the room, and one was to his left and right. He estimated the doors to be eight feet tall and six feet wide. Alongside each entry was a placard indicating what lay behind the door.

The sign beside the far-left door read Mission Control/Personnel Living Quarters. Mission Control\Electrical was written on the sign next to the middle door. Beside the last entry and in bold red block letters, a sign read Mission Control /Theater – Authorized Personnel Only.

Major Pittman walked up to a control panel below this sign and followed the same security protocols as in the first elevator. Once he finished with the eye scan, he pushed a large button next to the door-locking mechanism. A rather significant popping sound preceded the soft glide of metal sliding through metal. Then, a green light illuminated the control panel, which induced Pittman to begin pulling on the door.

"Joseph, through this door is your future, the future of our future – and our history. And as much of a paradox as all that sounds, it's entirely true. In the next several weeks, you will be briefed and educated for eighteen hours daily. And then, at ten a.m. on May 23, 1999, we will send you back to the same day and hour in 1943.

CHAPTER 9

As men moved through the massive doors, Campanella's eyes were assaulted by white. From this point forward, and all through the Mission Control Floor, the walls, the ceilings, and all the trim were brilliant white. A glistening, almost phosphorescent hue was emanating from an unusual polymer material. Even the floor was covered with a bright white gel coat. The whiteness was shocking.

"2001: A Space Odyssey," Campanella said under his breath.

"Excuse me?" Blackwell said.

"Oh, something just struck me. This entire facility reminds me of the film 2001: A Space Odyssey. Everything is so sterile-looking and as futuristic as anything I could imagine. Stanley Kubrick, eat your heart out." Barilla smiled at the comment and nodded his agreement.

The men continued down the long walkway and turned right at the end. They went another twenty feet until they came to another steel door. Pittman opened the door, and Campanella, Barilla, and Blackwell walked in, followed by the Robbins brothers. The rest of the men bid them farewell until later.

More astonishment greeted Campanella. This chamber was an explosion of electronic circuitry rivaling anything found at Kennedy Space Center. He counted thirty-two workstations in the theater-style room. Below these sat a ten-foot high by thirty-foot long viewing screen. The 6-inch-thick glass screen provided a transparent, unobstructed view of the facility's interior.

Barilla motioned Campanella to follow him as he made his way down a set of stairs leading to an open area in front of the viewing window. Once in position, he stood and gawked at the inconceivable scene on the other side. Campanella glanced quickly at Barilla and saw a man positively bursting with satisfaction. His twinkling eyes were those of a father gazing at his newborn child through a nursery-viewing window.

"Joseph, this is our mission control theater," Barilla said. "It's not necessary for you to learn about this part of the project, but I'm showing it to you for completeness."

Campanella nodded.

"The sending unit is in the middle of this part of the building. The tall glass apparatus, do you see?" Barilla asked.

"Yes. The unit looks like the one I saw from the footbridge, only this unit has an opening and no revolving mechanism inside," Campanella said.

"Correct! In this case, for you, it is a doorway to 1943. The walls, ceiling, and floor around the cylinder are solid granite, almost eight feet thick. We use granite because this ultra-dense igneous rock prevents electromagnetic interference with the portal and the mechanisms that support it. Getting the granite here was a massive undertaking. We needed pieces big enough to cover as much area as possible to minimize the number of seams. And even those had to be sealed with a high-density bonding agent."

Barilla shot a look up toward the ceiling while pointing upward. "Most of the working parts of this machine are on the level above, but all the functions required to operate the system are controlled from this room. Once the nuclear power plant is at eighty percent capacity, we energize and regulate the Worm Hole Pulse Generator output; those blue light pulses racing through the clear piping.

"The microgravity processor, which sits below the two oblong stainless-steel tubes you saw from the bridge when we entered the lower facility, is then engaged. When activated, an electronic dampening module is opened, allowing the fields of these two energy sources to combine. For the briefest of moments, this process creates a door of sorts in the space-time continuum.

"Now, I can't possibly explain to you how all this happens. I'll leave that to the minds who developed and built this machine. But believe me, the thing works."

"In fact," a technician who sat at a nearby workstation interjected, "we possess the ability, plus or minus one to three seconds and plus or minus the same number of meters, to send you to a precise location and time of our choosing. So, if you are standing in the center of the portal sensor pad at the exact calibrated moment, the system does the rest."

Campanella had turned to listen to the man. "What if I'm not in the unit at the exact calibrated moment," Campanella asked.

"Well, you may miss the selected time and or date, an indeterminable difference."

"Indeterminable difference. What the hell does that mean?" Campanella asked.

"As you might imagine, the energy needed to produce the wormhole is enormous. Because of this, we can only create the hole for a few brief moments at a time."

"And that means?"

Campanella noticed the beginning of a nervous creasing on Barilla's brow. "Well, if the portal remains open any longer than our designated *'safe zone timeframe,'* the hole starts to break down, and suffice to say, bad things can happen."

"Damn," Campanella mused while rubbing his chin.

"But don't worry, Joseph; we've got that covered. Now, let's get something to eat. You have much to learn over the next few weeks, and you'll need your strength."

CHAPTER 10

March 2, 1999

"He's here. I saw him in the cafeteria a few minutes ago," a grizzled, reedy man said nervously into an odd-looking communication device. "I don't know what happened, but obviously, your snipers failed." A bead of sweat trickled down the man's bony cheek. He swiped at it with his shoulder and repositioned the handset to his other ear.

The man was using a scrambled, untraceable phone mechanism smuggled into the facility soon after he arrived, some eighteen months earlier. The site itself was hard-wired for telephones that were accessible to all employees, but only approved numbers were allowed to be called, and even these calls were monitored.

As the familiar buzz of an open line sounded, the phone's encrypted microchip initiated a coded system that could only be understood by a handset with the same type of chip and set to the same frequency. Anyone else without a similar phone and the correct frequency would only hear static and believe the call unconnected.

When hired, the man on the phone presented credentials in the name of Kurt Shultz. His documentation stated he had been born in Woodbury Memorial Hospital in Woodbury, New Jersey. It also claimed he graduated from the Culinary Institute of America in New York. He was a chef; that part was true. However, his real name was Adalwolf Kaufman, and he was born in Braunau am Inn, Austria.

By no small coincidence, this tiny burg in Austria had also been the hometown of one Adolf Hitler.

During the short but horrific reign of the German dictator, the Kaufman family enjoyed a sheltered and, by most measures, privileged existence. Kurt von Kaufman, Adalwolf's grandfather, had been an aide in Hitler's inner circle. After the elder Kaufman's death due to a car accident, Adalwolf's father, Gunner, a chef himself, was added to the

Fuhrer's culinary staff.

In an odd moment of fate, Gunner had been one of the last to leave the room before the infamous Wolf's Lair assassination attack on Hitler on July 20, 1944. He had delivered a tray of meats, cheeses, and small pastries minutes before a bomb-filled attaché exploded under the German high command's meeting table. The attempt failed to kill Hitler, and during the early part of the ensuing investigation, Gunner was considered a prime suspect. Fortunately for him and the Kaufman family, the actual conspirators of the Valkyrie murder plot were soon unveiled, captured, and executed.

At the end of the conflict, and with Germany in ruins, Adalwolf's parents secreted him and his younger sister to the U.S. under assumed names. But even with this move, the Kaufman family remained loyal to Hitler and everything he stood for. Adalwolf longed for a chance to exact revenge on those who annihilated the Nazi way of life – his family's way of life. It wasn't until one Albert Farber arrived on the scene that he believed revenge possible.

Farber's father, Klaus, had been a Major in the SS during the war, and his mother, Magda, was a secretary in Heinrich Himmler's office. As the war was ending, Klaus slipped away from his command and attempted to make his way home to protect his family from the oncoming Allied forces. Knowing Berlin would soon fall, he discarded his uniform and changed into civilian clothes.

The plan worked flawlessly – until it didn't. Less than a mile from home, a Russian patrol happened upon the civilian-clad man and demanded his identification papers. Though they appeared in order, one of the guards became suspicious. After intense questioning, Klaus' deception became apparent. They arrested him, and soon after, he was executed. His capture occurred just one week before Hitler committed suicide.

Fearing potential retribution due to her husband's military status, Albert's mother traded most of her valuable possessions for passage out of the country. Though not without many obstacles, Magda and her young son eventually made their way to New York City, where her brother Hans lived. With false identifications that had been secured, the two began a life as American citizens.

A bright student, Albert became intrigued with studying atoms at a young age. When he mentioned this interest to his mother, she beamed with pride. She explained to him that one of the Fuhrer's deepest passions was science and that the German leader supported German scientists in many ways. This information made such an impression on her son that from then on, he ate, drank, and slept science, and more specifically, the science of atoms.

After many years of intense study and research, Farber had become one of the leading atomic physicists in the United States. But even though he was now a 'successful American,' his mother never let him forget his heritage. She reminded him that Hitler was a great leader, eulogizing him as a hero and visionary. Albert's mindset, molded from childhood, revolved around the fact that being a Nazi was something to be proud of. It was because of this belief that he became a member of a secretive Neo-Nazi organization. It was here that he met Kurt Schultz.

Though neither Farber nor Schultz had any idea of the true nature of the facility, it was Farber who convinced the project manager to hire Schultz. At the time, he did it with no ulterior motives. Call it fate or dumb luck, but the two men found themselves in a remarkable situation once together. One where *they* could be the heroes.

Farber became a participant in the facility's construction shortly after its inception. He initially helped oversee the primary placement of equipment and then was involved in the testing stages of the atomic processes. During this time, essential details of the facility's actual function were revealed to him.

While Farber was working in an obscure lab and hidden from view, Antonio Barilla and Cody Robbins entered an outer chamber. The two talked about financial appropriations needed for new equipment when Robbins mentioned aspects of Campanella and certain 'telling' particulars of the mission. At one point, the conversation centered on Campanella's body and whether it could survive the trip. Barilla talked of the time travel process and how Campanella's physical makeup made all the difference.

Farber only heard and understood that they intended to send the man back in time, but not why. Interesting, to be sure, but it didn't mean much to him personally – until a few moments later. As the two men started to depart, Barilla remarked how saving Churchill from the German assassins was the sole reason for the project and the facility. The system they were erecting must work, or all would be lost. If the project imploded and Campanella failed to return to the past, Germany's fate could, in fact, change.

Farber instantly saw his chance for Germany, or more importantly, Nazi redemption. From then on, he did his best to sabotage the project. Unfortunately, management fired him for overt dereliction of his responsibilities, preventing him from completing his scheme. And that is when chef Kurt Schultz became a prime cog in the plan to eliminate Campanella…

****

"Yes, when Otto and Bert didn't check in, I realized the sniper's attempt in the desert had failed. Now it is up to you," Farber said into the phone. After a few seconds of silence, he added, "You must be careful to do this at the right moment. We can't fail this time…it will be our final chance. Clearly, this Sergeant is more dangerous than we thought. We must stop him now," the man on the other end said sternly.

"I've got a couple of things I'm working on," Kaufman said. "I've stolen a level-five pass from one of the scientists. He contracted a strange flu-like illness. He's now in an oxygen tent in the health clinic. He's not even aware it's missing. I took some food to him and lifted it from his jacket hanging in the closet. If careful, I can get anywhere in the building undetected with this card."

"Any idea when the jump will take place?" Farber asked.

"It's going to happen soon. Management told me to lower the volume of food ordered as of June 1. When I asked why, they said half the staff would be leaving and adjustments needed to be made. It must be happening around that date," Kaufman said.

"Do you possess the device?"

"Yes, the C-4 was easy to get past the metal detectors. I smuggled the remaining items I needed in pieces or found here at the site."

"Excellent. This will be the most significant historical event anyone has ever achieved. The people of Germany will be the rule makers, the ones who dictate what happens, and all other nations will bow down to our supremacy. It will be as the Fuhrer envisioned."

"Yes," Kaufman said as he stood from his bed. "Albert, I must go. Dinner needs to be ready in an hour. Heil Hitler!"

"Heil Hitler!" Farber enthused.

CHAPTER 11

Over the next several weeks, Campanella spent almost all his waking hours learning to speak Italian and absorbing all he could about Italy. He surveyed and examined charts and maps detailing different terrains circa 1943. He studied the Barilla family history, the Italian resistance, the city of Naples, and the various western coastline cities he would be traversing in and through. All the while, they siphoned his blood daily and checked his vitals hourly.

The time traveler was trained, tutored, and educated as much as any human could be in the time frame available, and the man soaked in the information like a sponge. Blackwell monitored his progress and realized that his new physical acumen might only be trumped by the Sergeant's increased mental prowess.

As the night before the jump arrived, the team of specialists, along with Campanella, Barilla, and Blackwell, gathered at a conference table to discuss, one last time, the details of the operation.

Campanella sat to Barilla's right and Blackwell to his left. The three discussed Barilla's family, reviewing their characteristics and traits as much as was known. Most of the conversation fell on light and easy topics until Campanella asked Barilla, "So if I don't make it, what happens?"

The entire room went silent, and all eyes turned toward Barilla.

"Well," the man said in a reserved voice while looking down at his hands, "I guess everyone in this room will no longer exist. Not as we are right at this moment. Once you pass through the portal, all you see here will survive with you or simply disappear. And I guess as long as you stay alive, we will remain as we are. Once you stop the assassination, all should be well. If you don't halt the assassination, then who knows," Barilla said, his voice trailing off.

"Okay," Barilla said after a few moments of thoughtful silence. "It's eight-thirty. If we're not ready now, we never will be. So, I think it's time for a celebration," he bounded from his seat with a beaming smile for the men in the room. "I've asked the chef to prepare something special for us, plus I've also gotten us a little surprise – sort of a going away present for Joseph," he said while nodding at the waiter at the back of the room.

"Through some significant arm twisting, I've acquired three bottles of Glen Garioch Whiskey from their 1958 production. Though not the rarest, only 328 bottles were made that year. I'd like us all to celebrate our miraculous endeavors and drink this fine whiskey to the last drop," he said with an emphatic clap of his hands on each of the final two words.

At that moment, the waiter returned, wheeling a cart with the three bottles, fourteen glasses, and ice. He added the ice to the glasses of those who wanted it, then poured two fingers into each.

"Ladies and Gentlemen," Barilla said as he raised his glass in a toast, "I couldn't ask for a more loyal and dedicated group of people. Most of you gave up over five years of your lives to this project, and now we arrive at the moment that will forever be our destiny. Here's to all of you and your staff for going above and beyond." With that, the entire group stood and drank.

Turning to Campanella, Barilla lifted his glass once more. "Joseph, you honor us with your presence, unflagging effort, and dedication. Without you, none of this would be possible. Thank you." Everyone in the room chimed in with similar sentiments and drank again.

Over the next forty-five minutes, the men and women at the table imbibed, talked, and laughed until the last bottle stood empty. On this cue, Chef Schultz and his staff served dinner.

The first course consisted of cold gazpacho soup. The creamy, rich tomato-based soup was followed by a chopped salad with tomato, bacon, avocado, and delicious homemade blue cheese dressing. An eight-ounce filet mignon and two of the most enormous King Crab legs any of the men ever remembered seeing came next. Dessert was table-prepared Bananas Foster accompanied by a Hoyo de Monterey hand-rolled Cuban cigar. Finally, each person received a glass of ninety-eight-year-old Jenssen Arcana Courvoisier.

Chef Shultz rotated in and out of the room as each course was served. Campanella felt the man's eyes on him each time he came in. By the time dessert arrived, the sensation had made his skin crawl to the point that he needed answers.

Campanella leaned in toward Barilla and murmured, "Antonio."

"Yes, Joseph," Barilla said, smiling broadly.

In Italian, Campanella asked while nodding, "The Chef, what's his deal?"

"What do you mean?"

"What do you know about him, his background, where he's from, things like that?"

Barilla studied Shultz as he walked out of the room. "He's clean. As I mentioned, each person who came down that main elevator shaft received a thorough vetting. Why do you ask?"

"I'm not sure. But though the chef is trying to keep me from noticing, he's been staring at me each time he comes in until he goes out. I don't know what it is, but something isn't right."

"I'm sure it's nothing. As I said, everyone here has been checked and rechecked."

"You're right; I'm sure it's nothing," Campanella said, but his internal alarms told him something different.

At ten-thirty, Barilla stood up from his chair. He stayed that way momentarily, saying nothing as he scanned the room. He studied each person's eyes individually and then, with inner strength and confidence, said: "Gentleman, until tomorrow!" With that, the group rose and began filing out the door.

Campanella held back, wanting to be the last to leave. As he went to exit, he deliberately turned and saw Shultz standing on the opposite side of the room, staring. The man quickly averted his eyes and then pushed his cart out the door back toward the kitchen. Campanella watched his every step.

CHAPTER 12

Shultz listened as the phone rang three times, then hung up. He re-dialed, and Farber answered on the first ring.

"Yes, I'm here," Farber whispered into the mouthpiece.

"It's happening tomorrow," Shultz said confidently.

"How will you get the bomb in the room?" Farber asked.

"The control room staff will go to their stations at 0530 to start the final countdown preparations. That time is well before the regular breakfast serving time, so they've asked me to bring breakfast to them at 0630. I'll wheel the food in on a covered cart with the bomb concealed on the lower shelf.

"As I make my way around the room, I'll place the bomb under a desk in the back. The desk has two small cabinets with doors on the front, so I can place it toward the back of one of the cabinets and close the door. It will be completely concealed from view," Kaufman said.

"Excellent! The narration of our ancestors is about to change forever," Farber said. After a short pause, he added softly, "I'm sorry that history will not show what you will do tomorrow, my friend. But I believe the war's outcome will change positively for Germany because of it. Our families and our Fuhrer will be the benefactors. All I can say is thank you…"

****

Campanella leaned back in his desk chair and studied the maps of Italy, the various cities he would encounter, and a host of other documents and papers for the mission. He had long since memorized everything, but he re-examined them again anyway. As he lifted one of the papers, a picture of Berta, the eldest Barilla daughter, fell out and landed on the table before him.

He picked the photo up and examined it. Berta looked to be around age eighteen or nineteen, the age she would be when he arrived. She was sitting on a swing on the front porch of her grandfather's house. Her large brown eyes were full of energy and warmth, and her smile lit up the entire picture.

After a few more seconds of reflection, it hit him. Though he'd viewed this picture dozens of times before and always thought her pretty, he now grasped that she was more than pretty – the young girl was strikingly beautiful. Why hadn't he appreciated that earlier?

After a few moments, he put the picture and several maps into a small black body pouch. He grabbed his personal identification documents prepared for 1943 and put them in his bag. Lastly, he thumbed through a small black notebook, which detailed needed information regarding dates, names, and locations, and then placed the leather-bound object into the same carrier. These would be the only items he would be allowed to take.

He undressed, lay in bed, and turned on his IBM ThinkPad. Once it was powered up, he opened his browser and typed in Kurt Schultz. After a few additional clicks, he found one hundred forty-seven people documented with this name. Not all the Kurt Schultz's in the country, but it was as good a starting place as any. He began scrolling down the list, though nothing stood out.

Just as he was about to give up, he came across a Culinary Institute of America graduate named Kurt Schultz. He opened the website and found a small paragraph on the chef. It displayed a few places where the culinarian previously worked and one sentence stating his place of birth – Woodbury, New Jersey.

Campanella sat motionless for a moment. Something was gnawing at his intuition. For someone working in such a high-security position, the man offered limited qualifications...

Bolting upright in bed, Campanella decided to find out who this chef was. There was just too much about Schulz that didn't seem right. He slid on his pants and went to his closet. There, he found his ten-inch military knife and sheath. He attached it to his belt and moved to the door. After cracking the door just enough to verify no one was around, he slid out and moved down the hall.

The chef's quarters were at the opposite end of his. Campanella hurried in that direction. Each room had the person's name on a plaque next to the apartment's door. He searched each plaque, but when only two doors were left, he wondered if Schulz was billeted somewhere else. Maybe closer to the kitchen?

The next door he came to was for someone named Sherman Smythe. Campanella frowned. The last entry had two doors at the end of the hall facing him. The plaque, which was larger than the rest, read KURT SCHULZ. Odd, why did this man have what appeared to be a much larger room than anyone else?

Moving to the door, he leaned in and put his ear to the metal panel. He immediately heard several voices, all men, and they seemed to be having a party. Celebrating the time jump? Maybe. But there was something strange about the conversation. Straining to hear, he realized that all the men were speaking German. He also recognized Schulz's voice, "It will all be over tomorrow. Within thirty minutes after the fools eat breakfast, everyone will be dead. We will have stopped this insane time-travel scheme. Germany will win the war!"

Campanella pulled the knife from its sheath. He leaned back and slammed his foot against the door. It didn't budge. He tried again. Nothing. He began ramming his shoulder into the door, over and over. Bang, bang, bang...

"Joseph, we need you in the ready room in thirty minutes. Are you awake?" Antonio Barilla called out as he knocked on Campanella's door.

Campanella opened his eyes, his computer half on and half off his lap. He had fallen asleep and slept through the night in almost the same position. "Yes, I am. I will be ready," he said groggily. Sitting up, he tried to remember what he had just dreamt. Though the lingering moments of the dream began to fade, his concern about the chef did not.

At almost that exact moment, a voice over a loudspeaker system that echoed throughout the facility said, "Ladies and gentlemen, we are now at T minus sixty minutes…"

Chapter 13

Chef Kurt Schultz set the timer on the C-4 charge and placed it on a cake platter on the second shelf of the serving cart. He then put the matching stainless-steel cover over the device and positioned it in the middle of the shelf. Grabbing a variety of condiments and other foodstuffs from the counter behind him, the German plotter strategically placed them around the platter. He covered the whole cart with a white linen tablecloth and then wheeled the unit out of the storage room where he had been working.

After loading the top of the cart with trays of scrambled eggs, bacon, sausage, smoked salmon with capers, bagels, cream cheese, toast, and other breakfast items, he took a deep breath and walked to the control room as calmly as he could. As he exited the kitchen, he checked his watch. In thirty-two minutes, he would be changing the world for the better…

****

When Campanella arrived at the ready room, Dr. Blackwell smiled and asked, "You ready?"

"As ready as I'll ever be, I guess," Campanella said.

The two then headed toward the central transfer area of the time portal unit. They got on a nearby elevator, and Blackwell pushed the button marked with an M. As the doors closed, Campanella moved toward the elevator's back wall. Constructed of the same thick glass as all the other viewing areas of the facility, the panel furnished him with an unobstructed view of the interior of the building. Though he had observed the same vision dozens of times since arriving, this was the first time witnessing it with all facets of the time machine in full operation.

Unlike earlier, where only small bursts of the blue lights pulsed through the clear piping, a constant stream of brilliant blue light was now racing along the entire length of the cylinders. The central silo also blazed with the same throbbing, intense blue. It was a mesmerizing sight that again caused Campanella's jaw to slacken in awe.

The car descended two floors, and when the doors opened, Campanella walked into an area of about ten square feet. Directly before him was an immense steel door reminiscent of a Hollywood bank vault. Although Campanella had the run of the compound, he'd only visited this level twice before that day. Most recently, Blackwell and two assistants had brought him down for a dry run to show him where he would stand.

"I swore I wouldn't get sentimental, but I'd kick myself later if I didn't tell you this now. I am so very proud of you. And…well, I also want to thank you personally for doing this," Blackwell said. Before Campanella could reply, the small man grabbed the much larger Campanella and gave him a heartfelt hug.

After a moment longer, Blackwell backed away and then smiled. It was a smile of unabashed fondness. Blackwell shook his head slightly, reached into his pocket, and took out two sets of small orange earplugs. He handed one set to Campanella and put the second pair into his ears. Blackwell then entered a code to a small electric pad next to the large door. When he keyed in the last digit, the steel rods began sliding within the door. After a few seconds, they seated themselves with a clunk into a fully disengaged position. A moment later, the door started to slide open.

The deafening sound on the other side immediately assaulted Campanella's ears, even with the sound-dampening nodules firmly in place. Once inside, Campanella turned his head and glanced into the control room. Barilla stood plainly in view, as well as Pittman and several other military personnel with whom the Sergeant trained. They were all standing close to the glass, peering down, and watching as Campanella emerged into the portal area. The Sergeant smiled at them and gave them a reassuring thumbs-up. All the men in the group did the same, though their smiles seemed a bit forced.

Just as Campanella began turning toward Blackwell, he saw Schultz from the corner of his eye. Campanella spun toward Blackwell and pointed at the man. The Sergeant tried to alert his friend, but the thunderous noise of the machinery made communicating impossible.

"T minus twelve minutes," the loudspeaker announced.

Campanella shot another look at the control room, but Schultz was gone, as were the rest of the men. Dr. Blackwell grabbed Campanella's arm, and the two men made their way onto the platform, though the taller man kept looking over his shoulder toward the booth.

Once on this section of granite, Blackwell pushed a small black button on a panel next to the portal. The thick glass enclosure rotated slowly around until an opening appeared. Campanella smiled at the man and reached out to shake his hand.

He brushed the big paw away and bear-hugged him instead. The embrace lasted for several long beats before the two separated. Campanella smiled with genuine fondness and gave Blackwell a pat on his shoulder. He reached into his back pocket for his hat, put it on, winked at the spectacled man, and calmly walked into the cylinder.

As earlier instructed, he moved to a spot in the portal where a thirty-inch glass circle was positioned. During Campanella's training, Cody Robbins emphatically explained how he must stand unmoving in the center of this sphere until the portal was activated, and transportation completed. Looking down at the round glass object, he precisely positioned his feet as instructed. When he looked back up, he nodded at Blackwell. The smiling man nodded back and then re-engaged the button.

The cylinder silently rotated back toward its closed position. Once it stopped moving, a vacuum-like sound apparently signaled the cylinder had sealed in the desired way. This sequence ultimately closed out the world beyond the glass, and near silence descended.

During his training, this unit remained unlit and unremarkable because the actual transporting unit was not activated. Now, with the entire building abuzz with scientific overload, the structure's interior glowed brightly in a cobalt blue hue. He studied the cylinder, first along the bottom and then up and along the top. Every possible seam appeared sealed. There were no noticeable joints except where the portal's sliding door closed.

In the center of the top of the unit, he saw several rings of lights emanating from a circle that appeared to be just like the one he was standing on. The sphere throbbed with the same brilliant blue color, moving at light speed through the pipes above and the glass disk below.

Campanella gazed out toward the large steel door and watched Blackwell begin exiting area. Just as he was about to leave the chamber, the small man stopped, turned back toward Campanella, and offered the time traveler a small but purposeful salute. Campanella thought he saw a tear roll down the man's face before he turned and went through the door. As the door closed, he glanced up and saw a digitized clock on the wall above the jamb. The red digital numbers read 03:42 – and they were counting backward to zero.

Chapter 14

Schultz looked down at his watch. Up to that moment, he had been sitting in his room in a state of quiet and unnatural calmness. After positioning the bomb in the control room, he walked casually back to his apartment with no urgency. After all, there was no point worrying about getting to safety once the bomb went off.

With Montgomery dead, he wouldn't be alive in that specific time and place anyway. Nothing would be. This thought had filled him with an intense sense of pride and accomplishment, feelings which erased all thoughts of fear or fright.

That was moments before, though. Now, it was two minutes past the expected explosion time, and Schultz's heart was pounding in his ribcage.

"T minus three minutes," the loudspeaker squawked throughout the compound.

The mechanical drone of the announcement jolted Schultz, causing him to jump to his feet. He raced to his dresser and ripped the top drawer from its resting place. A large fourteen-inch butcher's knife sailed through the air and hit the ground several feet away. Schultz grabbed a towel on his bed and concealed the razor-sharp utensil in its fold.

"T minus two minutes..."

The noise outside the chamber where Campanella stood was now at an ear-shattering pitch as the results of five years of scientific research were now operating at total capacity. Equipment was banging, shrieking, and churning at a fevered level – yet Joseph Campanella heard little inside the chamber. The six-inch Plexiglas shield and surrounding transport portal equipment silenced most of the clamor. His ability to silence the outside world as needed quickly erased what noise was still filtering its way in.

He suddenly realized his heartbeat was elevated and his breathing slightly labored, so he began to meditate into a calmer state. Just as he was about to close his eyes, a flicker of movement caught his attention in the control room above.

"T minus ten, nine, eight, seven, six, five..."

In a moment of euphoric triumph, Kurt Schultz knew he was about to change the world: past, present, and future. He bounded down the steps toward the glass viewing area three at a time, stopping just short of plowing into the structure. Campanella saw him and took a small step forward in reaction. When he did, the toe of his boot extended a fragment outside the pulsating circle.

The time traveler glared at the chef with concern and malice. Schulz merely smiled back at Campanella, a victorious beaming grin, and then an explosion of brilliant blue light consumed the inside of the portal chamber...

PART 2

CHAPTER 1

A MAN'S BODY

May 23rd, 1943 - 10:00am

Diana D'Alba, Italy

The two young women approached the shaded and lumpen shape, and Maria, the younger and more excitable of the two Barilla siblings, thought it might be the remnants of a fallen tree in the tall grass. Her sister, Berta, nodded in agreement but wasn't so sure. With only a few feet to go, the two clasped hands tightly, edging forward on a sideways angle to give the object as wide a berth as possible. Suddenly, Maria gave an impossibly high-pitched scream, causing Bertha to scream in response.

Lying on the ground was a man's body.

The Barilla girls had traveled in the opposite direction on this same trail less than an hour before. On the return trip, a strange man was lying face down under an enormous Norwegian Maple tree. They were no more than a quarter of a mile from where they lived and discussed running home and getting help. It would be the prudent and cautious thing to do. But an odd and morbid curiosity kept their feet cemented in place and eyes glued on the body.

Maintaining what they assumed to be a safe distance, the two began speaking in whispered tones. At first, Maria suggested the man might be sleeping. But calls to the stationary form received no response. Berta bent down and picked up a small pebble. She aimed and tossed it, trying to hit the body for a reaction. Her toss missed, and the projectile bounced harmlessly across the ground.

Berta believed the pebble to be too light to get an accurate throw, so she retrieved a larger one. Maria didn't relinquish her grip and stumbled after her on the search. She brandished her find, more of a stone than a pebble and glanced at her sister. Maria nodded in nervous, wide-eyed approval. Her sister took a deep breath, aimed, and threw. The rock soared through the air and struck the body squarely in the back, making a solid thumping sound. Then silence.

The girls burst into manic speculation. Maria was sure that the inert man must have beaten, robbed of all his possessions, and left for dead. Berta, however, believed in a less grisly fate. She suggested a possible illness, or some accident could be the culprit. She pointed to a large flat rock near where he lay, explaining how maybe he fell and hit his head.

Over the next several moments, their young and febrile minds conjured up many possibilities for the man's appearance. Finally, though, Berta announced, "Maria, I think he's – DEAD!"

The notion staggered Maria, who hadn't thought seriously about death and had never been confronted with it. Yes, her father often cautioned her that death was inevitable in war, and she might experience those horrors one day. But his warning had not weighed on her carefree innocence.

Bertha decided they needed to investigate the man's condition more closely. She began moving toward the body. But Maria would have none of it. She yanked her hand from her older sister's grip as she started to pull her along. The younger girl had no intention of *investigating* anything. Besides, she couldn't move her legs or feet even if she wanted to go. She was too scared.

Berta turned to her sibling and glared at her for a moment. Her expression eventually faltered and softened, and she shrugged and edged tentatively to the man's side. She surveyed the area surrounding the body and noticed the ground around the man was undisturbed. Her father had taught all the older Barilla children the nuances of tracking animal spore and how the disturbed terrain revealed valuable information.

But if a struggle did occur, there were no signs of it. There were also no footprints – none. No impressions from a possible assailant nor from the man who lay sprawled on the ground. This made no sense to Berta. After all, the man hadn't fallen from the sky. *Had he?*

As that implausible thought crossed her mind, Berta's eyes narrowed. Although it was silly and stupid, she nevertheless looked up toward the tree. The long finger-like branches of the ancient maple hovered above in a protective shield. The limbs were thick and bulky, and she saw no movement though the wind was blowing briskly.

Berta studied the branch above the body and then looked back down. She contemplated the possibility the man had fallen from there. That could explain it. But the only access to the branch was to climb the tree. This didn't hold water. Though gnarly, with old limb wounds that might be used as handholds, a thirty-foot climb straight up the trunk to reach the first accessible branch would be needed. No, she thought as she shook her head; no one could do that. And besides, why would he?

Berta turned her attention back to the form on the ground. Something terrible happened to this man, but for the life of her, she couldn't figure out what. As she pondered, she used her foot to give the corpse a couple of investigative nudges.

Maria watched her sister prod the man with a vacant stare, her entire body rigid with fear. In a veiled fog of panic, she pointed in protest and attempted to talk. Only a croaking sound emerged. She swallowed hard and tried again, but her throat felt desert-dry, constricted shut. Moving her tongue around in her mouth, Maria did her best to produce a drop of speech-inducing saliva. She made an intense effort, and, this time, the words came out in a staccato, hoarse-throated fashion.

"Is…is…is he dead?"

Berta turned to look at her sister, glowering in irritation. "I don't know," she hissed through clenched teeth, "And for heaven's sake, keep your voice down. We don't know how he got here, if he hurt himself, or if someone else hurt him. And if someone did hurt him, they might still be near here. Now come over and help me roll him over," the older Barilla girl said as she positioned herself over the man's prone body.

Earlier, when the two had discussed a possible assailant, Maria hadn't contemplated that the potential attacker might still be nearby. Now that this was a real possibility, the cherub-faced girl's still bulging eyes began darting around in every direction. She was now in a state of near mouth-foaming hysteria.

"Maria!" Berta barked frustratingly, "I need you to come here and help me!"

This latest demand jolted the younger sibling out of her moment of detachment. Though slow-moving, she made her way over to Berta and the unmoving, possibly *dead* man.

The sisters strained to turn the limp form over, and eventually, momentum and gravity overcame the inertia of his weight. He flopped heavily onto his back, and Berta marveled at its size. Even on the ground, she could tell the man was incredibly tall, with shoulders broader than the trunk of the enormous tree that may have spelled his demise. His hands and feet were huge, and his arms bulged beneath his shirtsleeves. But the sheer mass of the man wasn't the only thing that caught her attention. His clothes seemed unfamiliar…odd looking.

At first glance, the shirt, pants, and boots he wore gave the appearance of clothes the men in her family might wear. But though they were similar, something was completely out of the ordinary about them. And the hat he was wearing was shaped like no other. The clothes were undoubtedly civilian styles, nothing military, that was for sure, and yet something wasn't right…

"He's a very big…" Berta started saying as she groaned from the stranger's weight, "…man," she finished as they got him on his back. "I think he may be a foreigner."

Maria jerked up and stumbled back in a panic. She tripped over something previously hidden under the man's body as she did. The object caused her to lose her balance, but she quickly shuffled her feet and regained her footing. At first, Maria simply gawked at the thing on the ground. She then shifted looked back to the man and then the object.

Though it appeared to be nothing more than a small, harmless pouch, her reaction was as if she'd seen a three-headed monster about to pounce. Without conscious thought, Maria began inching further and further away.

"What's that?" she asked in alarm while waving her arm at the object.

"I don't know. Pick it up and look at it," Berta snapped back.

"No way! You pick it up!" Maria said in defiance as she took another giant step backward.

"You're such a child," Berta said primly as she leaned over and snatched it up. She held it in her hands, surveying the odd bag. Unfortunately, the bravery shown to her sister had been more sibling bravado than real courage. As she examined the pouch, she once again felt as if she was viewing something entirely foreign.

The black bag was about ten inches long, eight inches deep, and five inches wide from front to back. Constructed primarily of leather, it had a zipper around the front and sides and small zippered pouches on each end.

An odd-looking strap was attached at the top of the left and right sides of the bag. It appeared made of a cloth-like material, though unlike any cloth Berta had ever seen. On the end of the left-hand strap, a peculiar-shaped black plastic buckle was attached.

Plastics were relatively new, especially in the area near their hometown of Diana d'Alba, and Berta only remembered a few things crafted of it, but nothing such as this. The end of the right-hand strap was torn and tattered. Although it looked like an animal had chewed it away, the girl figured a similar buckle should also be there.

She squeezed the bag in an investigative yet gentle way as if feeling a wrapped present to guess its contents. She couldn't recognize any shape she was feeling, though. She studied the pouch for a few more moments and then quickly pushed the bag away from her body, deciding that further exploration might not be such a good idea after all.

"Um," Berta choked, "Maybe we'll wait to open this…"

"Humph…" Maria muttered; victory achieved.

Berta stretched her arms far out and laid the pouch on the ground. Both girls watched the lying man intently for a few uninterrupted moments, studying his large physique in awe. At this moment, Berta thought she saw his chest rise and fall in a single breath. It was a slight movement, and she wasn't sure if she had imagined it, so she repositioned and refocused. The elder Barilla girl scrutinized in tension-filled anticipation for several seconds, waiting for it to happen again.

When she was about to give up, Maria jolted her with another panicked demand. "Berta, is he dead, or isn't he?"

Berta's body jerked in alarm, and her head twisted toward Maria. Her features, which usually remained soft, pleasant, and appealing, were now stone-like and icy. She glowered at her sister and said abruptly, "Maria, I said I don't know! Now stand still and be quiet!"

With eyes narrowed in anger, Berta returned to her self-appointed task. As she again focused on his chest, she subconsciously brought her hands up under her chin and began wrenching them back and forth. After a few more agonizing moments of nothing, Berta could not wait any longer and acted.

Although she didn't want to touch any exposed skin, she knew the only way to determine whether he was alive was to do just that. The girl crawled to his right side and got up on one knee. Grabbing the man's hand, she placed two fingers on his wrist and checked for a pulse. His skin was alarmingly cool, and Berta knew this wasn't a good sign.

Closing her eyes, she focused on the sensations at her fingertips. "I'm not sure…" she said with uncertainty. "Maybe…" the girl said with a grimace. She laid a hand on his chest and moved toward his shoulders. Her grandfather explained how finding a pulse along the throat was sometimes easier. Berta tried there. After a short pause, she exclaimed, "I feel something! It's weak, but I think so."

Though Berta was close to the man's head, she still couldn't see his face. His head was facing away from her, and his hat had slipped down when they turned him over and was now covering most of it. Once again, curiosity was getting the best of the young Italian, and she reached for the hat…

"Are you CRAZY?" Maria shouted in alarm. Berta jerked her hand back, and she lost her balance. Reflectively, she shot out a hand and caught herself on the man's shoulder to steady herself from falling. "For the last time, stop doing that!" Berta scolded her distraught sister.

"Don't do anything else, for God's sake!" Maria begged, ignoring Berta's insistent demand for calm.

"Maria, I want to see his face! What if it's someone we know?" Berta replied without hesitation, though she was confident he was not from their town. And with that, the older girl grabbed the brim of his hat and pulled it up and toward her with the man's head following. Just as she got his face to a viable viewing point, his hat dislodged and slid off his head.

"Oh, God," Berta yelped while falling back and landing flat on her backside.

"What? What is it?" Maria shouted as she shuffled backward in fright.

"The right side of his face… it's caked with dried blood…and part of his scalp is uh…kind of peeled back," Berta told her sister, the words jagged and edgy as they fell from her mouth.

After a few seconds of heavy breathing and thought, Berta acted. She hurried to the man's other side, closer to his injury. Once in position, she tore a narrow but long strip of material from the sash she wore at her waist. She wiped her hand on her dress and carefully pushed the skin flap back into place. She took the cloth and gently wrapped it around his head and the wound.

Maria stared in awe as she watched her sister nurse the unknown stranger, even as her body instinctively continued to move further away. She took a couple more steps toward a possible escape, arms and hands held back as feelers, when Berta spun in her direction. "Where do you think you're going?" she said in a chastising voice.

"Home. We need to get Grandpapa! He'll know what to do," Maria whined.

Four years had passed since Adolf Hitler, and his Blitzkrieg war machine had invaded Poland. And though the Barilla family had tried to avoid the conflict, Italy's involvement forced them to become unwilling participants. Now, the girl's father, their two uncles, and several other male members of the Barilla clan were off fighting in the war.

However, they were not soldiers in their country's army, nor were they in any allegiance with Italy's ally, Germany. In fact, they had joined a small band of Italian partisans who understood and detested the intentions of the Germans and Mussolini's dictatorship.

Unfortunately, with their men off fighting, the only males still at the Barilla home were the girl's two older brothers, Carlo and Arturo, their younger brother Antonio, and their Grandpapa, Santos. And because of these departures, their grandfather was whom the two turned to when in need.

Berta ignored her sister's panic and returned to the job. She tied the cloth so it would remain secured around the man's head. When finished, she took a moment to admire her work. Then she hesitated, frowning. The man must be enormously heavy. Too heavy for them to carry. Plus, she was unsure exactly what was wrong with him, so moving him could be dangerous.

"You're right, Maria."

"I am? About what?"

"We need Grandpapa's help. I want you to go get him while I stay here."

"You want me to go alone?"

"Yes, Maria, alone. Now go before it gets dark. And for heaven's sake, be careful – and be quick about it," Berta instructed as she took off her jacket and laid it on the man's chest, "And another thing. Don't go screaming and getting the entire family all worked up. When you arrive, gather some clean rags, bandages, and more fresh water. Once you have all those items, find Grandpapa and no one else. You must convince him to come without alerting the rest of the family."

Maria stared at her sister as her stunned brain processed Berta's demand. After a moment longer, her lips pursed, and her eyes narrowed. "I – wish – Papa – was – here!" she said defiantly as she stomped her left foot up and down with each word.

"Well, he's not," Bertha said more softly. "So got get Grandpapa. He will know what to do," Berta demanded as she pointed an authoritative finger down the path toward the Barilla farm.

"Great, just great…I don't like this one bit. Why don't we just leave him here and both go home," Maria barked as she wheeled around and trudged off. As Maria's light blue skirt swished back and forth from her exaggerated steps, she muttered and mumbled her disapproval of the situation. "She knows I don't like walking home alone. This whole thing is crazy! And he's a perfect stranger too; maybe even a German – or who knows what…" she continued, her voice trailing off as she moved further away and down the path.

As Berta watched her sister's irate form storm off, she frowned as she realized her sibling was a child in many ways. Though she was almost fourteen, her body only recently began to be affected by womanhood. Berta, now nineteen, was fully developed. But, more importantly, and unlike her younger sister, she was a woman of intellect and spirit.

If it weren't for the Great War, Paulo Gianelli and I would be married by now. She smiled wistfully and with the pleasure of one who hadn't known heartbreak.

She and Paulo had met as small children by the picturesque shoreline of Lake Vittoria, a mutual Gianelli and Barilla family gathering place. It was a spectacular summer's day, bursting with fun and revelry. As usual, the get-together had no lack of delicious food and flowing wine. He remembered that Paulo's father, Daniel Gianelli, brought a succulent smoked pig, a delicacy for which he was famous. There were also plenty of homemade side dishes of beans, potatoes, and fresh vegetables made by the wives of both families.

Berta's mother had baked loaves of hot, steamy bread, whose insides were as white and fluffy as the dainty clouds gliding above them throughout the day. Isla, Berta's grandmother, provided trays of pastries and cakes. The delicacies were smeared with gooey, sugary, sweet toppings dripping and oozing down their sides.

And then, of course, there were the Barolo wines. Boasting and bragging rights raged as the men argued over whose wines were best from that year's crop. And though not one of the gathered men would give into any other, the men seemed content not to crown a winner.

The children played games, and several of the adults joined in. Berta laughed as she remembered seeing Paulo Gianelli for the first time. Her beautiful Paulo, whom she'd beaten in a foot race, making him cry with frustration. They had run from the top of the beach line, where the coarse sand first started, to the water's edge some fifty feet away. Berta was as fast as a young filly and dove headfirst into the crystal-clear water well before Paulo. "Beat him by a mile," she would brag for years.

From that moment on, Berta was in love. Though he was a skinny, dark-eyed, dark-haired boy, barely seven years old, she was smitten forever.

Now, more than ten years since that day, the relationship had blossomed into a mutual expression of commitment. Well, she thought it had, at least. It was just that sometimes, things needed a little *push* to bring it to the surface for both parties. A few months ago, Paulo had done something special… he'd kissed Berta. She remembered the touch of his lips on hers. It felt as if he were taking the breath from them as a thrill pulsed into the pit of her stomach and down to her groin.

Berta had often dreamt of this exact moment with Paulo. But even her wildest fantasy was nothing compared to the physical sensations that overcame her as their mouths and tongues met in hungry passion. It was a defining moment. From that day forward, Berta was confident that she and Paulo would marry, and their life would be perfect!

No, Paulo hadn't asked for Berta's hand yet, but this simple fact didn't stop her from dreaming about their wedding day and all the delightful things she and her mother would do to prepare. In her mind, it would be the finest wedding ever held in their little town. She routinely fantasized about the actual day and how Diana D'Alba's townspeople would come to celebrate the occasion.

Friends, family, and even strangers would fawn over her and her new husband as they celebrated the magnificent event. Papa would erect streamers bought from Provenzano's market and colorful lanterns to light the night. Singing and dancing would echo through the hills, and people would put Liras in a hat each time Berta and Paulo kissed – and she would kiss him often. It would be a grand affair and a fantastic start to their married lives together.

Of course, the perfect wedding was only part of the ideal dream life for the soon-to-be Mrs. Paulo Gianelli. The couple would have four children. The first boy would be named Paulo, for his father, and then Santos would be born, named after her beloved grandfather. Two girls would come next. Genevieve, named after a character from her favorite childhood story, and Angelina because she always loved the name.

They would live on the Barilla family's land in a house Paulo and the men of her family would build. It would be high atop a hill between their home and the Gianelli's. She'd already picked the spot and the direction she wanted it to face.

The front of the house would look toward the setting sun, and the back, where the end-to-end covered porch would be, would open to Lake Vittoria and Nebbiolo Hill, the most beautiful and meaningful of vistas. Yes, it was all planned out, and it would be oh-so-perfect and wonderful. Once the war ended, that is.

"Mrs. Berta Gianelli," she mused aloud, momentarily ignoring the war's disruption of her plans, "what a splendid name…" Her moment of reflection evaporated as she heard voices coming from the path where Maria had vanished mere moments before. As the cobwebs cleared from her vision, she turned her head and watched for her sister and her grandfather to appear. The teenage Berta was sitting cross-legged next to the injured man with her hands in her lap. However, she sensed something odd.

As she began to understand what was wrong, her head slowly, but with purpose, tilted down. Somewhere during her daydream, she had picked up the man's hand and was holding, no, caressing it in hers. A breath of embarrassing realization rushed through her lips, and she gently lifted the hand and set it back on his chest.

The voices were now getting louder. Sensing that this was as good a time as any to move to a safer distance, Berta began to rise. Once standing, she casually straightened her dress and brushed away some debris clinging to the material. The girl suddenly noted something strange in the approaching voices and cocked her head, straining to listen. With a gasp, she recognized the harsh and clipped tones of German conversation. *It must be German soldiers,* she thought.

Berta stared down at the body on the ground and then glanced at her surroundings. Panic was rushing through her as she tried to decide what to do. Without thinking of her safety, the girl clutched the stranger by his wrists. She struggled as she turned the man and dragged him toward an area of dense brush. He was extremely heavy, and it took every ounce of her strength to pull the lifeless figure twenty-five or so feet to the hiding place, stumbling multiple times during the effort.

Grunting and groaning with each step, she reached the edge of the thicket. Stopping to catch her breath, she quickly glanced in the direction she'd heard the voices. At that moment, a gray helmet with the all too familiar German military flaring rounded the corner yards from where she stood.

Her mind raced with indecision. Was the man on the ground a German? Should she leave him where he lay and run home? No, she did not think so. Berta found a small gap in the bushes and pulled him through. After getting the body about six feet in, she dropped his hands and hurried to reposition the trampled foliage, so it blocked the opening. She knew that if someone looked closely, they would see something had been dragged there, and her pulse quickened in fear.

The men's voices were bearing down on where she knelt. She put her hand over her mouth, trying to stifle the sound of her own stress. Sweat dripped down her brow and along the bridge of her nose. She swiped at a bead on the tip and flicked it to the ground.

Berta tried to control her breathing as best she could, feeling the panic press against her ribcage. She closed her eyes and breathed slowly to calm herself. When she opened her eyes, Berta noticed the stranger's little black pouch lying on the path. In her haste to move the man, she had completely forgotten about it.

"I hear the women are deliciously pretty," the tall Private said to the Lance Corporal beside him.

"Yes, the mother and the older daughter especially," the other soldier responded.

The Private then gave his comrade a quick jab with his elbow and, with a laugh, added, "One for you and one for me, eh?"

Berta wasn't confident speaking German, but she understood reasonably well, and the men's comments caused a wave of nausea that began with a tingling in her scalp and swept down to her legs. Could they be speaking of her family? Was it her mother and her they desired? Or even her sister? It made her stomach spasm in revulsion to think of it. She shook the thought out of her head and refocused her attention on the black pouch. It was sitting like a beacon no more than twenty feet away. If they saw it, they would surely stop and pick it up. Then, they would search the area for its owner.

Maybe they wouldn't notice it,' she thought. No, that is foolish. How could they miss it? It was right in the open. Only a blind person would walk by and not see it.

Berta silently prayed that the soldiers would pass by and miss her and the bag. Sweat was now flowing everywhere. The sticky moisture was covering her body in a blanket of stress-induced dampness. She could feel tears begin to well up in her eyes. She would be caught for sure.

The men were still discussing their potential prizes as they were passing her. They walked past her position one by one, oblivious to her hiding place. The soldier's footfalls were deafening in her ears. Finally, as the fifth and last man passed, the foreboding sense of terror and impending capture began to ebb.

Soon, the men were out of sight and earshot. The relief was overwhelming, and Berta let out a shaky but cleansing breath. She closed her eyes and shook her head in disbelief. As hard as it was to believe, none of the men had detected her, the pouch, or the strange man lying in the undergrowth. She turned to look at the stranger with a smile of victory.

CHAPTER 2

"Fraulein!" a deep voice bellowed, causing Berta's head to snap back around. "Why do you hide from us?" Berta shrieked with fright as a hulking, thick-chested German grabbed her by the arm and jerked her to her feet. Before she could react, the soldier shoved her into the arms of the man next to him. He then half-dragged and half-yanked her away from the bushes, pulling her along until they stood in the exact spot where the stranger's body had lain minutes earlier.

The first soldier started to follow, but he glanced toward the ground as he was about to step out. "What is this?" he said as his eyes tracked the betraying path of heel marks from their origin to their end. Peering into the dense foliage, the eyes of the seasoned veteran of two wars narrowed. He took another step or two toward the brush and stopped. "Oh," he laughed as he saw the body. "Did you kill this man? Is that why you hide?" His grin was malevolent in its playfulness.

"This is a pity for you. Murdering someone is punishable by death," the man holding Berta said as he tightened his grip.

The other three men in the group now appeared from behind Berta. They surrounded the girl and expressed their sheer delight at the prize their fellow soldiers had discovered.

Private Reiner Diefenbaker, the man standing over the body, kicked the motionless form in its side. When there was no response, he made a tsking sound and turned around. "Yes, the drawbacks to murder are many. I'm afraid penance is due."

One of the other soldiers moved past the Neanderthal-faced Lance Corporal restraining Berta. He'd spotted the black bag on the ground and moved to retrieve it. He turned it over in his hands, half admiring, half puzzled, and opened the front zipper.

Scanning the contents, he pulled out various items tucked away in its recesses. He discovered a few maps and a small book of notes and writings. He examined the words but didn't understand them. Further searching exposed a compass, which he placed in his pocket, and a magnifying glass, which found a spot next to the compass.

The following item he pulled out was a picture of a girl. He studied it intently for a few moments and then glanced at Berta. "Well, well," he said so all could hear. He then walked over to where the girl was being held and asked, "Is this your bag, Fraulein?" Berta shook her head no. "The dead man's then?" Berta shrugged. "Hmmm...Well, it must be one of yours since I found a photo of you in it."

The young Italian girl's eyes widened as she stared in honest bewilderment. She turned toward where the man lay in the bushes and then back toward the soldier holding the bag and picture. Berta's scrutiny of the photo in the soldier's hand was interrupted by an unbuckling belt. The soldier grasping her chuckled as he spun Berta back toward the now-disrobing Private Diefenbaker.

Berta watched as the Private laid his helmet, gun belt, and knife on a large rock to his left. He was grinning ear to ear, and his eyes bore a wild, lustful stare as he started unbuttoning his tunic. A conspicuous bulge began to form in his trousers, causing Berta to shrink back in revulsion.

As the now erect soldier took two steps toward the girl, he unzipped his fly and reached into his pants. Grabbing himself, he started to moan with sadistic pleasure. At that moment, a massive set of hands grabbed him around the head and viciously twisted left and then right. A loud cracking sound filled the air like a branch snapped over someone's leg.

Before any of this could register with the assembled men, the unknown assailant had retrieved the discarded knife and gun belt from the rock. With a surgeon's precision, he threw the razor-sharp weapon straight toward the girl. The blade whistled through the air, passing no more than an inch or two past her head. Berta heard a sickening thwump and then felt the grip of the man holding her loosen and then fall away.

The knife thrower pulled the pistol from the gun belt and triggered the German luger three times in rapid succession. With accuracy as deadly as the knife throw, the bullets pierced each of the remaining German's chests just left of center, toppling them like dominoes.

The entire killing spree took less than ten seconds, and all Berta could do was turn her head from side to side as she watched each man drop around her. When she'd collected her wits and looked back at the stranger, he was sitting on the same rock that held the half-dressed soldier's weapons moments ago.

"Who—are—you?" Berta asked, stretching out the words as she did. But before he could respond, she quickly added, "And where are you from, and..." turning toward the dead soldier who had picked up the black bag, "And why was there a picture of me in that bag?"

The outsider put his hand up in a stopping gesture while closing his eyes tightly. He sat this way for a long moment, looking like he was trying to find an answer. Then, in slow motion, he toppled face-first to the ground.

CHAPTER 3

"Egli sta per wake," Berta's grandfather said. "Venite qui da me."

"Egli sta per wake," Berta's grandfather said. "Venite qui da me." Campanella vaguely registered the words, but they didn't initially translate. The person wasn't speaking English, and this confused him. His head was throbbing so badly he couldn't get his thoughts straight.

When Joseph Campanella opened his eyes, his vision was blurred. His first thought was to sit up. But for some reason, when he tried to move his arms, he could not. He tried again, one arm at a time, but they were held fast. He lifted his head and stared down. His arms were tied, as were his legs. He looked around the room, trying to focus on his surroundings. He noticed a man and two women standing next to him. This recognition instantly brought his brain back to the mission and the moment.

Speaking Italian, Campanella's brow creased as he asked groggily, "What's this all about? Why am I tied to this bed?"

"I'm afraid I'm going to be the one asking the questions, my friend," Santos Barilla said as he crossed his arms in front of his chest. "First," he offered while regarding Berta, "Thank you for saving my granddaughter. I shudder to think what might have happened without your intervention. For that, the Barilla family will always be in your debt."

Santos leaned against the table in the center of the rough-hewed hunting cabin and rubbed his chin. After a long moment, he seemed to decide. He grabbed a chair and walked with it toward the bed. As Santos moved, the two women shuffled close behind. Setting the seat six feet from the bed, he sat and began again.

"I need to ask you about what we found in your little black bag, though. I refer to my granddaughter's picture, the maps, and the various documents containing sketches of my home and vineyards. Not to mention the book with all the notes, which discusses me, my sons, and other family members. I would like you to explain all of this because it deeply concerns me."

Joseph took a deep breath. "Santos, I have much to explain. But I need to do this privately with you. However, if you could untie me first..."

"No, don't untie him," Berta implored her grandfather. "You cannot believe what he can do!"

Santos looked toward his granddaughter and held his hand up. "I have no intention of untying him. Not yet anyway." He turned back to the man lying out on the bed. He studied his bound guest again through squinted, searching eyes. Santos knew that a man's eyes couldn't lie, and he was an expert at reading them.

"I need you and Berta to go outside for now," Santos said after a pause. "I promise I will come out for you in a few minutes."

Though Berta started to protest again, her mother sensed not to question her father-in-law's decision and took her daughter by the arm. She opened the door, led her to it, and closed it quietly behind them without saying another word.

Santos moved his chair closer to Campanella.

"Okay, I'm listening," the mustachioed Italian said.

"My name is Joseph Campanella. And you are right; I possess much information on you and the entire Barilla family. And although the reason will be easy for me to explain, it will be difficult for you to accept."

"That doesn't make me feel any better, but I'm still listening."

Campanella had rehearsed this little speech dozens of times during his training, and though the lines were etched in his mind, he hesitated to say them. How could anyone believe what he was about to say when he wasn't sure he felt it himself? He swallowed hard.

"I've recently been sent here by a team of military specialists from the United States on a mission of the gravest importance. My country has received information of an assassination attempt on the life of Winston Churchill, and I must prevent it. But to accomplish this, I will need you and your family's help."

"You've come to us for help? Help to stop the assassination of the Prime Minister of England? You're joking, yes?"

"Santos, this is no joke. I already know some of your family is working with the Resistance. And I know that young Paulo Gianelli was wounded…"

"What?" Santos interrupted.

Joseph studied the man and realized the weathered-faced Italian comprehended nothing of what he had just said. He thought momentarily and then asked, "What is the date today?"

With a frown of disgust and furrowed brow, Santos said, "You've come here with this very grandiose plan, and you don't even know today's date?"

"Please, humor me. What is the date?"

"May twenty-fifth," Santos said as he shifted his weight in the chair.

"The twenty-fifth? It should be the twenty-third. I've lost two days somehow," Campanella said as he closed his eyes. He thought back at the instant of transportation. Had something gone wrong? Then he remembered the small step he'd taken when he saw Schulz at the viewing window of the time travel center. Could that movement have caused him to be sent to the wrong destination or point in time?

Santos interrupted his thought by saying, "It was the twenty-third the day we brought you to the cabin. But you've been asleep for the last two days."

"Well, that must be it," Joseph said, more to himself than Santos. "Okay, here's what's going to happen. Tomorrow morning, Paulo Gianelli's father will knock on your door. You will open it, and the man will practically jump into your arms to hug you. He will tell you and your family that Paulo is coming home. He will explain how his son was wounded and had to stay in a Milano hospital for a month.

"His injuries were not life-threatening but still required some recuperation. Now they are sending him to his parents. He will also tell you Paulo can stay for three weeks before returning to the front lines. But he won't be going back."

"He won't?" the old man asked with sarcasm. "And is this because he's going to be going with us on our mission'?"

"Yes."

Santos laughed, a big, boisterous laugh, and then said, "This tale of yours makes no sense, my young friend. I'm afraid you will need to do a little better."

"I'm about to. Please, do me a favor and get my bag. Inside, in one of the pockets, you will find a photo of a dark-haired man of about fifty."

Santos stared at Campanella with hesitant eyes for several seconds before standing and going over to the small table where the black bag lay. Using caution, he opened the bag, saw the pocket, reached in, and pulled out the photograph.

"And now?" Santos said.

"Take a thorough look at it. Do you notice any similarities to anyone in your family?"

"Well," Santos breathed out as he examined the photo, "it does look a little like my son Salvatore, but not exactly. "Plus," he said as he looked closer, "my son doesn't possess this scar on his chin."

"The person is not Salvatore, but it's someone in your family. And this person hasn't yet suffered the injury, but in less than two days, he will. And more to the point, it will be in that exact odd shape."

Santos began to laugh again, that infectious, deep belly laugh. "You own quite a vivid imagination, my boy," he said as he studied Campanella's face while still laughing. By now, he expected the young trickster to laugh, too, as the prank must surely have hit its crescendo. But the American didn't laugh or even smile. His face was impassive as granite, and his eyes were set.

"You're not kidding?"

"No, I'm not."

"Oh well...I was afraid you were going to say that," Santos said softly as he rubbed his grimacing chin.

"I'll make a deal with you. If you untie my legs and let me move around here freely, I promise you I won't try to get away or do anything that will harm you or your family. After all, saving Berta from those soldiers must mean something," Campanella suggested.

Santos sat down again and, for a few moments, only stared at the bound man. The Italian shook his head and said, "You know, you had me going for a moment. No, I think this whole thing is too much."

"Santos, please, allow me to prove what I'm saying is true. You have nothing to lose. If nothing I say comes to pass…well, you can turn me over to the authorities. No harm was done, and you're no worse for it. But what if I'm right? What if these events do happen?"

The winemaker fidgeted in his chair, popped up to a standing position, and started pacing the room. After making several passes across the small space, he walked over to the front door and opened it. He saw Berta and her mother sitting on the porch and said, "Come in. I've made my decision."

Once inside the cabin, Santos closed the door and began to speak. "Carmella, please attend to the man's wound. I will go down to the house and get a few things. I won't be gone for more than forty minutes. Do nothing more than tend to his injuries. Do you understand?"

"Santos!" Campanella pleaded.

Santos looked down at the American and said, "Mr. Campanella, after considering your story, I will do as you ask, though with some minor alterations to your request. Carmella and Berta will take care of you while I'm away. Please, do not argue with me, else I might change my mind."

No more words were exchanged as Santos headed out of the cabin with the two women following. Once outside and with the door closed, Santos reiterated his instructions. He then turned and walked away. When her father-in-law was out of sight, Carmella, with Berta hovering like a shadow, made her way back into the cabin and went over to the chair where Santos had been sitting.

Without turning toward her daughter, she said, "Berta, get the bandages and ointments from the bag we brought up from the house and bring them to me." As Berta walked away, Carmella stared at Campanella briefly, "You have kind eyes."

At that, Berta stopped in her tracks and spun around. "Mama!" she said in protest.

"Berta, you know I have a sense about these things. Don't worry. I'm not going to untie him. But I perceive no evil in this man's eyes. I see," she hesitated as her head tilted, "honesty."

"Thank you, Carmella. You're just like your..." Joseph suddenly realized he was about to say, *just like your son*. Turning his head away and closing his eyes, he said sincerely, "I value your confidence."

"Your wound was pretty nasty," Carmella said as she began to unwrap the bandages. "A big part of your scalp was torn back from your head, and you have severe bruising. My daughter bound it when she found you, and I cleaned and re-bandaged it after we brought you here. I think you are quite lucky. I don't know how you injured yourself, but this kind of thing can go bad extremely fast."

"I'm not sure what happened either," Campanella responded. "But your compassion and attention to my wounds are much appreciated." Carmella was peeling the last round of bandage, and as it came away from his head, she gasped and sprung from her chair in shock. She continued to take several awkward steps backward and finally came to an impactful thud against the wall behind her.

"Mama, what's wrong?" Berta asked fretfully as she ran to her mother's side.

"His...his wound," Berta's mother stuttered while pointing. "Look at it!"

Berta crept forward on weak knees.

"What, what is it? Is it infected?" Joseph begged in concern.

"This can't be," Berta said, turning to her mother. "That's not possible, is it?"

Carmella just shook her head. The color in her face had drained, and her eyes blinked rapidly as she tried to take in what lay before her.

"For God's sake, Carmella, Berta, what's wrong? What's happened?" Joseph asked, again pleading for some answers while trying unsuccessfully to move his arms to feel the wound.

Carmella walked over, sat back down, and said shakily, "No, it's not infected. It's almost completely healed!"

CHAPTER 4

As promised, Santos came lumbering up to the cabin some forty or so minutes later. He was carrying a big burlap sack over his shoulder, which swung back and forth with each step. As he neared the rustic structure, he saw Carmella and Berta sitting on the porch. Two troubled faces stared back at him as the elder Barilla stopped a few feet from where they sat. Dropping the sack on the ground, he said, "Is everything alright? He didn't get away, did he?"

"No," Carmella said, "he's still tied up just as you left him. But something is…well, strange."

"Okay, what is it?" Santos asked, unsure if he even wanted to hear the answer.

"Come inside. I must show you," Carmella said, rising to her feet as she did. Santos glanced at his daughter-in-law in confusion but didn't ask more.

"Grandpapa, wait till you see! Just wait till you see!" Berta said anxiously.

The three of them went in and walked over to where Campanella lay. "Look at his wound," Carmella instructed as she nodded at Joseph's head.

Santos eased himself down in the chair. He pulled his glasses out of his front pocket and opened the frames. Once they were properly affixed to the bridge of his nose, Santos leaned in and scanned the injured man's head. He immediately turned wide-eyed toward his daughter-in-law and granddaughter. He then turned his disbelieving gaze back at the injury.

"What does this mean? How can anyone heal so fast? The wound – it couldn't have gotten better this fast. It's just not possible," the older man said, stunned.

"May I explain," Joseph asked as he glanced up at the Barillas.

"Please do. I cannot wait to hear your next story," Santos said as he took off his hat and sat back in the chair, looking weary and old.

"Well," Joseph started saying while still eyeing each Barilla family member. "On second thought, it might be easier to believe if what I told you earlier occurs. Then, all I've said will make sense, including why my wound mended so quickly. So, I ask if you could put a little faith in me for the next few days."

Santos shook his head as he bent back down and stared in amazement at the almost healed man. Finally, he got up, put his hands on the shoulders of Carmella and Berta, and led them out onto the porch. After closing the creaking door behind him, he said, "Here's what I will do. I will secure one of his legs with a chain and lock I brought from the house. I'll make the chain long enough for him to move around within the confines of the cabin…"

Carmella opened her mouth to protest, but Santos raised his hand and stopped her before she could start speaking. "…I know you are concerned. But my intuition tells me we can believe this man. I want to allow him the opportunity to prove he's here to help us. We will leave him provisions, and I will check on him several times daily. I'll know soon enough if we can trust him. If not, we'll turn him over to the constable. Now, let's finish up here and head home."

PART 3

CHAPTER 1

Predictions Become Reality

May 26th, 1943

At just past five thirty a.m. the following day, a rooster crowed the morning's alarm, and the Barilla family began to stir. One by one, they awoke and prepared for their daily tasks, tending to the family's many acres of lush green vineyards. Before the fields could be worked, the animals needed to be fed, eggs collected, and tools and equipment readied.

When those chores were finished, Carmella came onto the house's front porch and announced, "Breakfast is on the table."

Santos didn't feel the usual gleeful pull in his heart at his daughter-in-law's summons. Instead, he wondered whether Daniel Gianelli would show as the strange man had promised. The sensation gnawed at his already raw nerves. Every noise, bump, or bang from man or animal startled the usually unflappable farmer. And yet, as each minute after protracted minute passed, no one came to his door. Finally, when Santos was convinced Joseph Campanella must be a liar, there was a loud banging at the door.

The pounding had a palpable sense of urgency. Carmella and Berta shrieked. Santos also reacted with alarm. He jumped up, sending his chair skidding backward.

"Please stay where you are," Santos tried to say calmly while gesturing with his hands for his family to remain where they were and for the standing women to sit. They all feared the new arrival would be a uniformed Italian or German soldier. Or even worse, it could be bad news about one of their men fighting in the Resistance.

The elder Barilla walked steadily but slowly over to the door. He grabbed the handle, turned the knob, and began to pull. The door burst open, with Daniel Gianelli pushing through and almost leaping into the old man's arms. The burly, overjoyed man gave the Barilla patriarch a gigantic and affectionate bear hug.

"Santos! Santos, my dear friend, it's Paulo! He's survived this cursed war and is coming home!"

The words hit the mustachioed Barilla like a sharp jab to the ribs. Thrilling news, to be sure. But what stunned Santos into a stupor was the realization that the first of Joseph Campanella's predictions had come true. Santos was left standing with mouth agape in disbelief.

As Gianelli jostled his neighbor in his exhilaration, Santos' legs felt heavy, like he was experiencing total muscle atrophy. Barilla might have dropped to the floor if Gianelli hadn't grasped him. He tried to calm himself and listen as best he could to his justifiably excited friend, but the words weren't registering in his frantic mind.

For the next forty-five minutes, Daniel Gianelli explained everything regarding Paulo's injury and hospital stay. In a vivid narration, he described how flying shrapnel from a nearby grenade tore through his son and two others. His comrades had perished from their injuries while Paulo lay near death, gaping wounds on several parts of his body.

Gianelli further described how Paulo had lost a lot of blood and was moving in and out of consciousness. He said that he would have died had he not been discovered by those sent to retrieve the dead. He was brought to a field hospital where he received lifesaving treatment and was moved from there to the Ospedale Maggiore in Milan, where he'd been recuperating for the last few weeks.

"My poor Paulo," Berta said as she wiped tears from her eyes.

"Don't worry, Berta, Paulo is fine. Be happy that he is coming home soon, any day, in fact," Paulo's father said, face beaming with anticipation.

Once Gianelli was gone, the Barillas talked with great excitement about the visit. At one point in the conversation, Maria made the sign of the cross and prayed aloud for the safe return of her father and the other Barilla members who were off fighting. The rest of the household did the same.

After the breakfast dishes were cleared, the family went about their daily work. Yet, three members did so absentmindedly. Throughout the day, Carmella needed to prod Berta and Maria to stop staring toward the cabin. Later in the day, Santos let Carmella know he would check on the southern vineyards, an area that hadn't been worked recently due to bomb destruction. This time, however, he would be checking on their strange visitor.

While he walked, Santos felt an edge of excitement for the conversation ahead of him. The man's story about Paulo's father had come to pass, and though he repeatedly tried to reconcile the event, how could he have known? He simply could not. Santos even considered the possibility that, somehow, the outsider had manipulated the situation.

But the more he ran Gianelli's visit through his mind, the more he became convinced the stranger was incapable of pre-staging and scripting such an incident. Especially with Daniel Gianelli showing up when he did and giving such a bear hug. How could he explain Gianelli's verbatim description of Paulo and the circumstances of his injury? No, nothing about what occurred made any sense at all.

****

Santos arrived at the cabin's front porch a short while later. He stood with one foot on the porch and the other on the ground, trying to collect his thoughts. He glanced at the door and noticed it was open several inches.

"Mr. Campanella," he called out, but he did not receive an answer. Santos looked around and saw nothing. "Joseph, are you there? Is everything okay?" Again, there was no answer from within the darkened structure. With caution, Santos walked up to the door. He peered in, but no one was there, just a dust-soaked ray of sunshine coating the cabin's floorboards.

"Joseph?" Santos said as he pushed the door a shade wider. He felt the hairs on the back of his neck stand up. With the door now open wide enough to stick his head in, Barilla quickly snuck in a peek. The first thing he saw was that the chain and lock holding his captive fast were now lying on the floor like a dead snake – curled, motionless, and attached to nothing.

"Santos," a man's voice beckoned from behind him. Barilla spun around and saw Campanella walking up.

For a moment, Santos only looked at the younger man. An expression of dejection enveloped his face. After sighing, he said, "You promised me you wouldn't leave, and you have broken that promise."

"Yes, and for that, I'm sorry. But we've got a bit of a bigger problem," Campanella said as he made his way past Barilla to a small window on the far wall. "I did intend to stay put and live up to my end of our bargain. However, just before dark, I was gazing out this window, and that's when I saw a patrol of German soldiers walking through the woods. I reasoned they must be looking for their missing men from the day I arrived. So, I…uh…slipped out of the shackle and did some recon work."

Santos glanced down at the empty and apparently useless shackles as Campanella continued.

"They camped about a mile away from here last night. But they'll be moving our way within a few hours. I speak German, and I overheard one of them say they would come to your home sometime today. They want to know about their missing soldiers and believe you or someone in your family might know something."

With a look of horror, Santos stared at Campanella but said nothing. Before Campanella continued, the Italian moved to the table and sat down. He put his head in his hands. The enormity of what this news might mean for the Barilla clan was evident, and Campanella could see him struggling to process it all.

After what seemed an eternity, Santos gazed up at the big man, his face sullen and apprehensive, and asked, "What can we do? I cannot allow my family to be blamed for what was done to those men. The consequences of the accusation – I can't even imagine."

"I have no intention of letting anything happen to any of you. Santos, I can take care of the Germans, at least for the immediate future, but…" Campanella began, though he let the thought trail off.

"But?" Santos repeated.

"Well, the honest answer is that I cannot keep them away forever."

In a moment of understanding, Santos looked into Joseph's eyes. "The mission?" he asked in a shaky voice.

"Yes, the mission needs to be completed. But that's not the only thing. You must see that once I eliminate these soldiers, the Germans will surely send more. Eventually, there will be too many of them for me to deal with."

"What must we do?"

"I will handle this patrol and meet you here tomorrow morning. Then, we will sit and chat, and I will explain everything from the beginning. Once I do, you will be able to decide whether you will help or not. But, either way, we will need to discuss arrangements regarding a way to keep your family out of harm's way."

The Barilla patriarch nodded but wasn't sure what he was agreeing to.

****

Campanella started gathering gear for his excursion. He retrieved several weapons from a stash that the Barillas had confiscated after they disposed of the German bodies three days earlier. The knife he used to kill the German Private went into its sheath and then on his belt. A Walther P-38 Luger and an MP40 Schmeisser machine gun came next, with ammunition to match. He added other miscellaneous items, including his compass and a thin rope of some twenty feet in length.

Once he was set, the two men walked out onto the hunting cabin's porch. They conversed briefly and then shook hands goodbye. Campanella walked a few feet and then stopped. He turned toward Santos and called out for the older man.

Barilla halted and looked back. Campanella said in a calm and reassuring voice, "I don't want you to worry about this. I will handle our immediate issues with the Germans and return here by noon tomorrow. I want you to trust me and to know I will protect your family with my life. That's a promise I am making and am intent on keeping." Santos smiled soberly, waved, and then turned and headed home.

As his mind grasped the task, Campanella went into his now familiar crouch, turned around and bounded up the slope behind the cabin. Within seconds, he had disappeared into the brush.

During his previous scouting of the German patrol, he'd found the same path the soldiers had used to get from one side of the mountain to the other. The rugged trail was about seven feet wide, furrowed, and overgrown. It encircled the small mountain, starting just above the cabin and running gradually up and back down to the other side.

Campanella reasoned the passageway might be a goat or cattle route formed by herders years earlier, perhaps using it to go from one set of pastures to the next. The pathway had fallen into disuse since the war and was now overgrown with chutes of forest undergrowth jutting from the earth. It was rutted from rain washouts and littered with dead branches and small stones, but the sure-footed Campanella easily traversed the terrain. He'd scouted the soldier's encampment the day before, and so he ate up the ground in huge chunks.

His eyes scanned his surroundings as he blazed along. His mind worked at sublime speed, providing him with the safest possible route, traveling at a sprinter's gait without fear of stumbling or falling.

Racing up the mountain, Campanella only slowed when he approached the end of the upper trail. From this point, the path altered its gradual slope and began winding down steeply until flattening out onto a large grassy field at the bottom. It was there that Campanella had observed the German's encampment from the previous night and where he anticipated they would still be.

He repositioned his gear and took a breath. Just as he was about to descend, he heard voices coming from below. His body tensed. He instinctively crouched down and raised his automatic weapon to shoulder height. He stayed frozen in place and listened for a long moment. The voices were faint but there, heading in his direction. Campanella studied his surroundings, and within seconds, his plan was formulated.

CHAPTER 2

"We will go to the top of the trail and then head back around the mountain to the other side," the patrol commander said. "I've seen a small cabin some forty meters below the trail's crest. We'll check it out first and then head to the main house."

The squad consisted of fifteen men. Sergeant Rolf Jaeger, a vet who'd arrived in Italy when the Axis agreement was signed, was leading the way. The soldiers were well-trained, and combat tested. They followed orders without questions or qualms. Private Bruno Kolb, a lithe, sinewy man of six feet tall, was at the back of the unit, about twenty-five feet behind the man in front of him. Though no issue was anticipated, Kolb kept an alert vigil to their rear.

The Private heard a sound just before clearing the crest of the ridge. It sounded like a small branch, or twig snapped somewhere in the bushes. Kolb rotated in a circle while scanning the area with trained eyes. His senses tingled ominously as he released the safety on his rifle and placed his finger on the trigger.

Sunlight sprayed strands of light on swaying foliage, giving the pathway an incarnate essence. When the Private's visual scan revealed nothing, he relaxed somewhat, reasoning that a small animal made the sound as it scampered over the dry woodland bed. Or maybe a dead branch seized that exact moment to free itself from the grasp of a tree and had fallen to the forest floor below. Maybe.

He turned toward Hans Gruber, the soldier he was following. Just as he was about to call out to Gruber, something closed around his throat. His head reactively dipped down, and the hand not holding his gun shot up to his neck. It was too late. The foreign object jerked tight, cutting off all ability to speak – or breathe.

Kolb dropped his gun as both his hands groped desperately at the wire wrapped firmly and savagely around his bleeding throat. His brain started racing as he struggled to understand what was happening. He dug frantically at his neck with his fingers, eyes bulging grotesquely.

Kolb tried to call out for help. But a barely audible gagging gurgle was all he could manage. Suddenly, he began to rise from the earth. It was as though he was levitating. He tried a last-ditch effort to kick his legs and feet, hoping this would free him. All this did was tighten the killing force of the thing suffocating him. And then, the conscious efforts of kicking gave way to uncontrolled jerking as the soldier's life ebbed away.

The strangled man's bulging eyes stared with terror, and his swollen tongue clogged his throat. As Kolb's head began a slow tilt backward and his arms dropped limply to his side, he momentarily focused on a man in the tree above. It was the last vision the soldier would ever see.

After a few moments, Campanella determined the dangling man was dead. He lowered the corpse softly to the ground. Then, in a move that evoked a jungle predator rather than a man, the American silently dropped down next to the lifeless form. He detached the rope from the German's chaffed and bloodied neck, then wrapped it up and put it in his belt.

Carrying the body as if weightless, Campanella walked a dozen paces off the path and deposited the Private in a patch of dense underbrush.

Turning his attention to the rest of the patrol, Campanella raced back to the ridge, moved left, and headed up and across the rutted pathway. Still moving with cat-like grace, he reached a spot just above the trail. Now in a 'high ground' position, he hid behind a blind of bushes and waited. He knew that the Germans would return to look for their missing man, and he didn't have to wait long.

"Bruno? Bruno, where the hell are you," Private Fritz Gruber called out.

"He probably stopped to take another piss. That guy pisses more than anyone I've ever met," the man to Gruber's left said. The three who had been sent back to look for their absent comrade now stood thirty feet from where Campanella lay hidden. Unlike the now-deceased Kolb, who had been tense and alert, these soldiers were moving in a much more relaxed manner.

Gruber shouted Kolb's name, but again, he was confronted with silence. Just as they passed Campanella's hiding spot, the American pulled his knife from its sheath. He slid down the slope, coming to rest on the trail some four feet behind the unsuspecting Germans.

The Private was slightly smaller and shorter than the other two. The man on the left was the biggest. He would be the first to go. The soldier to Gruber's right would be next, and then Gruber. Campanella prepared to execute his plan when Gruber called out for Kolb again. "Something's happened," Gruber said. "Go back and get Sergeant Jaeger," he instructed the soldier to his left.

Without hesitation, the man spun around. Just as he did, Campanella thrust his ten-inch knife into the soldier's throat, driving the blade through his neck. The man's eyes bulged, at first more so in shock than in pain, before his body crumpled as if devoid of bones.

Private Gruber and the second soldier turned toward the commotion. But, like the first soldier, their reaction time was hopelessly insufficient. In a lightning strike move, Campanella stabbed the man to Gruber's right straight through the sternum, with the knife sinking to its hilt. Without hesitation, and in front of an astonished and unmoving Gruber, the American pulled the knife out and slashed the Private clean across his throat in one smooth motion.

The cut almost completely severed Gruber's neck, passing through his flesh like a soft melon. Campanella's blade had just missed Gruber's vertebrae, which was all that kept the Private's head from toppling off his shoulders. As Gruber went reeling, he grabbed at his tilting and wobbling head. With blood gushing from the wound, he took two steps to his right and then plunged over the ridge and down the side of the mountain. Campanella picked up the other two men and tossed their bodies in the same direction.

With four unaccounted-for soldiers, the others would soon return to search for them. Campanella returned to his previous hiding place, again maintaining a high-ground vantage point. Once out of view from the trail below, he began inching along, ever vigilant, toward the patrol's line of march.

After several minutes of advancing parallel to the trail, Campanella could hear laughter and talking. He stopped and honed in. From the volume of their conversations, he could tell the balance of the German patrol was no more than twenty-five meters further down the path. After taking a few seconds to survey his surroundings, he devised a plan.

In snakelike fashion, he slithered along until he was positioned above the group. Before attacking, he counted the soldiers. One was missing. Campanella cursed under his breath as he realized his best opportunity to attack with the highest chance of success was ebbing away. Most of the weapons were leaning against various large rocks or trees, and they would need time to retrieve them. Those few heart-pounding moments would be all the time he required to take them out. But he needed to act now if he was to keep this advantage.

Campanella remained in place, watching, and hoping for the last man to return from wherever he'd gone. The patrol's leader began complaining about his missing men. He was clearly agitated, and it would be mere moments before he acted on their absence. Regardless of where the eleventh man was, he must strike.

Raising his Schmeisser machine gun to his shoulder, he tensed in anticipation of his assault – but a sound to his right stopped him cold. It was a shuffling of leaves, a grunt, a groan, and a flatulent bubbling as a man passed gas.

There he is, Campanella thought as he shifted his awareness to the disturbance. He twisted around and began moving along the ground toward the noise. After slinking this way for several feet, Campanella stopped, started again, and once more stopped. He gazed in the direction of where he heard the bodily gestations.

Through the foliage, Campanella saw the missing soldier. The man was enjoying quite a healthy bowel movement. Steeling himself against the smell, Campanella made his way behind him. In one swift and smooth motion, he reached up and grabbed his victim's head. He used his hand to cover his target's mouth and then jerked him backward.

As the soldier's head tilted back, Campanella took his knife and slid the razor-sharp blade along the German's neck, opening a gaping wound that immediately disgorged blood in all directions. A pungent line of urine sprayed up the gurgling man's chest and toward his head, catching his executioner on the side of the face.

After just a few short moments, soldier number eleven lay dead. Campanella rolled the limp body away and then wiped the yellow liquid from his cheek using the man's sleeve.

Excellent, Campanella thought. *The bastard shot me with his dick.*

After cleaning his knife on the soldier's uniform, he slid it back into its sheath and returned to his previous position. As a group, the Germans were looking down, and many were pointing into a deep ravine. Campanella had stopped at the same spot on his earlier expedition the day before. He'd seen that the gulch dropped about seventy-five meters, ending abruptly into an area filled with large, jagged rocks. A new plan developed in his mind.

Making his way back to the dead man, Joseph grabbed the body by its uniform's collar. He dragged it back as quietly as he could and positioned himself and the corpse just above where the other soldiers were standing.

With his machine gun dangling from a strap around his shoulder, he raised the body above his head. Taking three giant steps, Campanella heaved the dead soldier. A gap of ten to twelve feet of distance lay between his launch point and where the soldiers stood, but the limp projectile flew straight and true.

As the body soared through the air, one of the soldiers at the ravine's edge glanced backward and saw the body hurtling in his direction. In an instinctive reaction, he jumped back and straight into Private Curt Mueller, who went tumbling into the ravine.

The entire group seemed frozen in place as they watched the falling man flap his arms in a cartoonish attempt to fly back up. Before anyone could react to this surreal moment, the flying body Campanella had heaved slammed into three more, sending those men and the corpse over the side.

Instant pandemonium and panic erupted as the remaining Germans tried to respond to the unfolding event. Turning toward where the body had come, the survivors were now staring into the muzzle of Campanella's automatic weapon. Although some soldiers glanced at their guns, they could not respond in time to alter the outcome. One by one, the seven either went down in a heap or toppled into the gorge, riddled with bullets that appeared to come from all directions. In less than one minute, Campanella had eradicated the remaining balance of the patrol unit.

With smoke curling up from the gun's barrel, Joseph walked over to the bodies still on the ground and relieved them of anything of use. He then shoved each one over the edge to the bottom of the ravine with his massive boot. He gazed down at the mass grave of crushed flesh for several moments to be sure no one had survived.

What Campanella could not carry, he flung into the bushes. He slung the remaining items over his shoulder and headed back toward the Barilla hunting cabin.

****

The sun had risen to its noon zenith when Santos approached the cabin. As he neared the steps, he began to feel a pang of apprehension. Had Campanella returned? Was he able to accomplish his gruesome task? And if he was successful in killing so many, well, the thought added nausea to his already unsettled stomach.

As Santos stepped on the porch, the board creaked under his weight, giving off a loud moaning sound. Santos grimaced, though he was not sure why. After waiting for a sign or sound from within, he finally called, "Joseph…Joseph, are you there?"

A deep voice replied, "Yes, Santos. Come in."

With relief, Barilla made his way to the door and entered. As his eyes adjusted to the darkened interior, he spotted a large pile of weapons on the table. While staring at the stockpile, he said in an almost whisper, "I take it you were successful, yes?"

"Yes. For the moment, we don't have to worry about that patrol. Now, we must talk," Campanella responded as he bade Santos sit. "Santos, several key events are about to happen, and I need you to listen to what I am about to tell you before they do."

CHAPTER 3

Santos sat at the handmade wooden table while his cabin guest poured each of them a small glass of wine from a bottle Santos had brought up the previous day. Campanella took a sip, savoring it momentarily, and then leaned forward. "What I'm about to tell you will sound unbelievable, insane even, but I assure you it is all true," he said with all the sincerity he could muster.

Santos nodded cautiously, picking up his glass and deeply drinking the ruby red liquid.

"My real name is Brant Montgomery, and I was born…" he hesitated briefly, "…on July 5th – 1976."

The Italian leaned back in his chair and pushed his hat back on his head. His eyes narrowed, and his mouth dropped open as he stared at the man across from him. Not wanting Barilla to get up and run out, Campanella pulled his 1998 Florida driver's license from his black bag and handed it to the stunned Italian. With reluctance, Santos accepted the plastic card. Initially, he didn't look at the card as he could only stare at the apparently insane Campanella.

"I was sent here by an elite group of scientists, politicians, doctors, and military personnel on a mission of the utmost importance. The mission, which we will discuss at length in a moment, was the brainchild of another individual," Campanella paused and took a small sip of wine, "That person was your grandson."

"My grandson?" Santos croaked, the words barely forming.

Campanella nodded and responded, "Yes, your grandson, Antonio. He sent me here through a time portal on May 23rd, 1999, to enlist you and other members of your family to help me stop the assassination of Sir Winston Churchill…"

Campanella spent the next two hours explaining every detail about his journey up to that moment. He started with Antonio receiving the Journal Santos had written and ended with the jump through time. He included his concern about the chef and what possible interference he might have caused the mission.

Santos stopped him several times, sometimes with questions, sometimes with stunned laughter. But when Campanella finished, Santos was no longer laughing. He just slumped back in his chair with a blank, bewildered stare. Somewhere along the way, they had drained the bottle of wine, though he couldn't remember doing it.

The room remained eerily quiet as the gray-haired man contemplated this incredible story. With squinted eyes, he studied Campanella, searching for any hint that this whole thing was a joke. After a few tense moments, he stood and began pacing. He moved back and forth across the room several times, spun around in Campanella's direction, and proclaimed, "This is too much! How can this be? You traveled here from 1999? No, this is just too much! Joseph or Brant, or whatever your name is, this tale of yours is preposterous! Do you take me for a fool?"

"Of course not. Santos, I have the utmost respect for you and the entire Barilla family. And, believe me, I know how you feel. I'm still trying to accept this crazy story myself. But here I am in 1943. I could prove this to you repeatedly by telling you historical events that haven't occurred yet but will. However, I'm afraid that time is not on my side."

Campanella stood now and took a step toward Barilla. The elder Italian man, reeling from what he heard, reactively sank back in concern.

"I am asking, no, begging you to consider what I've told you. After all, the story of Mr. Gianelli's son and his return came true. Did it not?"

"Yes," Barilla said, filling his glass with more wine before drinking the liquid in two gulps. "But, come on, Joseph, you ask too much!"

"Look, two things come to mind. First, if we don't get your family out of here, you risk more Germans coming to look for them. And this time, they won't stop until they find you and force you to tell them what you know. Second, you will be compelled to consider the validity of my story if my other prediction occurs as I've described."

"Yes…. I mean, possibly. But even if I believe, my family will never believe!"

"It isn't necessary for us to convince them yet. But, over time, I hope to gain their confidence and prove that my reasons for being here are vital to everyone's future. I intend to join your Resistance group. Soon after, I will convey what we have discussed today and pray they will agree to be my guides to Naples."

Santos began pacing the small room again. The area was small, and the floor planks creaked and moaned with each footstep.

"I don't know," he said without stopping, "how could we ever convince them? They will question the entire story. Every single part."

"I understand. And I can only hope to answer all their questions satisfactorily, as I have done with you."

Walking to the cabin's lone window, Santos rubbed away months of hazy dust and grime and peered out for several minutes. At one point, he reached up and scratched his head. Then, as if that effort was the deciding factor, he nodded to the weary traveler. "Okay, for the moment, I will go along with what you are saying," the old man tilted his head. "At least until the time your next prediction is supposed to occur. Then we will see."

The two men discussed much over the ensuing hour or so. Their biggest decision was where to take the rest of Santos' family and get them out of harm's way. Once this was agreed to, the only other thing they had to do was contact the Resistance so Campanella could join them.

****

Santos explained to Campanella that members of his family had joined Dominic Patrelli's Resistance unit. Dominic had been a major in the Italian Army during World War One. His mindset then was that being allied with the Americans against the Germans was right and just. Now, twenty-plus years later, nothing had changed for him. The only difference was that he was much older and had to fight as a partisan, not an Italian soldier.

Barilla added that he and his brother Aldo had arranged for routine meetings before his family left to fight. Someone would meet with Santos at a designated rendezvous point every three months. They would discuss updates on the group's condition and assist with supplies or information.

Two separate locations and times were discussed. They would meet at the first site on the first Monday of each quarter. If either party did not attend this meeting, they would travel to the second site two days later. If either didn't show at this second place, Santos would try again three months later.

This arrangement worked well, and though it took Santos several days to get to the meeting locations, the news was mostly positive and reassuring each time he did.

Campanella chimed in here and explained it was no accident that he had arrived when he did. Santos' Journal was precise about when he would come. The date coincided with the elder Barilla's rendezvous time with the partisans. As was the plan from the beginning, Campanella was to join the Resistance. Once in the group, he was to familiarize himself with the lay of the land and get to know and earn the respect and acceptance of the Barilla men.

Santos and Campanella gathered all the weapons and hid them under the same loose floorboards Santos used for the earlier cache. They did a quick review of what their story would be and then headed down the mountain toward the main house. The two did not speak the entire journey. Santos was still reeling from the man's narration, and Campanella was silent in his thoughts about the future.

As they emerged from the wooded area above the house, Campanella slowed as he took in the beauty of the Barilla estate.

"My God. Santos, your home is beautiful!"

"Thank you. We are proud of our family's heritage and all our ancestors' accomplishments," the beaming Barilla patriarch said, a swelling sense of pride coming through loud and clear.

Berta was the first to notice the two men heading toward the house. She was sitting on the porch and jumped up to meet them. "Grandpapa, you are bringing him here?" Berta blurted out in astonishment.

Her grandfather put his hand up. "Yes. He is our guest and will be spending some time with us. Please advise your mother and aunts that we will have one more for dinner tonight."

"But…"

Santos shot his granddaughter a quick look, which was all that was needed. Berta turned without another word and went into the house. Campanella was once again taken aback by the young woman's beauty and found himself gawking as she went.

Berta didn't wear a lick of makeup, yet her face was stunning in every detail. High cheekbones, a straight, perfectly shaped nose, and lips that were full and red. Her hair, flowing down and around her neck and shoulders, was dark brown, almost black, and the morning sun caused it to glimmer and shine. And then there was her body…

Blinking away his thoughts, he turned toward Santos. "This will be odd. I know what your entire family looks like from the many pictures shown to me, and I've studied those images over and over. But to meet them all in person, well, it will be strange indeed,"

As the two men were about to step onto the porch, a loud crashing noise from the right side of the house stopped them in their tracks. They turned toward the racket, and as they stared, a loud child's shriek pierced the air.

Before Santos could lift a foot to move, Campanella was at the end of the porch. The older man was astounded by the almost super-human speed and reaction the American possessed. Within a blink of an eye, Campanella had rounded the corner of the house and vanished.

CHAPTER 4

As Joseph entered a rectangular staging area in front of the barn, he saw a little black-haired boy of about five or six heading in his direction. He was holding his chin with both hands as a shimmering flow of blood oozed through his fingers. The rivulets of fluid continued down his arms in red zigzagging streams that dripped from his tiny elbows in small, steady drops.

When the distraught boy spotted Campanella, he stopped as if he'd hit a wall. His eyes bulged in terror and began darting from side to side as they searched desperately for someone to help or somewhere to go.

Campanella held up his hand, reassuring the young boy that he was a friend, not a foe. But the bleeding child was a non-believer. He started shuffling backward while frantically forming a plan of escape. Just as he was about to turn and run, his grandfather and other family members came around the corner.

Campanella stopped and let the others pass. When Berta saw her brother and the blood running down his arms, she came to a skidding halt. With balled fists, the girl spun on her heels and stormed toward Campanella. When she got within arm's distance, she planted her feet and took a wild swing at Campanella's chin. Though he could easily have caught her fist mid-swing, he did not try to stop the attack. Campanella only tilted his head back, letting her blow land dead center on his chest with a loud thud.

He then stepped back and raised both hands in a gesture of forgiveness. "I'm sorry," he said haltingly. "Are you alright?"

Berta stared at the man's chest as a tear boiled over her eyelid and ran down her cheek. Her hand was throbbing and turning a bright beet red. It was like she had slammed her fist against a solid brick wall.

"I'm fine, no thanks to you!" she said through gritted teeth while rubbing the hand with her other one behind her back. But she was lying.

It hurt like hell.

Even though her first onslaught proved unsuccessful and rather painful, she was not done attacking the man. She repositioned herself and readied for her next assault. Due to her throbbing hand, her deluge was purely verbal this time.

"What did you do to my brother!" she demanded. Berta was pointing a condemning finger at him and doing her best to look intimidating. But her eyes betrayed her real emotions as they glistened with excess moisture, causing her to look more woeful than fierce.

"Me?" Campanella protested.

By this point, Santos had picked his grandson up and was carrying him toward the house. As he passed the two, he said, "Joseph didn't do this. We heard the boy scream, and he was running to his aid."

Berta glowered at the American but said nothing more and followed the rest of her family to the house. As she departed, a smile appeared on Campanella's face. It was not a smile of victory, arrogance, or humor but expressed his satisfaction. He knew where the injury would be on the boy and precisely what it would look like.

CHAPTER 5

Thirty minutes later, after Santos had introduced Joseph to the rest of the Barilla family, the American had taken a seat in an oversized leather chair in the family room. Though Santos had assured everyone they could feel safe around him, most family members kept a respectful and wary distance.   All except little Antonio, who stood right in front of Campanella, bandaged and apparently no longer in trouble for having been in the tool shed alone, staring at him with the intensity and wonder that is only possible in a young child's eyes.

Antonio did not blink as he stood mesmerized by the huge man's appearance. The boy had never seen anyone as big as this man. And although he was terrified when he first saw him, he was now utterly fascinated. Campanella, for his part, seemed equally enthralled by the diminutive youngster but for a far different reason. As he studied Antonio, he recognized in his young features the adult version he had come to know at the secret facility only a few short weeks before.

After several moments of this intense staring match, Campanella decided it was time for a tactical move. He leaned forward in his seat until his face was only a foot away from the boy. Antonio was not impressed by this challenging maneuver. He stood his ground without moving a muscle. After a few more seconds of glaring, Campanella began to narrow his brow while his eyes squinted, and his nose crinkled as he made a menacing scowl.

Little Antonio was clearly up for the challenge. Not missing a beat, the impish figure reciprocated with an almost identical expression. He then upped the ante, curling his lips and snarling like a wild animal. He clearly intended the growl to sound low and guttural, but his unbroken vocal cords were not up to the task. Campanella, who was many times Antonio's size and age, quickly reacted. At first, he mimicked the youth's facial expression and growl, and he then raised the bet again by sticking out his tongue and moving his head from side to side.

Stifling a giggle, the boy countered this effort by imitating Campanella's latest antics and then bringing his hands up in a claw-like manner and opening and closing his fingers in rapid succession. The two started bobbing and weaving with eyes bulging and cheeks puffing, each trying to out-terrify the other. At this point in their game, Berta approached them.

She wore a light blue form-fitting sundress, which accentuated every curve of her young body, and her hair was tied back in a neat, tight ponytail, which gave full license to her stunning features. Her brown eyes, already hypnotic, glowed with an alluring amber hue. Her cheeks bore a subtle rose shade, softly coloring her well-defined cheekbones. Her lips also appeared fuller to Campanella than when he'd previously seen her, more sensual.

Campanella swallowed hard and sat back in his chair, partially due to the impact of her physical presence on him and partially because of the look of utter astonishment on her face. He couldn't form words, so he simply held his arms apart, hands open and palms up, in the universal sign to ask, 'WHAT?'

Berta's eyes narrowed, and she was about to say something when Carmella, in a moment of flawless timing, announced, "Dinner is ready!" The big American sprung up from his seat, moved past Berta, averting his eyes from hers, and hurried toward the dining room.

Santos, who'd just returned from checking on the livestock, went to the front of the table and sat down. He motioned for Campanella, standing anxiously off the side, to sit to his left. Berta's sister, Maria, and brothers Antonio, Arturo, and Carlo came and sat down next. Also in attendance was Santos' daughter-in-law, Jenna, and her daughters, Rosalie, and Michelle. Each warily passed the visitor before sitting at their appointed seats.

The last two to sit were Carmella and Berta. Carmella moved to the open spot immediately to the right of Santos. In normal times, this was her husband's seat. Berta went past her mother and headed toward their dinner guest's position.

The hairs on Campanella's arms raised and sent a wave of tingles down his back as she hovered momentarily behind him. The moment seemed to last longer than it should. He was about to turn around when he caught Santos giving the girl a purposeful look. His granddaughter let out a small yet perfectly audible exhale before moving on and sitting in the last empty seat.

Santos bowed his head, as did the rest of the family, and gave a brief prayer of thanks. As soon as Amen left the diner's lips, the table came alive with a flurry of arms and hands. It reminded Campanella of the statues of Ganesh that he'd seen when on R&R in India. Plates began to fill, and lively and warm conversation mingled in the air with the alluring scents of sunshine, tomatoes, and mountain herbs.

Sitting as a passive observer, Joseph soaked in the scene. He did not utter a word while each Barilla family member added the relevant tidbits of their day to the conversation. That is until Carmella looked directly at him and decided to ask him the question she'd had since the first day they found him.

"Joseph, tell us again how you came to be here," Carmella said, her tone pleasant but direct.

The entire group immediately stopped talking and rotated to look at him. Total silence enveloped the room —the inevitable had arrived. Campanella knew that he would need to choose his words wisely. This was his chance to make believers out of the Barilla family assembled at the table.

Before speaking, he turned momentarily toward Santos. The Barilla patriarch looked at each family member momentarily before nodding his approval. At this sign, Campanella put his utensils down and dabbed a napkin at his mouth. After setting the napkin in his lap, he spoke.

"First, I want to thank all of you for welcoming me into your home. It is beautiful, and I am privileged to be here," he said in perfect, unflawed English. "I have arrived here from America for a mission of the highest importance." At this, the entire table gasped a sharp breath of shock.

The language the visitor used stunned the group. Up to this point, the stranger's Italian had been excellent, with only a slight hint in his accent and intonation that it was not his native tongue. Hearing him speak a language they knew but did not expect surprised them. But it wasn't speaking English that most shocked them. What amazed them were the six words – *I have arrived here from America*!

Maria's hands shot up to her mouth in a half-hearted attempt to stifle the yelp that had spurted from her throat. Berta, who had tried not to show the slightest interest in anything Campanella said, dropped her fork on her plate with a loud clang. Little Antonio, though listening, was not sure what the big deal was and decided at this point to shove a massive bite of lamb into his mouth.

"I was sent here a few days ago," Campanella said, now speaking fluent Italian. "Unfortunately, I was injured upon my arrival. I don't remember how because my injury caused me to black out." He glanced around at the family, gauging their facial expressions before continuing. "After an undetermined time, I stumbled down the trail…" he looked toward Berta and Maria, "…If not for the two of you coming along, I'd probably be dead, or at the very least, captured by Germans."

With this revelation, everyone gawked at the three for some explanation. It was then, after multiple interruptions from both Maria and Berta, that Santos chimed in. He explained how the two girls came across the injured man and the eventual rescue of Berta from the German patrol.

"For the last few days or so, we've been nursing him back to health at the cabin," he said.

"Yes, your family has been quite gracious in my recovery. I will be forever grateful," Campanella said, taking a much-needed sip of wine.

With a hint of sarcasm, Berta asked, "What kind of important mission? Are you a *spy* for the Americans?"

Campanella quickly answered, "No, I am not a spy… well, not really. But I can say this: the fate of many people, including yourselves, depends on me accomplishing my goal."

Berta was a bright girl, and this story seemed too convenient for her liking.

"Why will you not get more help? If the mission is 'SOOO'

important," she said, drawing the word out acerbically, "how could the Americans not send more men?"

Joseph studied the girl, and as he did, the light from the fireplace flickered seductively in her dark chocolate-brown eyes. "Well," he began again, clearing his throat as he averted his gaze, "the mission was planned and arranged with as few people as possible aware of its details. It was feared that the more individuals knew about it, the more chance the information would leak to the wrong ears. The truth is no one here in Europe knows anything about why I'm here."

"That is logical," Carlo said.

"Really?" Berta asked her brother.

"So," Carmella said, not giving her daughter a chance to interject further, "will you go alone and do the mission?"

"Yes. I have no other option," the American answered.

"What exactly is this mission?" Berta asked, unwilling to allow Campanella to get away with providing so few details.

Joseph scanned the room, looking each member of the family in the eye.

"For your safety and the mission's security, **I** cannot tell you what I must do. Suffice it to say, though, if I fail, it will change the outcome of this war – and not in a good way."

Arturo, who to this point had remained silent, put down his fork and raised his hand in a gesture to interrupt. "Excuse me," he said while turning toward his grandfather. "No offense to Mr. Campanella, and believe me, I'm thankful he saved Berta, but I feel that we place ourselves in unnecessary danger by having him here. I mean, those Germans have many friends. They must be looking for their missing men, and this will lead them to us."

Santos gazed around the table. His shoulders drooped noticeably, and he sighed deeply. "I'm afraid Arturo is right, which means some difficult decisions must be made."

Santos had already made these decisions, but he framed them as choices for the family. He suggested they might all travel the forty miles to the small farmhouse his father, Vito, had built. It was seldom used but maintained a leak-proof roof, solid doors, and unbroken windows.

Water was plentiful, and sufficient game could be found in the area. Everyone around the table readily agreed to the plan. Campanella felt a massive flood of relief that he wouldn't have to explain the unbelievable aspects of his presence to them until later.

The Barillas spent the next two days locking down and shuttering their buildings and houses. They gathered food, clothing, and other essential supplies, loading them onto wagons, carts, and trucks. Though they tried not to show it, each one of them was drowning in their own dread as they wondered when, if ever, they would return.

Campanella helped them with whatever he could. His strength to move large items and load the caravan of vehicles amazed the entire family. With his assistance and remarkable stamina, a job that would have taken five days was finished in less than half that.

On the scheduled day of the departure, Joseph arrived at the main Barilla home moments after the sun had risen. The boards creaked under his weight as he sat on the front porch, causing him to wince at the offensive noise. It was still relatively early, and he wanted to be quiet and not awaken anyone inside. Sitting there on the porch, he took in his surroundings.

The grounds of the Barilla compound were eerily silent as a breeze pushed tree limbs and leaves in gentle waving patterns. Campanella's senses homed in on nature's croaks, buzzing's, and susurrations. It was peaceful and serene, and he found it hard to believe that the greatest war in history was occurring. But a fierce and unforgiving war was being waged.

Evidence of this was immediately apparent in the massive pile of weapons, ammunition, and other gear he and Santos had salvaged from the dead German soldiers lying on the grass in front of the house.

Surveying the mound, he recognized that they needed help to carry everything collected. As Campanella considered options for transporting the weaponry, the main wooden front door and the outer screen door of the house opened, and Santos came out. He carried two cups of hot coffee and two napkins concealing still-warm homemade biscuits. Barilla walked over and sat down next to the American. Smiling weakly, he handed Joseph a steaming cup and a bulging napkin.

The pained expression on the elder Italian's face caused Campanella to want to ask if he was all right, but he thought better of it and only nodded and breathed in the aroma of the coffee. The scent wafted up his nose, and the smell roused memories of his time in Iraq.

A cup of joe was one of the limited things Sergeant Brant Montgomery looked forward to in that foreboding desert nation. And as he savored the rich coffee flavor, he suddenly remembered how it was only a few months earlier that he was in that barren country. It boggled his mind that he had come so far in place and time.

The two men sipped at the nourishing brew and discussed their upcoming trek to the rendezvous point. Campanella could hear the obvious concern in the older man's voice. He put a hand on Barilla's shoulder.

"Your family will be okay. I know you're concerned about this trip and how you will not be with them during this challenging time. But I can assure you that all will be well."

"How could you know that?"

"I just do…" Campanella said, his voice trailing off.

"But how? How can you be so sure?" Santos asked, his face twisted in distress. Joseph turned toward Barilla and stared at him for several seconds while tilting his head.

"You mean the future? You can say this confidently because you know what will happen?"

The American nodded before taking a slow, deliberate sip of the coffee. He tried to savor each drink of the heady brew and every bite of the delicious warm biscuit. He relished the moment because the biscuit and coffee were divine and might be his last hot food in a long time.

Soon after the men had finished their breakfast, Arturo emerged from the house, followed by his brother, Carlo. Unbeknownst to Campanella, the two had risen early to collect all the smaller animals on the property and loaded them onto cages and pens. They gathered six horses, two mules, four dairy cows, and twenty-five sheep from the fenced-in areas behind the main barn.

The farm's two tractors, harvesting wagons, and the family truck were moved to the front of the house the previous night. They proceeded to load these with food, clothing, and household provisions they would require.

"Boys," Campanella said while putting up his hand, "can you hold up for a bit?" Both young men stopped and turned their attention toward the American. Addressing the brow-creased man sitting next to him, he said, "Santos, I hate to say it, but the two of us will not be able to carry all the items we have here. A cart won't work in the terrain we'll be traveling, so I'm afraid we'll need help."

"Yes," Santos said in a strained voice, "I know, but..." He trailed off momentarily as he stared at the door to the house, "I fear for my family without both boys accompanying them."

The front screen door of the house flew open, and Berta came rushing out. She had been listening to the conversation on the other side of the window overlooking the porch from the dining room. When she heard what Campanella and her grandfather said, she dashed out to provide an answer.

"I will go with you, Grandpapa. I am the oldest child and the next strongest behind Carlo. With my help, we could take everything!"

"No!" her grandfather said. "Absolutely not!"

"But, Grandpapa, you said it yourself. The family needs both Arturo and Carlo to survive at the northern house. You know I am the most logical choice."

"Are you crazy?" Arturo said as he put his hands on his hips. "No way! You're too scrawny to carry anything, let alone a bunch of guns."

"Scrawny?" Berta snapped as she took a menacing step toward her brother. "First of all, I've been beating the vinegar out of you since you were this tall." She held her hand up a few feet above the ground, "And I'm three years older than you and two years older than Carlo. That makes me the best choice to go."

Santos sat silent, watching his grandchildren argue. While they verbally attacked each other with harmless though vigorous barbs, he turned and looked at Campanella. A smile appeared on his face, and Campanella sensed the pride filling the man's heart.

"Berta, grab a small bag of clothes and be out here in ten minutes, ready to leave. I will go and talk to your mother. You two will take the family," Santos finished as he nodded to the boys. Berta was excited and overjoyed as their route would pass right by Paulo Gianelli's house.

They spent the rest of the morning hours preparing for their respective trips and finalizing details. When the time arrived for the two groups to depart, generous tears flowed from all. For his part, Campanella bundled the various pieces of needed gear into somewhat manageable parcels. He managed most of the load, but Santos and Berta would carry their fair share.

Joseph stopped as the three approached the end of the road leading south from the property. He turned and watched the rest of the Barilla family as they rounded the bottom of the hill, heading in the opposite direction. Antonio was standing on the back of the last wagon, smiling and waving. Campanella stared at the small, bandaged youth and once again recalled with a fond smile the face of the man the boy would someday become.

CHAPTER 6

Campanella, Santos, and Berta walked a short time in silence, something Campanella relished until Berta ruptured the peaceful quiet.

"Grandpapa," she said.

"Yes," her grandfather replied, almost afraid.

"Well," Berta said, stretching out the word, "You know, since we go past the Gianelli farm, I was thinking."

"Yes?" Santos answered, knowing full well where this was headed.

"Well, shouldn't we check in on Paulo? I mean, it's the polite thing to do, right? The *neighborly* thing to do? After all, we don't even know how badly he's injured. Mr. Gianelli would be terribly upset if he knew we passed by their home and didn't stop."

Santos looked at Campanella and shook his head while offering a perceptive smile. "I don't know. What do you think, Joseph? Should we find time for such a visit?"

"Well, we're on a pretty tight schedule, but I think we could spare a few minutes if you do," Campanella said, almost chuckling as he did.

"I suppose you think you're funny, Mr. Big Shot Spy," Berta said curtly.

Campanella was about to respond but suddenly put a hand up and stopped the group.

"What is it? What's wrong?" Santos asked.

Campanella placed a finger up to his lips and gestured for the two of them to follow. As they hugged the tree line and cautiously rounded the hill overlooking the Gianelli property, Santos and Berta finally saw what had set off the American's radar. Though they didn't understand how he could have sensed the danger, a German troop carrier sat in front of the Gianelli home, and soldiers were milling about the grounds.

"How," Berta started to ask as she looked at the man towering above her. But Campanella shook her off. His military training was now in full gear, and he was surveying the landscape and formulating a plan.

As the three stood transfixed, they watched as German soldiers rushed Paulo, his father, mother, and two sisters out of the house. An officer came out last, yelling and gesturing, waving wildly back and forth as he followed them to a grassy spot near the front of the house.

When an overzealous Corporal grabbed one of the younger Gianelli girls by the hair, Paulo tried to intervene and was summarily bashed between the shoulders with the butt of a rifle. It knocked the youthful boy to the ground. While he writhed in pain, the soldier kicked him in the stomach, laughing as he did. This was all Campanella needed to see.

"Santos, take Berta into that brush," he said as he pointed to a place about ten meters ahead and to their left. "Stay there until I give you an all-clear," Campanella said as he grabbed their arms and herded them toward the prescribed hiding spot. Taking only a handgun and an extra knife, Campanella left the rest of his gear with the Barillas and turned to go.

As he brushed by Berta, the girl asked, "What are you going to do?"

"I'm going down to say hello," Campanella offered as he started down the path. Looking at Santos, he said in a firm voice that left no room for argument, "Santos, if things don't go exactly as planned, take a few weapons and meet up with your family at Vito's farmhouse."

Before either Berta or Santos could offer a protest, Campanella sprinted off. He headed down the trail for about twenty meters and then darted up the next rise and into the brush.

"He's so fast. How can he be so fast?" the stunned girl asked her grandfather. "Have you ever known anyone who could run and move like that? Her grandfather shook his head, just as baffled as she was.

With intense effort, the two dragged the gear bundles into the bushes. Once they had worked their way to an area they believed would be safe and out of view from below, they squatted behind the underbrush and waited.

As the two of them watched, it was apparent that the situation was grave. If Campanella was going to do something, he had better do it soon. But where had the man gone? Santos scanned as much of the grounds as he could, but from their vantage point, all he could see were the seven Germans in the front of the home. Others might have been inside the house, around the back, or in some other building, but there was no sure way of telling from where he and Berta hid.

"What is happening? Why is that man so upset? And why does he keep screaming at Paulo's father?" Berta begged, tears now pouring down her face.

"I don't know. We must wait and watch as Joseph instructed. Maybe they'll just leave," Santos said reassuringly, though he was inwardly terrified this situation would not turn out well.

As if his internal premonition was the precursor for the action to follow, a commotion at the back of the house triggered an immediate reaction by the officer. The German commander craned his neck toward the commotion and barked orders to three of his men. With raised weapons, the soldiers bolted for the back of the building.

The officer turned his attention back to the frightened family. Although Berta and her grandfather couldn't hear what was being said, they watched in silent dread as he moved within inches of Daniel Gianelli's face. His shouting soon became bellowing as he gestured in the direction the other soldiers were going. Then, in a flash of movement that made them gasp, the officer struck Gianelli across the face with his hand. The winemaker fell to the ground, and as he did, his son once again attempted a retaliatory move.

Paulo, bruised and battered from his previous effort, had barely gotten to his feet before being assaulted once again. The soldier that had previously bashed him in the back now slammed the butt of his rifle into his stomach. This buckled Paulo, dropping him to his knees as he coughed and gasped for breath.

This latest attempt by Gianelli's son sent the cantankerous German officer over the edge. His face contorted, and his jowls shook. He began racing madly back and forth, pointing fingers, and screaming orders.

Suddenly, the two soldiers not guarding Paulo raised their weapons to shoulder height, aiming at the members of the Gianelli family.

Paulo, who understood enough German to grasp what was commanded, was shouting at the soldiers, begging them to stop the insanity of what was happening. But his pleas were ignored. Still breathing like he was about to have a stroke, the officer doffed his hat and wiped his brow with a cloth he snatched from his coat pocket.

After taking a deep breath, he replaced his hat, pulled down on his sleeves, and straightened his coat. He then turned away from the scene and walked to the transport truck. With a nonchalant air of arrogance, the man ostentatiously got in the passenger side and closed the door.

Berta shifted side to side in agitation as she repositioned her hiding spot, trying to get a better look.

"Grandpapa, what's happening?" she beseeched frantically. "Are they going to shoot them? We must do something," she said as her hands frantically attempted to dislodge one of the guns in her bundle.

Santos grabbed Berta and pulled her beside him, pointing toward the house.

"Look," he said as he nodded to direct her gaze.

Campanella was gracefully and rapidly traversing the Gianelli roof. He was on the far left-hand eave line, located behind the troop carrier and out of view of the German officer and the men holding the Gianelli's. Once at the edge, the American crouched down with his arms out. Berta could not be sure, but it looked like he held a huge knife in each hand.

With the air redolent with an aura of foreboding, Santos and Berta watched helplessly as two soldiers shoved Mr. and Mrs. Gianelli and their two daughters toward a wall along the front of the house. It was now clear that the Germans meant to execute them.

Berta could feel a scream of panic forming in her throat. Sensing the eruption, her grandfather grabbed his granddaughter by the arm, admonishing her to stay quiet with a finger to his lips. The two watched as the guards dragged Paulo away and to the left of his corralled family. Clearly, he was to have a ringside view of whatever was about to occur.

The soldiers then used their rifles as prods to position the rest of the Gianelli's against the front wall of their home. Once they had them in place, those two soldiers turned and walked toward their firing site some fifteen feet away. It was the moment Campanella was waiting for.

CHAPTER 7

Campanella exploded in a blur of movement as if unleashed by a starter's pistol. He lunged forward, taking three huge strides and leaping from the roof. With arms raised above his head, the American hurdled through the air toward the two oblivious soldiers holding Paulo. For Berta and Santos, who witnessed the event from a spectator's vantage point, it seemed as if Campanella was capable of flight.

Once within striking distance, the airborne assassin used his momentum and body weight to plunge the knives deep into the back of the soldier's necks. The nearly ten-inch blades slid through the men's vertebrae before exploding out the front of their throats.

As Campanella landed on the ground, just inches from Paulo's perilous position, the grips of the two soldiers holding the young man released and their bodies crumpled lifeless to the earth. In stunned bewilderment, Paulo, confused about what had just occurred, gawked down at the two men lying on the ground. Although he didn't understand how it happened, he was sure his captives were stone dead. He sucked in a startled breath as a pair of massive hands grabbed him from behind and pushed him down.

Less than five seconds had elapsed from when Campanella leaped to when he killed the soldiers and shoved Paulo to safety. The arrogant officer sitting in the truck had witnessed the slayings. His heart skipped a beat as he drew out his sidearm and grabbed the door handle to face Campanella. He jerked on the lever, but the door would not open wrench as he might. He glared at the stubborn grip and yanked up several more times, using his shoulder as a ram. But still, the door fought his efforts.

When the German glanced out the truck window, he could only stare with wide eyes as Campanella pulled a pistol from a holster at his side and fired. Two flashes erupted from the muzzle, and the backs of the two soldier executioners' heads exploded. Shards of skull and flecks of brain erupted in volcanic fashion from the huge bullet holes and scattered on the ground.

The truck's door, which to this point refused to budge, now flew open. The unprepared officer fell sideways out the door, landing face-first into the dirt. By the time he had scrambled to his feet, the American was standing inches away from the confused man's face. Surprised and startled, the soldier took an unbalanced step backward. As he did, Campanella snatched the pistol from his hand in a deft, liquid motion.

When the officer regained his balance, he pointed his now empty hand toward Campanella. It only took the briefest moment before he realized he was empty-handed. Worse still, the man he intended to shoot was now pointing his own weapon directly at his head.

His uniform, with all the shiny medals and dignified insignia adorning it, did nothing to prevent his cowardice from showing. He held his hands in supplication, his face screwed into a terrified grimace. Suddenly, he began to sob like a child and begged the towering man for mercy. There would be none: the black stare of Joseph's eyes provided no solace.

In a final moment of panic, the officer remembered the rest of his patrol and started screaming for their help. But he received no answer. Campanella's lips curled into a chilling and broad smile with no hint of humor, and he motioned with the pistol for the German to move toward the wall of the house where the Gianelli's had stood moments before.

"Paulo," Campanella said as he and the officer approached, "Berta and her grandfather are up on that hill about two hundred meters up," he paused while pointing in their direction. "Please go and get them. They will need your assistance to bring down our supplies."

Though he couldn't imagine who this Savior might be, Paulo did as instructed and bolted expectantly to where the man pointed. Campanella detected a significant limp in Paulo's gait as he went, yet it did not hinder the young man's enthusiastic effort.

As Paulo scrambled up the incline, Berta dropped her gear and ran. She leaped into his arms, locking lips and arms with him in a frantic embrace. Tears streamed down their faces with the relief and joy of their reunion.

BANG

The pair immediately spun around and saw the German officer lying in a heap at the base of the wall in front of the Gianelli home.

CHAPTER 8

Santos introduced Campanella to the Gianelli family and then asked Daniel Gianelli and his son to join them for a private discussion. The Gianelli men explained how the Germans were trying to find out what information they possessed about their missing soldiers.

"We told them the truth, that we knew nothing of any missing soldiers," the elder Gianelli explained, "but the German officer would not believe us." Anger seethed in his tone. "The officer's name is, I mean was, Captain Rudolph Schmidt, something the bastard told us just before slapping me to the ground," Paulo's father sneered.

"Schmidt said that they had found a considerable amount of blood on a trail bordering my land. I told him I was clueless about that, how we were allies, and that I would harm any of his soldiers. I explained that Paulo was in the Italian army. But the man ignored me. He had decided to make an example of us for the rest of our neighbors.

"If you hadn't come when you did, well, I'm not sure we'd be talking to you right now," Mr. Gianelli said, a tear running down his face. One of his daughters, Giselle, ran over and jumped in his lap. He gazed at the young, dark-haired girl and kissed her cheek in loving adoration. Turning back to Joseph, he said, "I can't thank you enough."

"Now what?" Campanella asked.

"What do you mean?" Gianelli said, perplexed.

Campanella glanced at Santos, who read his mind.

"My old friend," Santos murmured as he put his hand on Gianelli's shoulder, "more Germans will come soon. None of you will be safe, not for a while at least."

"What will we do? Where will we go?" the man said, glancing between the two.

"Daniel, everyone from my home has gone too; we all needed to make tough decisions. Do you remember Vito's old estate about forty kilometers north of here?"

"In Benevello?" Gianelli asked.

"Yes. My grandsons took our women and children there. I'm to follow up in about four days. Please go there. The villa is large, with plenty of room for your family, too," Santos said, a warm, benevolent smile on his face. "We will help you dispose of the Germans, but as soon as we do, you must be on your way."

Gianelli, genuinely moved by this act of kindness, hugged Santos and shook Campanella's hand. He smiled at them both and then went inside his home to prepare for the journey.

Campanella loaded the dead Germans into their truck and then drove the vehicle into the woods. After he had returned, he advised Santos and Berta that they must leave at once. Berta nodded slowly and ambled to where Paulo stood. The two spoke briefly and then hugged each other with fierce intensity. Berta was the first to take a few steps away, tears streaming down her face, and then she turned and ran back to her grandfather. Her silent tears dropped like the beginnings of rain from her lowered head.

****

Campanella and the two Barillas walked for several hours, speaking only as needed. Santos had suggested it would be safer to proceed in silence and only to talk when necessary. Campanella, however, wasn't sure if it was due as much to a concern for safety as to spare them from his granddaughter's incessant inquisition about his mission.

The questioning had started the moment they'd left the Gianelli's and hadn't let up until Santos interrupted her with his instructions. It was only when the day was heading toward night that Berta decided enough was enough.

"Grandpapa."

"Hmm?" he muttered.

"Once we hand off *Mr. Spy* to the partisans, will we return to be with

173

the rest of the family at great grandpapa's house?"

"Yes, we will be going right back," he said, knowing the girl was thinking more about a reunion with Paulo than getting to her great-grandfather's farm.

A pregnant silence hung in the air for a few seconds, and then she added, "Will we be meeting up with Papa at the rendezvous site?"

"Maybe. Maybe not," Santos said solemnly. "Sometimes he comes, as do others. Often, though, it's your Uncle Aldo."

"Oh. Well, I hope all the men are there."

"As do I," her grandfather agreed, "as do I."

After Campanella secured a safe spot to camp, the three ate a small meal consisting of figs, dried meats, and some of Carmela's bread. Soon after, they decided to get some sleep. Santos would take the first watch and wake Campanella a few hours later.

****

After having slept, Santos opened his eyes. He blinked several times to get his bearings and was surprised that the sun was just under the horizon. Rising on his elbows, the sleepy-eyed Italian glanced expectantly over to the large rock Joseph had chosen for surveillance the previous night but saw that the man was not present. He looked toward his granddaughter; she was still sleeping soundly.

As Santos began to get up, he heard a commotion somewhere within the forest. He froze and listened. The elder Barilla stared toward where the noise came from, but now there was only silence, and he could see no movement. He crawled over to his granddaughter's side and gently roused the slumbering girl.

"What?" Berta groggily mumbled.

"Hush," her grandfather whispered while holding his hand over her mouth. "Somethings wrong. Joseph didn't wake me for my watch and now he's missing. I just heard something in the woods. It's probably him, but I'm not certain. Get up slowly and follow me."

174

Berta did so without hesitation. The two crawled along the ground, reaching the rock where Joseph had sat guard earlier. The sun's shadows had yet to materialize as its face was just creeping above the skyline. In the semi-darkness, they moved unseen to the hiding spot. Once behind the rock, Berta scooted her way around and behind her grandfather, huddling against him with her head buried in his back.

They stayed that way for several nail-biting moments and waited. For what they did not know. Berta was trembling from fright and the cool air. To make matters worse, she needed to pee so badly that she was afraid she couldn't hold it.

There was another rustling of branches and shrubs, although the clamor was much louder this time. The disturbance emanated from the opposite side of their small camp. Berta gasped and pressed her head harder into her grandfather's back. The older man almost fell forward but managed to steady himself with hands firmly on the ground.

"Berta," Santos said softly but forcefully.

"I'm sorry," she replied, easing the pressure.

They continued listening while Santos strained to see through the dim light. The clamor did not abate. In fact, it was getting much louder and closer. Santos glanced over at the bundle of weapons lying a few feet away.

And then the noise stopped. The silence was suddenly deafening in its intensity. Berta somehow got the courage to peek over her grandfather's shoulder, which is when it happened. She almost screamed but clasped a hand to her mouth as a massive black horse came crashing through the brush into the small clearing. It stood prancing nervously from side to side over the spot the two were sleeping minutes before.

The large mare was saddled and loaded with various supplies and gear but no rider. It was evident the steed had recently been ridden hard, as its breath was clearly visible in the chill morning air, jets shooting from its nostrils like a restless, chugging steam engine.

"What's going on?" Berta asked in a whisper.

"I have no idea," her grandfather said, while his shoulders shrugged slightly.

"What should we do now?"

"I have no idea," he said again, the words crawling out from his lips.

"I have no idea," he said again, the words seeming limp and helpless.

They didn't move, only huddled together, staring at this most peculiar of sites. Several moments passed, and the sun's rays began to light the clearing. Berta grasped her grandfather's shoulders.

"Is that? Could it be?" she asked. Her grip on her grandfather lessened as she started to rise. Her grandfather grabbed her arm and pulled her back down.

"Berta, no, you must stay down!"

"But I think that's Paulo's horse," she said.

"What?" Santos said in surprise. He spun his head around to look at her and then quickly twisted it back to look at the horse.

"Yes, I think it is," Berta said. Then she squinted at the horse, straining again for a better look. "Yes, I'm sure that's Bella."

They slowly stood and were about to walk toward the horse when a new commotion sounded from the bushes. Santos put his arm out, stopping Berta in her tracks. They took a cautionary step backward as they stared nervously toward the disturbance.

The bushes at the edge of the clearing began to shake and tremble as if a herd of animals was about to burst through. Campanella came barreling through with Paulo Gianelli slung over his shoulder, lolling with the dead weight of the unconscious man.

CHAPTER 9

"Oh my God, Joseph," Berta cried out. "What have you done to Paulo?"

Campanella rolled his eyes and didn't comment as he strode past her. He laid the boy down on Berta's dew-dampened bedroll and moved toward the still-startled horse. As he did so, Berta rushed to the lifeless figure and dropped to the ground beside him. The boy's face was ashen except for an angry red welt bulging from his forehead.

"I found him unconscious about a hundred yards down the trail. He must have been racing along in the darkness and didn't spot a low-hanging branch. It was right above where he was laying."

Berta was holding Paulo's hand now, and streaming tears ran down her face as she kissed his cheeks and lips. "Grandpapa, please, the water," she asked, pointing at the flask in their gear.

Santos hurried to their supplies, retrieved a canister, and brought it to the girl. Campanella watched as Berta wet a cloth she grabbed from her bag. She began dabbing Paulo's face, carefully avoiding the injured area. After a few moments, the boy started to rouse as his eyes fluttered and consciousness took hold.

"Paulo…Paulo, can you hear me," Berta said, her voice strained from worry.

His eyes opened, and he gazed up at Berta in grateful recognition.

"Berta?" he asked hoarsely.

"Yes, Paulo, it's me."

"Where did you come from?"

"Never mind where I came from, where did you come from, and what are you doing here?"

"I…I was worried about you," Paulo said weakly. "I convinced my father to continue without me. Some workers from the vineyard decided to accompany our family to your great-grandfather's home. So, he agreed to let me go and look for you…sort of.”

“Sort of?”

“Well, not at first, but he eventually gave in after a few hours of non-stop begging. I wasn’t sure how far you traveled, but I thought I could catch up to you before daybreak if I rode Bella hard. The last thing I remember is seeing a branch flying toward my face.” “Yes, you’re lucky you didn’t kill yourself,” Campanella said quietly.

Berta shot Campanella a quick dagger stare, then turned back to Paulo and said, “Well, you’re here now. We’ll let you rest, and then, when you feel better, we’ll take *you know who* to Uncle Aldo, and then head back,” Berta finished while giving a rapid jerk of her head toward Campanella.

The American looked at Santos with an expression of frustration and then nodded toward the rising sun. “We must go. We can’t afford to be late for the rendezvous,” he said, ignoring Berta’s suggestion.

Berta glowered at Campanella again and then looked over to her grandfather. “Paulo needs time to get better. He needs rest,” Berta demanded.

“We have no time to wait. I’ll put the boy on his horse and lead him along until he can ride home on his own,” Campanella said before Santos could.

With a groan, Paulo sat up, saying indignantly, “I’m not going anywhere without Berta!”

“And I’m not going anywhere without Paulo or Grandpapa. So, Mr. Spy, we are all going together – or not at all!”

“Jesus,” Campanella said in a puff of disgust as he threw one of the large bundles of guns over his shoulder.

“I’m alright now,” Paulo groaned as he stood, though he wobbled a bit as he did.

“Fine, then let’s get to it. At least we can put some gear we’ve been carrying on that horse,” Campanella said, disregarding the young man’s pain.

"Grandpapa, please, can't we wait for a little while?" Berta pleaded.

"No. Berta, I'm okay. I can do it," Paulo said.

Berta spun around and got to her feet, but she was spitting mad. She held Paulo until she was sure he was stable and then began gathering up her things to leave with begrudging slowness.

PART 4

CHAPTER 1

The Partisans

Although their country was allied with Germany during the war, most Italians were not for the partnership. It wasn't that they disliked the German people. They simply didn't want to fight – in any war, for any side. But here they were.

At the beginning of the conflict, those Italians not in the military took a somewhat uninterested stance toward their country's involvement. After all, hadn't their army rushed in and occupied Albania without incident? And wasn't the coordinated invasion of France a great success? But then the ensuing failed assault of Greece and the high costs of pre-war conquests, financially and for their natural resources, made the masses doubt Duce's guidance.

These later failures prompted wariness, but when the German began treating Italy like they owned it, the population's attitude soured quickly. The Nazis behaved like invading conquerors, confiscating crops, livestock, and other essential needs. They treated the Italian citizens like they were beneath them and used many Italian women as their personal sex objects.

Though the resistance groups realized they could not eliminate enough of the enemy to make a meaningful difference, they felt they could at least keep them off balance. That way, the Germans' real enemies, the Allies and their hordes of soldiers and weapons, could do something significant.

Dominic Patrelli's band of partisans was no different. They started out with ten men bonded together. Most were locals from his village, but some were laborers working the vineyards throughout the region before the conflict began. As they made their way around the northern part of Italy, the group inflated and shrunk depending on who joined, who was wounded, or who in the group needed to go home to tend to family issues. At the peak of their efforts, Patrelli's fighters contained almost thirty men.

Aldo Barilla, the brother of Santos, accompanied by his son Alberto and Santos' three sons, all enlisted with the partisans a couple of months after Dominic formed his original members. They were green and untrained initially but soon became hardened and efficient.

The Patrelli action plan was straightforward and simplistic. Hidden and undetected, his team would position themselves along roads and trails where they knew patrols traversed. As the German troops passed, they would unload dozens of rounds at their unsuspecting foes and then scatter before any real counterattack could be mounted.

The band of marauders would later meet at pre-determined rendezvous points and assess their efforts. If all was well, they would move on to another attack point. They enjoyed many successes with this guerrilla warfare style, buoyed by the rugged terrain that made it difficult for the Germans to counter their efforts.

All was going their way until one event changed everything.

On the fateful day that shattered their good fortunes, the partisans had chosen the roads in and out of Borgomale as their following ambush location. A quaint and idealistic Italian town before the war, Borgomale had become home to an entire unit of German infantry.

As in previous attacks, the small gang of freedom fighters sent two of their team to recon the Germans stationed there. After documenting enough of their foe's movements, the two returned to discuss a strategy for an attack. They had sketched details of the terrain so their comrades could see where to be positioned.

The partisan recons also revealed that the Germans were sending out regular patrols from the town. Each day, they had watched and noted the small groups of scouting parties leaving on routine patrols. Most often, these squads numbered ten to twelve. They would make their way down the road by 0700 every morning and return five hours later.

True to form, these Germans were systematic and methodical in their consistency. But while you could set your watch by the patrol schedule, they had become sloppy in their diligence, clearly feeling that the lack of partisan activities around Borgomale thus far would continue.

With the recon's information reviewed and dissected, Dominic led his group to the attack site right after dawn. The early morning sun cast thick and inky shadows below the treetop canopies, and the dense bushes and underbrush offered additional coverage. Each man found their killing zone, dug in, and waited.

At 0730, some forty-five minutes as expected, a patrol of Germans headed down the path toward their position. Their weapons were slung over their shoulders with careless indifference as they talked and laughed. An ambush this close to the town was not on their minds.

In the early days of the Partisan's efforts, this would be a moment of intense apprehension, even fear. But now, after months of their campaign, the men were almost literally licking their chops and waiting for the signal to fire.

As soon as the enemy squad moved opposite to where Dominic's men hid, the freedom fighter gave the command, and a hailstorm of bullets filled the air.

Mass confusion and pandemonium broke out as the Germans attempted to rebuff the attack. One by one, the small group of gray-clad soldiers was cut down. At one point during the melee, Patrelli saw an opportunity he couldn't resist. He brazenly emerged from behind his cover and took aim at the enemy's frantic German commander. The soldier, a big burly sergeant near the back of the patrol, was firing his weapon blindly toward his unknown assailants.

With such random fire, none of the Sergeant's deadly missiles had found a flesh-and-blood target, unlike the bullets aimed at him. One partisan shot creased his right thigh, while another took a chunk from his left forearm. Hurt and bleeding, he fought back with the ferocity of an injured animal as his pain was masked by fear and rage.

Patrelli, with lip upturned in victorious anticipation, resighted his careful aim. At this moment, fate and folly both decided to rear their ugly heads. With a sixth sense born from months of veteran fighting, the Sergeant turned at the same time Patrelli zeroed in. The two men's eyes locked, and the partisan's lips widened into a triumphant grin. He pulled the trigger...

Click.

The Italian's gun had misfired.

It was now the sergeant's turn to grin, eyes exultant and maniacal. The German shot, firing with a marksman's accuracy. The bullet whizzed through the brush, severing several twigs along its lethal path, and finally slammed into Patrelli's stomach. The Partisan looked down in surprise and saw a hole a few inches to the right of his belly button, not yet bleeding.

The leaden missile continued through his body and exploded out of the small of his back just above his belt line. As it exited, it left a wound twice the size of the entry hole. Both openings began expunging a steady stream of blood as rich as an aged bottle of Barolo. The German yelled a guttural roar of victory, his chest puffed out as he watched his adversary crumple down and out of sight.

The commotion around him was a raging chaos, but the Sergeant disregarded the anarchy in his sense of triumph. In that instant, a bullet struck the left side of the still-smiling Sergeant's head. The rifling slug hurtled through his skull and exploded out the back, with brain matter and bone fragments flying in all directions. The gigantic six-foot-four German was dead on his feet and none the wiser.

At first, he stayed upright in the center of the road, with only a red entry wound apparent on the right side of his head. But a significant portion of the left of his skull was now gone, including his left eye. His right eye, however, continued to stare forward in confused horror. Then his body went down, a mere heap of lifeless matter.

As fast as it had started, the attack finished. Only two Germans remained alive, and they lay moaning and jerking, clinging to life with short, spasmodic breaths. The Partisans, for their part, had accomplished what they set out to do. Yet they, too, experienced loss with Patrelli down.

The rendezvous location was miles away, and Patrelli was failing fast. When it was deemed safe to stop, Franco Marino, the appointed doctor of the group, did his best to administer first aid. He dressed the wound with a medicinal salve and wrapped Patrelli's waist with cloth bandages. He did this with incredible sadness, because Marino knew that nothing he did would change the eventual outcome.

For the entire trek back, each man contemplated the fate of their leader. A heavy atmosphere enveloped them as they reflected on Dominic's fate. Ambushing and killing Nazis from the safety of pre-positioned hiding spots was one thing. Watching when one of your own dies, especially your leader, well, that was something entirely different.

As Marino believed, Patrelli died that afternoon. The death triggered shock waves amongst their tight-knit group and caused many to rethink their part in the mission.

That day became a turning point in the team's fortunes.

To counter the constant harassment by this band of brothers, the Germans began stepping up their patrols. They also started sweeping local residences, searching out relatives and friends of known Partisans.

From the information they collected by strong-armed interrogations, the Germans initiated traps in anticipation of upcoming assaults. Their new strategy involved sending out two squads to cover the same area. Following at a safe distance, they would wait for shots to be fired and then rush in with additional troops to counterattack the ambushes. Almost overnight, the Partisan's forays, even with increased caution, became much more challenging and perilous.

As logic would dictate, the resistant group began losing more fighters. Wounds and non-life-ending injuries, whether from firefights or other activities, had always been part and parcel of the job. But now, men were slain or wounded at an alarming rate. These deaths gradually eroded the men's willingness to continue fighting for the cause.

Only the week before Campanella arrived in Italy, three were killed. Two days after those deaths, the Germans captured another. No Partisan had been taken in the past, and though dying in battle was a genuine heartbreak for the group, one of their own becoming a prisoner was almost harder to accept.

A resistance fighter caught by the Nazis would be executed. That was a certainty. But often, torture came before death, and this was terrifying. Rumors of reprehensible cruelty by the Germans during interrogation were legendary. This knowledge wrenched at the gut and heightened the growing uncertainty of the goals the freedom fighters hoped to achieve.

Tall, lanky, and pale-skinned, Abraham Paggio had only participated in three actions before capture. Nicknamed 'Pags' by one of the Marino brothers, the young Italian arrived after having fled his home a few weeks earlier.

Before Abraham joined the partisans, the only fighting of Nazis he'd done was in daydreams fueled by drunken conversations with his teenage friends. This all changed when he lost his parents.

Throughout many parts of Europe during World War Two, Jewish families were targeted for removal from their homes. At the onset of the Jewish elimination, the process appeared random. Then, as the war progressed and things evolved, the purging became a methodical obsession born of a disease-minded dictator hell-bent on erasing the Jewish race from the planet.

Fabricated justifications to appease the local non-Jewish inhabitants soon became unnecessary as the Germans rampaged through the homes and businesses of their targeted victims without any legitimate reason. One day, Abraham Paggio and his family were the targets.

At four a.m. on a rather unremarkable and peaceful morning, a German troop carrier rolled up to the Paggio home. An officer emerged from the front passenger seat while two other soldiers jumped from the truck's rear. The trio went straight to the residence and began battering their brightly colored door with their fists and rifle stocks. The intruders screamed anti-Jewish slurs, which careened and echoed hauntingly off the buildings of the small street.

Awakened by the disturbance, Abraham's father trudged groggy-eyed and disoriented down his stairs. Carrying a candle and dressed only in a nightshirt and slippers, he opened the family's front door in response to the commotion. Without word or warning, the two guards grabbed the pudgy, balding man and pulled him through the opening toward the waiting truck.

The elder Paggio tried to resist, protesting about the molestation and how they had no right. The burly soldiers paid no heed and wrenched the frail man's arms, causing the candle in his hand to drop to the ground. It extinguished in a puff of blue smoke, the hazy rivulets swirling up into the air before vanishing forever.

Mrs. Paggio, though warned by her husband to remain upstairs, heard his terrified pleas, and raced to investigate. As she arrived at the doorway, she was horror-struck as she realized what was happening. She was aware of others who had been taken away for questioning, never to be seen again, and Mrs. Paggio was sure this was about to happen to her husband. Without considering the consequences, she ran from her home, demanding in high-pitched Italian for the brutal tyrants to release him and leave.

Before Paggio's wife had moved five steps past the entryway of her home, the German officer turned, pulled out a pistol, and shot her in the head. Dying faster than she was falling, her hurtling body slammed face-first to the ground. With eyes and mouth agape in blind astonishment, her head whiplashed down and smashed with a sickening, bone-cracking thwack onto the ages-old brick road.

Hearing the tormented screams behind him, Paggio managed to twist his head around the moment the weapon fired. The incident seemed to happen in ghastly slow motion. The gun's muzzle flashed, and in a blink, his wife's head jerked back from the bullet's impact. Transfixed by shock and disbelief, he watched as the woman who had birthed his only son stumbled forward a step or two until gravity's inevitable pull induced her powerless body to crumple to the ground.

With obscenely wide eyes, Paggio met the lifeless gaze of his wife. They appeared to be staring into his soul. His legs failed him, and the guards holding the diminutive man released their grip, allowing the Italian to fall to his knees. The tyrannical trio watched and laughed as Paggio threw his balled-up fists into his clenched eyes. He sat rocking back and forth, sobbing incoherent ramblings as his body shuddered with convulsions.

Suddenly, he drove his fists onto his thighs. His neck and head stretched skyward, and he let out a blood-curdling scream of agony.

His gaze returned to his wife lying dead before him, and through bloodshot and tear-soaked eyes, Paggio jerked his head at his wife's executioner. With spittle flying, he screamed insults at the murderer. The soldiers merely laughed. Soon, they tired of his ranting. With a belittling nonchalance, the officer walked over and put the muzzle of his gun into the middle of the Italian's forehead. The German's mouth contorted in a sneer as he pressed the cold steel hard into the man's sweat-covered brow.

Paggio's executioner stared with uncaring eyes as the devout Jew began mumbling the Teshuva, the Jewish prayer of repentance, and waited for the inevitable. A click caused him to flinch. Paggio blinked and looked up in astonishment.

The would-be executioner laughed and said something to his fellow soldiers, eliciting similar chuckles. After shrugging his shoulders, the soldier re-cocked the gun and put the barrel back onto the reddened circle that had formed on the Paggio's forehead. With his other hand, he waved farewell and said, "Say hello to Yahweh or whatever his name is," and pulled the trigger. This time, the pistol erupted, sending a bullet smashing through his target's brow. Paggio's salt and pepper hair puffed out as bullet, skull fragments, and brain matter exploded from the back of his head, killing him instantly.

The officer holstered his weapon, and without another word, he and his band of murderers got back into the truck and drove away. Left on the cold, damp road were the inert and lifeless bodies of Joseph and Gina Paggio. They were dead for no other reason than their religion.

The town's inhabitants would be asleep at this hour on any typical night. But a sound night's sleep on this night was impossible. Many of the deceased couple's neighbors had been roused by the rumbling of the troop carrier as it arrived on the street so late. Recently, this disturbance had been heard often, and most knew what would occur, but who would it be? Now, no more than fifteen minutes later, they knew.

Throughout the onslaught, the slumber-eyed observers sat transfixed like the religious statues adorning their tiny homes. After all, they could do nothing to stop it. Even though the majority still living in this part of the town were not Jews, any defense of their friends could bring the same outcome for them. So, they watched and waited. Once the vehicle was out of view and they were sure the killers had gone for the night, the townspeople began spilling out onto the streets.

One by one, like a group of lifeless zombies, they ambled to the bodies. Some said nothing, merely weeping quietly. Others whispered hatred-filled raging's about those *'swastika-wearing devils.'* Still, others vowed to seek revenge without valid means or honest conviction. In time, everyone would meekly return to their homes, leaving the dead where they lay lest someone identify them as *'Jew lovers'.*

Abraham, the Paggio's seventeen-year-old son, had been visiting his aunt and uncle two streets away when word of the execution reached him. His father's brother suffered from gout and often could not manage the daily tasks needed to operate their small bakery. During these flare-ups, Abraham would spend the night helping with the early hours of baking. Had he not done so that evening, Abraham Paggio would have experienced the same fate as his parents.

As the devastating news was given, the boy broke down and sobbed. For a long while, the boy was inconsolable. But soon, grief turned to anger and outrage before morphing into thoughts of revenge.

Under the cover of darkness, Abraham went home and gathered clothes and other provisions, including his father's pistol. As he was about to leave, he glanced around with solemn sorrow and realized that his mother and father would never be there again – and probably neither would he. He cursed the Germans and his Italian government for what had befallen his family and country.

Abraham decided to seek out Giuseppe Andretti, the town's lone mechanic. He had heard rumors that Andretti was in touch with the local Resistance and provided them supplies and news of German troop movements in the area.

Unmarried, the mechanic felt unencumbered by family ties or fear of retribution and, therefore, helped whenever he could. And Abraham knew where he lived. He walked the three blocks to his house, found the man in his workshop, and begged for entry.

Though Andretti initially denied knowledge of the Resistance fighters, their activities, or their whereabouts, Paggio's story about his parents' murder soon swayed the mechanic into helping.

Gathering his weapon, he and Abraham slipped into the pre-dawn darkness. Andretti had explained that taking a straight route to their destination could allow them to be at the nearby encampment well before daylight, but doing so would not be safe for them or the Partisans. Instead, they would need to take a more circuitous path, backtracking at times until they reached a spot deep in the forest some four kilometers outside town. As instructed by the mechanic, they sat in total silence and waited. It didn't take long.

Franco Marino emerged from the woods as the sun began creeping over the horizon. Abraham stood and was about to speak, but Marino lifted his hand. He knew why he was there; the news of the murder had reached him almost immediately after it had happened. And so, though he was quite young, Abraham Paggio was welcomed with open arms.

Abraham fought bravely alongside the Partisans and cursed each German he killed while smiling through clenched teeth. Before this war, the thought of slaying another human being sickened him, but his sense of morality had vanished with the unprovoked killing of his parents. However, like his mother and father, fate was not on his side.

During his third outing with the group, and due to ferocious fighting, Paggio became confused and disoriented. Though instructed to stay with one of the team's more experienced members, he panicked and lost track of his companion. While ambling through the forest, he walked straight into an encampment of German soldiers and was captured.

Convinced Abraham was a member of the Resistance, the Germans tortured the boy until he could bear no more. In a semi-conscious state, Paggio divulged all he knew of his fellow comrades, revealing the number of fighters in the group, the names he could remember, each rendezvous location, and the weaponry they possessed.

It was clear then that the youth knew no more than what he'd already confessed, but interrogators beat him until he drew his last ragged breath. His body was hung on a pole in the town's square, a sign around his neck, "Death to Jews and Traitors."

CHAPTER 2

"Just as you predicted," Sal whispered to Aldo. "The Germans are at the second meeting point as well. Abraham talked." He scanned the area around their position and added, "We can't stay and fight. There are too many of them."

"No," Aldo agreed, "we should head in the direction your father should come from and hope we find him before the Germans do." Aldo pulled out a small map and surveyed the terrain. After a few seconds, he folded the paper and put it away. Signaling for his troop's attention, he motioned for them to fall back.

As the Italians moved around the perimeter of the German position, one of his men tripped and fell into a washout formed during the rainy season. He tumbled into the crevice, his right knee smashing into a tree stump at the bottom. Though the pain seared through his leg, he did not yell out, but the spill made plenty of noise as branches and twigs cracked and snapped. A German sentry, standing no more than thirty meters away, spun around to face his position and spotted the movement.

Then all hell broke loose.

The sentry shouted an alert to the rest of his comrades and began firing toward the Italians. The balance of the Germans took cover and joined in. Tracers from automatic weapons arced through the air, mixing with shots from bolt action Karabiner 98k's. And though Aldo's men did their best to return fire, they were hopelessly outmatched.

Salvatore realized their predicament and knew their only hope was to reposition. He signaled to two men on his right to follow him. Keeping as low as they could, the three crawled along the ground like frightened hermit crabs. The second man behind Salvatore, Giovanni Martello, a chunky box-shaped man, took huge gasping breaths as he scampered to keep up with the other two. At one point, a bullet whizzed past his face so close it caused him to lose balance, and he stumbled face-first into the dank earth. He immediately righted himself, spitting out a gritty mess of dirt and leaves, and then raced on.

For the first time since he joined the Resistance, Salvatore believed he might never see his family again. Bullets were zipping and cutting through the foliage, bouncing off rocks and burrowing into trees, often only inches away. At that moment, he stumbled across Alberto Denali. There was a bullet wound to his forehead, and his eyes were open and staring blankly skyward. A serpentine line of blood oozed out of the hole and followed the creases of his brow as it drained to the ground.

Salvatore moaned softly but kept going. He crawled over the dead man and sidled up to his uncle.

"The three of us are going to move to our left flank on that rise," Sal said, pointing toward a small hill. "If the Germans gain that access before us, and they'll try, we'll be defenseless."

Aldo surveyed the spot his nephew had indicated and nodded his approval just as a bullet split a branch right above their heads. At one time, the incident would have seen them both sprawling to the ground and looking for cover. Now, they barely flinched.

With the two others trailing behind, Salvatore nodded and moved on. The three trundled forward with care as they pushed through the brush. Eventually, they took up a spot twenty meters to the left of the rest of their men's primary position. From there, they opened fire.

The German reaction to this new attack was quick and decisive. An officer directed his troops to alternate positions and return fire toward this latest offensive. The barrage of bullets caused Salvatore to dive behind the tree to his right. His position had been discovered. His only recourse was to stay hidden and shoot his gun toward his targets without aiming, hoping for the best.

Salvatore's brother, Pietro, who had remained in place when Sal and the two others moved to their elevated position, realized that the repositioning of the Germans left him no direct line of the enemy. He dropped to his stomach and began slithering along the ground toward his uncle. After moving a few meters, he came upon Denali. The sight of his prone body napped Pietro out of his vacuous state. He scrambled over and away from the dead man and moved a few feet from his uncle.

Once near Aldo, Pietro got on one knee and raised his rifle to aim. As he did, a German stick grenade sailed over his head in a ponderous cartwheeling motion. Aldo also saw the flying object, watching dumbly as it tumbled through the air and landed with a thump behind them. Both reacted instinctively and dove as far away as possible before the explosion obliterated their surroundings.

The blast didn't kill them, but they lay disoriented, dazed, and motionless for several moments. When Pietro's head finally cleared enough to get his bearings, he tried to rise, but a sharp pain in his shoulder dropped him flat. Fiery hot shrapnel from the grenade had found its mark, ripping into his flesh.

In reaction to the searing agony, Pietro reached back and felt a stubby piece of metal lodged near the top of his left shoulder blade. Wincing, he searchingly slid his hand down and brushed over a second fragment protruding from his bicep. Both areas were saturated with his warm blood.

Pietro squinted through fuzzy eyes to see his uncle beginning to rise from the ground. "Are you okay?" he yelled. Aldo nodded, though shakily, and was about to return to the firefight when he observed a stain of blood now forming on Pietro's left arm. The wounded man locked eyes with his uncle and gave him a silent thumbs up.

Aldo nodded, rose, and began firing.

Pietro reached down to his arm and ripped apart his sleeve to reveal the shrapnel. He gritted his teeth and grabbed what he could to pull it out. The metal fragment was still hot, and it took some painful wrangling, but he managed to remove it. He gazed at the bloody chunk with a grimace for a moment before tossing it aside.

As the battle raged on, it quickly became apparent that the German's superior weapons and manpower would prevail. The Partisans were pinned down and getting the worst of the altercation. They would be doomed if the group's leader couldn't find a way to get his remaining team away and safe.

Turning his back to the enemy, Aldo began frantically searching the woods behind their location. Though his eyes darted in all directions, he could detect no easy avenue of escape. Multiple scenarios ran through his head, but most ended with his entire team wiped out. He thought all was lost but then sensed something odd happening. The rest of the group felt it, too. Guns still blazed from the German's position, but the bullets, for the most part, stopped coming toward the Partisans.

Salvatore inched his head around the tree he was using for cover and peered cautiously down to where the enemy had set up their defensive front. At first, he was unsure what had changed. But then he spotted something that made him blink. Someone else was engaged in the battle, firing from behind the Germans. He watched in astonishment as the men in grey uniforms scrambled to confront this new threat. They were too late.

A deafening explosion shattered the air with an intense shockwave, and the area instantly became smoke, and debris filled. It was now impossible for any Partisan to know what was happening. Salvatore heard Germans screaming at each other in panic as they attempted to organize.

Aldo called over to Salvatore, "What's going on?"

"I'm not sure, but I think another Partisan group has joined us in the fight. But I have no idea who they are."

A burst of machine-gun fire erupted, then another, and then a man's scream. Several minutes of silence ensued. Salvatore and Aldo sat and waited, scanning the area for any sign of what was happening. The two eyed each other, baffled. Aldo signaled for Salvatore to stay in position and checked the others for any casualties.

Aside from the dead Denali, two others were wounded, with Sal's brother Pietro's injuries being the most severe. The third Barilla sibling, Arturo, was now at Pietro's side and indicated to Aldo that his brother's wound didn't appear to be life-threatening.

At that moment, a man's voice broke the silence.

"Ciao, Ciao. Aldo! Are you there? Aldo, Salvatore, Pietro, anyone there?"

"Papa?" Salvatore answered in amazement. "Papa, is that you?"

"Yes, we're coming in, don't shoot."

Salvatore yelled back anxiously, "No, stay where you are! Are you crazy? There are Germans everywhere!"

A voice Salvatore did not recognize called out.

"It's Okay. All the Germans are dead." After a few seconds, Santos, Berta, and Paulo stood up. They were about fifty meters from where Salvatore crouched. As they walked toward him, they saw a stranger on the old man's left.

CHAPTER 3

"And that's when Joseph took off running," Santos explained to the Partisans. "After that, I'm unclear what occurred until he signaled it was alright to let you know we were coming in."

Aldo looked at Campanella in earnest appreciation and offered his hand. "I don't know how you did it, but we can't begin to thank you enough. I was starting to think we were done."

Before Campanella could respond, Salvatore said in amazement, "All that, and it was just you? No one else helped you?"

The big man did not answer. Campanella just nodded while extending his hand to take Aldo's. As he reached out, he felt a sudden surge of pain in the back of his shoulder. He winced as Aldo grabbed his appendage and shook it vigorously. Berta caught the agonized look on Campanella's face.

When the two finished shaking hands, Campanella clenched his right hand several times as it hung at his side. Berta worked her way behind him and saw a hole in his shirt about three inches below the top of his right shoulder. The opening was about half an inch in diameter and was blood-soaked.

"You're hurt," Berta gasped in alarm.

Campanella turned and looked at the young woman. Even though they hadn't seen eye to eye on much of anything, he recognized genuine concern in her deep brown eyes.

"Take your shirt off, and let me examine the wound," Berta said. It sounded more like an order than a request, and Campanella thought to protest. But he could tell by her tone and the look in her eyes that she was not taking no for an answer.

"I, uh…well, I have some scars. So don't be alarmed," Campanella said as he unbuckled his gear.

Berta watched in wary anticipation as the man removed his equipment and shirt. When Campanella's shirt was off, she could only stare in shock. Who was this man? He was like no other she'd ever laid eyes on. Yes, his skin bore scars, some of which were rather disturbing. But those healed injuries did not trigger her to take an unintentional pause.

Her astonishment was caused by his incredible muscular shape. It was as if sculpted with Carrara marble. Berta considered her father, brothers, uncles, cousins, and even Paulo. They were all in excellent condition, but their physiques paled compared to this man's. His was like the statue of David she had seen at the Accademia Gallery in Florence as a girl. But unlike David, Campanella's muscles appeared to have muscles of their own.

"I think you've been shot. There's a hole halfway up your right shoulder blade," Berta said.

Reaching into his pocket, Campanella pulled out a small pocketknife. He offered it to Berta. "Here, you might need this."

"What?" she blurted as she stared at the knife. "Are you nuts or something? I can't do that!"

"It's okay. I have a very high tolerance to pain."

"You might be tolerant to pain, but that doesn't mean I have any tolerance, whatsoever, for sticking a knife in someone!"

Campanella just smiled and waggled the knife at her as encouragement. At first, Berta didn't take it; she just stared at it like it would be fatal to the touch. After some seconds, though, she slowly reached for it. She gripped the knife between two fingers as if it were disease-ridden. Then, after a moment's more reluctance, she unfolded the blade. Once fully extended, she held the knife and examined it with wonder.

Berta turned it over several times, the blade flashing with each rotation. "I've never seen a pocketknife like this before. All the men in my family own pocketknives, but nothing like this. Where did you get it?"

"One of the dead Germans near your home," Campanella lied, trying to fend off more questions about his almost brand-new 1999 pocketknife.

"Really…" Berta said disbelievingly. She looked at the knife again, shrugged, and then laid her left hand on the American's shoulder to support her in the task of digging out the foreign object. "My God," she thought as she gripped his flesh, "was he made of marble too?" Shaking off the thought, she gently pressed the knife to the bullet hole. Taking a deep breath, she pushed the blade in and probed inside the wound. Campanella twitched in reaction.

"I'm sorry," Berta said, jerking the knife out. "I…I don't think I can do this."

"Here, I'll do it," Franco Marino called out. "I've had to do this a few times already, so let me."

Berta gladly handed the knife over.

With the rest of the group watching, Franco went to work. With some effort, the man half pulled, half pried a large bullet from the hole. He wiped it clean, studied it, and then showed it to Salvatore, who stared at it for several seconds before offering it to Aldo. After a brief exchange of comments, Salvatore looked to Campanella.

"I believe this is one of ours. Strange, though…" Salvatore said in bewilderment.

"I'm sure it was a stray shot from the fight. No one meant to shoot him," Berta said, trying to allay any fears that one of their men purposely shot Campanella.

"No, not that," her father said, shaking his head. "I find it strange how it only went into his shoulder an inch or so."

"Probably a ricochet," Campanella offered nonchalantly.

Salvatore was about to argue further, but Aldo stopped him by handing Berta additional first aid supplies. "Berta, close and dress the wound as quickly as you can. We must leave here at once."

CHAPTER 4

Outside of Montelupo Albese, Italy

It was late afternoon, and only a few hours of sunlight remained. Explanations of recent events would need to wait. It was time to move as far away as possible before the Germans could catch up. The burying of Alberto Denali had begun before Berta was finished nursing Campanella. The group was on their way once the American was tended to and the burial complete.

They headed south toward Montelupo Albese, stopping at a safe house for much-needed rest and food. The owner of the farmhouse, Bernard Calvino, permitted them to stay in his large barn whenever they were in the area, and no German or Italian troops were around. He was a sympathizer of the Resistance campaign and often kept a vigil on any troop movements to safeguard the partisan's activities.

Once at the farm, eating was the first order of business. The farmer's wife brought them a hearty homemade stew. After a diet of root vegetables, dried meats, and olives for the past month, this food tasted like it had been cooked by the gods. Campanella gratefully accepted a plate from Berta and sat down next to Santos and Salvatore. Nothing was said, but Campanella sensed a strong father-son bond between the two. He felt a pang of envy at the relationship.

Campanella hadn't known his mother. She'd died during his birth. And his father, though still around, silently blamed Joseph for his wife's death. He was an absent father for the most important events of his life. Ultimately, this lack of nurturing led Campanella to join the Marines, a decision that would change his life beyond all comprehension.

Once everyone had started to eat, Santos began detailing the occurrences at the family's vineyards since Campanella's arrival. He described Berta's rescue and his extermination of the two German patrols. He then discussed what had happened at the Gianelli farmhouse and how

Antonio had suffered a minor injury to his chin.

He reassured his son that all was well, and that the injury was not severe but then launched into an excited description of the American's efforts to ensure the boy was safe. What he didn't tell his son was how Campanella had miraculously healed from his horrific wounds. He thought about revealing it but thought better when he realized it was too soon to open Pandora's box.

The men sat in stunned silence as Santos laid out all that had occurred, often gaping at Campanella in awe as they listened to the tales of the Americans' feats of soldiery. Even Berta appeared to finally grasp what this man had done.

When Santos finished, Salvatore turned to Campanella. "I've heard the stories, and I admit that I would be skeptical of believing this fantastic tale if I hadn't witnessed what I did today. But still, how in the world did you kill those eighteen Germans? And so fast. I mean, it just all seems impossible." Salvatore looked to the other partisans for support, with each nodding in agreement.

Campanella gave his response and conveyed neither boast nor a hint of pride. "I did not kill eighteen. I killed fourteen. Your team took out the rest."

"Oh, just fourteen then…alright, how did you kill fourteen Germans? In fact, how did you know what was even going on?"

"We were about two hundred meters away when we heard a small-arms firefight," Campanella began as if providing a military debriefing. "Since we were close to our destination, it became evident that both your first and second rendezvous sites were compromised. Based on when and where Santos said you would meet, I thought it must be your group in the skirmish.

"I made my way around your left flank," Campanella said as he nodded at Salvatore before going on. "The spot I chose rose about ten meters above the action. This vantage point gave me a comprehensive view of the entire battle zone. I surveyed the enemy, saw they were in a direct frontal firing position, and decided to attack from their rear."

"But this would also put you in our line of fire," Pietro said with amazement.

"Yes, but it was a chance I had to take. The odds did get a bit better when three Germans tried to outflank you. As I made my way to my strike site, I saw them moving toward that position, so I established an ambush spot and waited for them to pass. That's as far as they got. After taking them out, I made my way behind the others. I saw the four you'd killed and planned my attack sequence on the rest."

"And that's all there was to it?" Pietro asked.

Campanella nodded.

"We found four killed by the grenade you threw, four dead from your automatic weapon, and three by knife wounds to the neck and back. Absolutely incredible!" Arturo shouted with a chuckle. "Mr. Campanella, I'm glad you're on our side!" Everyone laughed and voiced their agreement.

The fire embers gave off comforting warmth as the group continued chatting into the night. They expressed remorse about the dead, and Franco Marino told the story about the capture and killing of Abraham Paggio and Dominic Patrelli's demise. The mention of the leader's killing produced silent reflection by all, and then, as if on cue, Aldo spoke.

"I fear our success will diminish substantially without Dominic's leadership. To be honest, I'm concerned about even continuing with such a reduced contingent," the Italian said somberly.

There were a few more moments of silence as each man thought about Aldo's comment, and then Arturo decided to ask the question on everyone's lips.

"So, Joseph, where do you come from? I don't recognize your accent?"

Campanella looked at Santos enquiringly. When the older man gave him a slight, almost imperceptible shrug, Campanella turned his attention back to the rest of the group. Sitting around the fire were Santos' three sons, Salvatore, Pietro, and Arturo; Santos' brother Aldo and Aldo's son Alberto; two of Aldo's neighbors, Franco Marino, and Angelo "Sonny"

Marino; and finally, Giovanni Martello, a neighbor of Patrelli's. All were staring intently at the burly man – except for Paulo. The boy was next to Berta, and his attention was entirely on her. To his chagrin, Berta was hanging on every word from the American's mouth.

"I'm not from around here. In fact, I'm not from Italy. I am an American and was sent here on a mission of incredible importance."

Campanella proceeded to give only as much information as he felt was safe and would make sense. The American knew that giving these people the time travel specifics at this point would not result in willing acceptance.

As he spoke, he remained vigilant of Giovanni Martello. He remembered from his debriefing and from the Journal that this man would not continue with the group. The problem was that Campanella couldn't remember why. Santos' written accounts were usually vivid and detailed, but some events were omitted or vague, probably due to Santos's decision on what was essential and what wasn't.

When he'd finished, Joseph nodded in Santos' direction. "Santos and I have spoken at length about this. The mission's success depends on all of you participating." Campanella measured each person and said, "I am now confident that all of us in this circle will play a vital part in what needs to be done."

"Excuse me," Berta said as she waved a hand at the group. "You mean the men here – these men? Everyone excluding Paulo?"

"No, I mean everyone, including Paulo – and you."

With this statement, Salvatore began to rise in protest, but his father beat him to it and jumped to his feet first. His face was red with anger.

"Joseph, we never agreed to this! I do not intend to let my granddaughter or Paulo be involved. They will be leaving in the morning as planned."

"I'm sorry, Santos, but both Paulo and Berta must come, and I need you as well." Campanella turned to the rest of the partisans and added, "When I said I needed you all, I meant each person here. It is the only way." Turning toward the non-Barilla in the encampment, Campanella asked for a few minutes with the family to discuss the group's youngest members.

Some faces showed bewilderment but no hesitation as the Marino brothers and Martello stood and made their way to where they had previously laid out their bedding. Once they were out of earshot, Campanella turned and faced the man he now considered a friend.

"Santos, I know I didn't tell you about needing Berta and Paulo," Campanella said as he met the man's glare. "Honestly, I never intended to involve them. Not now or when we started. Even though my information, or more precisely your information, clearly stated they would be with us on the mission, I wasn't comfortable including them. In hindsight, I guess it worked how it was meant to be because here they are. Besides, would you have agreed to let them come if I told you they would be joining us?"

"Absolutely not," Santos said without hesitation, his face still blooming with anger.

Berta's father interrupted the two men before the conversation could escalate. "What do you mean, *your information clearly stated they would be on the mission'*. What information?"

The decisive moment was here. There was no getting around it.

"Santos, please sit." He put his hand on the man's shoulder and looked him in the eyes. "Please." Santos begrudgingly did so. Campanella found a spot where he could view every person. "What I'm about to tell you is for your ears only. It will be hard to believe, but as Santos has learned, it's the truth."

The small group stared at Campanella in stunned silence for nearly thirty minutes as he laid it all out. He held nothing back this time and told his story in minute detail. Though eyebrows were raised, no one asked a single question. When he was finished, Santos took the floor before anyone else spoke.

"First, I want it clear to all; I am angry and upset about Joseph's insistence that both of you be involved," he gestured to Berta and Paulo.

"This was not part of our agreement. And in different circumstances, I'd insist we all pack up and leave this man to whatever he needs to do." Santos stopped for a moment in contemplation. "However, there is more to this story, and I can't deny that. And I know what each of you are thinking. I know because I felt the same way you do. But you must hear what I have to say.

"In the last few weeks, Joseph has described events and situations that hadn't happened yet. He related places, people involved, and times – almost to the exact moment. And then those incidences occurred precisely as he detailed.

"He had to know what the future would bring. But something else also convinced me. Something Joseph is not even aware of."

Santos reached into the satchel that was almost permanently draped over his shoulder and pulled out a leather-bound book. He presented it to the group and allowed them to scan what was written on the pages.

"Your Journal," Sal said. "The one you started when Antonio was born."

"Yes, it is my journal. It is the very one Joseph just talked of, but I have yet to show him. In this book are documented events of which only I am aware. Yet Joseph has spoken of it as if he wrote the words himself."

"How can this be? Time travel does not exist," Berta said, still not convinced.

"No, not today. But in 1999, it does," Campanella said. "Remember my black pouch, my clothes, and the pocketknife. All made sometime around 1998 or 1999."

The young girl's brow furrowed, and her eyes began to squint as she studied the large man. She was looking for anything to suggest he was lying. Suddenly, she stood and strode toward him, causing him to take a small step backward.

With pursed lips, Berta pointed a finger. "Alright. If this is all true, and I don't believe it for a minute, then why haven't these 'scientists' of yours sent more people?" Before he could answer, she turned her head to the rest of the group for support. She then spun back and continued her barrage. "If time travel is possible like you claim it is, then why not send an army of American soldiers to handle this problem?"

Campanella gazed down at the girl and admired her tenacity. Her face was set in a stern demeanor, her eyes blazing in conviction. As he regarded her, a slight wind blew hair across her face. She glanced at it with slightly crossed eyes and puffed away the errant strands with a quick burst of air from her lips. Though the situation was at its most critical, the corner of Campanella's mouth drew up ever so slightly. Stifling what was headed toward a full grin, he cleared his throat.

"Let's just say I'm made up a bit different than most men. One of a kind, so to speak." This caused Berta to scoff. The much larger man started to feel a bead of sweat forming along his scalp, and he realized this slight-statured woman was making him nervous. "In other words," he went on as convincingly as he could muster, "no one else has the chemical and physical makeup I do. It would prevent anyone from surviving the trip without a similar molecular structure. You may have sensed I'm a little faster and stronger than most people you know."

Berta spent a few moments thinking about this. She recalled all the amazing things she'd already seen the man do. But even having witnessed his feats herself, she still couldn't fathom his explanation. Finally, to Campanella's relief, Arturo spoke, breaking her intense scrutiny.

"This is quite unbelievable," Berta's uncle said. "I mean, if what you say is even half true, then we have no choice but to go with you. If not, logic would dictate that the future, as it will eventually occur, might be different?"

Campanella stepped around Berta, thankful he could avoid her stare, and said, "It would seem so. But any of you could say no. I do not know what would happen, but it is written and documented by Santos that we all go."

"My biggest issue is the children. You say they must go. Why?" Berta's father asked, concern deeply embedded within the question.

"All I can tell you is the Journal says we are all in Naples on the first of October. It details how we find the assassins and stop them from killing Churchill. All of us – including Berta and Paulo." Campanella then shifted his gaze back toward the young couple. "I'm not sure why it happened, but you are both here at this now, and the Journal states that you go with us," Campanella said with sincerity.

"What about the rest of the men? Do they all go with us?" Pietro asked.

"All go but Martello. The journal reports he will not be with us. Sometime between now and then, he will leave us. The journal is vague on why. But he will be gone." With this announcement, several in the circle turned to look at Giovanni, who seemed unaware of their observation.

"So, what's next?" Santos asked wearily.

"As I understand it, we are going to Naples. The journey will not be easy as we will face many tests, but we will make it. When we arrive, I will check out the estate where the Prime Minister is supposed to stay. Once I have a clear lay of the land, we'll plan our strategy. Santo's writings give me a location of where they will be, but the specifics of what happens are…sketchy."

Campanella regarded everyone and saw the weariness in their eyes. "Now, I suggest we all get some rest. As I mentioned to the others, I will answer their questions, so sleep on it, and we will talk more tomorrow."

Santos stepped into the middle of the circle and looked each in the eye. He then settled his gaze on Campanella. "If we do decide to do this, we will do it as a family. If one wants out, we are all out. Is that clear?"

"Perfectly," Campanella said, adding, "I have one more thing, though."

Santos lifted an eyebrow.

"We must leave this place no later than two days from now, whether we go my way, or you go your way."

"Why?"

"Because…" Campanella hesitantly said, "…I'm afraid the Germans are coming, and this barn and house won't remain when they do."

CHAPTER 5

Morning came sooner than any of the exhausted group wanted. A small moan escaped from Berta as her left eye crept open and then her right. Once she got her bearings, she glanced over to where Paulo lay. He was still in a deep sleep. She scanned the rest of the barn and found all the partisans still in their respective sleeping spots – all except the American.

Berta rose, stretched, and approached the large wooden door leading outside. She slowly opened it and peered out. With all the havoc and upheaval war had brought upon the world, especially their small group of fighters, the girl was amazed at the serenity and beauty of the morning. She crept through the entrance and closed the door as quietly as possible.

The ground was damp with dew, and the new day's sun made it sparkle as she walked. After spotting two buckets sitting next to the barn, she decided to get fresh water from the well. Berta grabbed the buckets and headed that way. As she rounded the back corner of the building, her eyes caught a sight that caused her feet to come to a scrambling halt. Campanella was standing at the well, and he was practically naked. Though his back was turned toward her, the American had all his clothes off except his white undergarments.

The strapping man ran a wet, soapy cloth up and down his arms and chest and around his midsection. His muscles rippled with the movement when he raised his arm to wash under it. Just as when she'd tended to his injured shoulder, Berta marveled at Campanella's physique. He was spectacular in every sense of the word. As she scanned his body from head to toe, she wondered if all American soldiers could look like him. If so, the Germans and their Allies should surely surrender right away.

Berta cowered back toward the hiding shade of the barn, not wanting Campanella to know she was ogling him. Once out of his line of sight, she sat the buckets down and lowered her head. She stared at the ground while wringing her hands. Feeling embarrassed at what she'd witnessed, Berta thought of dashing back inside. But for some odd reason that she couldn't comprehend, the thought vanished almost as quickly as it had arrived. Instead, she lifted her head and turned slowly back toward the bathing man.

The young woman watched with a strange and excited anticipation as Campanella continued his early morning ritual. With the passing moments, Berta's breathing deepened as her eyes followed the washcloth move around the man's torso. At one point, as Campanella extended his left arm high in the air, Berta gasped and then held her breath as his muscles flexed and rippled. The undulating movements seemed surreal and grabbed Berta's total focus. She stared with bulging eyes as the bathing process continued – then the American did the unthinkable. He turned his body toward her, pulled his undershorts away from his waist, and ran the cloth inside.

Engrained moral instincts told Berta to forget the water and to turn and run, but she didn't. She just stood transfixed as she gawked. It wasn't until he removed the washcloth that she consciously took a breath or blinked. But now, the thin white cottony material of his undergarment clung to the outline of his manhood. It visibly and overtly defined every single detail. This was all Berta could take. She jerked her head away and spun back toward the barn.

Breathing fast and hard, the stunned Italian girl was now staring blindly. The vision she had just seen was burned in her psyche. Her face blushed, her cheeks got hot, and her body grew moist with tension. Clenching her eyes, the distressed girl did her best to shake the image. But all her mind's eye could see was Campanella's well-endowed body. He was a big, statuesque man. One of the biggest she had ever known or seen. But his…um…well, she couldn't believe it to be real.

She was struck with a glaring awareness of her own body's transformation. She hadn't detected it before, but now she was aware that her breathing was heavy, almost gasp-like. Her heart beat so hard in her chest that she considered running for help. On top of these strange changes, her stomach was flip-flopping, and her knees became weak.

Berta leaned heavily against the wooden barn for support and tried to control whatever was happening. Then, just as she'd convinced herself to race back inside, she heard a noise. She looked tentatively in its direction and saw that Campanella was now dressed except for his shirt.

The shirt Campanella wore when she removed the bullet from his shoulder had been discarded. A clean one was lying on the well, but he didn't put it on at first. Instead, he was studying a small vial he held in his hand. It appeared to Berta to be one of the ointments they'd found on the boat. She watched as he opened the bottle and dabbed some of the cream on a finger. He tried several times to cover the wound with medicine but with limited success.

After watching Campanella's futile efforts, she took a deep breath, patted her hair, tightened the sash around her waist, and then pushed off the wall. She picked up the two buckets and, with a straight back, made her way to the well.

"Good morning," she said, her voice cracking slightly.

"Good morning to you," Campanella replied as he turned toward the girl. "Did I wake you?"

"No, no. I just woke up and came outside to get water for everyone. Is your wound bothering you?" Berta asked, her speech coming faster than she wanted.

"No, not really. I was just trying to clean it some and apply some ointment. But I'm having a bit of trouble…would you mind?" Campanella said as he held up the tube.

"Uh…no, sure. I mean, yes, of course," Berta said, stuttering.

After setting the buckets down, Berta took the vial. She squeezed out a dab and applied the gel on the injury, rubbing it in and around the jagged opening, then covered it with a bandage Campanella had prepared. After she'd finished, he turned and thanked her. She nodded and thought he'd perceived something peculiar about her expression.

"Are you okay? You look a little flushed. Did you not sleep well?" Campanella asked.

Berta stiffened and gulped, "Huh? Yes, I'm fine. I mean, I slept fine." Berta was stammering, still shaken by what she witnessed while he bathed.

The image of him washing his private parts would not leave her mind, and she struggled to concentrate – or even talk. She certainly couldn't look the man in his eyes.

"Okay," Campanella shrugged. He put on his shirt and asked, "Can I fill the buckets for you?"

"Yes, thank you," Berta said and softly added, "Joseph?"

"Yes?"

"Can I ask you a question?"

"Be surprised if you didn't," he said with a grin.

"Yes. Well, anyway…" Berta said, trying to ignore his jibe, "…you said all of us are in Naples in October, yes?"

"Yep."

"Are we all safe? I mean, do each of us go home when this is over?"

Campanella had hoped this issue wouldn't come up, so he did what he had to do for the moment, and he lied. "Yes, as I remember it, we all go home safe."

Her face beamed with a huge grin. "Then I will vote we must go. Saving Mr. Churchill sounds like a fine thing to do."

"I'm glad you understand. Here, you take the ointment and my other shirt, and I'll carry the buckets. Okay?" The young woman's smile was so full of hope that Campanella felt saddened that he had to lie to make it happen.

"Let's go!" Berta said, her voice filled with gleeful elation.

As the two walked, they chatted about the beautiful morning, Calvino's farm, his hospitality, and other small talk. When they turned to go into the barn, they almost ran headfirst into Paulo. The youth was coming out as they were coming in, and he pulled up just before running into the larger Campanella. His surprise at the sudden encounter quickly changed into a look of consternation.

"Berta, where were you? You were not in the barn when I woke up," he said as he regained his composure. "Then I looked over and noticed

Mr. Campanella was not there either. I got, um – concerned something had happened to you. The two of you, I mean," Paulo said, though his tone did not appear to have as much concern in it as an accusation.

"I went to get water for everyone. Mr. Campanella volunteered to help," Berta answered.

"Yes, but I saw you get up and leave almost twenty minutes ago. When you were gone for so long, I got worried."

Campanella turned to look at Berta. She might have observed him bathing if she had been outside for any length of time. A slight discomfiture began creeping through him as he searched the girl's eyes for any sign of confession. But Berta ignored Paulo's question or Campanella's quizzical stare. She drew her shoulders back, stuck her chin out, and pushed past the two men, disregarding both. Campanella and Paulo eyed each other in bafflement and then glanced back toward the girl as she stormed off.

"You've got your hands full, my young friend," Campanella said to Paulo as he laid a big hand on the boy's shoulder and gave him a wry and consoling grin.

"Yes, I do. I do indeed…" Paulo agreed with a thoughtful seriousness.

Over the next thirty minutes, the rest of the group woke and soon went about their morning routines. After Campanella had delivered the buckets of water for Berta, he moved to his bundle of belongings and began inspecting each of his weapons. After tinkering with a sticky firing pin on his handgun, he noticed several men had assembled just outside the barn door.

Santos and Salvatore were there, as well as Franco, Sonny, Alberto, and Giovanni. The property owner, Bernard Calvino, was also amongst the group. They were animatedly talking, and although Campanella was twenty meters away, he could hear everything. He shook his head in anguish at what was being discussed and was about to return to what he was doing when Santos glanced his way and motioned him to join them.

Campanella grimaced. He didn't want to be put in a position to reveal anything about the future. More specifically, anything suggesting he might be asked to change the future. He set his gun on the rag he was working with, stood, and slowly walked to the men.

"Joseph," Santos said as Campanella approached, "Bernard here is a fine man, and he hates the Germans as do we. But..." Santos paused here for effect and, with genuine anxiety, said, "With all the German activity going on, I believe his family's safety is at risk. I have been trying to convince him it would be best if he comes with us."

"Yes," Campanella said with conviction, "Things will get rather ugly here very soon, and your family will not be safe. It would be wise to pack up as much as possible and leave with us now."

The danger was real. Of that, there was no doubt. If the Calvino family stayed, they would indeed be executed, so packing up and going was the best, if not the only option for survival. But Campanella also knew something no one else did. Neither Calvino nor any of his family was supposed to leave with them.

"Santos," spoke Bernard, "as I said, I deeply appreciate your concern. But no Calvino has ever abandoned this farm due to war, battle, or civil strife. I just cannot leave. Although I thank you for your offer, we must stay and defend our property."

"Please, be reasonable," Santos begged. "It is not safe here."

Santos persisted for several minutes longer but eventually realized that Bernard Calvino would not go, no matter what he said.

The group moved on to preparations that needed to be completed before they could depart. Once they'd finalized these, Calvino said his farewells and returned home. Santos shot a meaningful look at Campanella, which the American immediately understood. It was time to settle the critical issue at hand.

CHAPTER 6

"I realize we haven't had much time to digest what Joseph has asked us to do," Santos said to the rest of the partisans, "but as he says, time is of the essence. So, I shall ask each of you now whether you want to do this. Before I do, let me be clear and remind each of you, it is our decision and ours alone. No pressure nor shame comes with either choice," Santos paused for a moment so that the message could sink in. "Sal?" Santos asked first.

Berta's father stepped up. His lips tightened as he eyed the rest of the family. Taking a deep breath and then exhaling, he said, "To be honest, the entire story seems to be a crazy thing to me. Though we fight and do our best with what we have, what is now being asked of us appears to be well above our abilities. I know we take chances with our lives each time we go on a raid. But I feel like this is suicide." He stopped and appeared deep in thought as he prepared what to say next.

Campanella recognized that Salvatore's reasoning made sense. Based on this man's statement alone, he might vote no if he were asked. And if it went that way, it would be unlikely any other vote would occur.

With a grim demeanor, Salvatore glanced around the group, straightened his back, and said, "But Papa, I look in your eyes and see you believe. And if you believe then that is all I need to vote yes. I am in."

Campanella released a small breath of relief as Santos turned to his eldest son and said, "Pietro?"

"Me, too," he said, nodding. "Stopping the Germans, at any cost, is what must be done. It's what we've been trying to do for months. At least now we possess a set goal: a mission to stop a major evil."

"With your injuries, are you up to it?" his brother Arturo asked.

"It's only a flesh wound," Pietro said while looking down at the bloodstained hole in his shirt. "It will not stop me from doing my part," he said, flexing his muscles as proof of his words.

Santos continued, giving each their turn to speak. To a person, they all agreed what needed to be done would be done. Once they'd reached a consensus, Salvatore spoke up again.

"Pietro is right," he said while scratching at a several weeks-old beard, "Stopping this assassination would truly be a difference-making act."

"Then it's settled," Santos said.

"Not entirely," Paulo replied, stepping to the forefront of the group. "My father and mother will die of worry if we don't return soon. It's the same with all your families. So, if we must go on this quest, someone should return and tell them what we've agreed to do."

"You are right, my boy," Santos agreed. "But who shall that be?"

"I will go," Giovanni Martello said, stepping up from behind Arturo. "I know I agreed to go to Naples, and I believe in what you all are doing. But unlike some of you here, I've not been with my family for over a year. I don't know whether they are safe or even…" He hesitated momentarily, not wanting to say what everyone else was thinking or fearing for his or her family. He then finished, "I'll go and tell each of our families what has happened. And though I know I cannot relate what is still to come, I will assure them you were safe when I left."

"Giovanni will go, and we thank him," Santos agreed. And he embraced the man warmly.

****

Campanella was the first to rise just before dawn the following day. He prepared his gear for the journey southward, carefully packing each item in his travel bag. Salvatore stirred, and when the Italian opened his eyes and saw daylight was upon, he was surprised that he had slept through the entire night. The Barilla patriarch smiled with contentment, closing his eyes softly again.

The decision for Giovanni to go back to reassure the families of their group's safety had lifted a huge emotional weight from his shoulders. The relief of this burden had allowed him his first profound and restful sleep in many months. After a moment or two indulging in the warm embrace of rest, Salvatore looked over and saw Campanella moving about the barn. He watched the American methodically pack his gear and prepare and arrange other provisions for the group's departure.

Clearly, this man was a trained professional soldier, he thought. And in the next instant, he felt immense gratitude that the American was with them, supporting their efforts. But he was only one man, a thought that sent a shiver of concern down Salvatore's back. He forced himself to smile and close his eyes again to banish his worry.

A few minutes later, with gray hair shooting up in all directions, Santos sat up. He stretched his arms and legs with a gigantic and slow moan and then slowly put on his boots. With some effort, he rose from his seated position, grabbed his satchel, and motioned for Campanella to follow him outside.

In the shadows of the early morning sunlight, the two chatted about Calvino. Once again, Santos insisted on convincing his dear friend to pack up and leave with their group. Campanella warned him of the possible consequences, though his voice did not stress the conviction he should have projected.

"Okay," Campanella said in resignation, "but let me do something first."

Santos watched as he grabbed the MP40 Schmeisser, his Luger, and a few other miscellaneous items. He approached Santos and, with a nod, said, "I'll be back in one hour. Everyone needs to be ready to go when I return."

Campanella was off and running before Santos could ask where he was going.

CHAPTER 7

"What do you mean he's not here? Where did he go?" Salvatore asked his father.

Raising his hands, palms out in mock defense, Santos replied, "He said he'd be back in about an hour, and that was…" he paused and checked his watch, "…about an hour ago. That's all I know."

Santos' son glared off in the direction of where his father said the man had gone. He vacantly began to scratch his left ear.

"Well, that's just crazy," he muttered. The two stood together for several more minutes as they stared toward the woods. Santos thought about *'when'* the man would return, with Salvatore wondering *'if'* the man would return.

At that moment, Calvino came out of his home with supplies of bacon, salt, dried beef, and loaves of freshly baked bread. He headed toward the two Italians with a broad smile on his face. It was now or never, and Santos had prepared for the encounter. He was about to begin his *"You must come with us"* speech when, as if on cue, Campanella came racing out of the trees to their left.

"Look at…" Calvino started to say, his jaw hanging low in disbelief.

"Yes, the boy can run quite fast," Santos said in a deadpan that suggested he had seen this display many times.

"Santos, Salvatore, we must go now!" Campanella demanded as he approached the three men.

"Why, what's happening," Calvino asked in confusion.

Campanella turned his attention to the concerned landowner. "Mr. Calvino, I speak a little German, but more importantly, I understand spoken German very well. I went out this morning to make sure the area was clear of patrols before we left when I ran across a company of Germans just beyond that crest," Campanella said, pointing to the northwest. "I saw at least fifty German soldiers camped in a small clearing, and they are preparing to come here."

"What? What do you mean, come here? Why?" Calvino asked. The man's hat was tipped back, exposing his brow, which was now profoundly creased.

"They know about our group and that you are helping us. I overheard the group commander explaining to his men their plan to come here, question and torture you and your family for information about us and burn down everything here. In two hours, no building will remain, nor will any living thing be left alive. I'm sorry, but you must leave with us now."

Calvino stood in stunned silence for a long moment. He turned toward his home and began shaking his head in disbelief. With trembling lips and a cracking voice, he said, "Five generations of my family have lived here. All they possessed and all I own is right here. There are a dozen lifetimes in that house."

The Partisans remained silent as they viewed the man's home and farm in anguish. Finally, Calvino looked at the three standing with him. The dangers of destruction had drained the color from his face. But, as quickly as his color had left, a scarlet tinge began boiling up his neckline and soon filled his puffy cheeks. His frightened look had vanished, and now a scowl of a determined and furious man appeared.

"I can't let them do this; I just can't. You must stay and help me defeat these evil devils. This is what you do, is it not?" Calvino implored.

Santos walked up next to Calvino and touched the farmer's shoulder. In an honest but firm manner, he said, "Bernard, we could, and most certainly would remain to fight. But to what end? Undoubtedly, the Germans have reported our position and your participation to their superiors. If they don't finish the job today, more soldiers will come to finish it for them tomorrow. And it won't be fifty who will come...it will be one hundred or more.

"These fiends won't stop until every person here is dead and your property is razed. They will erase you and all your family's history from this earth. I'm afraid the choice is clear. For the sake of your wife and children, you must come with us now."

Calvino's face changed once again. The now beleaguered Italian, with eyes welling up, stood for a moment without speaking. Then, with resignation, he assented. "I will do it. I will go. But I will go to my brother's, and he and I will get others. We will come back and fight. We will drive these men from our lands. And if not, we'll die trying."

The farmer turned toward the entire partisan group now assembled in the small clearing next to his home and said, "I know you must go, and I can't blame you for not staying. You've done much and sacrificed much. Don't worry about the Calvino's!" he shouted. "We'll outlive this scourge that has darkened our homeland. I guarantee it."

Calvino turned back toward his family's 250-year-old home, raised his hand, and made a fist. He began shaking it fiercely and, with a voice exuding the power of deadly conviction, declared, "We will survive this! We must!"

Racing into his home, Calvino instructed his family to pack quickly. The partisans pitched in, too. Some rounded up the livestock and other animals. Others assisted with the packing and loading of belongings and food.

At one point, Santos walked over to Campanella and calmly said, "That was quite a show. And your plan to exit through the woods as Bernard came out of his home was nothing short of a stroke of genius. You weren't kidding about convincing him to leave. Were you?"

"If I'd planned a ruse to get him and his family to come with us, I'd say it was indeed a stroke of genius. But I'm afraid what I said is all true. We must go very soon because the Germans are coming."

Santos froze statue-like and blinked several times. "You didn't plan what happened? You weren't hiding in the trees waiting for Calvino to leave his house?" Santos asked, his arm moving back and forth toward the forest and then the Calvino home.

"Well, yes and no. I concocted a similar idea, but I also decided to do some actual recon while the rest of you were packing to leave. I came across the German patrol I spoke of and overheard their plans. They must have had this farm under surveillance because they knew of Calvino's relationship with the partisans.

"I followed them to their encampment and counted at least fifty men. The company also had a half-track vehicle with a 50-caliber machine gun on top and two howitzer cannons attached to light trucks. Their camp is there," Campanella said, pointing toward a spot in the woods, "no more than two to three kilometers away. They are coming, and I'm sorry to say they're going to destroy this farm."

"My God," Santos said as he removed his hat and made the sign of the cross on his chest.

****

The Calvino family and all the possessions they could load on their wagons and trucks followed the partisans down the south exit of their property. It was a silent trek filled with unspoken emotion and despair. After an hour of traveling, the group arrived at a fork in the road.

"That is the way to Genoa," Calvino said as he pointed to the right, "and this is the way to my brother's," now pointing to the left. He looked at each of the faces staring up at him and said through trembling lips, "I wish you all the luck in the world and pray we meet again soon. And I hope when we do, this God-forsaken war will be over, and we will all be safe."

Everyone said their final goodbyes, waving as they did, and started in their respective directions. Campanella let his team travel ahead as he stayed and watched the Calvino family move around a slight bend in the road and then disappear behind the tree line. He could not help but feel deep sadness as they went, knowing that what they were leaving would soon vanish in a pile of smoldering ashes. He kicked the ground in frustration before turning to follow his team.

Once Campanella made it back to the partisans, he glanced back toward the farm one more time. A significant pillar of black smoke billowed high into the air, indicating that the German war machine had indeed consumed the Calvino home as prophesied.

PART 5

CHAPTER 1

Death From Above

June 25, 1943

Apennines Mountains

Northern Italy

July was fast approaching as the partisans made their way along the foothills of the Apennine Mountains. The path they traversed was often slow and arduous due to densely overgrown wooded areas. Despite the difficulties, this route was essential to avoid unnecessary contact with the enemy. Yes, the partisan's original mission was to harass and disrupt the enemy, but they could no longer afford to risk anyone being killed or captured.

The troop worked their way south as unobtrusively as possible. Boredom often overtook them as they wended through the beautiful, if not somewhat shadowy, topography. Not until a squadron of bombers passed overhead did everyone's demeanor change.

The droning sound of the engines caused each to crane their necks skyward, but the broad-winged planes were unidentifiable through the thick green canopy looming above their heads. However, it soon became evident whose side the aircraft were on as the ground beneath them began to shake and rumble, coinciding with monstrous explosions that felt too close for comfort.

The partisans didn't know the area and were unaware of the target or what damage the blanketed onslaught produced. However, if the bombing lay along their path, they would need to know how to avoid the carnage. Campanella suggested they take a much-needed break while he, Salvatore, and Arturo went to investigate.

After fifteen minutes of brisk jogging, the men slowed as they smelled burning destruction. Campanella saw a clearing a few dozen paces away and motioned to proceed at a cautious walk. After a few more tentative steps, he held up his hand. The trio went into a crouch. In stunned shock, they said nothing. The bombings had annihilated a production factory and destroyed or damaged dozens of surrounding buildings.

Flames shot thirty meters above the bombed-out site, causing the structure to resemble a colossal bonfire stoked by whatever flammable substances the facility stored. And though the rampaging blaze was a considerable distance away, the heat nipped at their bare skin with surprising intensity.

Acrid smoke caused their eyes to blur and their noses to run. Pulling back a little, Campanella led the group along the edge of the clearing until they approached a littering of tiny homes. After several minutes of watching the grounds, they could detect no signs of life or movement in or around the houses. Believing the area to be safe, they moved toward the closest dwelling.

At first glance, this house appeared undamaged. They thought the structure might have been far enough away from the bombs' actual target to allow it to escape much of their destructive wrath. The three dashed over to its entry. Arturo tried the handle and found the door unlocked, which suggested a quick departure by the inhabitants. They slipped in and searched for essential items.

As they would find in most of the houses investigated that day, this one held the meager personal belongings of a small family. Salvatore commented at one point how surprised he was that no one remained. "How did these people escape so fast without warning?"

Arturo noted that the bombings occurred during working hours. This might account for the laborers being in the factory rather than at home.

Sound logic, to be sure. But where were their spouses and children? Although it was evident the residents must have received some alert, none remembered hearing any sirens or alarms.

Each dwelling they entered was littered with shards of porcelain dishes, cups, and shattered glass. Tables and chairs were overturned or broken; in some homes, walls or ceilings had collapsed. On the occasions they did discover undamaged items, such as canned foods, matches, or other foodstuffs, they only took what they needed. By the time they finished searching the remaining houses, they'd been fully reminded of how utterly grim and emotionally draining this war had become.

The men assembled and were about to head back with what they had foraged when they spotted one more dwelling near the exit point of their search area. They glanced at each other, nodded, and made their way over. Though they could not know it, their decision to investigate this one last home was a choice that would forever haunt them.

CHAPTER 2

The house's exterior walls appeared undamaged as they approached, but upon closer inspection, the entry door seemed out of kilter. After a moment of examination, it was apparent that this part of the structure had been jarred just enough to be the cause of the altered door frame. Salvatore tried the handle, but the slight shift in the casing had jammed the door tight.

While he and Arturo worked on getting in through the front entry, Campanella checked out the back of the house. He quickly looped around the perimeter, looking for another egress point. He saw that the only possible way in was through a door in a part of the house that appeared to be an addition added after the original construction. The issue was that a buckled roof blocked access to the door.

"There's a door in the back, but the roof has collapsed and blocked it. What about this door?" Campanella asked as he approached Arturo and Salvatore.

"Well, there's a slight crack running from the top of the door's left-hand corner to around three-quarters of the way down its right bottom corner. The door is unlocked, but it won't budge. Sal and I were about to force it open," Arturo said.

Arturo and Salvatore eyed each other and then made several valiant attempts of shoulder-to-shoulder ramming – but to no avail. The disjointed frame and surrounding wall had immovably wedged the door. The two stepped back and stared at the access in discouraged defeat.

"That thing's not moving. I guess we should return with what we have," Salvatore said, shaking his head while rubbing the top of his arm.

"Let me try it," Campanella said as he moved past the two. "Whoever lives here won't be able to get in without this door opened either." He turned his back toward the wooden door and leaned in. The American then put his hands against the inside of the frame and wedged his heels on the cement stoop. He nodded at the two Italians and then began to push. The veins in his neck throbbed, and his muscles bulged through his clothes, threatening to burst through the material.

With his teeth clamped, Campanella thrust back with all his strength. Under this incredible Herculean onslaught, the door creaked and groaned in protest. This ghostly moaning grew louder and more profound as his exertions increased. Salvatore and Arturo, suspicious of the strange sounds, took a half step back as they watched the incredulous scene unfolding before them.

After a few seconds, the door started to bow inwards. All at once, and with a noise like a small explosion, the door split down the damaged fault line and blew inward. Three sections of the door jettisoned across the interior floor as if shot from a cannon. Campanella's body likewise flew back, but with uncanny catlike reflexes, he grabbed the door frame with his left hand and saved himself from a tumble.

Salvatore grasped his hat and swung it over his leg, producing a loud thwacking noise. "That surely was something! I've never seen anything like it!" the man exclaimed in delight.

"You two must have weakened it for me," Campanella said with a pleased chuckle as he cleared away the debris of the broken door.

"Yes, of course we did," Arturo scoffed as he frowned at the now-shattered opening.

After the three entered the dwelling, they saw a similar simple design as the other houses with only modest differences. There was a stone fireplace and concrete flooring, with just enough glass windows to let in some natural light.

The interior walls were smooth plaster with whitewashed finishes, giving them a clean and bright appearance. All contained a common room with a kitchen, a bedroom to the left, and one to the right. There was one lavatory outfitted with piped-in water, and each room was wired with electricity. The house was small, but the open-air cathedral ceilings gave the rooms a spacious feel.

The three surveyed this portion of the house and realized that, despite the damaged doorway, nothing appeared out of place except a fallen picture and an overturned lamp. Salvatore and Campanella wasted no time and began searching the kitchen cabinets and pantry located behind a round dining table. They found several candles, more matches, and a few tin cups. Salvatore grabbed a bag of sugar, something they hadn't had for a long while, and some dried beans. He also uncovered bars of soap, some towels, and clean rags.

With the other two men exploring the kitchen, Arturo walked through the open bedroom door to his right. He searched the dresser and found two pairs of socks. Good socks were an appreciated find. Several team members owned pairs that had seen better days.

Finding little more, Arturo went to the opposite bedroom. He grabbed the door handle and tried to walk through but banged his face into an unmoving door. Rubbing his nose, which throbbed from the impact, he attempted to use his shoulder to push through. But the door resisted and only moved a few inches.

Peering inside, Arturo saw a large dresser on the ground, blocking the door. Beyond the dresser was a foot or two of clear floor space. If he could shove the door that distance, it would allow him enough room to squeeze through.

Though he stood much shorter than the American, Arturo was broad in the shoulders and thick across the chest. Emulating Campanella's earlier effort, he turned, put his back against the door, and began pushing. The stout Italian strained for several seconds, pushing for all his worth. Yet all he received for his labors was a couple of inches of movement. He shot a glance at Campanella, who watched from the kitchen.

Not giving up, Arturo set his jaw and gave it his all. He groaned and grunted, exerting every ounce of strength until the door opened the needed distance. Smiling triumphantly, he looked over to Campanella for recognition of his extraordinary efforts. But the American had returned to his own task and had missed his victory.

Arturo frowned at his comrade's apparent lack of interest. Still, at least the American hadn't noticed he was exhausted and out of breath. He took the moment to take several deep breaths of much-needed air. Once he felt recharged, he stood and slipped through the small opening.

After righting the fallen dresser and moving it out of the way, Arturo examined the room's interior. Unlike the rest of the house, this room was completely wrecked by the blast impact. Lightening-like cracks shot up and down the walls in jagged zigzagging patterns, and the windows were either cracked or completely shattered.

Arturo also saw that a woman's touch was evident in the decor. The bed had a lace-trimmed bedspread and matching sleeping pillows. At the foot of the bed lay a hand-woven woolen blanket folded in a perfect square positioned in the center of the mattress. Small hand-embroidered throw pillows lay near the headboard, and the room's two windows had yellow curtains with little blue flowers that matched the blue of the bed's blanket.

An overturned vase lay next to the bed on a wooden nightstand. Fresh flowers were strewn about the stand's top and on the floor below. A pewter picture frame had toppled over and lay alongside an empty silver candle holder. A half-burned candle lay under a foot-sized piece of plaster next to the bed on the floor.

Just then, he noticed something different than all the other homes they'd been in. There was an extra door in the left-hand corner of the room. Arturo thought that perhaps it led to a later addition of a closet or storage area. Making his way to investigate, he grimaced as he maneuvered around large chunks of fallen ceiling plaster. The white, chalky debris was scattered around the floor, making crunching sounds under his feet like walking on eggshells.

Hanging on the left wall next to the bed, Arturo passed photos hung from one end of the wall to the other end. The first three were of a man and woman standing next to what looked like the same tree before a modest wooden home, though he was sure it was not this one. In the fourth picture, the couple appeared slightly aged, and a tall, gangly boy of about ten stood next to the woman. From there, the fair-haired boy seemed to mature a few years with each proceeding photograph. In the last three pictures, a young girl appeared with the family, and in the final one, she looked about six or seven.

A chill began to slink its way up Arturo's spine. In his mind, this home could have easily been his own, and knowing that a stranger could be rifling through it like he and his comrades were? Well, he suddenly felt too intrusive. This internal feeling weighed on his conscience, and he decided they needed to go.

As he moved to leave, he considered the extra door. His chest tightened as he pondered it. He didn't want to see what was there for some reason, but his curiosity got the best of him, knowing that this was the only house with it. Arturo shrugged his shoulders. He walked over and attempted to go in. However, as with the door coming into the bedroom, this door only moved a few inches.

Then, Campanella stuck his head in the room and suggested they leave. Arturo nodded and was about to oblige when he gave the door one more try. He began pushing, but the door resisted his efforts. With the other two men now looking on, Arturo considered giving up. Then, just as he thought to pull back, the door skidded open.

Once inside, Arturo glanced around and realized this room was a small bedroom. A young girl's bedroom, he thought. However, in stark contrast to the rest of the house, this one showed utter devastation. An entire section of two walls had collapsed inward, with the roof hovering mere inches above his head.

The room was dark, with a hazy mist of dust floating from floor to ceiling. This effect made it almost impossible for Arturo to see the rooms contents. He moved cautiously and noticed several children's toys and stuffed animals amongst the debris to his right. He also discovered clothing suited for a young girl and a toppled dollhouse that lay in pieces. It was then that Salvatore and Campanella walked up behind him.

"My God," Salvatore said in a gasp.

"This is the room I saw when I circled the house earlier," Campanella added in a strained voice. "There was a large crater from a bomb about fifteen meters away. I'm surprised it's standing at all."

At first, the damage appeared only structural. Only when Arturo pulled back a wooden panel lying nearby did they find out how wrong they were. As he lifted the board and tossed it to the side, the men noticed a woman's shoe protruding from underneath a small mattress – with a woman's foot still attached. They hurriedly cleared away the mattress as well as other rubble. The discovery of what the debris hid stopped the three mid-effort. Two females, a mother, and daughter, it seemed, lay deathly still in a shroud of dust.

The woman had clearly used the mattress for protection when the bombing started, but the weight of the roof and walls from the wreckage was too much and crushed them.

Salvatore could bear no more. He spun around on his heels and ran from the room. He felt nauseous as a shiver of disgust raced through his body. Moving to one of the two windows in the outer bedroom, he grasped its sill and closed his eyes. Thoughts of his wife and children filled his mind as tears streamed down his cheeks.

"What a waste," Salvatore said, his voice just barely above a whisper.

"What?" Arturo asked as he entered the room.

Salvatore glared at his brother. "What a waste!" he screamed. "I hate this war. People dying. Property destroyed. Whole towns wiped out. And for what? So, generals can play their war games while they sit around like self-congratulating slobs drinking wine and smoking cigars?!"

Salvatore gazed through the window at the factory building, still burning out of control. "And this building here. An Italian business is now demolished, and there is no telling how many men and women have perished. And…" his voice trembled, and he waved his arm weakly towards the small outer bedroom, "a man's wife and daughter, dead from no fault of their own. Even if the man survived the factory's destruction, he would come home to this. What a horrible, immeasurable loss – for NOTHING!" and he collapsed onto the floor, head cradled in his hands.

CHAPTER 3

By the middle of July, the partisans had arrived and set up camp on the outskirts of Pisa. The town was well-known by all in the group. For Campanella, though, the appeal was far more significant. At the age of twelve, he was fascinated by a picture of the famous Leaning Tower that hung in the living room of his childhood home. He had studied the building with almost fanatical zeal and authored several detailed reports about it for school.

Campanella smiled at this recollection. The pleasant image of the tower was vivid in his mind when Santos jolted him from his reverie.

"Can everyone give me their attention?" the Italian asked. The partisans shifted their focus. "For a while now, I've been concerned about our pace of travel. I was fearful we might not make Naples on time. Now, I'm sure of it," he stated firmly.

He turned to Campanella and added, "I've done a little calculating. Since we move mostly at night to avoid any trail or path that might put us in harm's way, we'll likely not get to your destination by the time you say we must. Surely you know this. You must know we are not moving fast enough, but you say nothing…"

Berta spoke before Campanella could answer. "We could travel more during daylight hours," she suggested. "And if we get into a tight spot, we'll fight our way out."

With a slight frown, Campanella shot her a glance, ignored her suggestion, and turned his attention back to Santos. "You are right. If we continue the way we have, we won't arrive in Naples in time. So, starting tomorrow, we'll be heading to Marina di Pisa," the American said matter-of-factly. He looked at Franco and Sonny Marino and nodded at them conspiratorially.

"What?" Franco asked as he stared at his brother for an answer. But the stout man shrugged in bewilderment. Then, as if a light bulb had turned on in his head, Sonny snapped his fingers and laughed. He gave a surprised Franco a quick backhanded slap on his shoulder.

"Of course…Alfonso!" he crowed to the whole group.

Franco's eyes grew wide as he, too, realized what Campanella was trying to get at.

"Yes indeed – Alfonso!" he agreed with intense vigor. "Sonny and I have a cousin who lives along the docks in Marina di Pisa. And here's the best part! He owns a big, beautiful fishing vessel. Once we explain what we're doing, I know he will take us to Naples."

Whooping and hollering erupted as the thought of riding in a boat instead of walking to Naples provoked the entire team to smile from ear to ear – all except Arturo. A pained expression of concern enveloped his face.

The first to notice her uncle's consternation was Berta.

"What is it? Uncle, what's wrong?" Berta asked.

Arturo was sitting but got to his feet to address everyone. He stood rigid and unspeaking momentarily before glancing Franco's way. "This is a foolhardy plan, much too dangerous."

"Why," Franco responded in disbelief. "What do you mean too dangerous? What could be more dangerous than what we've been doing?"

Arturo walked over to the small but warming fire and began rubbing his hands together inches away from the flame. As the air became tense, he turned toward Franco. "First, with all the bombing in the area, we don't know if Alfonso is alive, or for that matter, if his boat or the city still exists. And when we get to the town, we risk being caught by soldiers stationed there. And we all know what the Germans do to townspeople who aid partisans."

Arturo added, "And listen…If somehow their cousin is still there and willing to take us on his boat, there are naval vessels at sea, land lookouts, and artillery positions up and down the coastline. We'd be sitting ducks out in the open ocean."

In a tone tinged with anger, Sonny stepped forward.

"Alfonso knows those waters better than anyone. I'm sure he knows when and where to go so we won't be discovered! And, if we're all being honest here, we don't know what to expect each time we walk around the next corner or tree. If it weren't for Joseph, we'd have been caught and probably shot by now. So how much more dangerous can it be? If we're behind schedule, then maybe we should try."

In a whisper, Santos asked Campanella, "Do we go to his cousin's and get him to use his boat to ferry us?"

"Yes, we do."

Campanella decided to take control of the moment and stepped in between Franco and Arturo.

"My friends," he said in a concerned but not panicked tone, "if we stay on this course and continue on foot, we'll likely be late to Naples. And if we don't arrive by October, we cannot stop the assassins." The mood in the room was slowly shifting. "Going by boat, especially if we move at night, will give us the best chance to get there unseen and on time. Even if we can only travel this way for a short while, it can take weeks off our time."

"There's only one real issue," Franco interjected.

"What's that?" Santos and Campanella asked, nearly in unison.

"The Arno. We'll need to get across the river to be able to get to the town. And that won't be easy. Though it is almost summer, the water temperature is quite cold and the current very strong."

They talked this over, but when no other alternative could be offered or defended, they set out for Marina di Pisa and Cousin Alfonso's boat.

****

The small band made it to the Arno two days later. When they arrived at its shoreline, the town of Marina di Pisa sat on the other side in picturesque calm. After finding a safe place to stay for the night, the partisans discussed the next phase of the plan, which included swimming across the Arno.

A lively debate struck up about Franco or Sonny being the better swimmer. Sonny insisted it was Franco and vice versa, but eventually, Campanella nominated Franco to accompany him to find Cousin Alfonso. The rest of the group would set up a camp and gather food and water while they waited.

With darkness approaching on the night of the proposed crossing, Berta and Paulo joined Campanella and Franco at the river's edge. Berta bent down and touched the swiftly moving water with her fingertips. She jerked her hand back as if burned by a flame and jolted upright.

"Oh, my Lord, the river is freezing," Berta exclaimed. She walked over to where the men were preparing and stared Campanella in the eyes. "Joseph, this is ridiculous. How will you make it? Your body couldn't possibly handle the cold and the current. You'll both end up drowning halfway across," she said with sincere concern.

Campanella reached into a pouch he'd been carrying since he, Salvatore, and Arturo had searched the bombed-out factory site. "I found this," he said, holding a large can he pulled from the bag. "It's filled with animal lard. I'll be fine crossing the couple hundred yards to the other side, but Franco should smear this all over his body to help insulate him from the cold. I will also tie us together with a rope for safety. We'll be okay. I promise."

Berta took a few steps closer until she stood a breath's distance from the brawny American. She then raised her hand and, pointing her finger straight at him, said with an intense look of anxiety, "If you die on my birthday, I will never forgive you!"

"It's your birthday?" Paulo asked, stunned.

"Really?" Campanella said.

"Yes. Today. And I will be furious with both of you if something happens! I refuse to have a memory of this kind on my birthday each year from this day forward!"

"Well, we can't have that now, can we?" Campanella said warmly. "Believe me. I have no intention of letting anything happen to either of us."

Paulo walked over and touched Berta tenderly on the arm. "I lost track of what date it was. I'm so sorry I didn't remember today was your birthday. How will you ever forgive me?" the boy begged, almost in tears.

Berta grasped Paulo's hand and walked him over to the water's edge out of earshot of the others. They stood for several minutes chatting until Berta raised herself on her toes and gave Paulo a short kiss. In reply, Paulo grabbed the girl with fierce gratitude and hugged her.

After Franco stripped down to his undergarments, Campanella handed him the can of lard. While he slathered it liberally over his body, the American fashioned a twelve-foot rope to connect them. He secured one end around his waist and, once Franco was re-dressed, tied the other end below the man's armpits. As the two were about to wade into the river, the remainder of the partisans arrived. With grim looks of determination, Franco and Campanella nodded at their team, took deep breaths in anticipation of the chilly water, and waded in.

The water was indeed frigid, and both let out audible gasps. Knowing that every second in the water was one second too long, Campanella took the lead using long, powerful strokes of his arms and fluid kicks with his legs and feet. At the halfway point, he sensed Franco beginning to falter.

The possibility of the young man's demise ignited something within Campanella. To Franco's astonishment, his swimming partner began to move faster and even stronger than before. It got to where he barely needed to paddle, which was a godsend as he was almost incapable of moving his numbing limbs.

They made the distance to the other side quicker than expected, the current helping rather than hindering their efforts, and the pair soon walked up the far embankment. Franco teetered on legs weak from the frigid water temperature, supported by Campanella, who strode with strength and vigor. Once on level terrain, they turned to the others and waved. In the bright moonlight, they could see their comrades raising their arms in response.

The two men crept away, keeping a low crouching profile to hide their silhouettes. After continuing this way for about fifteen minutes, they came to a place parallel to the city's first buildings. They climbed the final rise of the shoreline and traversed a hundred meters to a point next to a rock wall opposite a small outbuilding.

"Which way now?" Campanella asked.

"As I said, I've only been here one time. I think we go down the main road before taking a right at the second street we come to. We go down that road, heading back to the river. We turn back toward the sea, and Alfonso's house should be ahead on the right…I think."

"On the river?" Campanella asked, confusion evident in his voice.

"Yes," Franco said, though his reply was not convincing.

"Well, when we crossed the river, why didn't we follow the shore until we got to the house?"

"Because I don't know how to get there that way since I've only come from the street."

Campanella sighed as he moved up the embankment to the avenue leading into the village.

Like most towns and villages in Europe during the war, residents of Marina di Pisa were required to black out their homes during evening hours. Nighttime aerial bombings were as common as daytime attacks at this point, so all light needed to be extinguished to ensure they couldn't be used as a homing beacon for the bombers.

The men maintained their low profiles as they crept along the right side of the road, staying close to the storefronts and weaving in and out of the natural crevices. All was quiet, and they moved without incident until a door unexpectedly flew open directly across from them. A sudden flood of light bathed the street, forcing the two men to jam themselves into the niche of a shop entry. If someone leaving that building glanced in their direction, they would be spotted as the niche only partially hid them.

Campanella pulled his knife, preparing to act if need be. Thankfully, a highly inebriated Italian soldier came through the opening, said something over his shoulder, and laughed as he headed in the opposite direction. Campanella slowly sheathed his weapon, and Franco remembered to breathe again.

Suddenly, the soldier stopped. He turned and looked around. For a heart-stopping moment, the man gazed their way. He wobbled, unbuckled his pants, and urinated on the side of the building. After finishing, he re-buckled his pants and stumbled down the road.

"Santa Maria," Franco mumbled as he made the sign of the cross on his chest.

"You said it," Campanella whispered.

The two then edged forward until they came to the corner of another intersecting road. They could see the moonlight reflecting off the ocean at the end of the town. Campanella nodded toward the road between them and the water.

"Okay," Franco whispered, "we go right at that corner and follow the road to the end."

The two headed down the street, moving along the buildings for fifty meters. Suddenly, Franco jolted to a stop and spun toward Campanella. "I just thought of something," he said quizzically. "How did you know about Alfonso and his boat? I don't remember Sonny or me ever mentioning his name or anything else about him."

"Is this really the time?" asked Campanella, anxiety edging into his voice.

"I'm sorry. It just occurred to me," Franco shrugged.

"Fine," Campanella whispered. "Listen, the one thing I haven't explained to everyone is that the Allies have set up some rather valuable relationships here in Italy," Campanella lied. Though he had previously described his time travel to the Barilla family, the others were still clueless about how he had arrived. "With Santos' help and one of these connections, I found out about your cousin. It was my intention all along to come here, but only if we made it this far with you and your brother still with us."

"Ah," Franco said somewhat vaguely. "Makes sense...I think."

The burly Italian turned back in the direction they were going and started walking again. After a few more steps, he whirled around with another question on his tongue, but Campanella's hand shot to the man's mouth, stifling his words.

Startled, Franco attempted to pull the massive paw away. But the American's grip was vise-like, and he couldn't budge it. He tried to speak, but Campanella put a finger up to his lips in a silencing gesture. He turned the man and pointed at two Italian watchmen standing in the road. They were within rock-throwing distance.

Campanella and Franco watched as the Italian guards walked back and forth, and back and forth. After twenty minutes of this trudging routine, Campanella became impatient. It was time to move things along. With his incredible knack for accurately estimating time, he calculated it took ten minutes for the sentries to make the trip from one end of the boardwalk to the other. He would wait until they met in the middle again and then make his move.

Gesturing for Franco to crouch down, and said, "We can't stay here any longer. It's getting late, and we need to find Alfonso now. Stay here. I will take those two guards out when they return from this trip. Then we will find your cousin's house."

"Are you going to kill them?" Franco asked.

"Not if I can help it. They've done nothing to us, but we need to move this along."

When the two sentries approached the middle of their route, Campanella prepared to pounce. With his knife in hand, he nodded at Franco and readied himself for the task. Before he could act, a match flared and illuminated the faces of the two guards. One of the men lit a cigarette, took a couple of puffs, and handed it to his compatriot. Inhaling deeply, they savored the tobacco and resumed meandering to the dock's edge.

With their backs now turned, Campanella saw his opening. But instead of attacking the sentries, he grabbed Franco by the collar and lifted the man to his feet, motioning him to follow. The two snuck their way down the road and around the corner, unseen and unheard by the two watchmen.

Marino began searching the houses lining the river. After a short time, he stopped and pointed. "There. Right there," Franco said. "That's my cousin's house…I think."

Campanella rolled his eyes.

"Okay, we'll cross over and stop next to that picket fence. Do you see?" Campanella finished while pointing at the whitewashed wooden barrier running alongside the house.

"Yes. I got it. Now?"

"Okay. Go and stay low."

The two men crossed the street and squatted down next to the fence. Franco's breath was quick and shallow, his adrenaline pumping wildly as he gawked at Campanella for instructions.

"Take a few deep breaths," Campanella said, trying to calm the man's nerves, "and then go to the door. Knock softly, but do not call out to them even if they ask who it is. Try to get them to open the door without making any noise. When they answer, don't explain anything while standing outside. Once you're in, tell him what we need. If he agrees, come and get me. Now go," Campanella commanded.

As Franco headed to the door, Campanella moved along the fence and wedged himself between its end and the corner of the building. This spot gave him good cover and an excellent line of vision up and down the street.

Franco was trembling as he walked, stiff with anxiety, toward the door. His head jerked in panicky unease as he glanced around for anyone who might be out. Finally making it to his destination, the Italian stood rigid for several tense moments and rubbed his palms on his chest. He stole a nervous glance over to where Campanella waited. Taking in a deep breath, he knocked softly on the door. He paused, heard nothing, and then knocked again. No response. Marino stared over at Campanella, raised his hands, and shrugged. Campanella signaled him to try again.

Franco did so, but again, no one came.

He waited a few more seconds and was about to walk back when the door opened, though just an inch or two. Whispering, a man's voice asked, "Who's there?"

"Alfonso? It's me, Cousin Franco. Let me in." The door slid open a little more. After apparent recognition, the door swung fully wide, and a large hand grabbed Franco by the shoulder and dragged him in.

Campanella sat in his position, waiting for a signal to follow when he observed one of the patrolmen walking his way. Alfonso's house was about fifteen meters past the man's usual routine, but the guard ignored his previous stopping point and was heading directly toward the American's hiding spot. Campanella moved further back into the darkness, hoping to go undetected. As he wedged himself in, a slight scraping noise sounded as the ten-inch blade of his knife emerged from its sheath.

The patrolman was almost on top of where Campanella lay hidden. Though his knife was ready for a swift kill, Campanella remained in place as the soldier passed him by without the slightest hint of acknowledgment.

The guard came to a halt only a few feet later. Turning in Campanella's direction, he removed a box of matches from his jacket and lit another cigarette. He held the match aloft while fumbling in the pocket of his pants. Pulling out a small watch, he nodded, and flicked the match onto the ground. He then walked directly to the same door Franco had entered moments earlier.

The patrolman faced the door, briefly glancing to his left and then back at the door before turning his head toward where the other guard stood at the far end of the street. He raised his hand and waved.

Campanella could clearly see the soldier's face at Alfonso's door. Oddly, he was sporting a massive grin. Campanella turned his head and looked toward the second guard near the pier to determine what, if anything, the patrolman's expression might infer. He winced at the discovery. Now, three guards, not one, were standing together.

Did the patrolman alert these new men to help in a raid of the seaman's house? Campanella thought it through and realized two things in this equation didn't add up. First, how did the guard alert the two without him hearing them, and why were they not on their way? Whatever the reason, Campanella was in attack mode, ready to make any move necessary to ensure a quick and deadly strike.

The nearby sentry, oblivious to Campanella and his deathly intent, produced a baton from the belt at his waist and knocked three times in rapid succession. After a few seconds, the door opened. But this time, no one called out. Instead, a man with curly black hair and a spectacular handlebar mustache, came out of the house.

Based on Franco's earlier description, Campanella knew him to be Cousin Alfonso. The man was holding a tarnished tin pot of hot coffee. As he handed the urn to the patrolman, the two exchanged pleasantries. After a moment, Alfonso patted the sentry on the back, turned, and retreated from whence he came.

The tension in Campanella's muscles began to ease until Alfonso spun on his heels and called back for the man to wait. The fisherman almost ran the short distance between them, grabbed the uniformed man by the forearm, leaned in, and whispered something in his ear. This exchange elicited a hearty laugh from both but also re-ignited Campanella's concern about a ruse. Staring hard, he watched as Alfonso glanced conspiratorially over his shoulder.

"Damn it," Campanella said under his breath. He searched around for a better angle of attack. It was then that Alfonso reached into his inner jacket pocket and pulled out a small glass flask. The guard studied the bottle and then laughed, giving Alfonso an appreciative slap on the back.

The sentry poured some of the decanter's contents into his coffee, and then continued toward the other guards as Alfonso returned to his house. When Alfonso was standing opposite Campanella's hiding place, he stopped and lit a cigarette. "After I go back in," he whispered, "come around to the back of the house. I will open the door for you." He puffed a few times on the hand-rolled smoke and then crushed it under his shoe, turning and walking calmly back into the house.

The back door to the home opened just as Campanella reached it.

"Joseph," Franco called, "come inside quickly."

Campanella entered and followed Franco through a small kitchen, the family room, and finally into the couple's bedroom. "Here," a woman said as she waved her hand, "sit in this chair."

"Joseph, this is my Cousin Alfonso Marpese, and this is his wife, Mariana," Franco said as he turned to the smiling woman. "I had only begun to explain what we need to do when the patrolman interrupted us. Alfonso was supposed to bring him coffee, but by showing up, I delayed him." Franco laughed nervously. "That was a close one." Alfonso nodded his agreement, making the sign of the cross above his chest. "Anyway, I didn't have to say much because as soon as my cousin heard we were on a mission to rid Italy of the Germans, he volunteered to help however he could."

"Yes, of course I will," Alfonso said, jumping into the conversation. "I hate these bullies! I fish all day, and then they take most of what I catch. I come home exhausted and am forced to be a patrolman at night." Alfonso's face was flush with anger. "I am bullied and pushed around. But not only me. The bastards also harass many others in our town. They have even killed people I know for no reason. They make our lives a living nightmare!"

"They are evil people," Marina said with disdain.

"They are indeed, and we hope to help rid these people from here and all of Italy," Campanella said. "Alfonso, I'll come right to the point. We are hoping you could take us just north of Napoli in your boat. We must get there as soon as possible without being stopped."

"That will not be easy, Mr. Joseph," the fisherman said respectfully. "The waters are patrolled up and down the coast with gunboats, and most areas where someone could land are heavily mined. There are more lookout posts along the coast than I care to count. No, it's no easy task at all."

"Are you suggesting you can't do it?" Campanella asked.

"Can't do it? Who said such a thing? My beautiful Carina and I can do it! I only say that it won't be easy," Alfonso said with not a little pride. "When do we leave?"

"Sometime during the following three days," Campanella responded. "…who is Carina, may I ask?"

"My boat!" Alfonso exclaimed. I named it after my dear mama."

"Ah!" Campanella exclaimed with a smile.

CHAPTER 4

Once Campanella and Franco had made their swim across the Arno in search of Marino's cousin, the remaining partisans had returned to hiding for the night. The following day, as previously decided, they would return to the shoreline just before sunrise and wait. If all went well and Alfonso agreed to help, the boat would show up by dawn to pick them up. If the boat failed to arrive that morning, they would wait at the same time the following two days.

If no boat arrived after the pre-arranged three-day pickup time frame, they were to assume that something had gone wrong. They were to discard all excess weapons and anything else, tying them to the Resistance. All begrudgingly agreed on the plan.

"After all," Santos had said, "the mission would be unachievable without Campanella. There would be no reason to stay."

With forty-five minutes still needed for the sun to rise the following morning, the group was at the shore, gear in hand. They waited as long as possible, but they retreated to their hidden camp when sunshine illuminated the land.

The second day of the waiting process saw the temperatures plunge, creating a dense fog blanket. The partisans cautiously made their way again to the riverbank. But, like the previous day, no boat came as the sun started to rise. Disappointed, they gathered their gear and were about head back to camp when Berta thought she heard something.

"Wait!" she alerted the team. "Listen." She gazed into the mist with brow furrowed in concentration though she saw nothing. The fog was pea soup thick. The rest of the partisans readied their weapons, unsure of what or who might be heading their way. As the team searched the haze, the bow of a boat emerged from the mist. At first, no one moved. Then Pietro exclaimed, "It's them! I see Campanella!"

"It is Joseph," Berta said passionately. "He's alright." The words burst from her mouth before she realized what and how she said them.

When she did, she turned her head toward Paulo. He was staring blankly
back.

CHAPTER 5

The captain of the Carina deftly slid the bow onto the soft shoreline. Once stable with mooring ropes flung from the deck, Campanella lifted the group's gear onboard as if they were sacks of hay and not filled with heavy weapons, clothing, and other supplies. Next came the partisans. Each member climbed aboard one by one until only Pietro and Arturo remained in the knee-deep water.

Pietro attempted to pull himself up and on, and though he made a valiant effort, his wounded arm caused him to fail. Arturo shuffled over and helped boost Pietro into the Carina before climbing on board.

Alfonso put the engines in reverse and revved the throttle, but the boat did not budge. He pushed the level to full, but the vessel remained stuck. The Carina had bogged down in the sand and was going nowhere. The captain throttled down and placed the boat into neutral.

"I can't risk pushing the engines any harder than I have. Maybe a few on board should jump down and push?" the boat Captain suggested.

Campanella held up a hand and then jumped into the water. He positioned the bow along his left shoulder and instructed Santos to move everyone to the rear of the boat. Once in place, he signaled Alfonso to put the boat in reverse and throttle up. As the engine whirred into a roar, the American took a deep breath and began to heave.

Every muscle in his body tensed, straining against the seemingly immovable object. He could feel his feet sinking into the sand that wedged the Carina. Within seconds, the sand was halfway up to his knees.

"Somebody needs to help. Joseph can't move this whole boat alone," Berta shouted over the engine while staring intently at the rest of the men on board.

Arturo and Salvatore headed to the port side and were about to get into the water when the bow began to rise, and the boat slid backward. The Carina was free from the muddy embankment, and Campanella had pulled himself back on board. Once again, the man had done the impossible, and all on board marveled at his strength.

The experienced fisherman maneuvered the vessel and brought the bow to bear, heading out of the river and into the sea. Initially, it was slow going. The fog completely obscured their view. After twenty minutes of moving slightly above idle speed, the sky cleared, the waves calmed, and Alfonso shifted to cruising speed.

Campanella and Franco gathered with the group. With some prodding from Sonny, Joseph detailed the events as they had occurred after they crossed the Arno. "…and once the patrolman returned to the dock and I entered the house, we explained what was happening to Alfonso. But before we got close to giving him all the details…"

Franco interjected enthusiastically, "Cousin Alfonso volunteered to help just like Sonny, and I said he would!"

Campanella smiled at the big Italian and went on. "Yes, he was quite eager. Alfonso also explained that he would need at least a day to prepare the boat. And since he couldn't involve his usual crew, we were required to assist him in organizing what was needed.

"Diesel fuel in Pisa is rationed like everything else, so Franco and I had to steal some last night. I'll admit this was risky, but we were fortunate that Alfonso is a patrolman on the docks. He was our lookout while we collected the gear and supplies.

"Getting the fuel was our final preparation, so we were ready to leave after we loaded it on board. We got a bit of restless sleep, but when we woke and saw that crazy fog this morning, I thought we'd have to wait another day."

"Yes, but Cousin Alfonso could sail these waters with his eyes closed. So off we went!" Franco said, unable once again to contain his excitement.

"A useful skill, to be sure," Santos said, nodding. "But now what? What is the plan to get to Naples?"

"Alfonso said that caution is the key. The area within a hundred kilometers of his home port should be fine, as most harbor patrols know his boat. But after that, we'll be open to boarding anytime," Campanella said.

"Not to mention the possibility of being spotted by enemy shore batteries when we come in to tie up," Alfonso added from the pilot's seat.

Campanella ignored Alfonso's comment and reached over to a ladle hanging on a hook above a freshwater barrel on the deck. He knew of the artillery placements but wanted to downplay the peril as much as possible. There were dangers, and they would face several while on the Carina. But it was best if those played out as written. He dipped the scoop and took a long drink of water before continuing.

"The plan is for Alfonso to pilot the boat on a course straight out from Marina di Pisa for about twenty kilometers. Once we reach that point, he'll take the most southerly route possible, moving along the coast near Populonia. Then, he'll set the trawler up like a typical fishing day as we cruise through this region. We'll pretend to work the nets up to an hour before sunset.

"After this, Alfonso will store all the gear for the rest of the voyage and head south under the cover of darkness. From then on, we will only travel at night. During the day, he will find a safe place for us to tie down. If we don't see patrol boats in the area, we'll do the whole process each day until we reach Lido di Licola, a small port town north of Naples. Alfonso said it's impossible to get any closer than this because there's heavy naval traffic in the seas below that area."

"What will we do throughout the day?" Arturo asked.

"We'll hide as best we can. It will also be our only time to find food, water, and anything else we need. Once darkness approaches and the coast is clear, we head out again. Alfonso says it'll be tricky, and timing is crucial, but he knows several places where we can tie up and be hidden from view."

"How long will it take?" Arturo asked.

"God willing, we'll make it to Lido di Licola sometime in mid to late August.

Part 6

CHAPTER 1

The Voyage of the Carina

July 19, 1943

The Mediterranean Sea

"Oh God," Paulo moaned before sending another spray into the churning sea below. He'd been heaving off and on since Alfonso got the Carina on plane just after the last remnants of the fog evaporated.

The day was chilly and somewhat blustery with roiling ocean waves, which often tossed the vessel around like a toy in a bathtub. The captain guided the boat as if it was part of his very being, but his efforts did little to help Paulo, and the boy's body was protesting the only way it knew how.

"Poor kid," Santos said, nodding towards the sick boy.

Campanella lifted his gaze and looked at the shrunken form. He frowned but didn't respond. The young man was curled up next to Berta with his eyes closed. His skin had a sickly green pallor, and he often swallowed back refluxes of bile. Berta tried to comfort her friend, speaking in a soothing tone to keep him distracted. But not much more could be done beyond that. Once the sea wrapped its tentacles around you, the only real cure was to return to solid land.

It took five hours to reach Alfonso's southernmost fishing area. After arriving, the fisherman prepared for an average day of trawling. He didn't let his lines out far, lest they need to haul them back in quickly. Most of the partisans stayed below when their help was not needed. But the lower decks reeked of fish, which was hard to take, especially for Paulo.

After boarding the Carina, Campanella, and Santos took turns checking Pietro's condition. He had been sleeping on a cot ever since they got onboard. Before Alfonso had arrived to pick up the group, the area around the wound only had a slight red hue surrounding it. However, the latest check revealed how much worse the situation had become. The injury was now a deep scarlet color, and there was puss boiling up where the shrapnel had entered. Pietro's entire body was flushed, and his forehead felt feverish.

"I'm concerned about him," Campanella said to Santos as he walked up. "His arm is getting infected, and if things continue to deteriorate, as it appears they might, gangrene could set in."

"Yes, I too am worried," the man's parent said as he wiped his brow with his handkerchief. "What can we do?"

"We must find a doctor soon. If we wait too long, it could be fatal." Campanella rubbed a knuckle on his chin in thought and added, "If we could get him some penicillin, the medicine would react rapidly and stop any infection from doing permanent harm."

"What is penicillin?" Santos asked, confused. "I've not heard of it?"

"It is a revolutionary medication the United States possessed in 1944. I mean, will possess in 1944," Campanella said, catching himself. "It kills harmful bacteria like nothing that existed up to this point in history."

The two said nothing for several anguishing minutes, and then the American's eyes lit up. "Hold on," he said as he snapped his fingers, "I just remembered another possibility. The medicine is Sulfonamide, and the doctors here in Italy should have it."

During his training, Campanella learned that the United States military received penicillin sometime in 1944, though only they and their allies had regular availability. So, if he needed an antibiotic, he should look for Sulfonamide.

"Sulfonamides saved tens of thousands of soldiers during the war. In fact, the drug healed Franklin Roosevelt's son and our primary objective of the mission, Winston Churchill."

"Yes. That will be a wonderful thing. But Joseph, to get it for Pietro means going ashore and finding it," Santos said, concern evident in his voice.

Both understood the perils of going ashore to hide during daylight hours. They risked being found and captured each time they did. However, leaving the boat to search for medicine would increase that risk substantially and could mean ultimate disaster for the group and the mission.

Moments before the sun dissolved into the watery skyline, the makeshift crew of the Carina pulled in the craft's fishing nets. Alfonso stared down at his passengers in anticipation, got a nod from his cousin, and moved the throttle forward. Once the boat was on plane, he adjusted the engines to 2700 rpm. In this setting, he would be running at a safe and steady speed to navigate the seas at night, while also conserving fuel.

The boat's Captain set his course to take them along the Italian coastline until they were just north of Marina di Alberese. The fisherman had traversed those waters many times before and retained knowledge of a small cove about three kilometers above the city. Though it wasn't much of a port, consisting of barely enough depth to handle the vessel, it was relatively secluded.

The trawler moved along at a steady clip with the ocean waves a tolerable one to two feet. Still a bit green, Paulo seemed to be over the worst of his sickness and was now sitting upright at the bow. He silently noted how Berta clasped Paulo's hand, comforting him with encouragement as he moaned in response. Campanella smiled softly and went into the wheelhouse. He carried two cups of coffee and gave one to an appreciative Captain Alfonso. He sat beside the skipper and began sipping while gazing into the night sky.

As the small craft rocked in harmony with the rolling ocean, Campanella became mesmerized by the beauty of the stars filling the darkness. This moment of almost pure serenity caused him to drift off a bit in contemplation. He recalled his time at the training camp in New

Mexico. And though the event occurred only a few months earlier, so much had happened that he felt he had lived a lifetime in the interim.

He remembered how the night had been filled with a similar starlight spectacle. The night's radiance had caused a similar sense of awe as he'd walked out of Major James Pittman's office after meeting Antonio Barilla. The beautiful stars were strewn across the sky like a glittering carpet, and the moon crowded his vision, a glowing sphere so huge that he'd felt he could almost reach up and grasp it with his hands.

He chuckled softly and then began to laugh harder. This memory of his, which had taken place just a few months ago, wouldn't happen for another sixty years! The whole situation was still incredible, and Campanella didn't think he would ever feel the reality of it all.

Here he was, bobbing along in the Mediterranean Sea during one of the deadliest times in the planet's history. A handful of insane humans hell-bent on controlling the world had brought death and destruction, the likes that had never been seen before. When it was all over, some seventy-five million people will have perished. It was like something straight out of a science fiction movie. But the war was real, and he and this small band of volunteers were crucial to its outcome.

As the Captain continued his heading, he and Campanella chatted about fishing around Italy and what the effects of the global conflict had done to the man's way of life. At one point, Joseph asked what Alfonso typically used for bait. He was about to answer, but his gaze shifted, eyes narrowing and brow furrowing.

"What is it?" Campanella asked as he stood and looked out into the ocean. He scanned the darkened space but, at first, saw nothing. Then, the Carina crested a wave, revealing a faint but definite glowing light in the distance.

"What do you think…" Joseph started to ask when the sky exploded as if someone had ignited a massive cache of fireworks. Santos rushed in at that moment.

"Oh, my Lord, what in the world is going on?" he exclaimed as the next round of explosive carnage erupted.

Campanella knew precisely what they were witnessing. The barrage was automatic gunfire– and lots of it. Multiple arcs of tracers were lighting up the skyline in rapid and ongoing succession. Campanella didn't know who was shooting or how far away they were. The vacuous, inky night and equally dark sea made it almost impossible for him to get his bearings. But he did know one thing for sure. Whatever the unknown aggressors were firing at, it was taking a lot of heat.

Alfonso had backed the throttle down the moment the glowing white anomaly appeared. Now, the Carina was moving forward at just above idle speed. As the boat rocked in a lulling gentleness, the men stood frozen and silent as they peered into the night. The sky settled back into its obscure stillness for a few eerie moments. Then, as if the attackers knew an audience was nearby, the tracers lit up the gloomy blackness again.

"If a one-sided firefight," Campanella said.

"What do you mean?" Alfonso asked.

"The shooting is coming from one side only and moving in one direction. Whoever is firing is not receiving return fire."

As they watched, Salvatore and some of the others came up from below. "What's wrong? Why have we slowed?" Santos' son asked.

"There's a gun battle ahead. I'm not sure who's involved or how far away they are," Campanella said while nodding toward the disturbance.

"It's no more than a few kilometers," Alfonso offered dryly.

"Look," Santos said as he pointed to the confrontation. By this point, each person on board, with the lone exception of Pietro, had come on deck to investigate the commotion. Some stood near the wheelhouse, others at the bow.

The lapping of the waves against the Carina's hull and the droning hum of the engines became an eerie backdrop to the moment as no one spoke a word. Only Campanella had ever witnessed such a sight, which both awed and frightened them.

The barrage stopped after what felt like an eternity but was only a mere minute or two. "Is it over?" Santos asked. Before anyone answered the unanswerable, a small red light materialized and floated through the air from the direction of the gunfire.

"Looks like the attackers sent someone over to whatever they were attacking," Alfonso murmured.

"Yes, a boarding party, I'd say," Campanella agreed.

The Carina was now drifting silently on the ocean as Alfonso had extinguished the engines. As the waves moved the boat at their leisure, the group stared in apprehension at the red undulating glow. Suddenly, three or four white beams of light came on. These new ghostly aberrations danced on and off without regular pattern. Then, one after the other, these lights extinguished.

"They've gone below," Salvatore said.

After several long moments of calm, flashing bursts from what Campanella suggested to be small arms fire again gave the scene illumination. The shooting sequence occurred multiple times over the following ten minutes, and then they stopped. The dancing beams briefly reappeared, but then they also were extinguished.

The passengers on the fishing boat watched in anticipation, unsure what to expect next. Then, the floating red light reappeared and glided through the darkness before disappearing a few moments later. Several white lights came on in the same general area where that light had vanished. However, these were random in their placements, hovering stationary in the air. After remaining motionless for what seemed to be an eternity, they began moving…and heading straight for the Carina.

"Am I crazy, or are those lights coming right at us," Franco said, staring at the strange apparition.

"Yes, and I believe whatever those lights are on is big, very big," said Berta, now edging her way back toward the wheelhouse.

The small boat's Captain was about to start the engine when

Campanella stopped him. "If they've spotted us, we won't be able to outrun them," he said as he grabbed the captain's hand before it could engage the starter. "Let's wait a moment. I'm not convinced they know we're here, and I don't want to give our location away unless we must."

As the lights got closer, all but Joseph and Alfonso began moving to the rear of the fishing boat – as if that would be the safest place to go. Abruptly, the silhouette of the vessel carrying the lights came into focus. A gasp could be heard from all on deck. The advancing object was a massive German warship.

"Stay quiet," Campanella said in a whisper. But it wasn't necessary to warn the rest of the team, as fear had stifled any thoughts of comment or noise. At that moment, Pietro punctured the tense silence with a moan of agony that echoed loudly from the lower cabin's door.

Berta ran to the door with Paulo behind her, their faces contorted in panic. The assembled partisans stood frozen, hearts racing and faces pale, waiting for what they felt was certain discovery and destruction.

CHAPTER 2

"Shall I get weapons?" Salvatore asked. "We can at least take some of them with us."

"No," Campanella whispered without hesitation. "They would simply do to us what they did to the poor victims on the other boat. We need to try to reason with them if we get the chance."

The warship picked up speed, cruising through the ocean directly at the defenseless Carina. Just as it looked like the towering craft would grind them into a watery grave, it began turning away. The huddled group of frightened people watched wide-eyed in anticipation as the hulking ship slid past them, no more than thirty feet separating them.

After a few breathless minutes, the silhouetted mass vanished. It was as if the blackness of the night had swallowed the warship whole.

"They didn't see us! My God, they didn't even see us," Paulo muttered as he emerged from below.

Once he was sure the larger vessel was far enough away, Campanella motioned to the captain. "Alfonso, can you take us to where they were shooting?"

"Yes, right away," the fisherman replied. He fired up the engines, added some throttle, and powered forward.

The Carina moved just above idle speed for about ten minutes when Salvatore called out, "There. Over there. Floating off the port side, do you see?"

Everyone shuffled to the bow to look. As they stared into the night, the darkened silhouette of a majestic cabin cruiser began to materialize. It was at least forty meters long, and though it was damaged beyond repair, it was clear it had once been an exquisite craft made of the finest hardwood teak and brass materials. The word Ruach was painted in block letters on the bow.

Arturo and Salvatore grabbed two gaffing poles as Alfonso maneuvered alongside the gently rocking watercraft. Once the two boats were close enough, they used the hooked ends to reach the railing and pull the Carina to it. Two things were immediately apparent. One, the boat had received massive damage from hundreds of bullets. And two, it was listing badly from the onslaught and would soon sink.

"Salvatore, Arturo, come with me," Campanella said as he jumped on the other boat. Alfonso handed down one lantern and two flashlights. The American regarded the captain. "We will see if there are any survivors. But be ready to leave at a moment's notice if we need to."

Berta watched the men go, and as she did, she noticed a plaque affixed to the forward part of the yacht's large main cabin. The words Yasher Koach was etched on it. She was about to ask her grandfather if he understood what it meant, but when she turned, he, too, had climbed on board. Before she could utter a word of protest, he had disappeared down the passageway. She turned to Paulo and said, "Do you know what that means?"

"No," Paulo answered, shaking his head.

"In this case, I believe Yasher Koach means strength. And Ruach can mean spirit, breath, or wind," Franco Marino said.

"Huh," Berta said softly. She turned to Franco and said, "How do you know what it means? What language is it?

"It's Hebrew, and I just do."

****

Campanella unhooked the strap on his holster and pulled out his handgun. He turned to ask for the lantern when he saw Santos rushing up.

"Joseph, maybe there will be medicine for Pietro. I will go below and search, yes?" the man said urgently. Campanella nodded, handed him the lantern, and said, "But be careful, and keep the light dimmed until absolutely needed. Out here, a light can be seen for many miles, and we don't want a lookout on that warship to spot us."

With eyes wide in understanding, Santos nodded and headed down stairs to his left. The others continued toward the back of the vessel. Everywhere they went, broken glass, chunks of wood, and canvas shreds were scattered everywhere. The beautiful teak decking and walls were pock-marked by hundreds of rounds of large caliber bullets. Where picture frame windows had once lined the main cabin, there were now only empty openings with jagged glass shards along their outer rims.

Being cautious, Campanella made his way to the open-air aft section of the boat. It was about twenty feet wide and twenty feet long and surrounded by an ornate brass railing. Remains of deck chairs and tables were everywhere, and the delicate blue canvas that once hovered above as a protector from the sun's rays was a fluttering menagerie of tattered strips. But that was not all, as Campanella sensed something else.

He was about to give the area a quick bath of light with the flashlight, but Arturo hurried past him. Campanella tried to grab his sleeve when the man's silhouette vanished. He had tripped over something and fell face-first to the deck, moaning in pain and anger.

Arturo snapped on his flashlight and irritably aimed it at the object on the ground. A man's mangled face with glazed-over eyes was staring back at him. He scrambled away, an involuntary shout escaping his mouth. "A dead body," he said, pointing down to the corpse.

"Yes. One of many, I'm afraid," Campanella said, waving his light in a sweeping gesture. Eight dead were there, all riddled with bullet holes.

The murderous projectiles left gaping wounds all over their victim's bodies. Appendages were blown off and lay several feet from their previous hosts. One corpse had a large hole in the front of his head, with the top and back parts of his skull obliterated. Remnants of bone and brain matter were splattered on a piece of white canvas from a deck chair.

"Poor souls," Salvatore said softly as he made the cross sign on his chest. "They never had a chance."

He was right. As they walked through the cabin door. They saw more bodies, but each of these victims had received pistol gunshots to the head.

""Oh no…" moaned Salvatore.

"Listen," Campanella said with authority. "We need to check the rest of the boat. Once we get below, you can use your lights a little more generously. If the rooms have portholes, you will need to cover them with something. We must hurry. This boat hasn't much life left in it, and we don't want to be on it when it goes down."

Salvatore led the way and began checking the cabins on the boat's starboard side. He opened a storage cabinet in the hopes of finding needed supplies. What he found instead was a man, woman, and small girl slumped in a group hug, three small-caliber bullet holes in each of their foreheads.

When Santos had left the other three, he had descended a set of stairs toward the boat's bow. He entered every door, looking for a medical supply storage unit. After feeling like the task was a lost cause, he came across a door marked with a red cross at the end of the hall. He opened it – *Jackpot!*

On shelving to the left were four small boxes, all with the same red cross as was on the door. In a glass-fronted cabinet on the other side of the room were several varieties of medicine bottles. There was gauze, scissors, and various tapes, and bandages. He put everything in an empty canvas bag he'd found and started hauling it up to the Carina.

During his search, Campanella came across the captain's quarters. He stepped in and gave the room a quick once over. Though a few useful items of clothing hung neatly in a bureau, he couldn't bring himself to take any. As he left the cabin and moved back into the hall, his feet splashed through water that hadn't been there when he went in. He shined his light on the floor and saw seawater racing down the hallway.

Campanella shouted for everyone to get back to the Carina as he sprinted through the corridor. He could tell the boat was now inclining purposefully, and they didn't have much time. As he was about to go up the stairs, he spotted Santos splashing his way from the opposite direction.

"Where are Arturo and Salvatore?" Campanella asked.

"I'm not sure. I thought they were still in the aft section, but when I went to tell them I was taking the medical supplies back, they were nowhere to be found. I turned around to look for them and noticed water coming down the passageway, and then I saw you," Santos said.

"Okay, time for us to get off this boat. I'll find the other two and meet you on board the Carina. Now go – and hurry!"

As the two men headed off in their respective directions, Campanella called back over his shoulder, "And make sure the mooring lines between the two boats are free. When this vessel starts to go down, we don't want our boat tied to it."

Santos nodded anxiously in understanding, and he re-energized his efforts to lug his find up the staircase and back to the Carina.

Campanella, for his part, ran as best as he could in the opposite direction, hoping to find the other two. But even for him, the effort was a struggle as the listing boat and rising water hampered his progress. He shouted the missing men's names as he checked each cabin. However, when he reached the passageway's end, he found nothing but a closet containing boating supplies. He was about to return the way he came when he heard yelling for help.

The seawater was now almost to the top of Campanella's knees and climbing, and when he glanced behind him, he understood why. The wooden craft was beginning to lift upward, causing the water to shift and rush his way. There was no time to lose, and he knew it.

"Arturo, Salvatore, where are you?" he called out.

"Here. We are here. Something is blocking the door, and we can't get out!" the two men shouted.

Though Campanella clearly heard their pleas, it was obvious that they weren't on his side. In fact, the shouts were coming from the starboard side. He remembered an exit about ten meters down the hall and dashed toward it.

"Okay, I'm on my way. Hold tight!" He ran up the inclination until he came to the passageway. Using his right hand to keep his balance, he splashed his way to the other side of the yacht. When Campanella turned the corner, he immediately saw the problem. A wooden joist had dislodged and fallen across the doorway. The door was open as far as it could go, and he could see two pairs of hands sticking out.

"I'm here. Don't worry, I'll get you," Campanella said, sloshing his way to where the men were trapped. He examined the situation and how it was positioned and formulated a plan.

"There's a broken ceiling joist in the way. I will lift it up and out of the way. Once you think you can squeeze through, step past me. Then go straight up to the deck and don't stop for anything, including me. This boat is about to go down."

"Okay, we're ready," came the simultaneous unseen reply, the men's voices gasping with anxiety.

Campanella squatted down and got under the beam. In this lowered position, the frigid water swirled menacingly around his waist. Without hesitation, he began to lift. At first, the thing didn't budge; it only moaned and creaked from his effort. With gritted teeth, he dug deep and doubled his determination. Yet, even with his incredible strength, the wooden roof support stopped solid after only a few inches.

He lowered the beam back down. After a moment of inspection, he saw where the joist collapsed in a way where it was now impossible to move it in the direction he was trying to go. He calculated that the beam needed to be moved about six inches toward his body first and then raise it. If he could manage that, there was space to push it several inches straight up. From there, he should be able to shift it two feet or so to slide the beam left and out of the way far enough for the men to escape.

"What's wrong?" Salvatore begged.

"I'm trying it again. Get ready to MOVE!" Campanella shouted back.

The water now lapped just below his armpits, rising with each labored breath. Campanella repositioned his body for leverage and lifted with his legs. He lifted with his legs, but it felt as though the beam was more wedged than the first time he tried. He began to lose hope: nothing was happening, no matter how much pressure he applied.

Closing his eyes, he strained to envision every muscle in his body. Knowing the three would surely die if he didn't move the obstruction on his next attempt, he exploded all his energy to shift the blockage. The beam jerked and began to give. Campanella took this advantage and changed the angle of his efforts, pulling it back and then pushing the beam upward and outward away from the door. It moved about a foot. He then straightened his legs into a standing position.

The rising water made the door more challenging to maneuver, but with both men shoving, it swung open, and they came struggling out.

"Quick, go to the first stairs on your left, just on the other side of that next hall," Campanella grunted as he nodded down the passage. "That stairway goes up into the dining area. Go right when you come out, and the Carina should be in front of you. Now HURRY!" Campanella urged in a strained groan.

"What about you?" Salvatore asked.

"I'll be right behind you! Go!"

The two turned and dashed up the passageway and out of Campanella's view.

Arturo and Salvatore would soon be safe and back on the Carina, but Campanella had a problem. The beam had wedged him against the wall, and he couldn't summon enough strength to move it off his shoulder. He was stuck.

CHAPTER 3

"Where is he? Where is he?" Salvatore shouted in panic as he stared toward the doorway from which he and his brother had emerged moments before.

"Why isn't he coming out?" Berta shouted back equally in alarm. "Wasn't he right behind you? The boat is about to sink. What's happening?" Not waiting for an answer, she raced to the vessel's edge and was about to jump on the other vessel when her father grabbed her by the shoulders and pulled her back.

"Are you mad? Stay put! You can't help him now. If he can be here, he will be here. You know that." His daughter did, but the notion didn't bring comfort because the girl was now in panic mode, and her only thought was to save him.

As Campanella had instructed, the men on the Carina freed their lines from the cruiser and directed Alfonso to move away. As the boat slowly backed off, each person onboard watched slack jawed as the front of the yacht, with their friend still on board, started lifting into the air. It was soon almost perpendicular, with the water churning and bubbling like a boiling cauldron. Then, as if someone cut a string, the yacht began to plummet…

****

The bow rose rapidly as the seawater made a mad dash to fill every crevice of the sinking cruiser. As it did so, the entire skeleton of the ship shifted, including the load of the beam pinning Campanella. He felt the change and twisted his body sharply, sliding the joist off his neck and shoulder. He felt a rush of adrenaline flood through his veins. He was free! But now, it was a race to get out before it went under.

Grabbing the handrails on either side of the passageway, Campanella lunged up the steep grade until he reached the stairs. Wedging his foot against the riser and wall, he began climbing toward the dining level. Even with all his strength, he felt like he was moving in slow motion. The stairs were steep, and the flooding water was trying to drown him. He continued to grope along and made progress. Too slow, he thought. If he didn't move his ass, he would end up at the bottom of the Mediterranean.

The doorway that led out of the stairwell was now only a couple of feet away. Usually, this would have been an easy reach, but the feat seemed almost impossible as water was hammering him from head to toe like a fire hose. Campanella planted his foot on the brass railing and squatted down. Digging into every ounce of strength, he jettisoned through the onrushing torrent toward the opening.

The gushing deluge battered Campanella's torpedoing body, and he feared he wouldn't make it. Then his hand hit solid wood, and he grabbed it and held on with all his might. With his grip secured, he pulled himself out of the stairwell and onto the dining room floor. Getting to his feet, he sprang to the opposite side of the vessel leading to the outside deck. Lamps, chairs, books, and all manner of items from inside the cabin sailed by in uncontrolled mayhem as the yacht's bow rose higher and higher. A large glass bottle narrowly missed his head, smashing into the bulkhead behind him.

Sensing death breathing down his neck, the American scrambled with a hell-bent fury to the exit door. From this vantage point, he could see that the Carina was no longer tied alongside the yacht. Its shadowy figure was now bobbing up and down a safe distance away. On its deck, lit by a small lantern, nine people stared at him with terror-stricken faces.

The sinking vessel had stopped moving and was now almost perpendicular. It was hanging in the air as if unwilling to go down. The moment was surreal, and time seemed to stand still...Then, the craft began to nosedive.

Jerked back to the reality of his situation, Campanella lunged at the yacht's outer grabrail. Gripping the brass bar, he swung his body up and placed his feet on one of the railing's crossbars, his hands grasping the boat's rooftop. The terrified partisans watched as Joseph sprang from the railing and plunged into the sea.

The pitch-black Mediterranean swallowed Campanella like the biblical whale swallowed Jonah just as the bow sank below the water's surface. As he plunged under, the drag of the one-hundred-foot cabin cruiser pulled at his legs and torso, beckoning him to follow it to its watery grave. Realizing what was happening, he kicked his feet and thrashed his arms in a furious dash toward the surface. But he wasn't moving. He was stuck in deadly limbo like a fly in amber.

The seconds ticked by without any discernable advance, and it soon became apparent that Campanella wouldn't make it. He felt himself giving in to the inevitable and decided to stop his efforts. At that moment, he felt something hit his hands. He made a desperate grab and latched onto the object. His body, seconds away from certain death, started moving forward and upward. When Campanella broke the ocean's surface and gasped the night air like a newborn taking its first breath of life. After clearing water from his eyes, he gazed up. The intense faces of Arturo, Salvatore, and Franco peered back. They were holding the other end of the long pole that Campanella was grasping onto for dear life.

After being pulled alongside the Carina, Campanella glanced back over his shoulder. Only bubbles and a swirling sea remained as any proof that the once beautiful cruiser ever existed. It had disappeared. He shuddered as he realized how close he had come to the same fate.

The boarding party estimated they'd seen around fifty bodies on the yacht, either killed by the automatic weapon fire from the warship or by execution by the German executioners who came on board after the initial attack. It was sick, gruesome carnage, an unnecessary and unprovoked killing in an unnecessary and unwanted war.

Though tragic beyond description, the event merely reinforced to all onboard just how vital it was for them to be successful in their mission. But the Carina's voyage was now behind schedule, and Captain had wanted to get to his designated safe port before daylight. This was now impossible because the sun would be on the rise when they got there, risking the boat being exposed to the shoreline lookouts and the batteries they controlled.

And then there was the tide. Alfonso knew the tide was at its highest point just before sunrise. Unless they entered when and where the water was deep enough, the small coral reef blocking much of the egress to the cove would scuttle the vessel. There was no other option, though, as it was too dangerous to navigate in the daylight, so they continued knowing the risks.

The fishing boat was moving again and back on plane. With the vessel at a somewhat level ride, Santos and Berta decided to examine the first aid boxes found onboard the cabin cruiser. Once Campanella described the proper medicine to look for, they began searching for it but couldn't find what he had described in the first container. There were valuable medicines that could come in handy, but not the ones Pietro needed. After examining several vials in the second and third boxes without success, Berta doubted whether their efforts would bear the desired results.

Reading each label took time, but it was necessary to ensure they didn't miss anything. In their desperation, they found themselves rereading the same containers over and over. Berta had nearly given up, but picking up a vial she could have sworn she'd examined before, read the label once, blinked, and reread it. "FOUND IT!!" she shouted excitedly. "SULFONAMIDE!"

Santos and Berta wasted no time, rushing to Pietro to gently wake him from his feverish slumber. He had been sleeping for hours and missed almost the entire episode of the attack and sinking of the cruiser. Now awake and somewhat cogent, Berta administered a single dosage to the man with a glass of water. He took it without regard and announced he was hungry. Berta gave him bread and some dried fish.

While her uncle nibbled on the bread, he listened in astonishment as Berta related the details of all the events since they pulled in the trawling nets the day before. His niece vividly recalled each moment until Campanella leaped from the sinking ship. Pietro sat entranced, hanging on every word. Finally, when the tale was over, he looked at Berta earnestly and said, "Who is this man? How does he do what he can do?"

With no possible explanation that made sense, Berta just shrugged her shoulders and handed Pietro the glass of water. It was now in the early hours of the following day, and though Pietro wanted to rise and stretch his legs, Santos suggested he wait until sunrise. In fact, he recommended to anyone who still needed sleep that they should turn in. No one knew what the ensuing days would bring, and rest might be a luxury.

Joseph offered to stay with Alfonso in the wheelhouse to keep him company for the balance of the time it would take to get to shore. However, Sonny and Franco protested. The man had barely survived the recent ordeal, and they insisted he get some sleep.

Though Campanella required only a few hours of sleep a day, hours had turned into days since he got any true restorative shuteye. Truth be told, he was glad the two made their way in when they did. He was fatigued and welcomed the changing of the guard. Once below, he found an empty spot and stretched out on the floor. As he closed his eyes, he feared that sleep would come. He needn't have worried. With the lulling aid of the rocking boat and the exhaustion of his earlier efforts, he was out in minutes.

Sometime during his sleep, Campanella dreamt. It was a startling vision that would be burned deep into his consciousness for days to come. The dream revolved around Berta and began as a garish, all too realistic abduction. The seizure happened right in front of him, and he was unable to prevent the girl from being taken. German soldiers had herded her off through a cobbled street full mobbed with people, though nowhere he recognized.

Immediately giving chase, Campanella did all he could to catch up, but the crowded streets kept him at arm's length. At one point, he went from being inches away to ending up on the opposite side of the street. He was stunned by the occurrence and tried to race back to the other side. But he was steadfastly stuck in place and could only watch as the group of leering soldiers encircled the terrified female.

A large crowd of people crossed past him and blocked his view. He jumped up and down, trying to glimpse what was happening, but to no avail. When the throng finally passed, the group of soldiers had been reduced to one lascivious soldier. He stood a breath away from the disheveled girl. Reaching out, he grasped the material of her dress and ripped it down, leaving her naked and exposed. She instinctively tried to hide her nakedness by folding her arms across her chest, bending, and twisting her legs in a knee-locked attempt at modesty.

Campanella urged himself to race to her aide, but some invisible force still prevented him from moving. It was as if his feet were planted inside the sidewalk.

Unlike most of his dreams, which came to him in two-dimensional black-and-white spectrums, this vision evolved into a vibrant three-dimensional panorama. With eyes wide in embarrassed reaction, he gaped at her body in stupefied awe. Her skin shimmered like she had just emerged from a warm pool of water. This strange glistening provided a splendor of sensual shadings along her luxurious curves.

Her hair was a velvety chocolate brown, and it flowed down her back in gentle, luminous waves. His eyes followed the length of her back, inching down until they locked onto her perfectly formed behind. In what could only be described as a feminine miracle, he marveled at its delicate form. After a few awkward moments, he shifted his gaze toward her long, well-toned legs. He was spellbound, and his subconscious dream self could only gawk at her like a lovesick schoolboy. And though ashamed of his lustful stare, embarrassed even, he just could not look away.

It was at this part of his erotic trance that the assailant began to morph and alter. Campanella watched in confusion as the leering kidnapper's face dissolved away and was replaced by – his own! Then, he found he now stood where the German had been. He glanced back to where he was standing a second before, but the street and sidewalk had vanished.

Turning back to Berta, now only a breath away, Campanella realized that she was facing away from him. He wanted to reach out and turn the young woman around, but his arms felt like lead and wouldn't move. He stayed stock-still and helpless, only able to stare at the woman's backside. Without request or motivation, she slowly rotated until the two were face to face with her smoldering, inviting if not alluring, eyes grabbing at his very soul.

The big, imposing man, who rarely felt fear, stood mesmerized and weak in the legs, unable to do anything but stare. Then Berta smiled. This innocent action released him from the cement-like bond that had kept him from moving. She then opened her arms in invitation, exposing her bare body to him, no longer embarrassed by her exposure. Campanella had never seen anyone so beautiful or bewitching; surely God had handcrafted this woman.

"Joseph…Joseph…" she called softly while gesturing for him to embrace her. "Joseph…" she repeated, his name on her lips burrowing a hole into his heart and melting his brain…

Then reality began to push its way through, forcing his eyes to flutter open. As he blinked away the dream, a face foggily appeared in front of him. But it wasn't the face of Berta Barilla; it was the lined and weathered face of her grandfather standing stiffly and completely unlike the vision of the girl of his dream.

"We are getting close to shore. Alfonso said you wanted to be awakened when we arrived."

"Yes," Campanella said hoarsely as he cleared his eyes of sleep. I'm up. Tell him I'm on my way." As he began to rise, he couldn't shake the clarity of the dream, which grasped him like a vice. He felt confused…and concerned.

CHAPTER 4

The sun was minutes away from rising when a faint hint of a coastline appeared. Alfonso maintained the engines to as close to full throttle as he felt safe, urging the boat forward to enter the bay before the sun's rays allowed them to be seen by shoreline observers.

"Are we close?" Franco asked his cousin. He and Sonny were there, as well as Arturo.

"Yes. A small rocky crag should appear just to the north of the entrance to the inlet, over in that area," Alfonso said as he pointed off in the distance. "There will also be a portion of marsh just to the south. The opening is just wide and deep enough to allow us to enter. Once we get in, we'll go about five hundred meters more until we arrive at a section of trees and dense brush. There is an overhanging tree canopy we can tie up to for the day."

"Makes me a bit nervous," Franco said while staring vacantly toward the shore. "Coming this close to land with all the trouble in the area..." he added. Campanella arrived with hot coffee, repeating Franco's question and receiving the same answer.

The group stood silent, sipping the rich, scented brew, and searching for some hint of the inlet. Then Campanella eagerly pointed, " I think I see it."

"Where?" Alfonso asked as he intently scanned ahead.

"About eleven o'clock," Campanella said while gesturing at the position along the coastline.

"All I see is a bunch of nothing," Sonny said. "Are you sure?"

"It is there. Head for that rocky outcropping," he said as he continued to point. "There is an opening about fifty meters to your port side that I think is your inlet."

Alfonso throttled back to half speed for a hundred meters, and then he saw the cove's entrance. Not taking his eyes it, he said, "I must navigate south and travel along the cliff line to avoid the highest points of the reef. When I find my mark, I will make a sharp turn and cross over its lowest point. That is the tricky part," the Captain said, with the last sentence being uttered under his breath.

With deft hands and a steady confidence, Alfonso maneuvered the boat alongside the reef. With the sun coming up, and the water a crystal-clear blue, the danger became apparent to everyone. At certain spots, the coral formations were just a couple of feet below the surface. Running across those areas would cause untold damage to the boat's hull.

After a few moments on this heading, Alfonso tensed and said, "Here we go, hang on." He added throttle speed and spun the helm hard to port. The vessel leaned significantly during the turn before straightening out as the captain rolled the wheel back. The vessel slid over the trouble with no issue. Once past the reef, the men in the wheelhouse breathed again, realizing they'd not done so since the beginning of the maneuver.

The captain headed back to the inlet's entrance and steered the boat in. There was a loud scraping noise beneath them as the boat passed into the cove. Everyone except the pilot stared at each other in alarm.

"Not to worry," Alfonso assured his passengers. "It is but the sandy bottom to the cove's entry the props have stirred up. We've made it just in time. In another thirty minutes, we would not have been able to enter the bay.

Once past the shallow access, Alfonso reduced the throttle to just above idle speed. From here, he piloted his way inland with the precision of a surgeon.

Those that had been below, were now on deck, including Pietro. The encounter with the German boat and the senseless killing of the people on the yacht had been intensely upsetting. Having time to rest, regroup, and have a meal together was needed.

Campanella joined the others on the bow. As he scooted down the stairway, he looked back at the boat's passage. A roiling cauldron of sandy debris swirled around the surface where the scraping sound occurred, and he realized they were fortunate to make it through safely. Shaking his head at the thought, his eyes moved up the cliff. His gaze froze on bluff's peak above the cove's entrance. He involuntarily sucked in his breath and blinked several times to be confident of what he was seeing. Then, he was sure. At crest of the precipice sat a massive gun emplacement overlooking the sea.

"Santos," the American called out in a soft whisper to the Italian.

"Yes, Joseph, what is it?" the man said as he made his way over.

Campanella nodded toward the guns, and said, "Trouble."

CHAPTER 5

Once Alfonso found a safe landing spot, he cut the engines and let the Carina glide to a stop next to a large stand of trees. While the group moored the vessel, Campanella and Santos went forward to inform the team of their predicament.

"We have good and bad news, everyone," Campanella said sternly. The bad news is that a German gun emplacement is nestled in the cliffs overlooking the bay." Before anyone could say anything, he continued. "The good news is they clearly haven't spotted us…yet. But we can't take a chance that we will be lucky again when we try to leave." "What shall we do? We can't stay here indefinitely; we don't have the time," Salvatore said.

"You're right. We have no choice but to disable the guns and the soldiers manning them. I will gather some gear and see to it. If I'm successful, we can leave unseen and unreported tonight as planned," Campanella replied.

"What does that mean, exactly? How will you do this? And will you do this *'disabling'* all on your own?" Berta asked.

Campanella turned to answer, but the image of seeing her naked in his dream made him glance away. He was about to explain his plan without looking at her, but Franco and Sonny spoke up in unison before he could reply. "Whatever his idea, no way he goes alone."

They looked at each other and grinned at their synchronicity. Then they both nodded, and Franco continued, "We are now a team. And besides if something happens to you, we are done, and the mission is over!"

"We should all go," Salvatore said. "After all, fifty or more of the enemy could be up there."

"No. There won't be enough cover to hide everyone as we make our way up. If anything, a smaller party has a better chance of success," Campanella said.

"In that case, Sal and I will go, along with Franco and Sonny. It is settled," Arturo said with resolve.

"Okay," Campanella agreed in resignation. "Let's get some weapons and gear. Once we're set with what we need, we'll scout the situation to decide how to execute our objective. Before we passed beyond sight of the gunnery, I spotted several outbuildings. We can use them as cover during our approach. We'll head out near noon and hope to catch most of them at lunch. It should increase our odds a little, at least."

After gearing up, the five men jumped from the boat and made their way around the cove. The going was slow along a marshy shoreline full of thorn-filled bushes. It took them over thirty minutes to reach a spot where the terrain began progressing to the top of the rise. The upward trail was littered with huge boulders and crevices, a perilous trail but one that offered plenty of natural hiding places.

Campanella was at the head of the group. His experience of combat in the Middle East gave the partisans an edge they sorely needed in their fight for freedom. His confident leadership and decisive direction made it easy to see that the American had skills the others didn't possess.

Once at the top, Campanella moved to a secure place in the rocky terrain within fifty meters of the nearest building. The structure was a windowless four-sided wood-framed building and looked like a storage shed. The American raised his hand in a stopping gesture and turned to the men and motioned them to gather into a small circle.

"Okay, from here I'll make my way to the back of that shed," Campanella said while pointing with two fingers at the closest building. "Once I know it's safe, I'll motion each of you to come over one at a time. We'll then move from the back of the shed toward the front. We should be able to survey the entire camp from that spot. From there, we will at least recognize what we're up against. Understood?"

Everyone nodded in response. Satisfied that he'd been clear, Campanella turned toward the first building, watched for a moment, and then darted from the crease in the rocks. He made it to the back of the building in six or seven huge strides. The partisans were again amazed at how he could move for such a big man. Not only faster than seemed possible but agile to the point that it didn't look like his feet were hitting the ground.

With caution, Campanella snuck a peek around the corner. After a few heart-pounding seconds, he glanced back and signaled for the first partisan to cross the distance to his position. Arturo went first. Salvatore, Sonny, and Franco followed. When they'd all made it, Campanella stuck a finger to his lips. He motioned for them to stay put, waiting a moment or two to be sure no one had seen them. He raised a hand, pointed forward, and moved around the building, with the rest following close behind.

After arriving at the front left corner, Salvatore and Campanella surveyed the camp. It was empty. Not a single sentry or lookout.

"Where is everyone? This is rather odd, don't you think?" Salvatore whispered to Campanella.

"Yes, odd, indeed," he agreed, continuing to scan the surroundings.

After watching the deserted grounds for a few more minutes, Campanella turned back toward Salvatore. Whispering, he said, "There are four artillery positions on the plateau. Currently, no one is manning them. Twenty meters to the right of the last weapon is a covered storage garage containing two German troop carriers and four small Italian utility vehicles. So, even though we don't see anyone, I'm betting plenty of soldiers are nearby."

Unexpectedly and without warning, an ear-piercing bell began clanging throughout the compound. Campanella cringed and looked above his head for the source. The offending alarms were attached to the top corner of the shed. The group didn't have time to think when the front doors of two buildings to their right burst open.

With the partisans glued to the side of the outbuilding and with trigger fingers twitching on their guns, they watched as nearly two dozen men raced out of the buildings, rushing toward their artillery position.

"Apparently, we missed catching them during lunch," Salvatore said sarcastically.

With a slight frown, Campanella nodded.

The gun squads consisted of six men. All were dressed in black apparel except for one at each site. Those men were clad in white jumpsuits and wore headphones with a microphone attached. As the men in white barked orders, their crews loaded and aimed their weapons at some unknown target in the sea beyond.

Then, as suddenly as the clanging started, it stopped. An eerie stillness followed in which the assault team appeared to shuffle backward in anticipation of what might come next. Campanella was captivated despite the danger. He watched in awe as the 1940's wartime scene unfolded before him. The firing routine was something he'd seen in movies or documentaries, and they were remarkable on film. But now, seeing these men and weapons live was indeed a marvel.

The radiomen concentrated as they listened to instructions over their headsets. After a pause each man began barking new orders to the gunners. The arsenals were realigned, and once in position, the order came – FEUER!

The massive cannons erupted in ear-deafening blasts, causing all but Campanella to inch back even further toward the rear of the shed.

The American sat still in thought for a moment and then turned to gesture his next commands to his team. Salvatore was closest, but he was now six feet or so away. He studied the man and then the rest and saw fear in their eyes. None of these men expected this. It wasn't a situation they had previously dealt with or trained for, so Campanella gestured for them to move to the back of the building.

"Trust me, we can do this. They have no idea we're here and won't be expecting anyone to come up from where we did. Those guns," he said as he nodded at the blasting arsenal, "they can't harm us. Yes, their crews are well-trained, but they're not ready or prepared for our surprise attack.

"I'm going to make my way over to that spot," he said, pointing toward the next closest structure. "Once in place, I'll motion you to follow one at a time as before. From there, we'll go around to the front corner. Understood?" They all agreed, but less enthusiastically than before. The reality of the situation had begun to alter their eagerness.

"Okay, safeties off. Be ready and focused," he added. The group moved to the end, and Campanella scanned the area between the two buildings. Seeing the coast clear, he sprang forward.

The four partisans watched in breathless anticipation as the American rushed to the adjacent building. Once in place, he waited several moments again to be sure he was unseen and motioned to Salvatore. He, too, made it across safely, though, again, much slower than the team's leader. Franco was next, and then the other two.

The group crept to the right corner of the building, hearts racing. When they were all still, Campanella took out a small mirror from a pocket in his shirt and positioned it to see the front of the structure and most of the surrounding area.

Standing in the structure's doorway, just a few feet away, was a shirtless soldier watching the gunnery in action. Campanella reached down and pulled out his knife. He looked back at his team and pointed with two fingers toward where the man stood.

Campanella handed his automatic gun to Salvatore. He gestured for the men to stay put, crouched low, and prepared to strike. Salvatore watched as the veins in the American's neck and temple began to bulge and throb, and the muscles in his arms seemed to expand substantially in volume without flexing. Then Campanella was gone.

Salvatore shook his head and was about to ask the rest of the other three if anyone else had seen what he had when a soldier's body came flopping down at his feet. His throat had been slit ear to ear.

"Holy Shit," Franco mouthed silently while looking at the dead corpse and then up at Campanella.

"Okay. Once we enter, there are three soldiers to the right. They are watching the gun teams go through their exercise. Along the back is a radio man. He's facing the wall and won't see us come in. Salvatore, you take him out, and I will take care of the men at the window. The rest of you will guard the door and cover our backs. Ready?" The men nodded. Campanella nodded back and slid around the corner of the building and through the open front door with his team following.

Salvatore had only killed a man from a distance with his gun. Killing someone up close by sliding a knife in their back, well, that was not going to be easy. With his heart pounding in his chest, the Italian pulled his knife and followed his leader through the door. As the two were about to reach their targets, one of the soldiers at the window turned toward the radioman with a broad grin and spotted the intruders. He was about to yell in warning, but Campanella rammed his knife straight into the side of his skull.

The other two soldiers barely had time to turn their heads to grasp what was happening when the assailant's ten-inch blade ended their lives as well. The three lay crumpled down into a pile with blood spewing and flowing from life-ending wounds. The American paid them no mind as he turned toward the radioman. Salvatore had completed his job but stood over his victim in stunned silence. His chest was heaving, and tears were flowing from his eyes.

Campanella walked over, put his hand on the shaken man's shoulder, motioning him back to the doorway. "We did what has to be done in wartime," Campanella said as he cleaned his knife on a coat hanging by the door. "We need to check out the other buildings before we take on the gunnery positions.

"Sal, stay here with Arturo in case someone calls in. If they do, and he doesn't answer, one or more of them will come to investigate why. If this happens while we're gone, you must kill them. We can't afford for the others to be alerted. I'll take Sonny and Franco with me. If all goes well, we should return in no more than ten minutes."

Salvatore and Arturo nodded, Sal moving to the radio and Arturo taking up a position at the window.

"Okay," Campanella muttered as he faced the Marino brothers, "after I confirm the area is clear, I will make my way out the front door. I want the two of you right on my heels. Do not hesitate. Got it?" Both men nodded again. "Here we go," Campanella said as he reached up to open the door. As he was about to pull it open, Arturo began wildly gesturing to them to stop and for Joseph to come to the window.

"What's wrong?" Campanella asked as he scurried over.

"Look at the soldier in white at the first gunnery position. He's talking into the microphone and keeps glancing our way. I think he's calling in and getting no answer."

Campanella stared at the gunner. He turned and considered the dead radioman. He winked at Salvatore and said, "Worth a shot." Dashing to the radio, he grabbed the headset and put it on.

"Stiegler, are you drinking again? You stupid bastard, where the hell are you? It's been fifteen minutes, and we're supposed to be done with this exercise. Can I call it a day or what?" one of the gunnery men shouted.

Campanella thought momentarily and answered in his best German, "No, there's still ten more minutes." There was silence from the other end.

"What's he doing," Campanella asked Arturo.

"He's staring at us, not moving, only staring. Um…"

"What?" Campanella asked.

"He just unplugged his headset and is coming this way," he said as he ducked down.

"Well, that didn't work how I'd hoped," Campanella said as he tossed the headphones down and moved back to the window. Peering through the grainy dirt-encrusted glass, he saw where the man in the white jumpsuit was a little more than halfway to the building. He wasn't rushing over but would be at the entrance in less than a dozen strides.

"Sal, he's going to walk through that door any second!" Campanella said as he moved to the Salvatore's side.

"Stiegler, what the fuck are you doing in here?" the soldier said as he opened the door. In a flash of movement, Campanella grabbed the soldier's head and, with a motion almost too quick to see, violently twisted. Even with the noise outside, the snap of vertebrae could be heard as the man's spinal cord severed.

Franco brought his hand to his neck and squeezed it in reaction. He turned to Sonny and, with teeth gritted and brow furrowed deep, said in an anguished tone, "Marone."

Not giving his actions a second thought, Campanella dragged the lifeless body over to the pile where the other three men lay and tossed it on top.

"It looks like things are going from bad to worse," Arturo said from the window. Campanella dashed over and peered in the direction he was indicating. Another of the white-suited soldiers was now eyeing the building. They could see him speaking in his mic. After not receiving the expected response, the soldier walked over to the radioman at the next gunnery position. Now, they were both looking in the partisan's direction. Perplexed, they turned toward their respective men and signaled for the crews to cease fire.

"Oh shit," Campanella said. "That's not good. "Okay, change of plans. Check your weapons for ammo and load new clips if you must. Here's what we're going to do...."

****

Campanella crouched down and got into a runner's three-point stance with Salvatore, Franco, and Sonny close behind. He grasped two hand grenades in each hand with six more in his pockets. He glanced over to

Arturo, who was still at the window, and asked, "What are they doing now?"

"The two men in white are standing at the third gunnery position, sharing a smoke. The resto of the soldiers are still at their stations, but the way everyone keeps looking toward us, I doubt they'll stay where they are much longer. It's now or never."

Campanella nodded. "On three, ready?"

"You sure this is going to work?" Salvatore asked.

"We're about to find out. Remember, wait for the first two blasts before making your run," Campanella said. Then he hesitated and shot a look at Sonny Marino. He was about to say something when Arturo interrupted his thought.

"One of the guys threw his cigarette down and pointed at us. I think he's going to head our way."

Campanella grimaced at the news. He needed to say something to Sonny, but time had run out. He closed his eyes briefly in resignation and refocused on his task. He looked up at Salvatore and nodded. "One…two…three!" Salvatore swung open the door.

They all watched in astonishment as the hulking figure exploded from his crouch and raced toward his target. It was like watching a human rocket being launched from a cannon, and they knew when this was all over, nobody would ever be able to fully grasp the incredible sight of this man in combat. The ferociousness with which he attacked was frightening to witness, yet at the same time genuinely inspiring.

****

The second gun station radio man had made his way to the third gunnery station. He had his back to Campanella. But the soldier there was facing the onrushing figure. For a moment, he wasn't sure what he was seeing. "What the…" he gasped as he pointed toward the hurtling American. When the other soldier turned to see what he was gawking at, someone was flashing by the second artillery position.

In less than four seconds, Campanella had sprinted more than sixty meters. He'd streaked by the first two cannon emplacements, sending two grenades into each. A blink of an eye later, he had reached his third goal.

The two radiomen stared in bafflement, and when he threw two more grenades toward the cannon next to them, they didn't have time to register what they were. When the first two grenades exploded at the first cannon, they knew. They instantly ran for the shed at the end of the gunnery. Before they were halfway to the structure's safety, the third and fourth grenades detonated at the second cannon position.

Several members of the crews manning the first destroyed locations already lay dead. Those still standing began scrambling around for a way to battle the intruder. While they searched for weapons, Salvatore, Franco, and Sonny were on them, opening fire with a barrage of automatic gunfire.

One of the soldiers in the fourth gunnery had been tending to his Howitzer. His rifle sat in a built-in gun slot attached to the guardrail surrounding the emplacement. After the first explosions occurred, he grabbed the gun, checked the safety, and leaped over the railing. As he was landing on the ground, one of the grenades tossed at his post exploded just below his feet.

The concussive blast almost vaporized the soldier's left foot just above the ankle. Hot, searing metal shards ripped into his groin as well as into and through his arms and torso. The man and his weapon catapulted backward, flying over the cliff's precipice and into the sea.

By the time the last two grenades had detonated, Campanella was sliding to a stop and had gotten into a firing position, pistol in hand. Two precise shots had the two fleeing radiomen's bodies crashing down in a cloud of exploding dust and gravel. Swiveling back to the gun emplacements, he saw three men lying on the ground, dead from the blasts, yet two others he'd seen as he passed the final two gunneries weren't visible.

Moving with caution, he made his way back toward the smoking ruins. Crouching low, he shuffled to the entryway of the last gunnery platform. Peering around the wreckage, he spotted a body draped over a crumpled section of railing. At that instant, his heightened sense of perception kicked in. He dove behind several large crates just as a shot rang out. The bullet, like a buzzing bee, whizzed by his head so close it singed the hair on the back of his neck.

After hitting the ground, he rolled to his left and found an opening between the boxes wide enough to spot a pair of boots shuffling from side to side. At one point, the person stopped and raised up on his toes. Campanella took the opportunity and squeezed off a round, hitting him in his ankle. The soldier screamed out in pain and tumbled onto his back, holding the destroyed ankle in anguish. He rocked back and forth as the agony of his wound caused him to momentarily lose awareness of the situation. Soon, though, self-preservation took over, and he rolled over and got up on his knees.

Using his rifle as a crutch, he pushed himself up and got his uninjured foot under him. Once steady, the soldier turned toward the sound of the shot. His eyes bulged in horror as a knife came hurtling toward his chest. Before he could even blink, the 10-inch blade bore through his sternum, only stopping its forward momentum when the hilt of the weapon smacked against his rib cage.

Campanella scampered over and pulled the blade from the prone body. He knew the other partisans were in a blistering firefight with the survivors left from his grenade attacks and needed help.

As he surveyed the action, he realized that enemy assaults were coming from multiple directions. The survivors around the damaged guns had been joined by another five or six with good firing positions in the garage and at the far side of the communications building.

Campanella had to act fast, or the current three-pronged crossfire would decimate his friends. A plan formed in his head. Spinning on his heels, he raced back toward the shed where he'd killed the two radiomen. Jumping over the dead soldiers, Campanella ran behind the structure, sprinted across the divide, and moved past the two middle buildings before skidding up to the back right-hand corner. He took a calming breath, leaned over, and peered around the edge. Two soldiers were no more than five meters away.

On the other side of the compound, he saw three more of the enemy crouched down behind vehicles parked in the garage engrossed in attacking the partisans. Campanella didn't hesitate, moving slowly toward the two soldiers nearest him. As he approached the crouching men, he slid his still bloody knife from its sheath. It was an almost silent action – almost. One of the two caught the telltale sound and turned, swinging his rifle in the direction of the noise.

At the very instant the soldier's finger pulled the firing trigger, Campanella dove to his right. His reaction was lightning-fast, but this time, the bullet was faster. The deadly projectile sliced through the American's shirt and opened a large gash along his chest an inch or two below his left shoulder.

The wound did little to slow the American as adrenaline and training kept him moving. In the time it took the soldier to blink back the amazement of seeing his target's unimaginable agility, the man was back on his feet and lunging. Campanella propelled his knife into his foe's throat at the same time as wrapping his massive arm around the neck of the other soldier. The man tried to shout, but Campanella squeezed with a boa constrictor's intensity, and only muffled gurgles came from the dying man's vocal cords.

After a moment of this intense pressure, Campanella heard a sound like a brittle twig snapping, and the man's squirming body went limp. He dropped the corpse on top of the other dead man. Using the piled mass as cover, he retrieved one of the soldier's K98 bolt-action rifles and a few ammo clips. With weapon in hand, he set his sights on the three Germans in the garage.

Peering down the sight line, he moved the gun's barrel until he found a target positioned in the deepest recesses of the garage. He took a breath, held it, and squeezed the trigger. The bullet struck the soldier in his left temple, slamming him against the wall and to the ground. The other two soldiers turned toward the dead man, his head a grizzly mess, and then to where Campanella lay. Their mouths hung open in shock, not expecting this additional angle of attack.

Campanella had already gone through the bolt-action process and was pulling the trigger again before the men could react. As if a switch controlled his body, the second soldier tumbled over and down into a heap, killed by a shot dead center in his chest.

Then, a bullet thudded into the corpse in front of Campanella as the last man standing regained his wits and retaliated with a round of his own. After the shot was away, he repositioned himself behind one of the troop carriers. Campanella took aim but had no clear shot.

Keeping a sniper's intense focus, Campanella breathed out slowly and deliberately, forcing his heartbeat to slow. Then he waited. Subconsciously, awareness of his surroundings took over, and he realized the raging firefight of a few moments earlier had ended. He knew the conflict was over but maintained his focus on the final target.

The hidden soldier also noticed the quiet. Feeling triumphant, he called out to his comrades, anticipating their inevitable victory over the assailants.

"This is Hanz. I need help. I'm pinned down in the garage. I have only one attacker, and he's at the right front corner of communications," the soldier yelled. "Come up from behind, and you will have him! Heinrich, Jorgen, do you hear me?"

There was no response for a few tense moments, and then Campanella heard Franco yell back, "Sorry, all your play pals are dead."

Whether the soldier understood Italian or not, he reacted instantly. A gunshot echoed out from the garage, and then the man burst from behind a vehicle and went running down the road away from the camp. Campanella took a bead on the fleeing figure. He pulled the trigger and the man tumbled face-first onto the roadway.

Chapter 6

"Clear?" Campanella called out in question as he peered from his hiding spot.

"Clear," Salvatore responded, though his voice sounded strained.

As Campanella moved from around the building, he saw Salvatore and Arturo standing over a crouched Franco. The stocky Italian's shoulders shook as the man sobbed while he tended to a body on the ground.

"Was this in your precious Journal? The killing of my brother?" Franco asked accusingly as Joseph raced up.

Campanella thought about this for a moment. He wasn't sure exactly when it would happen, but he knew it was. Even so, he had to lie. He reminded himself that if he had told of Sonny's death beforehand, it could have altered all the events before this and certainly after. Following the actions as they were written was something drilled into his head day after day – and yet, though he understood why it had to be this way, his heart ached with a burning ferocity.

"I'm sorry. Nothing in the Journal implied this would happen," Campanella said, kneeling beside Sonny's body on the opposite side of Franco. In the dead man's chest was a large caliber bullet wound as well as a stunted flow of oozing blood. Campanella watched the three men somberly. He wanted to say more. Help with Franco's agony. But he didn't have the words.

There was an uncomfortable silence broken only by stifled sobs coming from Franco. Salvatore touched the man's shoulder. He helped his friend stand while Campanella and Arturo moved Sonny beneath a gunnery-sighting canopy. Franco sat down, grasped his brother's hand, and put it into his own. "It was that last shot. The one the soldier fired as he fled the garage. How is that possible? The very last shot..."

The three left the grief-stricken man alone with his thoughts and spent the next fifteen minutes rigging the cannons with sticks of dynamite found in an ammo storage shed at the far end of the camp. As Campanella entwined fuses together, the others made their way to a safe distance. Once they were clear, he lit the fuse and ran to their sides.

The explosions were immense, and as the dust settled, it became clear. The one-time instruments of death were now useless mangled pieces of steel.

The task of disposing of the bodies came next. Campanella insisted they be thrown over the cliff into the sea below so that when more Germans came looking and found no one, it would take them much longer to figure out what happened. Unsurprisingly, Franco engaged in this task with grim gusto.

When they were done, the partisans disposed of any weapons they couldn't carry, sending them to the same fate as the dead. They collected food and water and then headed back toward the Carina. Campanella insisted on carrying Franco's brother himself. He handed Salvatore his weapon and lifted Sonny over his shoulder.

It took quite a bit longer to get back as the trip down the expanse was trickier, especially with the added burden. As they rounded the final bend in the path and came into view of the boat, Berta saw them first. She beamed a broad smile and raised her hands excitedly to wave – until she noticed Sonny's body draped over Campanella's shoulder. She gasped, and her hands dropped to cover her open mouth.

Paulo, who'd been fishing, heard the sound and moved beside Berta, touching her arm. "Are you okay? What's wrong?"

The girl couldn't answer, only nodding toward the returning men. As he turned to look, she leaned into him, put her arm around his waist, and held him tight. The two stood in frozen anguish as Campanella lifted the body over the side and into the waiting arms of the others.

CHAPTER 7

Arturo and Salvatore told the others the story of the cannon fortifications and their battle with the Germans. When they reached the killing of Sonny, Campanella felt the need for damage control. He rose and moved to Arturo's side. The expedition's leader looked to both men and then turned his attention to the rest.

He took a deep breath and said, "The death of Sonny is very puzzling and disturbing for many reasons. I'm deeply saddened by what happened and wish there was something I could have done differently. But this does bring up other concerns as it is now obvious how events can change, and the Journal is not absolute. The fact that Franco's brother was killed, and it wasn't written in the book, is confusing.

Looking toward Santos, he went on. "All the occurrences documented in your writings so far were accurate. And yet," he said with his palms open, "what happened on that ridge today showed that we can't totally rely on its contents." Everyone stood in silence pondering this."

Campanella then went on. "And even though we've lost Sonny, I know that we must stop this assassination so that history does not change for the worse! We must stop it for Sonny's sake."

No one said a word, all too grief-stricken to process what had happened. Finally, though, Franco spoke up.

"I, for one, will not let my brother's death go to waste. I don't know why he had to be the one to die." The big, burly man stopped here and swallowed back an emotional moment. He blinked away a tear and said softly but firmly, "But I do know this. I will kill every German myself if it helps to fulfill our mission!"

****

The sunset was as beautiful as any person had ever witnessed, but it was scant consolation to the saddened hearts of the partisans. As the Carina churned out of the secluded inlet, all minds were on their fallen comrade and his brother, Franco.

They discussed what to do with Sonny's body and decided that they had no way to stop it from decomposing. So, after they had traveled far enough from shore, they wrapped him in a blanket, tied it with a rope, and sent it gently overboard. Franco wept as it slipped over the side, as did most of the others in the group. Santos said a short prayer as Sonny Marino's body disappeared into the icy blackness.

Over the next few weeks, Alfonso dipped the trawler in and out of small bays and inlets. The weather sometimes prevented them from traveling, and they had to stay harbored. On several occasions, a German patrol boat was spotted cruising the shoreline, causing them to remain hidden and anchored until the captain of the Carina deemed it safe to move on.

Toward the end of August, Campanella sat on the boat's bow with Arturo and scanned the ocean. After a moment, without looking Arturo's way, he said, "The Invasion is coming,"

"What invasion?" Arturo asked in alarm.

"Right about now, the Allied forces have stepped up the bombing of the area around Naples and along Italy's southern coastline. The assault of Salerno, and soon after, Naples, is only weeks away; we must hurry and get ashore as the sea will no longer be a safe passageway."

"I knew it was coming," Arturo said with a sigh, "but the thought of the death and destruction is very frightening. I sometimes wonder if all of this is worth it."

PART 7

CHAPTER 1

The March Inland

September 9th, 1943

After a few hours of restless sleep, Berta and Campanella made their way aft. The two had exchanged morning pleasantries but little else since. Then, Berta saw a massive black cloud growing in the sky. "There, do you see it?" Berta said, pointing to the sky while shading her eyes from the rising sun.

There was just enough light to discern shapes, but Berta wasn't entirely certain of what it was. Campanella had also seen the ebony mass, and he knew that the dark, moving formation was an enormous silhouette of Allied airships. The aircraft, consisting of many bombers and fighters, were heading inland from the direction of Sicily. Based on what he knew of the timing of the Italian invasion, he was sure they were friends and not foes.

"Yes, Berta, I see them," he said as he took stock of the balance of the group's remaining supplies.

"What is it?" she asked while looking in awe.

"Allied bombers advancing toward Calabria, I'd think," Campanella said with disinterest.

Stunned, the girl glanced his way and then back up at the incredible number of planes. This time, she used both hands to shade her eyes, straining to make out the individual machines. "But they look as though they fill the sky. Are you sure?"

The gentle rocking of the sea was interrupted by a rogue wave. The upsurge was strong enough to shift the vessel's movement with a pronounced jerk. This sudden change of rhythm caused Berta to lose her balance. She rocked once toward the open ocean, arms waving like a tightrope performer, before overcompensating and falling back toward Campanella.

Unable to stop her momentum, Berta plopped straight into Campanella's lap, causing her legs to fly up in the air and her dress to slide to her thighs. Campanella was now gazing into her eyes, which were huge with embarrassment. He responded with as little emotion as possible.

"Yes, I'm sure."

Berta struggled to right herself, but as she shifted her weight back, it became almost impossible to do anything but flounder. After a few awkward moments, Campanella tilted her back into an upright position, allowing her to jump up and out of his arms.

She used her hands to push the dress back down while shuffling back toward the side of the boat. Once steady, she brushed several strands of fallen hair from her face, now flush with redness, and grabbed her dress at its waistline, wrenching it back and forth, trying to restore order.

As she was twisting, Berta briefly glanced at Campanella. She stopped and glowered at him. Her lips tightened, and her eyes narrowed in a menacing challenge. Though Campanella tried not to react, the corner of his mouth rose slightly, so he dropped his head and refocused on the job.

He cleared his throat and continued his response as if nothing had happened. "On September 3rd, the Allies will start a three-step assault of your country with one prong spearheading through Calabria. Two more will move to Taranto and Salerno on the ninth. Once these areas are secure, they will head north along both coasts as they move to Rome. What you're witnessing is just one of many pre-invasion bombings," Campanella finished.

In a moment of contemplation, the young woman stared at mirrored water with unfocused eyes. Berta stayed this way for several moments before emitting a deep sigh. She turned back to Campanella and gazed at him with pursed lips. After a few seconds, she nodded as if she had decided something.

An empty bucket lay under the boat's gunwale next to her feet. Berta retrieved the bucket, repositioned it across from Campanella, and eased into a sitting position. This gave her a direct line of vision into his face. She was now staring directly at him, though he did his best to ignore it – until he no longer could.

He stiffly raised his head in her direction. As he did, she reached over and grabbed his hands into hers.

"Joseph, it's so odd how you know things before they happen," Berta said, her eyes blazing with emotion. "I mean, it must be difficult to cope with this knowledge when incidents are going to occur – good or bad – and then deciding what to tell and what not to tell. It must be an enormous burden to carry around with you."

Campanella sat with his lips pressed together as he watched the girl's face portray several emotive and empathic expressions. These expressions were subtle, but Campanella realized their intentions at once. She hoped to steer him toward discussing information he might be holding back.

The American attempted to avert his eyes from hers while trying to get her to release his hands. But Berta was not easily ignored. She held him fast and leaned in, forcing him to re-engage her stare. He resisted this tactic as best he could. But when she dropped one of his hands, reached over, grabbed his chin, and brought his face in line with hers, he knew he couldn't escape the situation.

"Please, talk to me," Berta begged.

"Berta, I'm sorry…I, uh," Campanella said, stumbling over his words as he went. The girl mesmerized him. Her eyes were big, beautiful, and full of questions.

With head tilted, Berta searched his eyes for the secrets hidden in his mind as if she could divine them through these portals. He felt the desperate urge to get up and jump overboard, anything to release himself from her gaze. Thankfully, Berta released his chin before he could do anything stupid, only to re-grasp his hands.

After a moment, which seemed to last far longer than it should, she said, "Joseph, though I know we are doing what must be done, you need to understand something. My family is all I have. If something were to happen to one of them, I don't know what I would do. Franco's brother died on that cursed hill a few days ago, and I can't stop thinking about it. Every time I look at him, it brings me to tears. And I'm not even related to him."

Her face softened a bit though her voice became even more impassioned. "Papa, Grandpapa, my uncles, and the rest of the men in the group don't deserve to die this far from home and their families. This war wasn't our war. We didn't start it, but here we are." Berta glanced at the now-vacant sky and then returned her eyes to his. "Yes, here we are, following you on a quest that seems impossible."

Campanella watched as she swallowed hard in an apparent effort not to cry. "You are an amazing man, and though I don't quite understand how you do what you do, I am grateful for those actions…but…" she stopped mid-thought and stared at him like she had forgotten what she was saying.

At that moment, a glistening tear rolled from the corner of Berta's right eye and streaked down her cheek. She turned her head and used one of her hands to wipe the droplet away. Campanella heard an audible gulp, sniffle, and clearing of her throat before she turned back to face him. When she did, he was surprised to see a total change in her face. It was set with conviction and renewed strength. She leaned closer and said, "Do you remember when I asked you if everyone would get back alive, and you said yes?"

Campanella considered himself able to handle intense situations with dispassion. Still, when he gazed at this woman struggling with inner turmoil, his emotions clawed at him, and he could feel his own eyes begin to mist over. Though he did his best to keep his feelings in check, he could only nod in response to her question.

"Well," Berta said as another tear spilled out, "From this moment forward, I'm going to hold you to that." She gave him an impassioned gaze that seemed to last forever. With the tear still on her cheek, she released his hands, stood, and walked away.

Campanella sat motionless as he stared somewhat blankly in the direction of the girl's departure. As her words flooded his mind, two things hit him; one, he would have to face her someday with the truth, and two, Paulo's name wasn't mentioned in the list of people she was concerned about…

CHAPTER 2

The Carina cruised toward shore just as the sun began its age-old routine of rising in the East. Alfonso had been running just above idle for thirty-five minutes, doing his best to maneuver through the fog and dangerously shallow waters. Marveling at his constant manipulation of the controls, Campanella was reminded of the sacrifices the man had made to get them this far. He had left his loved ones behind, giving them no guarantees he would be back.

Fishing was Alfonso's way of life and how he fed his family. Now, he had laid his livelihood and life on the line by exposing the Carina to possible search and destruction. But he had done so willingly and without hesitation. Yes, the captain had done his job and done it well.

In any case, this portion of their journey was soon over, and they would switch back to moving on land. Campanella knew the Allies would have countless naval vessels in the area as part of the invasion forces. Add the fleeing German and Italian ships to the equation, and Campanella concluded it was time for the loyal captain to head back. So, when Alfonso found a suitable landing spot, Campanella and the partisans would unload their gear, say their goodbyes, and send him home.

After another thirty minutes of searching though, they still could not find a safe place to land.

"Okay, we must adapt to what's happening and fast. As we head south, the risk of being spotted will increase dramatically. So, here's what I propose," Campanella said after the group gathered. "Once Alfonso gets as close to shore as possible, we will set the Carina's life raft over the side. We'll tie a rope to it, fill it with as much gear as it will hold, and then slip into the water and swim while pulling the life raft with us. When we reach shore, we will empty the raft's contents, and Alfonso will pull the raft back."

"Swim?" Pietro said with concern evident in his tone after their last river outing.

Campanella nodded. "I will be at the prow of the raft to steer. Two of you will be at the stern and will kick with your feet. The rest will hang on the sides, swimming along as we go. Does anyone have any objections? Or a better idea?" he asked as he considered each person. They took some time to consider his questions, but no one responded.

"Right then, let's get to it," Campanella said as he stood and headed to the raft.

CHAPTER 3

Emotions gripped everyone as they said goodbye to the Carina's captain. After the last hugs and handshakes, Alfonso sighed in resignation and climbed up to the helm. After giving the high sign, he maneuvered the boat at low speed until the vessel floated about thirty meters from shore. Campanella shot a look at the captain and nodded, then gave the man a quick salute. Then he turned back toward the group.

Each partisan was assembled at the stern of the boat and went over the edge into the crystal blue sea one by one. The water was icy cold, and everyone gasped as they entered. Pietro, Santos, and Berta, with Paulo at her hip, grabbed onto one side of the raft, with Alberto, Franco, and Aldo hanging on to the other. Salvatore and Arturo moved to the stern, with Campanella making his way to the front of the small boat. Once in place, he pulled the end of the retrieval rope through an eyelet and wrapped the rope around his waist. He gave a thumbs up, and everyone began to paddle and swim toward the shoreline.

The raft made it within a few minutes, and the team made short work of unloading it. Alfonso maintained his position at the helm, keeping the rocking craft from moving any closer or further from the drop zone.

Before the team entered the water, Campanella handed the captain one end of the rope, and the man kept a firm grasp on the line, waiting for the pre-arranged signal tugs. As soon as the rope jerked three times, he dropped to the deck and reeled the raft back in.

After onboarding and storing the raft, Alfonso dashed back to the helm and maneuvered the vessel toward the open sea. He glanced back once, made the sign of the cross on his chest, and prayed to God that each partisan remained safe.

The Carina's motors could be heard fading away as the partisans collected their gear and headed up the shoreline. A dense tree line came almost to the water's edge in many places, but they soon found an opening in the thick foliage. The gap appeared to be a rarely used horse-drawn cart path. And though it was overgrown and in rough repair, it was passable.

Campanella and Salvatore stopped the group here to review their route. Based on an estimation from Alfonso, they believed they were somewhere near Lido di Licola. "Okay," Campanella said while pointing inland, "If we are correct about where we are, we should come to Lido di Licola sometime this afternoon. The town is about thirty-five kilometers from Naples. When we arrive, we will try to find a place to camp until just before October 1st. Then …"

"October 1st; why wait so long?" Arturo interrupted.

"For one essential reason," Campanella said as he turned to face Arturo. "The Allies will soon be invading the Italian mainland. And when they do, all hell is going to break loose. We don't want to be anywhere near that area when that happens. Once the city is in the Allies' control, we'll head there and begin the next phase of our plan." As Campanella finished, a low but perceptible rumbling could be heard to the south.

"The bombers," Berta said in a voice filled with awe and dread in equal mixture. Without another word, the partisans began moving inland, straight toward the sound of the rolling thunder.

CHAPTER 4

The terrain they were now traveling was pristine and uncorrupted by the travesties of war, but Campanella understood all too well that things would change as they moved inland and closer to Naples. The ex-Marine had witnessed the ravages of war more than once, but he was worried that his band of fighters hadn't yet seen the full extent of what would happen to their country and countrymen.

Campanella turned back and stole a glance at the faces of the group. When he got to Berta, she was staring straight into his eyes. She smiled, a tired, almost despondent smile, and he smiled back with great effort.

The group's anointed leader began to wonder if it would be best to warn them of what they would soon see. He questioned if he should try to reason with them, to explain how things would eventually get better. That the cities and country would be rebuilt and would someday be coveted places to live again and prized destinations for tourists. But he decided against it. Nothing he could say would counter the stark reality of the destruction ahead.

The group had been walking in silence from the moment they left the shoreline. Campanella had explained the need for caution more than ever as the chances of encountering the enemy were higher than at any point in their mission. This declaration from the seasoned soldier was almost debilitating for the team's already frayed nerves. To some, it was like walking through a field loaded with landmines, knowing that any wrong step could be the end.

For others, being unable to talk also offered unwelcome time for reflection. Uncontrollable thoughts of loss and sacrifice endured on their mission sliced at their hearts. Dominic Patrelli's demise. The woman and child dead in their home at the bombed factory. The death of Sonny Marino and the killing of the Jews at sea made their stomachs lurch in agony. Mixed in with those raw emotions was the warning of what horrors lie ahead. Even seasoned military veterans struggled with these types of feelings.

But the war and the Churchill mission had forced them to act in a way none had been trained for. This life-altering transformation was a bitter pill to swallow. Their very existence, as they had known it, was long gone. Lake Vittoria and summer afternoon picnics were distant memories. And though this day was as bright and sunny as any of those wonderful, carefree days, no one walking on the bug-infested trail seemed to be able to appreciate it.

At one point, Campanella went ahead to scout, leaving Santos to take the lead in his absence. After the small party had traveled about a mile, the Italian patriarch glanced over his shoulder. The anxious faces troubled him. Everyone looked aged far beyond their actual years.

Though Santos couldn't see his own face, he could imagine how its creases had become more defined due to the stresses of recent times. He sighed deeply and decided everyone needed a rest. As they descended the overgrown path, he lifted his hand to stop the team just as Campanella came rushing back with the news that Lido di Licola lay just ahead.

"I found a spot above the town from where I could see the village and much of the surrounding area. As we move down the hill, we will pass a few farms along the way," Campanella said after he brought the partisans into a circle. "There are some outbuildings on some of the properties. These appear to be storage sheds, barns, and root cellars. We'll check the ones closest to our route and see if we can find some food and other supplies."

Campanella took out his map and located the small city. Displaying it to the group, he said, "I will take a team of four down this path to recon the homesites. If we can, we will gather any provisions we might discover. The rest of you will go south of Lido di Licola," he added while running his finger in a circular motion on the map. "From what I could tell, the grounds appear covered with extensive foliage and trees. I hope you can locate an area inside the forest to set up a camp."

Shifting his footing, Campanella turned in the direction he'd just scouted. "As soon as we round that bend," he said as he pointed down the path, "the tree line ends. From there, a blanket of high grass flanks the route I've chosen, so we'll still have reasonable cover. Now…" he paused a moment in reflection, "…for some reason, the town is a beehive of activity. Townspeople were running up and down the street with loud music playing. There's some type of celebration going on.

"There were no enemy soldiers in sight, but I'm concerned there may still be some around. So…" he hesitated here before saying with conviction, "…I cannot stress enough how careful we must be from now on. We do our jobs. Cover each other's backs. And we do nothing reckless. Any questions?"

Santos eyed the American briefly and was about to suggest a food break. It had been almost a full day since they had eaten. But the city's proximity had boosted everyone's spirits, so he said nothing.

"Good. Alberto, Marco, and Arturo come with me. The rest of the team will go with Santos and head toward the other side of town. Once you've found a safe spot to camp, send someone to the edge of the trees and have them wait for us to arrive. Whoever comes for us, be sure you stay well out of sight."

Campanella nodded before checking his gun for ammo. Alberto, Marco, and Arturo did the same.

The two groups started out as one for about fifty meters. When they arrived at the clearing, Campanella and his team went left while the rest of the partisans went right. Santos led his group due south, following the tree line until they reached the far side of the city. After finding a break in the undergrowth, they shuttled their way into the forest to scout for a campsite.

Campanella's route took them above Lido di Licola and opposite the first farmhouse. He motioned for the other three to hunker down in the concealing grasses. The American pulled out a pair of binoculars and began setting the focus. They were big and bulky, unlike the modern kind he was used to, but the lenses did their job and provided him a clear view of their first target.

"No movement on the outside of the house nor near the barn or root cellar," he whispered as he continued peering through the glasses. "We'll make our way down until we arrive at the first property. From there, we will go to that stand of trees," Campanella said as he indicated a grouping of Italian Cypress some twenty meters away.

"Arturo, when we get to that spot, you and Marco will head to the barn. Alberto and I will go to the root cellar." He pulled the binoculars down and glanced back at the three men.

"We take no unnecessary chances. We see anyone, man, woman, or child, and we move on to the next house. Is that clear?"

The group nodded. Campanella turned and, without another word, moved serpentine down the hill with the others close on his heels. They moved with stealth through each phase of Campanella's directions right up to the point where they were crouching behind the cypress stand along the side of the first house.

Though they were only forty meters from the main house, Campanella used the binoculars again and scanned the grounds, doing his best to peer in through open doors or windows. He could see no movements of any kind. With a quick nod, Campanella gave Arturo and Franco the green light to head out. The two men sped off past the trees and across a fifteen-meter open area to the back of the barn. The held in place momentarily and then scurried around and into the front entrance.

Campanella headed toward cellar. Once again, his agility and lightning speed shocked Alberto. He was twenty-nine years old and reasonably fit, but he found it impossible to keep up. He'd seen the man's incredible abilities several times before but still couldn't get used to it.

Once at the entrance, Campanella dashed down the steps to the door, opened it, and entered the cellar. The enclosed area was dark, and if not for the light from the sun, he wouldn't have been able to see anything. As it was, the space was mostly empty, save for a dozen or so potatoes, four or five bundles of carrots, and some sprouting onions. He also unearthed eight or nine large round molds filled with cheese.

Shaking his head at the slim pickings, Campanella pulled a cloth sack from his shirt and collected a few items. After a minute or two more, he tapped Alberto on his shoulder, notifying him it was time to go. Just as they were about to head back up the steps, Campanella spotted a wooden crate in the darkened corner to his right.

He grabbed Alberto by the arm to let him know to wait and went over for a look. Despite his keen eyesight, he couldn't see what the container held, so he used his hands and began running them along and down its surface. He felt about a dozen glass bottlenecks protruding from several openings. Grabbing one, he brought it to the light…WINE! He showed his haul to Alberto and could make out the man's happy grin in the gloom.

Moments later, they returned to the tree line with the bottles of wine in their bags and met Arturo and Marco, who were already waiting. Both men displayed looks of disappointment.

"Nothing?" Campanella asked. They shook their heads no.

"And you?" Arturo asked.

"Some cheese, and a few vegetables, and…these!" Campanella said as he held up the wine. The others beamed with delight at the discovery.

"Well, isn't that a pleasant surprise," Arturo said as he examined the wine.

"It is, but not exactly what we need. We'll check one more house. Maybe we'll get lucky," Campanella said.

The men skittered down the right-hand side of the structure before moving on a diagonal across an open patch of yard. After going about forty meters, they found another area covered in high grass. This time, however, they were on the same side of the expanse as Santos and the rest of the group would have traversed.

The next house was now only fifty meters ahead, but the open yard around the dwelling was much larger and more revealing. They were forced to stop short of the intended target to stay out of sight of any residents.

Campanella once again went through the motions with the binoculars. Their vantage point from here could have been better as he could only see a small portion of the grounds. He had no clear sight of the house's front or right side. But the barn and the cellar were close, eight to ten meters away.

Compared to seeing the buildings from the hillside, things now appeared quite different. The distances from the outbuildings to house were much shorter, which caused Campanella to have second thoughts about taking the risk. He considered other options for a moment, but those posed their own issues, being closer to the town's perimeter and so at higher risk of exposure.

"I'm going to head in that direction…" Campanella pointed toward the right-hand side of the house, "…along the grass line so I can see if anyone is there. I need to know what or who might be nearby. Stay here but keep a sharp eye on me. If things look safe, I'll give you the *all clear* sign and guide you over."

Campanella made it to the far side of the house in a few gaping strides and found a hiding spot behind a small shed thirty meters from the home's main entry. He moved around the structure to view the front of the house.

He didn't like what he saw.

A German staff car was parked out front with a canvased-topped troop carrier truck sitting next to it. To make matters worse, six soldiers were milling about. He knew he had to cut the scavenger hunt short. He didn't want to risk the team unnecessarily.

Campanella was about to turn and return from where he'd come when the front door opened. A tall, thin man came out dressed in a dark tailor-fitted suit, a white shirt, and a slim black tie. He wore shiny black shoes and a black felt hat, whose brim was drawn low over his eyes. He moved down the steps and headed toward the car.

Straining to get a better look, Campanella watched the man walk away from the house, but he couldn't see his face clearly. A few seconds later, another man came bursting out of the door, pulling on a pair of suspenders, which he snapped over and onto his shoulders with an audible 'thwacking' sound. The action seemed to express some kind of victorious moment, and this was proved right when the man began to whoop and holler.

This bit of revelry ignited a rousing response of similar whoops and hollers from the six soldiers who, moments earlier, had appeared quite sullen and disinterested as they skulked about the truck. The suited man ignored the shared celebrations from the gathered men though as he made his way to the passenger side of the staff car.

The soldiers spoke German, congratulating the man in suspenders on whatever he'd meant to have just achieved. It was then that the house door opened again, and a young petit brunette filled the doorway. She seemed to be in her early twenties and was clasping a robe tightly around her waist and neck. Her face was red, and her eyes were swollen. She also appeared to have a sizeable burgeoning bruise on her right arm.

The man in the suspenders turned back toward the house when he heard the creaking of the door's hinges. He spread his arms wide, bowed to the girl, and thanked her for her obliging participation.

After returning to the car, he reached in through the window and pulled out a jacket and hat. Campanella could see various German military insignia on the jacket's shoulders as he put them on. The symbols indicated that he was an officer – a captain. Taking his time, the man straightened his attire while continuing to boast of his accomplishments in rather vulgar detail.

As Campanella regarded the captain's total indifference for the girl's distraught form, he felt an overwhelming impulse begin welling inside his body. His instinct to right an obvious wrong urged him to burst from his hiding spot and use his weapon to mow down the entire pack of German animals. He imagined walking over to them and spattering them with gunfire. After they were a mass of bullet-riddled bodies, he would turn his attention to the perverted sex offender. Using only his fists, he would beat the man into a senseless pile of worthless flesh. It would feel good to do it.

Suddenly, he was jolted back to reality by a new voice, clear and distinct. It was as if the wind had shifted, causing the group's conversation to funnel directly and intentionally into Campanella's ears. Campanella repositioned himself and honed in. It was no longer disgusting, raw sexual innuendos he heard. What drew him in was the language of the man in the suit. The slender figure was directing his thoughts toward the captain, but he wasn't speaking German. He, in fact, was talking in perfect English, tinged with a rather distinctive public-school role-play drawl. It was neither clipped nor laconic but suffused with a dripping condescension.

The English-speaking man had said he either wanted something or had seen something. This comment caused an instant reaction as the German Captain began spewing orders while pointing at the shed. This directive triggered a Corporal to dash straight for where Campanella hid.

In one quick motion, Campanella pulled his knife and slid to the back of the shed. Once hidden from view, he readied himself for the killing. At that moment, he glanced toward the forest. And there, sitting in the brush, the rest of his team was there. The men were staring anxiously in his direction, and Campanella thought momentarily about dashing to their side. But he could hear footsteps nearing and knew he could not cover the distance without being seen.

As he waited, he felt that unmistakable power rushing through his body as his muscles tensed in preparation for whatever might come his way. He was now used to this feeling. The incredible rush of adrenaline and muscle response coursing through his system at lightning speed felt like an old friend.

Throughout his recuperation from his operations, this strange physical alteration had startled him. There were times when his newfound strength often caused an over-exaggeration of movements and actions. But now his body had harnessed the flow, and the feeling became as normal as breathing.

The German soldier pulled up as he reached the shed that hid Campanella. He took a moment and looked back at his captain. The officer angrily motioned with his hand for him to get on with it. The Corporal turned toward where Campanella lay in wait, but instead of confronting the American, he opened the shed door and went in.

After a few moments, there was the sound of glass tapping together, and then the soldier was out. The shed door slammed shut with the help of the Corporal's boot, and he raced back to his commander. Campanella moved to watch what came next, just in time to see the soldier hand the captain two bottles of crystal-clear liquid.

The officer jerked the cork from one of the bottles and took a deep pull lasting several seconds. As he swallowed, he began to cough and gag. After spitting and blinking his eyes in surprise, he started sucking on the bottle again.

Once he'd had his fill, he belched loudly and then barked new orders at the few men still not in the truck. They scurried like rats as they hustled into the back of the vehicle. The captain nodded at the suited man, and both got in the car.

Campanella felt his muscles ease as the two vehicles drove away, a cloud of dust trailing behind. He turned his attention back to the house, where he saw the slender girl sitting on the steps, her face buried in her hands.

CHAPTER 5

With grief for the abused woman weighing heavy in his heart and anger toward the German still pulsing through his veins, Campanella watched the unmoving figure. He wanted to help, but he couldn't think of anything he could do that wouldn't risk his mission. He shook his head regretfully and sprinted back to his group in the trees.

Once in their midst, they agreed it was too risky to continue their searches, so they returned to their camp for the day. They went south, following the tree line for about fifty meters, and came upon Berta and Paulo crouched in the bushes waiting. Nodding to the approaching men, they led them to their temporary base.

After the foragers dispersed the provisions, the partisans sat and ate. While they savored the cheeses, potatoes, and especially the wine, Campanella related the events of their expedition as they unfolded.

"And then the man in the suit spoke – in impeccable English! And with a British accent!" Campanella exclaimed as he got to the end of the tale. "Now, it isn't unusual for someone from England to be in Italy, even with a war going on, but him? And being with those soldiers and that Captain? This appearance was no coincidence."

"Would you recognize the men again if you saw them?" Salvatore asked.

"The man in the suit? Unfortunately, no. I didn't see his face. But the German officer – I'll never forget him," Campanella said with evident emotion. He glanced over at Berta and felt sure she and the girl on the step couldn't have been much different in age. They were also both strikingly beautiful. Women like these were easy and desirable targets for the filthy-minded Germans.

Renewed anger grew in Campanella as he imagined what had happened to the poor Italian women he'd seen. He felt his blood boiling and tried to stop the images from dancing in his head. He couldn't shake them, though; it would be several hours before he calmed. The impressions had burrowed deeply into his permanent memory.

The provisions they amassed only lasted a week, even with the usual rationing all were now accustomed to. Twice more, the group sent out a search party to steal more supplies. During these two ventures, Campanella made sure he checked on the woman. When he did, she was outside hanging her laundry or working the small garden on the side of her house.

On one of the trips, Campanella watched as she carefully moved in through the garden. She whistled and sang softly to herself, bringing joy and sorrow to his heart. She was alone in this house, but if she did have a special someone, they were almost certainly away fighting in the conflict.

****

The echoes of the war continued to haunt the partisans for their entire time in hiding. The deep resonating explosions got closer and closer with each passing day. Campanella tried to alleviate the stress of the experience with words of encouragement about the future. But these were proud Italians. The fact their country was being pummeled with landscape-erasing efficiency was disturbing, and the days leading to the twenty-fourth passed like treacle through an hourglass. In one week, they would be heading to Naples. But first, they needed to deal with and hide from the expected onslaught of evacuating German militia.

Assembling the partisans, Campanella explained the process of the upcoming German withdrawal. He related how their army and equipment would head north toward Rome and stressed the need to stay hidden at all costs. Everyone knew the Germans wouldn't hesitate to execute any partisan they encountered during their retreat. To lift their spirits in any way he could, he assured the team that by October 1st, most German soldiers would be gone from Southern Italy.

Campanella made daily trips to the tree line to gauge the volume of the fleeing German traffic. He would go to a secluded spot in the morning and return each afternoon to the team to report the activity. During the first few days, hundreds of vehicles of every kind and thousands of soldiers moved northward toward Rome. Campanella watched as a steady stream of vulgar and angry Germans stomped past and through the little village. On multiple occasions, he witnessed the destruction or theft of civilian property as the Germans displayed their disgust for their Italian Axis partners, who were failing to help them beat back the Allies.

Campanella forced himself to hold back on more than one occasion as local townspeople were beaten for trying to protect their valuables. The urge to race over and pummel the bastards was often overwhelming. But circumstances allowed him only to watch in almost unbearable frustration.

On the morning of September 29th, Campanella made his way to his usual lookout position for what he thought would be the final time. This belief was partly because the previous day's activity had only produced a handful of vehicles. If this day were similar in movement, he would head back and inform the others it was time to pack up camp.

As he rose, a lone vehicle emerged from over the horizon. He gave it little notice and was about to blend into the forest when a glance back stopped him cold. The same German officer he'd seen at the Italian girl's home the day they arrived in Lido di Licola was driving the car.

Suddenly, without conscious thought, he mirrored the vehicle's path as it barreled into town toward a destination Campanella had already guessed. A vision of the girl in the intruder's hands exploded in his mind, triggering an instant reaction. His resolve consumed his every thought and movement as he tore up huge chunks of ground. Campanella occasionally glanced to his right, and though he could see he was close to keeping pace with the car, which was only slightly ahead of him, the German would arrive before he did.

After only a few minutes of this torrid pace, he reached a point opposite the shed next to the young woman's home. The officer had arrived, and as he attempted to get out of the car, his trailing foot caught on the door's sill. He stumbled and almost fell to the ground. He cursed and shouted at the car, then laughed and guffawed like a town drunk, pointing at the offending ledge like it had purposely grabbed him.

The officer's coat and hat were already off, and he was pulling his shirt from his waistband, with the folds of fabric hanging loose and rumpled. He held an opened bottle of wine in his left hand and a German Luger in his right.

When the man arrived, the Italian woman had been tending to her garden. At first, she didn't hear or see the vehicle's appearance. But as the car door slammed shut, she turned her head. Recognition was immediate, and sheer terror rushed across her face. She dropped the small trowel she had been using, jumped to her feet, and started running toward her door.

"Where do you run to, my young fraulein?" the foul-breathed soldier said as he chased the fleeing girl. "You can run, but we've played this game before, and I know where you hide…" he bellowed, the words slurring out in lust-strewn overtures.

Campanella was ready to attack, and though the Luger didn't scare him in the least, especially in the hands of a drunken animal, he didn't want to chance any retreating troops might hear a gunshot. So, he waited and watched for the right moment.

After the girl raced to the house and dashed inside, Campanella caught the faint but definite sound of a door lock slamming into place. This attempt to slow or stop the intoxicated soldier bore little to no effect on the outcome. Once he arrived at the entryway, he raised his foot, kicked the door open, and stormed in.

Campanella leaped from his hiding spot as if the German's entrance had been the crack of a starter's pistol. Before he had taken his first step, his knife was out. Six long strides later, he was at the door. Glancing in, he could see the back of the teetering man a few feet inside the house. Just beyond him stood the frightened woman.

When Campanella walked up the house's stoop, his size filled the doorway. The woman's expression of terror changed to a look of confused shock. The soldier noticed her look and made an awkward attempt to turn to see what had caught the girl's eye. Campanella acted before the officer could focus on the hulking figure behind him.

In a move neither the German nor the woman could follow, Campanella snatched the arm holding the Luger and wrenched it violently back and down. A loud popping sound of separating bones occurred, which caused the immediate release of the gun. The soldier screamed in agony as the weapon fell to the floor and bounced backward and under a chair.

The horrific crunch of the injury, followed by the scream from the German, made the woman shriek, and she backed hurriedly away. She gaped in disbelief as Campanella grabbed the man by the head and lifted him high from the ground before tossing him like a rag doll through the air. The man landed face-first with a sickening thud. The room went eerily quiet for several seconds.

Campanella then commanded the soldier in his best, though somewhat broken German, "Roll over on your back, hands, and arms under your body. Do it now and do it slowly."

Only a groan came from the German's mouth. Impatient, Campanella kicked the soldier in the thigh with his size fourteen boot and repeated his order. The soldier groaned again but, this time rolled onto his back. He'd brought his left arm under as instructed, but his right arm was out of its socket at the shoulder, and he couldn't move it.

"You broke my damn arm! You will pay for this!" the German grunted through gritted teeth.

"You should be glad that was all I did," Campanella replied, this time in English.

The officer focused his watery, bloodshot eyes on the American, who still held the large razor-sharp knife in his hand and said, "Englander?"

"American," Campanella answered back.

"American!" the surprised girl blurted.

Campanella turned to her, "Yes, the first of many to come."

In a thick German accent, the soldier asked in English, "Are you part of the invasion force?"

Campanella thought for a moment before answering, "You could say that. But I'll be the one asking the questions from this point forward." He moved around to where he was opposite the man's injured shoulder. "So, if you don't want to experience pain worse than you already have, your answers had better be the truth."

The German only glowered in response.

"Several days ago, you were here with another man in a dark suit and about a half-dozen soldiers. I want to know who the suited man was and what he is doing here in Italy."

The German laughed, a snide, lascivious laugh, before gloating, "Yes, I've been here many times, but…I have no recollection of any man in a suit. Besides, I come for only one reason: to take advantage of the hospitality this young Fraulein offers." He stopped, turned his gaze toward the woman, and added, "I don't allow others here as I am not one to share my special prize."

"He lies. He did bring a man here. He was as much of a pig as this man," the girl said in disgust and bent and spit on the German's face.

Before the soldier could react to the spray of spittle, Campanella slid his knife in front of the German's flaring nostrils. The man's eyes widened in terror. For a moment, Campanella considered shoving the blade through the rapist's nose and into his brain. It would be easy and well deserved, but he kept his composure and kept the razor-sharp knife suspended a hair above his face.

Thinking momentarily about how to remind his captive of what would happen if he lied, Campanella moved his knee and placed it on the German's separated shoulder. He applied a tad bit of pressure – or maybe more than a tad. It was all he needed to do to get his captive's immediate and full attention.

The German clenched his eyes and let out another shriek of pain. He began groaning a list of incoherent curses. Adrenaline caused sobriety to rush through his body as his head swung to the left, and his eyes shot open, blazing a look of hatred into Campanella's. But this fury only made Campanella's smile broaden even more and his knee pressure increase. The German grimaced and contorted, but he kept silent.

"I will ask you one more time. If you don't tell me what I want to know, I will take this knife…" Campanella said while again lowering the blade to the man's face, "…and shove it into your mouth. And I will not stop pushing it in until it comes out the other side of your head."

The woman gasped, and the eyes of the soldier narrowed as he watched the knife move to within a few inches of his face. To prove his point, Campanella deftly flicked his blade down and through the man's right nostril, slicing through the outer flap of his nose like the node was warm butter. This time, the German's shriek was followed by a stream of blood flowing from the wound like a faucet.

"Who is the man, and why is he here!" Campanella demanded.

"I don't know what you're talking about," the German said through blood-drenched lips and teeth. Campanella placed the knife blade on the un-pierced side of his nostril and applied a small amount of pressure. However, before the blade cut skin this time, the soldier yelled, "Okay, stop! I'll tell you what I know."

Campanella nodded for the officer to continue. The man's face and neck were now completely blood-soaked, and when he tried to answer, more flowed into his mouth, causing him to choke and spit up a thick mixture of red slobber. He turned his head and spat a large glob to allow him to speak, "I'm not sure why he's here, only that his mission is vital to the war effort."

"What is his name, and where is he now?" Campanella demanded while adding a bit more pressure with his knife.

"His name is Paul Jones," the German spewed. "He's from England, and the last time I saw him, he was in a small villa near Pozzuoli. But with the Allies invading, I believe he has gone. Now let me up – YOU SWINE!"

Campanella regarded the woman and said, "Think he's lying?"

The girl's eyes widened as if she was about to answer. But all she was able to muster were raised eyebrows and shrugged shoulders.

"Yeah, I'm not sure either."

"I am telling the truth," the soldier barked adamantly.

"Well, maybe you are, and maybe you're not. But really, it is no longer important. Now get up," Campanella said as he stood and moved away.

The officer did as he was told, but awkwardly, as the arm under his back was numb from lying on it, and his right arm was useless. The German raised his left hand to his nose as he got to his feet and gingerly inspected the damage.

The bleeding had slowed, clumped, and clotted, but his neck and shirt were now a soggy, soaked mess. The wounded officer winced as he dabbed at the damaged nostril. He dropped his hand and turned to glower at Campanella. "You're a dead man for doing this to me," he said. "Do you know who I AM?"

Ignoring the soldier's obvious threat, Campanella looked the woman's way and said, "We will be leaving. From now on, you won't ever have to worry about this man or any other German again. I give you my word. Oh, and sorry about the blood on your floor." The woman shook her head to say that the apology wasn't necessary as a tear formed in her eye and rolled down her face.

Using his knife, Campanella motioned for the German to move toward the door. The officer hesitated for momentarily before thinking better of his situation and obeying with a glower. Moving through the door, he glanced back at the woman and leered. As Campanella saw this, he kicked the man in the ass.

The German was propelled violently through the opening and windmilled his uninjured arm to stay upright. Somehow, he maintained his footing and balance and used the momentum to start a mad dash toward his staff car. The distance was no more than twenty meters, and he reasoned the shove had given him enough impetus to race to the car before the American could catch him.

The German had gone less than two steps when a hand clamped down on his shoulder like a vise. Though a stout man over six feet tall and weighing over two hundred pounds, the American jerked him backward and cleaned off his feet as if he were no more than a small child. The soldier landed flat on his back with a crashing thud that knocked the wind from his lungs.

Suddenly and shockingly, the man was again staring up at

Campanella. This time, his one good arm was grasping at his chest. His eyes bulged wildly, and his face turned a bright burgundy red. He tried desperately to regain the life-giving breath violently expunged from the impact, but his attempts could only produce tiny gasps. After a few seconds, the German took a small breath and then another. Before long, he breathed more steadily but with a burning, bursting sensation in his chest. Then he collapsed again on the floor.

The girl had witnessed the whole episode from her doorway, watching in disbelief as Campanella made up the distance between the two in lightning speed. With her hands at her mouth, she stood on her stoop, staring at the two men. The American was again towering over the German, lying on the ground in pain and agony.

This time, however, Campanella said nothing as he reached down, manhandled the soldier by the collar, and dragged him back to the corner of the house. He tossed the soldier through the air and watched as he landed with a crash and crumpled up into a ball.

"You've made a grave mistake, I'm afraid," Campanella said as he glanced at the human heap. He considered the girl before saying, "You might want to close the drapes inside. I don't think you want to see what I'm about to do."

The woman's face turned steely, and her eyes narrowed. Campanella could see her body go rigid as she said in anger, "This man is a monster. He has raped me for months and deserves to die. No, I will not turn away as I want to watch him take his last breath."

Chapter 6

Campanella was greatly affected by the young woman's desire to view this man's execution. He wondered how it may affect her. Regardless of the consequences, though, he could tell from the look on her face that she was determined to follow through with her wish, so he jerked the stupefied man to his feet and directed him to the barn.

The soldier's body wobbled, and his eyes were vacant and glassy, but when Campanella ordered him to walk, he did. The three moved to the small barn behind the house, with Campanella giving the German several guiding shoves as they went. Once inside, Campanella pulled his knife from its sheath and turned toward the blood-soaked soldier. The gleaming metal blade in his assailant's hand appeared to be an immediate stimulus. "You cannot do this! I am an officer of the German Army. I demand you…"

"Your demands mean nothing to me, so don't waste your breath," Campanella said, drowning out the man's pleadings. He walked over and spun the soldier to where the man was facing away. He wrapped his left arm around the soldier's head and raised the knife to run the blade across his neck when the girl suddenly spoke.

"Wait. Please," the woman said, holding a hand up in protest.

Campanella stopped and gazed her way in bewilderment. If she was about to ask him to spare the fiend's life, he couldn't allow it. He wasn't willing to take a chance the soldier would tell others about him and jeopardize his mission. "I need to do something first," she said, a sorrowful pleading in her voice and eyes. "Please...will you hold him still for me?"

Campanella nodded, assuming the girl planned to slap, hit, punch, or inflict some other kind of physical harm. Anything to alleviate the sum of the cruelty the Germans had done. But what she did next shocked him.

Facing the disheveled soldier but not saying a word, she reached down and unbuttoned his pants. She grabbed the top of his trousers and jerked them to the ground. The woman did the same thing with the German's undergarments, which left him exposed, his flaccid penis hanging limp and ridiculous in front of her.

The soldier was momentarily confused but, after a moment of thought, said through an arrogant smile. "See American pig. The woman likes my superior Aryan cock. Now release me!"

However, when Campanella looked into her eyes, he saw something else entirely. The girl stuck her hand out but not toward the man's penis. Campanella hesitated and then understood what she wanted and handed her his knife – and that's when the German understood, too.

The smugness exhibited by the officer only seconds before gave way to sheer panic. He jerked back and tried to wriggle and free himself from his captive. His struggles did little to loosen Campanella's vice-like grip that kept him cemented in place.

"Please, do not let her take my dignity. If I am to die, I must die a man," the officer blurted in a terrified whimper.

"You lost that honor the first time you assaulted this woman," Campanella replied with cold steel in his voice.

Ignoring the useless pleadings of the German, the frail-looking girl glowered down at her abuser's sexual organ with blazing rage and hatred. She gripped the rapist's penis with her free hand as she raised her fiery eyes again to his. At that moment, her face, previously a mask of animosity, was transformed.

Without taking her eyes off his, she smiled. And though she was beautiful and the smile undoubtedly radiant, this was not a smile of happiness. It was one of bitter triumph. The German's terrified eyes moved to the knife as the girl placed the razor-sharp edge across his penis and, with a quick and precise motion, sliced it off.

Moving quickly back, holding the man's flaccid member in her hand, she watched in satisfaction as blood spewed and shot out of the gaping hole where the once dangling organ hung.

With eyes bulging in shock, Captain Peter Von Gerber's entire being jolted with existential horror. His penis was now in the woman's hand, six feet away. A blood-curdling scream ran up his throat, but like a vice, Campanella stifled it back with the crook of his arm. After a few seconds, he could feel the man's weight increase as the soldier's legs had lost their ability to hold him erect. Campanella let the bleeding man fall to the ground.

The mutilated soldier started rolling back and forth, muttering in mostly unrecognizable profanity. His good arm and hand had frantically thrust to his groin to stem the blood's gushing flow. But the effort did no good as a torrent of thick red fluid continued to pump out between his fingers.

The surreal event had taken Campanella aback. He stood and stared, mouth slightly open, until he was brought out of his trance when the Italian woman walked past him. She avoided the gathering pool of scarlet liquid and stepped toward the squirming body on the ground. Without emotion, she threw the limp flesh into the screaming man's face. It slapped against his cheek and bounced directly into the dirt before his agony-filled eyes.

The woman glowered at the officer for several seconds before gazing at Campanella. She said nothing, and her face was now sullen, drawn, and compassionless. She suddenly appeared many years older. After moments of silent staring in which nothing was said, but everything was communicated, she calmly returned the knife and headed toward the barn's exit. A shovel was leaning to the right of the door, and she grabbed it as she walked out.

Watching her leave with shovel in hand, Campanella tried to grasp what the girl had done. He thought a good punch in the face would have been reasonable. Or maybe a kick in the groin – or even two kicks. But taking his knife and slicing his thing off was not what he was expecting. Not at all. He grimaced.

After a moment of slightly shocked reflection, he turned back toward the still agonizing soldier. He understood full well what a monster this man was and that he deserved to die. But at that instant, he felt a bit unsettled for the now emasculated officer. Campanella cocked his head slightly before deciding to discard the thought. He grabbed the officer by his hair, jerking him up and into a kneeling position.

The injured man groaned as the blond hair in Campanella's grasp began ripping from its roots. After Campanella had the man stable, he wasted no time. He pulled his knife across the German's throat and released his grip. The man's body slumped to the ground, blood boiling out of a gaping five-inch wound.

The soldier's hand, at his groin seconds earlier, was now squeezing around this new assault in a desperate attempt to stop the unstoppable. He was staring up at Campanella with shock-stricken eyes while gurgling noises emanating from his mouth. Campanella smirked and said, "In America, we have a saying – paybacks a bitch!"

As he strode through the barn's doorway, Campanella spotted the woman struggling to dig a hole in the middle of her immaculate garden. She was not trying to save any of the plants sprouting from the ground. She just stabbed, stomped, and scooped the dirt in a pile.

Walking over to where she toiled, he held out his hand in an offer to take over, but the woman ignored him and kept digging, now with reckless abandon. Abruptly, without any outward warning, her raw emotions exploded as her body convulsed, and she began sobbing in deep heaves.

Campanella gently pulled her into his chest. At first, she tried to pull back but soon gave up and melted into his grasp. She stayed this way for a long while, weeping in uncontrolled spasms. Campanella did not try to console her; nothing he could have said would have provided comfort.

In time, the crying subsided into slight yet perceptible shivers, at which point she leaned back and moved away a couple of feet. She searched Campanella's eyes for an instant before relinquishing the shovel. The emotionally drained woman walked over to a wooden bench near the corner of the house and sat.

As he was about to turn the first spade of dirt, Campanella regarded the woman, and asked, "Are you sure? Right here in your garden?"

"Every day for the rest of my life, I will be stepping on this man's grave and throwing manure over his remains. On days when his foul memory fills my mind, I will come out and spit where he lies. Yes, I am sure."

The two didn't speak again as Campanella made short work of the hole, digging it several feet deeper and larger than necessary. When finished, he leaned the shovel against the house and walked back into the barn. He retrieved the body – and the extra body part – and tossed both into the makeshift grave.

The bloody form crumpled into a lifeless ball at the bottom of the pit in the dank earth. Campanella refilled the hole three-quarters of the way and then began cleaning up the large pool of blood on the barn's dirt floor. He scraped up as much of the affected soil as possible and shoveled the mixture into a small wheelbarrow. Returning to the grave, Campanella dumped the contents into it and filled the rest of the cavity with the remaining dirt.

After putting the shovel away, Campanella grabbed his weapon and headed for the staff car. It was vital to dispose of the vehicle, or the girl would be at serious risk. He would drive it into the woods and hide it with tree limbs and loose brush. As he got into the car, the girl exited her home and walked to the driver's door.

"Is it over? The war, I mean," she asked in a monotone voice, her eyes sad and despondent.

"It's almost October. So, for you and this area of Italy, it soon will be," Campanella said as he nodded toward the town. "Stragglers might still come, but you have seen the last of more German soldiers for the most part."

"May I know the name of the man who saved me?" the woman said as she laid her hand on his arm.

Campanella looked up at the woman, unsure of how to answer. After considering, he said, "I'm afraid it would be safer for you if you didn't. If I can, I will come back and check on you. We can talk then if you would like. Unless your husband…"

The woman's eyes narrowed as she quickly answered, "He is dead. Killed in Greece when that idiot Mussolini tried to invade."

"I'm sorry," Campanella offered.

The two looked at each other for a moment longer without speaking. Campanella started the car, engaged the clutch, and pulled the vehicle around and behind her house. From there, he traveled across the broad expanse beyond her yard, following the tree line. Finding an opening large enough, he drove as far as the foliage would allow. Once he finished camouflaging the car, he headed back to his team.

Chapter 7

September 29th, 1943

"Mussolini arrested?" Salvatore asked as he scratched the top of his head in amazement.

Campanella nodded and said, "It happened this past July."

"And we've given up; surrendered?"

Again, Campanella nodded. "Earlier this month. But the Germans will force many of your troops to continue fighting and will hold much of northern Italy until the war's end. Your government will soon switch sides, though, and those still able to will fight alongside the Allied forces. The partisan groups will expand and multiply, and in time, Hitler's army will be defeated."

The group gaped at each other. There was a palpable silence while everyone considered the impact of this news. After a few minutes, Santos stepped up, "Joseph, what do we do next?"

"It will be October 1st in two days. That is liberation day for Naples and the beginning of the end for Germany in this country. We will head to Pozzuoli and start the search for the British man I saw in the dark suit. He will either be the one we want or will know who it is we're after."

****

The partisans spent that last night in their camp before leaving at first light the following morning. They traveled south for three days, and the devastation from the Allied bombings and the German retreat became increasingly apparent. The destruction saddened at times and sickened at others. And though Campanella knew life would get better for everyone in this part of the world, the rest of his party couldn't come close to fathoming the possibility of returning to the way things were.

After moving in and out of the woods and around other smaller towns, the partisans finally found their way to the outskirts of Pozzuoli. Campanella went ahead of his team as a precaution. He needed to be sure the town and its people were free of any enemy influence.

When he arrived at the entrance to the tiny burg, Campanella heard music – loud music. He slipped past several buildings and down a few shadowy alleys until he found a sheltered vantage point to see the middle of the town. From this darkened recess, Campanella moved to the edge of the building and peered out. The scene in front of him was truly amazing. Hundreds of people were dancing and singing in the streets.

Though most were civilians, Campanella spotted a dozen or more Italian soldiers intermingled in various stages of military dress in the crowd. To his left, a man and a woman kissed with evident passion, only to turn and do the same to others nearby. People raised their arms and hands, shouting, cheering, and reveling in the festivities.

Campanella left his hiding spot and moved down the street. As he approached the rowdy and rambunctious throng, a woman came bursting out from a building to his right. She was an attractive brunette, somewhere in her mid-thirties, Campanella thought, with dazzling eyes and a magnificent, blissful smile that lit up her face.

The woman noticed Campanella, locked eyes with him, and raced his way. The American took a small step backward. The delighted woman leaped into his arms and wrapped her legs and arms around the towering man. She kissed him long and hard, pulled back, and kissed him several more times with lip-smacking enthusiasm. Then, just as suddenly as she had started the embrace, she dropped to the ground, spun around, and ran back toward the center of the big crowd, whooping and hollering.

Campanella, happily stunned, smiled, and followed her into the multitude. He was half-mauled in joyous revelry as he slowly moved through the crowd. Then he spotted a small bistro on the street's corner to his right that caught his eye with its cheerful exterior.

The little café appeared open but empty. Campanella walked in and, at first, saw no one. He was about to call out when he heard a shuffling noise to his left. He could just make out a man in the semi-gloom. The

Italian was no more than five feet short, wearing black pants, a long-sleeved white button-down shirt, a black tie, and an apron. He held a broom in his hand and pushed it back and forth in a rhythmic motion.

The man's hair was thick and bushy on the sides and back of his head, with only a few wisps growing along the top. He had an abundant mustache curled up on the ends and a tapered beard hanging four inches below his chin. His belly bulged pleasingly in his shirt, a mark of health rather than excess.

As the broom pusher gazed out the window at the people in the town's center, his feet were moving to and fro, here and there, and up and down. His arms went out, then they were up, and then they were waving back and forth. He did this for several moments, then turned and looked in Campanella's direction.

The man stopped dancing and gazed at the newcomer, not saying anything. Suddenly, a big smile erupted on his face. He leaned the broom against the wall and began dancing again. This time, instead of dancing in place, he danced in a side-to-side back-and-forth shuffle toward Campanella, arms raised above his head as he came.

When he got a few feet away, he opened his arms wide to his side and said, "Welcome. Welcome to my Bistro! Isn't today a magnificent day!"

"Yes, it most certainly is," Campanella replied cheerfully.

"The German swine have fled like the evil scum they are, and we are once again free," the man said without any prodding. He laughed aloud, executed a surprisingly graceful pirouette, walked right up to Campanella, and, still dancing, stared straight at the American with wild, boisterous eyes. He was full of spit and vinegar, and Campanella could feel his own feet start to shuffle as if being commanded by his host's physicality.

"I'm passing through on my way to Naples. I've been fighting with the partisans in the north until recently, so I don't know what has happened," Campanella said as he danced.

"Oh! Well, my boy, just look around," the restaurant owner said as he danced out the door. He got to the sidewalk's edge and swung his arm in a fanlike gesture. "We are free, free Italians once more. Two days ago, we woke up, and they were gone. Every one of them just up and left! We've been rejoicing and reveling ever since!"

The man winked at Campanella, began to do a little rumba, pirouetted again, and made his way out into the street to join the rest of the celebrators.

Campanella watched for a few minutes, smiled genuinely for the town's freedom, and went back to his small band of anxious partisans.

CHAPTER 8

Once Campanella had returned to the group with the good news, it took all of five minutes for them to load up their gear and head out. As they traveled the short distance, their conversation flowed like the wine they would soon drink. They spoke of how they would sing, dance, and soak up the excitement.

Berta kept shaking her head in agreement after each gleeful exclamation. And though she was excited at those prospects, her thoughts were of one thing – a bath with hot water – and lots of it. She hadn't bathed in a hot tub since they'd left their farm many weeks before.

Once the group secured a place to clean up, eat, and sleep for the next few days, Campanella and Santos went back to the bistro. The last time Campanella had visited, only the proprietor was there. This time, the cafe was full of people who looked to be on an uncontrollable liberation high. Singing, dancing, and a constant flow of alcohol had propelled the crowd into a frenzied state of mind. It was deserved and justified, and Campanella soaked it in with great pleasure.

After observing the townspeople bask in their glorious freedom for a few moments, Campanella directed his attention to finding the bistro's owner. He passed through and around the throng to the end of the counter, and there he was. The little man was racing from end to end, serving his townsfolk with the same verve and grace Campanella had seen earlier in the day. In time, the owner turned and saw the two partisans.

The huge smile that had been on the proprietor's face the day before was back again with a vengeance. Without being asked, he snatched a bottle of clear liquid and three glasses from under the bar and headed their way.

His smile was still ear-to-ear as he walked up. "Sambuca," the small round man said with conviction. His voice was deep and passionate, resonating bigger than seemed possible. "They never found it." After filling their glasses, he handed the two men theirs, grabbed his, lifted it high, and shouted, "Viva Italia!"

Campanella and Santos raised their drinks and, as if on cue, joined the rest of the patrons and yelled out with a voluminous roar, "VIVA ITALIA!"

In less than an hour, the balance of Campanella's partisans had stumbled in, with Berta and Paulo bringing up the rear. They were hand in hand as they entered, but no one was looking toward Paulo. Everyone's eyes were transfixed on Berta Barilla. Her hair flowed to her shoulders. It shimmered from the light as it framed her olive-toned face, which glowed as if lit from within. As Campanella gazed her way, he knew few, if any, that could rival her stunning looks.

Throughout the night and into the wee hours of the morning, the Bistro owner never allowed anyone's glasses, including his, to be empty. Dancing and singing reigned, and though multiple chances arose to strike up a conversation about the dark-suited man, neither Santos nor Campanella brought it up. They were too busy bonding over the Allies' triumph and Italy's liberation.

Chapter 9

Most of the partisans saw the sun come up before their revelry ended. Pounding headaches and soured stomachs would rule the day, but no one would complain. These were the wonderfully bearable pains of freedom, and they all welcomed the release from anxiety and physical hardship they'd endured for endless months.

Campanella and Santos were up and ready before the others, and they made a beeline straight to the cafe to gather information. They weren't sure if their new acquaintance would be up, but to their amazement, the door was open, and they could hear whistling from within. They walked through the door and saw the diminutive man with the big smile sweeping the floor. Campanella smiled in amusement and then offered the proprietor a hearty good morning.

"Ah, my dear friends, and very good morning to you. Please, come and sit. I have coffee, my wife has baked bread, and I have freshly churned butter. Made it myself."

Hot bread slathered with creamy butter had never tasted so fantastic. And the coffee, well, the time traveler had never had any better, not in 1999 or since.

For the next hour or so, the conversation went back and forth between the partisan's travels and travails to the little town's survival of the German occupation. The proprietor's name was Pasquale Marconi, which seemed to Campanella to be an entirely appropriate name for the little bistro owner. His wife was Angelica, and they were the proud parents of two sons, both of whom were off fighting with the Italian army.

As the couple discussed their children, the air grew dark and sedate. They were understandably on edge as they hadn't heard news of their well-being in months. As the noon hour approached, other patrons began to file in. The café proprietor would soon be busy, so Campanella took the moment to seek information about the man he was seeking.

"Pasquale, may I ask you a question?" Campanella said.

"Of course, my friend, anything."

"I saw a man in a nearby village. He was tall, maybe a few inches over six feet, thin, and spoke with an obvious British accent. I asked around and was told he had stayed in a local villa. Have you seen anyone matching this description?" Campanella tried to ask as if the answer were a trivial matter to him.

The change in the little man was instant and unmistakable. His forehead creased, and his bright smile evaporated. "Why do you ask after this man?" the man asked, his eyes narrowed to slits.

Campanella knew his answer would need to satisfy, or he risked being thrown out. There was no mistaking the immediate loathing in the Italian's demeanor. He decided to tell the truth – or a version of it. "This man and a group of German soldiers attacked a woman in the town where we were staying. He violated her in unspeakable ways. We followed him here to bring him to justice," Campanella said, his face now one of determination.

"Pasquale," Santos interjected, "this is not our town. We don't live here. But we are all Italians. What this man has done to one of our women cannot be tolerated. We need to find him and let the authorities deal with him. We promised we would at least try to take him back."

The bistro owner stared at the men seated before him. His gaze searched for deception. After what felt like an eternity, he spoke calmly and in an even tone. "That man is a bad man. He is an Englishman and should not be friends with the German pigs. But he is. He was here, in this very bistro, many times. He drank my liquor, not the good stuff..." Pasquale added with a quick wink, "...and ate my food. But worst of all, he talked with pride of Germany, Hitler, and the fascist animals who have ruined our country. All the while, he did so as if they were his family." To emphasize his point, Pasquale spat on the floor in disgust.

Santos leaned forward and said with conviction, "He will pay for the betrayal of his country, our country, and everyone he has hurt. We just need to find him. Do you have any idea where he might be?"

"Sadly, no. The last time I saw him was the day before the Germans cleared out. But…" Pasquale stopped for a moment as he gazed toward the street.

"But?" Santos repeated.

"But I know he spoke for a long while with Tomaso Bellini, our ex-town mayor."

"Ex-town mayor?"

"Yes, ex-mayor, as in he is no longer. He was nothing but a puppet for the Germans. A co-conspirator to all the corrupt and evil things those people brought to this town and our country."

Where is he now? Can we speak with him?" Campanella asked.

"He is in our blacksmith's barn – chained to a post," the barkeep said with a grin. "If you want to go, I will need to take you. He is being guarded by those who would not let you see him if you went alone."

"When can you take us?" Campanella asked.

Pasquale pulled a pocket watch from his vest and read the time. "It is twelve-thirty now. Meet me here at, say…three p.m., and we will go," Pasquale chuckled. Santos and Campanella gazed at the man, perplexed, not understanding the humor displayed by their new friend. But, as he turned to go, the little bistro owner's sense of humor became clear. "This is going to be interesting…and fun," the proprietor said between chuckles as he went behind his counter.

CHAPTER 10

That afternoon, Santos and Campanella returned to the bistro to find Pasquale sitting at a table with his wife. The woman looked as short as her husband, maybe shorter, but she was quite attractive for someone Campanella estimated to be in her sixties.

Pasquale and his wife's eyes lit up when the two men entered. "Three p.m., right on time!" the café owner said.

"Yes, and we are anxious to get started," Campanella replied.

Pasquale leaned in, kissed his wife on the cheek, and headed for the door. The two partisans nodded toward the woman, with Santos tipping his hat, and followed her husband. The trio walked down a much quieter street than the day before. It appeared the previous night had put a temporary pause on the celebratory mood.

Pasquale made his way to a boot shop some one hundred meters down the road. With his feet moving at twice the rhythm of Campanella's, he passed the shop's entrance and turned left at the following corner. He headed down an alleyway toward a large barn with a stable attached. In front of the stable was an anvil positioned next to a water vat. Standing by the anvil, Campanella could see a massive man feverishly hammering away at a red-hot piece of iron.

"Theo, I bring friends," Pasquale said once the blacksmith noticed their arrival.

The disparity between the two Italians was amusing. The blacksmith towered at least a foot and a half over the smaller man and easily outweighed him by one hundred pounds. He wore suspenders over a sleeveless shirt, work pants, boots, and a thick leather apron. In his right hand, the blacksmith wielded a fifteen-pound hammer. Muscles bulged as the thick-handled tool made precise strikes on a glowing piece of metal that he deftly maneuvered to his design.

At first, Theo Rossi didn't respond; he just stared at Pasquale and the two strangers coming his way. Once the three stood before him, he grumbled, "Pasquale," and nodded.

"Theo," Pasquale answered jubilantly. "This is Santos Barilla and Joseph Campanella."

The hulking man appraised the two for several long moments, "What can I do for you?"

"We must see Tomaso," Pasquale said. "Santos and Joseph need to ask him questions about the Englishman. It seems our town wasn't the only town his kind raped and pillaged."

The blacksmith turned and regarded his barn. As he did, Campanella noticed the arm and hand holding the hammer tensed. Turning back, Rossi cocked his head and nodded toward the barn door. "Go ahead. If you have any trouble, let me know, and I'll take care of it."

Once through the large wooden door, they saw a shackled man stooped in the corner of the manure-smelling stable. He was dirty – filthy, in fact – and his clothes were torn and tattered. His shoes were gone, his feet were bare, and his face exhibited red blotchy patches around the eyes and mouth. It was apparent that Tomaso Bellini had been through the wringer.

"Pasquale, my dear friend, please tell my people I only had their best interests at heart. Never once did I do anything to cause harm to anyone," Bellini begged in his defense.

Ignoring the man's pleas, Pasquale pulled up a hay bale and sat down. "Tomaso, these two men have a few questions to ask you. If you answer with the truth, I will let the town elders know, and maybe they'll do something about your conditions."

"Oh, yes, splendid! Please, ask away," the man said with pathetic eagerness.

"Mr. Bellini, my name is Joseph Campanella. I'm here looking for a man. But before I describe this person to you, I must say this so there is no confusion. If you lie, I will know it, and things will go very, very badly for you. You get one chance. Do you understand me?"

The man nodded in agreement but with evident trepidation.

"Fine. Now, you were seen talking to this man the day before the Germans evacuated your town. He was a tall, lithe Englishman. He wore a dark suit and Fedora. He was with a German Captain named Gerber, and I've been told they stayed in a villa near here. Do you recall meeting him?"

Bellini, who moments ago was nodding his head like a bobblehead toy, was now starting to shake his head back and forth. His face began to contort, and his brow wrinkled like someone was twisting his nose.

"No, you are mistaken. I know no one like that," the man said. Campanella eyed Pasquale and then shot a glance toward Santos. He brought his attention back to Bellini.

"Wrong answer. And this was just my first of many questions. Quite discouraging. Maybe I wasn't clear about being honest," Campanella said with raised eyebrows.

Then he said nothing for several moments, staring silently at the disheveled man, appearing to be contemplating what to say or do next. Without speaking, Campanella got up and left the barn. As he went, Bellini trailed after him with inquisitive eyes. When Campanella returned a few seconds later, the American held a glowing red-hot shaft of metal in his hand.

"Wait, what do you intend to do? I am the mayor here!"

"Ex-Mayor," Pasquale reminded.

Campanella went straight to Bellini and put the scalding rod up to his pale, blood-drained face. The heat it produced made Bellini jerk back and cry out. Campanella ignored his dramatics and moved the bar until it was only an inch away from his trembling jowls.

"Now, we will start again. But before you answer this time, I want you to know you have used up your one mistake. If you lie again, and I will know if you do, I plan on taking this rod and shoving it into your right eye. I will fill the socket with this blazing hot poker until the only thing remaining is a gaping hole. And let me remind you, we already know you did talk to this man. So, do you remember the conversation? A simple yes or no will do."

The man hesitated, but when Campanella inched the bar closer, the man blurted, "Yes, yes. Come to think of it, I do remember the man you speak of. Now, please take it away." Campanella pulled the bar back, but only a little.

"See, that was easy. Now, let's continue. What was discussed?"

The once cocky and prominent mayor closed his eyes and bowed his head. Campanella thought he was making an all-out effort to remember. But instead of talking, the man started blubbering like an infant and seemed unable to speak. Campanella shook his head in disgust. He took his booted foot and gave the crying man a quick jab to the leg. This small but unexpected action produced an effect in the man akin to being jabbed with an electrical cattle prod.

"Please! I cannot say. If I tell you, they will kill me," Bellini said through gulping sobs.

"And I will blind you in both eyes, which, believe me, will be worse than death."

As a means of emphasis, Campanella brushed the man's exposed arm with the hot metal. Bellini screamed as if shot. The voluminous shriek caused the blacksmith to poke his head in for a look. The sobbing man saw him and raised his arms in a pleading gesture. But the man didn't come to the ex-mayor's rescue, Rossi just smiled at the sniveling man and closed the solid wooden doors.

"I want answers, and I want them now. You'll lose your right eye if you don't speak the truth. While you're screaming and bellowing in agonizing pain, I'll ask you another question. You'll lose your left eye if you refuse to answer or tell me another lie. Either way, you will confess to me what I want to know. The only difference will be whether you do so with two good eyes, one good eye, or completely blind."

This declaration appeared to focus Bellini, and he blurted out, "The Englishman's name is Paul Jones. He's some type of attaché to the Prime Minister of England." As he confessed, Bellini's body began to jerk and shake. Occasionally, a snot-induced bubble would emanate from his nose, and the little politician would wipe it with one of his tattered sleeves.

"And why was he here in your town?" Campanella asked.

"He said he was stopping here only for a rest and a meeting before heading to another city near Naples."

"What city?"

"I don't know if he even said it. If he did mention it, I paid no attention to it as it did not concern me."

"Okay. We'll get back to that in a minute. Now, with whom did this man meet while he was here?"

"Well…I'm not sure of their names," Bellini said hesitantly. But when Campanella moved the bar closer, he quickly added, "But I did see them!"

"You saw the men Jones was talking to?" Santos asked.

"Yes," Bellini replied while agreeing vigorously.

"Were they from around here, someone you know?" Santos asked.

"No, no one from our town," the man choked out.

"Were they soldiers, either German or Italian?" Campanella asked.

"Not Germans. I am quite certain they were Italians, but they were dressed in civilian clothes. But like I said, no one from here."

Campanella glanced at Pasquale, but the man just shrugged.

"Okay, back to the city. I need you to think and think hard. What was the name of the city where the man was going?" Campanella asked.

"I don't think he said it," Bellini cried as Campanella pushed the bar closer. "I swear I'm telling you the truth, but…"

"But?" Campanella asked.

"But he did say something…it was…a place, a hotel – yes, it was a hotel!"

"Yes! Finally, we're getting somewhere," Santos said in satisfaction.

"But I can't remember the name," the dejected Bellini said as his head drooped.

"You must; you must remember. Try harder," Pasquale hollered as he jumped up from his hay bale. Campanella looked at the small bistro proprietor, who returned his gaze, shrugged, and sat back down.

"Bellini, you face some dire consequences here. The fact you were supporting the enemy will not go well for you. So, it is imperative to know where this man went. He told you the name, so it's in your head. Now think!" Campanella demanded.

Bellini covered his face with his hands and began to moan and cry again. His interrogators looked at each other and were about to give up when Bellini shot up from his seat.

"I'VE GOT IT!" the man yelled as he wiped his face and eyes again, "The Palazzo Turchini Hotel! That's what I heard him say - The Turchini. I'm sure of it!"

"Bravo Bellini. Bravo!" Pasquale exclaimed.

"Yes. Excellent," Campanella agreed as he got up. "And you're sure he said the Palazzo Turchini, no doubts?"

"None. I am positive," Bellini insisted, a smile of triumph on his face.

Campanella nodded to the rest of the group and headed toward the door with Santos and Pasquale in pursuit.

"Wait, what about me?" Bellini pleaded.

"I will let elders know you have helped. Maybe they won't hang you after all," Pasquale said as he winked at Campanella.

"Hang me? What do you mean hang me? Who said anything about

hanging me? I've lived my whole life in this town. Everyone knows me – they wouldn't dare," he blustered unconvincingly.

Do you know this hotel, the Palazzo Turchini?" Campanella asked Pasquale as the men walked back toward the bistro.

"No. But I know someone who will," Pasquale said. The bistro owner's short legs quickened their pace as this new train of thought gave the stubby appendages invigorated motivation.

Campanella and Santos followed as the small rotund man made a beeline to a building a few blocks past his cafe. The plain white stucco structure bore the name 'Francona's Fine Foods' written in Italian on a sign above the entryway. They entered a store that would have, in normal times, been filled with all manner of foodstuffs. But now, with the war raging throughout Europe and the German occupiers having confiscated all they could carry when they left, the store contained a bare-bones inventory of merchandise on its shelves.

The shop's owner, Anthony 'Little Tony' Francona, was perched on a stool behind a long row of cabinets at the back of the store. He was reading a bill of lading when he noticed the men approach.

"Pasquale," Francona said with genuine fondness. "Welcome. Another glorious day for our town!"

"Yes, hello, my friend. A great day indeed. But I have important business," Pasquale said as he hustled to where the man sat. He went about explaining the situation and the conversation with Bellini. When he got to the part about the Turchini, Francona's eyes lit up.

"I have stayed in that inn. It is a splendid little hotel near the Bay of Naples. The last time I visited, it was still quite beautiful and in operation, but…who knows now," Francona sighed as his shoulders rose and lowered like an ocean tide.

Campanella and Santos smiled at each other and asked the man for directions. After he had provided them with the necessary details, they thanked the shopkeeper and headed toward the door with Pasquale at the lead. As Pasquale's hand reached for the knob, Francona said matter of fact, "Those men the Englishman met with, are they important, or just the Englishman?"

Campanella spun back in Francona's direction. "Why, do you know something about them?" he asked.

"Well, one came in to buy coffee. Since he wasn't from around here, I kept an eye on him. When he pulled out his money to pay, his identification fell onto the floor behind my counter. I picked it up for him and noted his name when I did. Not sure why I did it, but I did."

"Do you remember it?" Pasquale asked as he hurried back to where Francona sat.

"Of course! I said I looked at it, didn't I?" Francona said, somewhat dismayed at his friend's question. "His name was Angelo Palmira. I'm certain of it."

"Can you describe his appearance?" Campanella asked.

"Oh, about five feet six inches tall, black hair, mustache…"

"So far, that's about ninety percent of the men in this part of Italy," Pasquale said with disdain. "Tony, think carefully, please. It's important. Did he have any unusual scars or facial features? Something we could look for?"

"Well," Little Tony said in contemplation, "he had a large nose. In fact, rather enormous for his face and quite crooked teeth."

Pasquale shot a look at Campanella and shrugged in resignation. The information seemed too vague to be truly helpful. The American thought otherwise.

"Excellent," Campanella said to the shop owner. "You've been a big help. Thank you."

Campanella and Santos walked back to the bistro with Pasquale, where they also took their leave to meet with the other partisans and relay all they'd learned. As Campanella related the story, he realized he was staring at tired, undernourished, and exhausted people. With no protests expected or received, the group decided to spend one more day of rest before heading out.

The Journal said they were close to confronting their inevitable date with history, and Campanella knew much was yet to be done. But first, the healing powers of sleeping on real beds and eating hot meals were required.

PART 8

CHAPTER 1

THE ASSASSINS

October 17, 1943

Naples, Italy

When the partisans reached the outskirts of Naples, an Allied security checkpoint was in place, and the freedom fighters were required to show identification papers to get into the city. They all nervously waited while the officials checked their credentials, but eventually, they were allowed to pass. It was evident Naples was liberated, but only to the degree that the Germans were gone. Order still needed to be preserved, and the Allied troops were now policing the city.

As they walked the streets, the group glared in amazement at the bustling throng of activity. The Allies were pouring more and more soldiers into and through the city, along with truckloads of equipment and supplies. There was a somber air about the city that contrasted markedly with the celebrations they'd seen in Pozzuoli a few days earlier.

Most of these inhabitants moved like zombies. Many, in fact, didn't even look at the partisans as they passed. They just kept at the task of clearing and combing through debris as they searched for any possessions they could salvage.

This part of Naples had been a grand and beautiful area. But now, that grandeur lay obliterated due to the relentless bombings leading up to the invasion. No words could describe the grim reality of what had happened: the city had been bombed more than any other Italian city in the war. Campanella spotted a man with his arm around a black-faced dog. He was sitting in front of gutted and debris-strewn remains of a row of shops and other buildings. He walked over to the disheveled man, spoke to him for several moments, and returned to the partisans.

"The man says the Palazzo Turchini is not open, damaged too much during the invasion. In fact, he said he knows of only a few businesses still in operation.

"Now, what do we do?" Salvatore asked.

"The Englishman and Palmira have been in town less than a week, so we ask everyone we see about them. We'll work in groups of three and comb the city blocks near the Villa in quadrants," Campanella said. He checked his watch and added, "It will be dark in an hour, so we need to find a place to sleep for the night. We'll get some rest and begin searching for Jones at first light tomorrow.

The group found an empty building and settled in. It was a far cry from the comfortable beds they were lucky enough to have in Pozzuoli, but they had slept in much worse.

Once the sun had risen the following day, Campanella assembled everyone outside to discuss a plan. He pulled a map of Naples from his pouch and opened it on the hood of a burned-out automobile sitting on the road. He segregated the groups and their areas of search by grids, giving each party a similar amount of the city to cover.

With instructions discussed and understood, the various teams headed out. Campanella, Paulo, and Berta would explore an area along the Bay of Naples. This route would bring them past the Villa Rivalta property. He chose this course so he could scout the manor and the grounds while looking for the Englishman.

It took a little over thirty minutes to reach the bay. They saw many people as they traveled and asked several about the individuals they sought. Most seemed numb to the questions and answered with a muted *"no"* or just shook their heads.

As Campanella surveyed his map, Paulo and Berta took in the unbelievable vision of the bay before them. Besides an area being cleared by the Allies, the inlet was nothing more than a body of water filled with damaged or destroyed seagoing vessels. The formidable piers and marinas one would expect in a harbor such as this were now mostly charred and floating timbers, crumbling concrete, and ravaged buildings.

As they were about to move on, Paulo motioned out to the bay. "Look at that." About two hundred meters from the shoreline, two men with fishing gear paddled through the waterway on a rigged grouping of tires, crates, and salvaged lumber. Berta grabbed Paulo's arm and pulled close to him. As the fisherman struggled to row their makeshift raft to the sea, she made the cross sign on her chest.

"This is awful," Berta said as a tear fell from her eye. "The fact anyone survived this destruction is incredible enough, but now they have to do this to feed themselves and their families…"

The three watched a few minutes more, and then Campanella motioned for them to go. They followed Via Nuova Marina Highway southwest toward the Villa. After forty minutes and three more turns, they arrived at the driveway to the home, which sat on a bluff overlooking the bay.

"The Rivalta," Campanella said as he nodded at the white stucco manor.

"Are we going up?" Paulo asked.

"Yes," Campanella said as he began to walk up the drive.

"What will we do when we get there?" Berta asked.

"We will take a good look at the grounds. See where the various entrances are and if any natural areas to hide can be found."

"We'll be looking for hiding spots?" she asked.

"For us, and possibly someone else. I don't want to be surprised if we return."

Berta frowned as she followed the big man up the drive. When they were about a hundred meters from the home, a slight bend in the roadway lay before them. Just as they were about to navigate this stretch, a car's engine could be heard starting somewhere close ahead. The three eyed each other and then dashed into the thick brush to their left. Once in and concealed, Campanella turned to view the car as it passed.

The automobile was a sleek, undamaged black Alfa Romeo. For the time traveler, it was a beautiful example of 'antique' Italian car designs. He'd only seen these vehicles at vintage auto shows or in magazines and was taken by its lines. This momentary appreciation for Italian craftsmanship vanished when he spotted the Englishman, Paul Jones, sitting in the front passenger seat.

The sight of him provoked an overwhelming urge in Campanella to pull out his handgun and kill the man then and there. But though his hand moved toward the weapon, he thought better of it. From all the in-depth briefings he'd received, he knew that if he killed Jones now, all hope of finding the other conspirators could be lost.

Berta's eyes widened as the veins in Campanella's neck bulged, and the muscles in his arms flexed in a sinewy show of power. She'd seen it before, more than once. Everyone had. And because of that, she knew the American was about to do something remarkable and tensed in anticipation. But the car passed, and he did nothing.

"What's happening?" she whispered.

"It's the Englishman. He's in the car," Campanella said without looking at her.

Berta lifted her head above Campanella's shoulder, with Paulo looking over her shoulder. She caught a quick glimpse of the rider and said, "Shouldn't we do something?"

"Yes, do our best to watch where he goes," Campanella replied. He turned to the two and said, "I'll try to track him on foot. Maybe he'll lead us to where they are staying. The two of you go back and meet the rest of the group at the rendezvous point. I'll follow you soon after." And before either could respond, he was gone.

"Shouldn't we go with him?" Paulo said as he began to stand.

Berta rose and pointed at Campanella as he sped away. In an instant, he reached a pace neither of them could have dreamt of keeping up with.

"You first," she said through a chuckle.

Paulo stared in the direction of where the car and Campanella went. The car was no longer in sight, and within a blink of an eye, neither was the American.

"Uh…," was the only word the stunned Italian could say as he somewhat stumbled out of the dense foliage.

CHAPTER 2

Campanella sprinted down the drive and then went right onto the roadway. At first, he didn't spot Jones, but after sprinting for several minutes, he saw the Alfa Romeo turning left a couple of hundred meters ahead. He reasoned he could stay close, as the car would need to reduce speed or stop due to debris still littering the roadways throughout Naples.

It wasn't long before his intuition proved correct. He turned at the same corner and almost ran up the back end of the slow-moving vehicle. The car was forced to decelerate as it weaved in and around several sections of a collapsed building.

Campanella dashed down a side street to his right, allowing him to avoid a potential confrontation. Making his way to the edge of the concealment, he peered past the corner and watched as the car progressed down the road. When it was safe to move, he left his hiding spot and followed. Several times he had to duck behind buildings, parked vehicles, and other obstructions to remain unseen.

He tailed the car this way for what seemed to be close to two or three kilometers, and then the car came to rest in front of the L'Hotel San Marco. Though not devoid of damage, this area of Naples was in far better shape than the parts of the city along the bay and to the east.

Coming to a stop, Campanella watched from about thirty meters back as the Englishman and his driver got out of the car and went inside the inn. A few shops and stores were on the same side of the road, and these were still in operation or at least still standing. He stopped in front of the business closest to the San Marco and waited. After about ten minutes of no movement, he decided to return to the partisan's rendezvous point and advise the others of his discovery. But a flicker of movement at the inn's entrance caused him to pause. Four men exited the building and stopped on the sidewalk. Campanella leaned a shoulder against the storefront's wall and watched and listened.

Being downwind, and thanks to his extraordinary hearing, he could catch that they had seen him following the Alpha Romeo. Now, they planned to confront him and take care of the situation.

The men chatted briefly, deciding how to approach the stranger and who would do what when they arrived. One man nodded, the others nodded back, and then the group turned and headed toward where he stood. As they advanced, they attempted to appear unconcerned about the lurking man.

As the four neared, Campanella scanned each for any outward physical traits of interest. Nothing appeared out of the ordinary. The only noticeable difference was that one man owned a nose well out of proportion to the rest of his face. *Could this be Angelo Palmira?*

The big-nosed man and the companion to his left slowed until stopping just before Campanella. The other two passed by but stopped a few feet behind. The position of the men, and him knowing of their intent to confront him, had the hair on the back of his neck standing on end. He could feel a massive adrenaline rush racing through every fiber in his body, yet he showed no outward sign that he was interested in the men.

Smiling broadly, the big-nosed man revealed a jagged row of teeth that reminded the American of a poorly carved jack-o-lantern. The man said in a calming tone, "Please, we want no trouble from you."

Campanella moved away from the wall to face the man, and when he did, felt a gun press into his back. He eyed the jagged-toothed man and smiled back. "You'll get no trouble from me. What's this all about?"

"They call me the Nose," the man said.

"No kidding? Why's that?" Campanella said with mock confusion in his voice that elicited no reaction from the man.

"Just follow me to the San Marco," the man said, motioning toward the three-story structure, "and we can talk in private."

Without waiting for a response, the Nose turned toward the inn. Campanella felt a nudge from the man with the gun and, though he was sure he could disarm his assailants, merely followed the lead man.

As they walked, Campanella knew that these men represented a contingent of the plotters but also understood he needed to find out if the rest were holed up in the inn. Upon entering, he quickly surveyed the interior of the building. Even though the inn was dark, and the windows shuttered and closed, his eyesight still picked out a man sitting alone in the shadows next to the registration desk.

The Nose led the group past the righthand side of the reception counter and continued down a long corridor to a door at the back of the hotel. As he opened the door, light flooded the hallway, making it difficult to see outside. Campanella blocked the glare with his hand, giving him a view of a sizeable open-aired courtyard beyond the doorway.

Solid, sound-inhibiting brick walls enclosed the area on all four sides. Two walls comprised part of San Marco's buildings, with the other two being that of two different structures. There was a marble fountain in the center. A few wooden shrub boxes with various bushes and flowering plants were positioned along three of the walls, and an ivy-covered trellis obscured the fourth wall.

It was secluded and private, perfect for an interrogation – or worse. Campanella almost smiled at the thought that this would be the most idyllic torture chamber he could ever imagine. To his right were several small tables and chairs. These were overflowing with men. Within seconds, he had registered each man in the courtyard and seen, at the center table, facing him and wearing the same dark suit, was the Englishman.

CHAPTER 3

Without Campanella's map and guidance, Berta and Paulo got lost returning to the rendezvous location. This cost them about an hour, but eventually, they happened upon their fellow travelers. Though relieved they'd finally found the partisan team, they were also disturbed when they realized Campanella was not among the group.

"Joseph hasn't made it back yet?" Berta asked her father.

"No," he said, perplexed. "Why? Isn't he with you?"

"We went to the Villa Rivalta during our search, and when we did, the Englishman was leaving the manor by car. He drove right past us. Joseph raced after him, but before he left, he told us to return here to advise you of what we saw. We would have gotten here much sooner, but we got lost," Berta said, concern clear in her voice. She turned, gazed off toward where she and Paulo had come, and added, "Something must have happened. Joseph should have made it back to us by now."

"I don't like this one bit," Santos said as he stared at his son Salvatore. "Without Campanella, we're finished."

"What will we do?" Berta asked her grandfather.

"Did you see which way they went?" Santos asked the young couple.

"Only a general direction from the Villa," Berta said. "He left us on the Villa's drive, and though we chased after him, we only saw him for a moment. He went right at the drive's end and raced down the road until he disappeared from our view. You know how fast he is…"

"Yes. Okay…" Berta's father said as he pulled a timepiece from his pants pocket. He studied it for an instant, "We will wait here for thirty more minutes. If he doesn't return, we will start a search starting from where you were last with him."

****

"Is this your man?" the Nose said to the Englishman.

"Indeed, he most certainly is," Paul Jones said as he turned his attention to Campanella. Jones wore a friendly, if not forced smile as he considered the man from head to toe. He stared at the American, marveling at his size, before saying, "First, you are more than a little rapid. In fact, I can't believe how fast you are, especially given your size. We saw you come down the drive at the Rivalta. We sped away, but each time we glanced back, you were visible in the rearview mirror for nearly two kilometers. How is that possible?"

"Good genes," Campanella answered smugly.

"Quite…" the man said. He leaned back in his chair, not saying a word until the unconvincing smile on his face transformed into what Campanella could have only described as a scowl. "Who the fuck are you, and why were you following my car?"

There were eleven men, including the Englishman. Campanella thought he might be able to take them all out…but he might not. He returned his focus to Jones and said, "My name's Campanella. When you passed me, I was standing at the street corner near the Rivalta. I noticed your right rear tire was low, so I wanted to let you know. When I caught up with you, the tire was fine, so I stopped at the building next to the inn to catch my breath."

Jones' eyes narrowed even further, and then the smile returned as he said, "I don't think so." Jones nodded at one of the men standing behind Campanella. He was a stocky, broad-shouldered thug with big meat cleaver hands and bulging Popeye forearms. Campanella had noticed the Englishman's subtle nod and realized what the gesture meant. Already in a heightened state of readiness, he was able to tense his torso muscles just as a fist slammed into his lower back.

Campanella's body was alert, but the blow made solid contact near his left kidney. A loud thud from the impact elicited a yelp of agony, but not from Campanella. He did wince, and it did weaken his knees, but the cry of pain came from the man delivering the punch. Jones registered a look of surprise and leaned over to look around Campanella. His man was holding his hand like it was broken.

Jones cocked his head in disgust. Sighing, he said, "I'm going to ask you again, and if I don't get the answer I want, it won't be a fist coming your way. So, why were you following me?"

Campanella, who had been speaking in Italian, now spoke in perfect English. "I'm an American. I was part of the Allied invasion forces now in Sicily. Once things settled a bit and I found out what was next, I realized it wasn't for me. During a training exercise, I was able to slip away. I went to Messina, stole a boat, and traveled to the mainland.

"I've been lucky so far, but I know I'll need assistance to get out of Naples. That's when I saw you drive by. And, well, I didn't take you for a German or Italian, so I decided to follow you to see if you could help me."

"A deserter," Paul Jones said with a derisive chuckle.

"Call it what you want."

Paul Jones studied the man, and though Campanella thought his acting job was damned impressive, he didn't think Jones was buying it. He glanced around the room one more time and began to coordinate in his mind a method to kill the entire group. He would take out the two assassins behind him with his knife. As they were going down, he would take the pistol from the back of his waistband and fire at the others, using one of the two dying men as a shield.

It would be a gamble, but one he thought he might have to take.

"So, American deserter," Jones repeated with his refined British accent, "Where is it you want to go?"

Campanella didn't hesitate with his answer. "North, I'm thinking France or England, if possible."

"There's a war going on, you know. Going in that direction might be a problem. You've heard of the Gustav Line? No one's getting past there anytime soon."

"Maybe, but isn't that where you'll eventually be going? Why can't I tag along with you? You could use a capable bodyguard."

"I'm afraid I have enough bodyguards," Jones said as he glanced at the Nose and the others in the courtyard.

"These guys?" Campanella said with a chuckle.

Upon hearing this, the thug who hit Campanella earlier decided to get revenge for his sore hand. Though Jones gave no acknowledgment, the man swung his uninjured hand at his intended victim's head. Campanella sensed his advance. In a lightning-fast move, he ducked out of the way. His attacker spun in a circle from the momentum of his swing, at which point his back became exposed. Fair play, in Campanella's mind, meant a blow to the exact spot the man had struck him earlier.

This time, the punch resonated throughout the enclosed courtyard, with the ensuing scream of pain from the man even louder and more ferocious than when he hurt his hand with his punch. The Italian fell to his knees, gasping and grabbing hopelessly at his back.

To Jones' surprise, Campanella faced him again as if nothing had happened. "Well," Jones said as he blinked in amazement, "Maybe I could use you after all. But…"

"But?" Campanella echoed.

"But you need to know I trust no one and will be watching you closely. If I don't like what I see, I won't hesitate to have you removed from our team at any time. Do you understand?"

"Of course," Campanella answered.

"Where are your personal belongings?"

"Nearby."

Jones eyed the Nose, nodded, and said, "Mr. Palmira will accompany you to get them. Once you do, you'll come back to the hotel."

CHAPTER 4

With reluctance, the partisans waited the thirty minutes Santos had allowed. When Campanella didn't show, they followed Berta and Paulo to the spot where the three had parted ways.

After arriving at the Villa Rivalta, Berta pointed down the road. "He went that way, but I have no idea where he went after that," Berta said as she looked at Paulo, who nodded in agreement.

Santos removed his hat and scratched his head. His face wrinkled, and he said, "I guess all we can do is head in that direction and look for him. If we come to any intersections, we'll set up a rendezvous location and time and split up. I can't think of any other way unless someone else has a better plan."

Each team member looked at the others with a hopeful gaze, but no one could offer any alternative. Santos shrugged and turned to head where the two youngest members had indicated. He'd only taken two steps when he saw two men appear over the rise of the street two hundred meters in front of them. At first, it was difficult to determine who it was.

Soon though, Berta released a cry of joy; it was Joseph walking their way. Berta pushed through the group to greet Campanella, but her father grabbed her by the arm. "Wait," the elderly Barilla said to his granddaughter.

"Why, what's wrong?" Berta asked.

"We don't know the man with Joseph, and he's had plenty of time to recognize and signal to us but hasn't..."

Santos turned toward the rest of the partisans and gathered in a circle. "Keep your eyes on me until Joseph either stops here or passes. We will decide what to do once we know what is happening."

They waited in uncomfortable silence for the two approaching men to near them. When the two were only a few meters away, Campanella struck the Nose with a hard chop to the carotid artery in his neck. The lithe man seemed to cave inward, and he lost consciousness. Campanella caught the folding Italian in mid-descent. Like a sack of potatoes, the American tossed Palmira over his shoulder and walked over to his companions.

"Uh…" Salvatore said as Campanella approached, "…friend of yours?"

"Soon to be a friend of ours or a friend of a long dirt nap," Campanella replied.

"A long dirt nap?" Paulo said, puzzled.

****

Campanella threw some water on the Nose's face, causing the man to reactively snort the liquid into his lungs. The man choked and gagged as he began to rouse. Self-preservation took over as the Nose gasped for a breath of air. Once his wheezing stopped and he got his bearings, the assassin strained his eyes to see what was happening. Campanella leaned in until he was only a few inches away.

"This time, I will be the one asking the questions," Campanella said, and as he did so, he reached over and gripped Palmira's neck. After a brief second or two, the Nose's eyes bulged in response to Campanella's fingers closing like a vice.

"With one hand, I can crush your throat, killing you in seconds. Do you believe that?"

The terrified man nodded his head.

"Okay," Campanella said as he released his grip slightly. "Taking a page from your boss's playbook, I have a few questions. If you answer with the truth, you live. If you don't…" Without removing his hand, he said, "First question. Were all of Jones's men there today, or does he have others?"

The Italian blinked and hesitated, but as Campanella started squeezing again, the Nose managed to choke out, "One more man! He has one more, and he works at the Villa."

"Excellent start. Next question. What are Jones' plans regarding Churchill's visit?"

The Nose's eyes bulged again. This time, however, Campanella hadn't tightened his grip. "How do you know about Churchill? No one knows about him," he said, his voice hoarse and forced.

"Well, I think I've proven that statement false. Churchill is due here soon, and Jones and his band of traitors are plotting to kill him. I need to know every single detail."

In stunned defiance, the man said, "You call me a traitor; I call myself a businessman."

"I'm going to call you a dead piece of shit," Campanella said as he squeezed the man's throat as an exclamation point. "Now, what is Jones planning to do?"

CHAPTER 5

"Okay," Campanella said to his group as they gathered close, "If our friend here is telling the truth, then I think I know what we must do. It won't be easy, and some of us may die," he let the statement hang in the air while it sank in. "There are more of them than there are of us, but these men fight a different way to German soldiers, no matter how disgusting the Germans have acted."

"What do you mean?" Arturo asked.

"These men are ruthless thugs. Assassins with no morals or scruples and would kill any of us without cause or reason," Campanella said before pausing. He took in a deep breath, and his lips tightened. After a moment of reflection, he sighed and said with unaffected sincerity, "None of you are like these people in any way. It's hard for me to say this, but if we're to be successful with our mission, we may have to sink to their level."

Campanella expected some resistance to this statement, but no one said a word. They only stared back at him with concerned but determined eyes. "Getting them all in one place as I saw them today might not happen again, so we will have our work cut out for us."

He motioned the group to follow him as he moved to an area of loose soil. Squatting down, he said, "Here is the street with the inn." He began to draw in the sand with his finger. "Several buildings line the opposite side with above-average vantage points. But I think we can only use one of them."

Campanella made dots on both sides of the street and pointed to a place on his makeshift map. "Most of these buildings have operating businesses in them except for one right about here," he said, indicating a spot almost opposite the San Marco. "Though the aerial attacks wrought minimal damage in this area, this building suffered enough to render it vacant. It's boarded up, so setting up our base there is likely safe.

"From this point forward, you'll take turns keeping an eye on the inn. I'll briefly describe each man's appearance, so we'll all know their faces.

Hopefully, we can get an idea of who's coming and going to see if there are any patterns. When someone leaves, one of you will follow, but not too close. We don't want anyone to know we are watching. If you lose them, come back, and we'll wait for the person to return. And remember, others may join these men, so report any new people you see to me."

"So, you are going back?" Franco asked.

"Yes. I need to be around the assassins as much as possible, especially the Englishman. I want to know everything he's doing."

"What are we going to do with this one?" Santos said as he nodded at the now gagged and tied up Palmira.

"I'm afraid that he's outlived his usefulness."

Berta's head spun around to look at Campanella. On occasion, the American had shown intense kindness and compassion. But at other times, like this, he all but admitted he would have to kill this man and could do so without a care. She was about to say something when Paulo interrupted her thoughts.

"What will you say when you return, and he's not with you?" the young Italian asked.

"Let me worry about that," Campanella said. He turned to his map in the sand and brushed it away with his foot. Berta eyed Campanella, and though she felt the need to say something, her mouth remained firmly closed.

After delivering his instructions, the partisans split into several groups and headed toward the inn. Campanella suggested they do this to prevent suspicion as they moved through the city.

The first two to leave were Salvatore and his brother Arturo. They would find a way behind the vacant building and look for an egress to be used to get in and out of without being detected. Once this was done, Salvatore would head to a front viewing window and start the surveillance of the San Marco. Arturo would go to a building a block south and wait for the following groups. As they arrived, he would guide them to the lookout's entrance.

This process took about forty-five minutes and went off without a hitch. As soon as Berta was brought in, she began exploring their temporary home until she came to the doorway of the room where her father stood. She gazed at him through eyes that appeared to have aged several years, but at the same time, she was still his little girl. She walked to his side, said nothing, and wrapped her arm around his waist.

CHAPTER 6

Campanella watched as the last of his partisan family disappeared from his view, leaving him and the Italian assassin alone. He paused and then turned toward the man whose life he was about to end. He frowned at the thought.

Campanella did not consider himself a cold-blooded murderer; in any case, he was truly disgusted by what he was about to do – must do. Despite taking no pleasure in this course of action, he had to resign himself to it. If circumstances were different, he could turn him over to the authorities. But no explanation that wouldn't cause suspicion to fall on Campanella himself could be given.

As Campanella approached the bound man, a look of knowing terror filled the Italian's deep-set eyes. The Nose began squirming and tried to scream, but the gag in his mouth made the sound muffled and unintelligible. Palmira started shaking his head in violent rebellion against the inevitable. Campanella ignored the pleas.

He snatched his captive up with little effort and tossed him over his shoulder again as if the man was weightless. With Palmira continuing to squirm and groan for help, he carried the man toward a group of trees just to the left of the Villa Rivalta. It seemed fitting that the assassin's life would soon end at the same spot where he and his band of thugs hoped to kill Churchill.

Less than two minutes later, the American re-emerged – alone.

He spent a few moments cleaning his knife and gathering his belongings before he headed for the inn. Campanella retraced his route to the villa to confirm something he'd seen along the way. There was a small tavern he and the Nose passed, which could provide the cover story he would need for Palmira's disappearance.

After walking about a mile, Campanella arrived at the bistro. As he was about to enter, he sighted the man he had punched in the back earlier sitting at a table on the restaurant's terrace. Campanella recognized the man's profile, and something intuitive told him not to go in.

As Campanella stood and watched from the opening, he could tell the goon was inebriated. He was loud and obnoxious, swilling and slopping more beer down his shirt than in his mouth. Two women sat with him, and in between gulps, he would grope and paw them. An idea popped into Campanella's head. It wasn't perfect, but it could work.

****

The man with his face buried in the newspaper he'd seen when he was first brought to the hotel was now standing behind the desk. Campanella gave him his name, which prompted the attendant to turn around and retrieve a key from a pegboard. He turned back and slid the key across the counter.

The bored proprietor reached into a drawer, pulled out an envelope, and handed it to Campanella. No words were spoken during these transactions, and no signature was asked for or given to provide him access to his room. The attendant nodded toward the corridor to his left. Campanella nodded back and headed to his room.

The key bore the number nine. He located the room and went in. Once he put his things down, he retrieved the envelope. Inside was a note with the number twenty-one written on it. Campanella left his room, went to the end of the hall, and saw an arrow pointing up a flight of stairs. On a sign below the arrow were the numbers twenty to thirty.

He went up the stairs and found room twenty-one and knocked. He was greeted for several seconds by silence before the door creaked open. A man he recognized from the terrace earlier stood in the doorway glowering. Campanella walked by him without acknowledging his presence.

As he entered, Campanella spotted the Englishman, Paul Jones, sitting on a small sofa next to a young woman wearing a thin negligee – a ridiculously tiny and flimsy negligée. One of the girl's legs was draped over Jones's, and the other leg was on the floor. In this pose, it was apparent what the girl wasn't wearing under the frock. When she saw Campanella's unfamiliar face, she quickly lowered the left leg alongside the other. But if modesty was her aim, it was too late.

Jones appeared amused by her reaction to the newcomer. But when he glanced up at Campanella, the humorous expression disappeared. He glowered past the American. "Where is the Nose?"

"Well, by now, I'd say he is either getting drunk or getting laid," Campanella said with a chuckle.

"What the hell are you talking about? Where is he?" Jones demanded.

"There's a little tavern a few blocks from here. The Nose said he saw one of your guys inside and told me to come here, and he'd be along in time. I watched him head in and go straight for a table with a man and two women sitting at it. I recognized the man as the one I got acquainted with earlier in the courtyard. I didn't ask any questions and headed here as instructed."

The girl put her hand in Jones' lap, but the Englishman brushed it away and stood. His body was rigid, and his face reddened as he blazed at the man who opened the door for Campanella.

"Bruno, do you know the tavern?" Jones asked the man.

"I do," the burly man said.

"Then go get those two idiots and bring them back here – NOW!" Jones shouted. He sucked in a breath and turned to Campanella. "I told Benedetti not to go back there. And the Nose, he should have known better," Jones said, as his face contorted into a scowl.

After a moment or two of contemplation, Jones glowered at the woman and said between clenched teeth, "You'll need to go. Get your things and get out. I'll see you tonight at the usual time." The girl started to object, but Jones' intense gaze caused her to shrink back and stay quiet.

"Sit," Jones said to Campanella as he got a cigarette from a case in his jacket pocket. He offered one to the American, but he refused. The Brit drew out a match and lit the cigarette. After a few deep pulls, he explained, "We have a job to do, a rather important one. It will take us about a week or so to complete, and then, well, we'll see about getting you to wherever you want to go. In the meantime, you'll be helping us with our little task."

"What is this little task?" Campanella probed, almost as an afterthought. Of course, he knew what they were here to do, but any other information he could wrangle from Jones would be helpful.

"Your job is to do whatever I ask you to do. Unless you have a problem following orders?"

"Nope," Campanella stated without hesitation.

"Good. Now, once the Nose returns, we'll begin," Jones said as he took another deep pull from his cigarette. Campanella studied the room while they waited for the man who would never appear. They were in a small sitting area. The room had an exterior door leading to a balcony and a second door. Campanella guessed that it led to the man's sleeping quarters. A writing desk, the sofa Jones had been on, a rectangular wooden coffee table, and a bulky cloth-covered chair finished off the furnishings.

The balcony overlooked the street in front of the inn. This view meant the structure the partisans hid in had a perfect sightline for surveillance. The building had a second floor, but Campanella wasn't sure the level was safe.

After a few moments, Jones started to pace. The veins in his neck began to throb, and he appeared ready to implode. Then came a knock at the door. Jones hurried over to it and grasped the handle. Before he opened it, he called out, "Yes?"

"It's us," a voice from the other side answered.

Jones yanked the door open and, without a glance, turned and walked back toward the chair where Campanella sat. Once behind Campanella, he spun expectantly back in the door's direction, prepared to rant. To his surprise, not only was the Nose not there for him to berate, but the man he sent to retrieve the scraggle-toothed Italian now stood in the room's entry, bloodied, and bruised.

"What the hell?" Jones snapped as he pulled the cigarette from his lips. "What happened to you?"

"Ask this asshole! I repeatedly asked where the Nose was. And he repeatedly told me to go screw myself. Finally, I insisted he return to talk to you about it with me. He again told me to go screw myself. And when I put my hand on his shoulder to get him up to go, this drunken bastard tried to kill me," Bruno said.

Jones was livid, turning shades of red as each second ticked by. Campanella watched the whole scene unfold in silent amusement.

"Where…is…the…Nose?" he growled through grinding teeth.

"Like I told this persistent pain-in-the-ass, I haven't seen that little dipshit since earlier today," the bar brawler spewed.

"Really?" Jones responded as he sidestepped the chair Campanella sat in. Now, almost snarling, he said, "The American says he and the Nose saw you at the bar. He said the Nose entered and went directly to where you were sitting. So, I know you were there and with him. Now, do you want to re-think your answer?"

The man shot a blazing look of hatred at Campanella while he reached around and touched the painful reminder of their previous encounter. "Neither the Nose nor this asshole came into the bistro, so I don't care what he said," the man insisted as spit mixed with blood flew from his mouth.

Jones considered Campanella, who only lifted his shoulders and rolled his eyes. This small gesture triggered an immediate response in Jones. His brow began to narrow, and deep rage-filled creases materialized. A long moment passed, and Jones walked toward the two men by the door.

Bruno recognized that the rage on Jones' face wasn't directed at him, so he slid deftly out of his way. This move opened a clear path to the other man.

"Claudio, I have tolerated your drinking, vulgar treatment of women, and lack of intelligence because you possess certain attributes I desired. But the numerous run-ins with the Nose and the fact he is now missing, and you were the last to be seen with him, leaves me no choice. I've decided your services are no longer needed…" Jones said flatly. And with that, a switchblade appeared from somewhere hidden in his sleeve and into the palm of his hand.

The Englishman plunged the knife into the larger man's chest so fast that his victim had no time to react. The Italian, innocent, at least for this latest crime, stared down in horror as blood began spewing from the knife wound. Benedetti's legs buckled, and he fell to his knees while clutching vainly at his chest. Campanella, though surprised by Jones' faith in his made-up story, watched impassively.

The wounded man wobbled a few times before falling face forward. Instinctively, he reached out with his hand to grab something to stop his fall. The only thing within his reach was Jones, who merely sidestepped the dying man's grasp.

The barrel-chested man hit the ground with a hulking thud. A pool of red ooze began to form around his upper chest, under his face, and into his capacious Nose. Still breathing, though just, he started inhaling the blood, causing him to snort and choke. This desperate drowning lasted a few more moments, and then the man expired.

Two down, Campanella thought as he forced himself not to smile.

"Joseph, as you can see, I cannot tolerate nor allow anyone or anything to disrupt my plans. This man has been a problem since he joined our team. Now, the problem is no more. Please take heed."

Campanella nodded, though his facial expression showed no fear of the apparent threat.

"This changes things," Jones said to Bruno. He turned and entered a room, which Campanella reasoned was the bedroom. After several minutes, he reappeared with a note and handed it to Bruno. "Take this to our contact. You know where to go?"

"Yes," Bruno acknowledged, and he headed out the door.

Jones checked his timepiece and said to Campanella, "You're done for today. Go down to Gino at the desk and ask him to fix you something to eat, and then go to your room and don't leave. I'll send for you in the morning."

Campanella nodded, got up, and did as he'd been told, though with a slight change. He got the food and went to his room, but he didn't stay there. He went straight to the rear window and crawled out on the ledge. Then, using a drainage pipe he'd seen earlier, he slid down the conduit to the alleyway below. Once on the ground, he crept to an area just south of the inn.

After being sure he wouldn't be noticed, he dashed across the street and behind the building where the other partisans were hiding. He tapped on the back door and was soon greeted by Santos. Upon entering, he gave the food to Berta and then gathered the team to describe the events in Jones' hotel room.

"…I don't know where, but they disposed of the body," explained Campanella. He hesitated momentarily and then said, "First, thank you all for your sacrifices to help me with this mission. There is no way I could have gotten here without you. But we are now at a critical stage, and certain things need to be discussed."

Though I have thought our situation might be different by now…" Campanella hesitated and looked at Berta and Paulo, "…they are not. So, here it is in a nutshell. According to the diary, the assassins will be eliminated in six days."

"Six days? How? How does it happen? And how are we involved?" Berta asked.

"The exact details are not clear. But your grandfather's Journal explains that an explosion will occur at the San Marco. The entire team of assassins will be killed, except for Jones and one other man. Those two somehow are not in the building when it happens."

"Well, this brings up two important questions. One, who is the other man? And two, where are they killed?" Salvatore asked.

"We don't know the other man's name. The Journal doesn't reveal it to us. But we do know they die at the Rivalta. So, I believe the second man is the person already working for Jones at the villa."

"Okay, here's a question. Does the Journal say who kills those two men?" Berta proposed.

There was a long pause here as Campanella considered what to say. He realized his response would bring an outpouring of rage that, though deserved, he wasn't looking forward to. The American took a moment and surveyed the group before fixing his gaze on Santos. Campanella believed he would be the angriest with his following words and wanted to address him directly.

Before Campanella could start, Berta walked in front of him, forcing Campanella to speak to her. She asked again with an abrupt manner, "By whom, Joseph? Who kills these horrible men?"

Campanella stared straight into the girl's eyes, "By you, Berta."

Stunned by this statement, Berta took an unbalanced step backward and said, "By ME…are you crazy?" She expected the answer to be anyone else in the group but her.

"I'm sorry. But according to the Journal, it is, in fact, you who kills Jones and the other man," Campanella said ruefully.

"Joseph, this can't be true. You never once mentioned this at any time when we talked. I would never have let her come had I known. And I will not agree or allow her to kill anyone," Santos demanded as he took a few animated steps in Campanella's direction.

Campanella's mouth opened to speak, but Salvatore stepped in between them and began a protest of his own. Within a blink of an eye, Paulo joined the fray, and soon, the rest of the partisans were verbally assaulting him. Berta, who had been in Campanella's face seconds earlier, now found herself behind the shouting throng. She had gone pale and was now staring blankly at the American.

The American held up his hands and asked everyone to stay calm and give him a chance to explain. The room hung thick with anger-stricken faces, all glaring with malice toward Campanella.

"I didn't say anything before because I hoped I could change the events. I wanted to remove Berta from the equation by keeping her away from this whole thing. In fact, before we left your home, I tried…" Campanella stopped and swallowed hard. His throat had gone as dry as the desert he'd fought in before his accident. He had to tell the truth, though, because everything, including the death of Marco's brother, was in the Journal.

"I know you all are angry, and you have every right to be. But it was drilled in me that if I changed anything or prevented any of you from coming, it could and probably would produce unimaginable consequences.

"Unfortunately, Berta somehow managed to join us and be involved with everything we did along the way. It has been and will continue to be my objective to spare any of you harm or pain, but I only know what the Journal says happens. No matter how I try to prevent her participation, whether Berta is involved in these men's deaths may be out of my hands."

"Well, maybe you can't keep her out of this, but I can," Salvatore fumed. "For the next six days, she stays here under guard. She can be a lookout, but Berta will not leave this building until things are resolved. And I must tell you, I am extremely disappointed in you for deceiving my family and putting Berta in harm's way. You have asked for trust. Trust in unimaginable things, and we've given to you only to be lied to."

"Santos, I am truly sorry. But you must understand, I had no other choice. From the start of this mission, even as far back as when I visited Antonio to bring him your Journal, every step of the way had to happen as it was written. It had happened already. Don't you see? You wouldn't have written it had it not. But listen to me. I totally agree with keeping Berta here and out of the way. I don't want any harm to come to her, nor do I want her to do this awful thing," Campanella said with conviction, though he was pretty sure it wouldn't make a difference.

"Now, here's something else playing out as written," Campanella added with controlled emphasis. "Jones told me he would be going back to England for a few days and would return around the middle of November. He says he will be leaving on the twenty-fourth," Campanella explained.

"Six days from now," Santos said slowly.

"Yes, the same day as the explosion," Campanella said, preempting

Santos' next thought.

"The explosion must be caused by the bomb Palmira talked of, the one to be used to kill the Prime Minister. Have you seen it? Do we use it on them, or do they do it to themselves?" Arturo asked.

"I haven't seen it, but Santos wrote that the bomb was in Jones' room. He wrote about a struggle between one of Jones' men and me right before the detonation."

"Are you injured?" Salvatore asked.

"No, not severely."

"Great, and then what? If this kills everyone, how does Berta get thrown together with Jones?"

Somehow, Jones comes across Berta and takes her to the villa," Campanella said.

"Well, I can tell you for certain that this will not happen. I will not let Berta out of my sight," Salvatore said, and Paula nodded in agreement.

CHAPTER 7

October 22, 1943

At noon on Saturday the twenty-second, Campanella was in his room cleaning his handgun for the seventh time. Then, as he checked his watch for the tenth (or was it the eleventh?) time, there was a knock at his door. He put the gun in the back of his waistband and went to the door. Standing outside was Paul Jones.

"I need you to come with me," he said as he glanced around the American's room. "Meet me out front in ten minutes."

Ten minutes later, Campanella emerged to find Jones waiting for him in the same black Alfa-Romero sedan he had followed a few days earlier. "Get in," Jones said from the backseat.

Campanella got in the opposite side, and then the car sped off. No talking occurred between the two as the driver made his way to the Villa Rivalta and stopped in the driveway.

"Do you know this place?" Jones asked as he pointed toward the villa.

"No," Campanella replied.

"It's called the Villa Rivalta. You may not believe it by looking at it now, but this was a grand manor at one time," Jones said with a strange hint of pride. "Though still structurally sound, it has become a bit run down. I'm afraid the war has taken a toll on the old girl."

"Okay, times are tough, but why show me this?"

"Right to the point, I like that. I'm showing you this because the villa will play a big part in your future and mine, old chap. You see, an extraordinary man is coming here soon, and the estate owners, people I am quite close with, have asked me for some help. Specifically, they need someone to clean up the grounds and spruce up the place a little. I told them I possessed the perfect man for the job – you."

"Me?" Campanella said, surprised.

"Yes, you. As I mentioned, I'm scheduled to leave in a few days, and when I'm away, I want you to do everything you can to get the grounds in order. And while you're here, and this is the important part, I'd like you to keep track of who comes and goes. Can you do that?"

"Sure, I guess so."

"Jolly good," Jones crowed. "Okay, the morning before I leave, I will bring you here to introduce you to the owner, and you will settle in. They'll give you a room, and you will go to work. Do whatever is needed until I get back. Understand?"

"Understood," Campanella said.

****

That night at eight p.m., Paul Jones walked out of the San Marco on his way to visit to his local Italian concubine. He stopped to light a cigarette, and as he did, he happened to glance across the street.

At first, he stared at the boarded-up building without reaction. But as his mind focused on a broken window in the building's lower left corner, he thought he saw something. He reached into his jacket and retrieved the handgun he kept there. While dragging heavily on the cigarette, he crossed the street and walked over.

The Englishman leaned in, but the broken pane's opening was barely large enough for half a person's face to fit, and he could not get a good look. He began to wonder if he'd seen anything after all. He looked again – but still nothing. Jones straightened and took another pull on his cigarette. Frowning, he pocketed his gun, took out his lighter, and lit it. He put it through the opening but could see nothing unusual, only the lighter's flickering flame. Jones scoffed in frustration, extinguished the lighter, and walked away.

The entire time that the Englishman was hovering above the window, Berta had been inches away, crouched below and to the left of the opening. Campanella had been watching, too. Expecting Jones to depart for his nightly rendezvous, he had climbed through his window and down

370

the same drainpipe he'd used the first day he'd arrived at the San Marco. He intended to hide in the shadows, waiting for Jones to leave the inn, and then go to the man's room to look for the bomb. All had gone to plan until Jones pulled the gun. When he saw this, Campanella silently unsheathed his knife.

As Jones moved toward the partisan's building, Campanella shadowed him while remaining hidden. It would be dangerous if Jones attempted to search the partisan's hiding spot further rather than just peering in. Once the Englishman departed, Campanella made his way to a trellis running up the outside wall. The wooden framework led to the balcony of Jones' room. Like a cat burglar half his size, Campanella scampered up the latticework and stood beside the French doors leading inside.

A table lamp lit the assassin's room, and in the soft glow of yellow light sat a man in a cloth-covered chair – it was the behemoth, Bruno.

Campanella stood silent, contemplating what to do. With only two days before the bomb's supposed detonation, he hesitated to wait any longer to see if Bruno or another of Jones' men would be in the room. On the other hand, if he didn't delay and acted then, he'd have to kill Bruno and dispose of his body. Not an issue. And yet, if he did eliminate Bruno, Jones would be suspicious of another man from his team disappearing, of that there would be no doubt. Neither option seemed to be advantageous.

After waiting another few moments, Campanella decided the timing of the explosion was too close to take a chance. So, if Bruno had to die, he had to die. He scanned the room and determined that that the man's back would face him the entire time if he entered from the correct angle.

Pulling his knife, Campanella prepared to move when another thought raced through his mind. If he didn't manage to kill the man cleanly and a struggle ensued, both their blood could be spilled. This messy scenario would be nearly impossible to explain or ignore. He put his knife back in its sheath. His next alternative was to sneak up to the man and snap his spine. The only problem with this was Bruno's size. With such a thick, muscular neck, killing him may not be instant, and so was inherently risky.

He'd have to risk it, though. Even if his spine didn't sever in the attempt, it should cause enough damage to allow Campanella to subdue him. He grabbed the doorknob and began to turn. At that very moment, a knock sounded at Jones' outer door. Bruno jumped up and worked his way over.

If Campanella stayed where he was, he'd be seen by whoever walked in, so he slid back to his original spot on the balcony. When Bruno opened the door, three men from his group came in.

They laughed and talked, and one of the three went straight for a cabinet opposite Campanella's hiding place. The man retrieved a liquor bottle, and Bruno grabbed four glasses from the desk. Campanella glanced down at his watch as the man with the bottle poured. It read 12:24. "Screw it," he thought and went back over the railing and down the trellis.

Once on the ground, Campanella dashed over to the partisan's building and went through the back entrance. He went to a room at the back right-hand side where the group set up their sleeping quarters. As he entered the room, he saw a disturbing look on everyone's face. "What's wrong with you all?" he asked. "What's happened?"

"We think Jones may have seen us," Santos explained. "Berta was taking her turn watching when he came out of the inn and lit a cigarette. As he smoked, he stared at where she had been, then came straight over and looked in. Berta had crouched down and to the side but couldn't leave the room before he got to the window. She doesn't think she was spotted, but she can't be sure".

"Yes, I was watching from the south end of the hotel. Jones did see something, but I don't think he was sure what it was. If he decides to investigate, it won't be until tomorrow, and I'll know about it," Campanella said.

"You saw?" Berta asked.

"Yes, I did, and I think we're okay."

"Were you able to check out his room?" Salvatore asked. "Did you find the bomb?"

"No. Four of Jones' men were there, and I didn't want to risk it. I'll try again tomorrow."

"What if they show up then, too," Marco speculated.

"If that happens, well, I guess I'll have to make a different decision," Campanella replied. "Listen, everything is going to work out. With only a day or two left, we'll soon have this behind us."

Campanella remained with the team for another fifteen minutes before leaving for the night. As he walked out the door, Santos followed him.

"Joseph," he called.

"Yes, Santos," Campanella answered as he turned back to the older man.

"Remember, Berta stays here. She is out of this from this point forward. I can't let anything happen to my granddaughter."

"I know. And I hope you know and believe this: I'd give my life to save her or any of you. Now, get some sleep. Things might get rough soon, and we all need our wits about us."

The next day went without incident. If Jones did have any ideas about what he might have seen, he didn't mention it to anyone. Had he sent someone to go into the building to check the place out, the situation would have gotten messy.

That night, like clockwork, the Englishman was out the San Marco's front door by eight p.m. Once again, he stopped at the entrance, lit a cigarette, took a deep drag, held it in, and let the smoke drift out of his mouth while re-inhaling it through his nose as it rose. Jones glanced across the street and thought of the events from the previous night. His mouth twitched in consideration, and then he blew out the remaining smoke from his lungs and headed off.

As with the night before, Campanella observed Jones from the same darkened recess at the south corner. When he was out of sight, he climbed the trellis to the Englishman's balcony. Moving to get a good view, he saw that the light was on again, and Bruno was sitting in the chair, again. Before he'd made his descent, Campanella had decided. If Bruno were there, he would dispatch him before anyone else joined him. Now, assuming the role of assassin, Campanella slid over to the door and grabbed the handle.

As fate would have it, someone knocked on Jones' door, just as they had the previous night. Campanella stood in frozen astonishment as the déjà vu moment unfolded. But this time, instead of inviting the men in, Bruno forced the group to turn around and go back out. Though they moaned in protest, Bruno walked out and closed the door behind him.

Campanella didn't hesitate. He opened the unlocked door of the balcony and entered the room, which was neat and in perfect order. Campanella needed to search the room as quickly as possible, so he would have preferred a bit of a mess. He didn't want it to look as if someone ransacked the place. Now, he'd have to be careful and take his time – as best he could.

Using only the light from the outer room, Campanella scanned the area. He saw nothing out of the ordinary. No boxes or crates or anything that might contain a device. He moved to the closet and pulled on the door handle. The door's hinges creaked in defiance as it swung open. Campanella gave it no mind.

The closet contained a grouping of organized and arranged clothes. Jackets first, then shirts, and finally pants hanging from a wooden rod. Below the hanging clothes were three pairs of shoes, side by side, in perfect order. And there were two hats on the shelf above the hanging clothes. The man was undoubtedly obsessive about his tidiness. Campanella examined every nook and cranny, top to bottom, tapping on the walls, the floor, and the ceiling, looking for hidden compartments. But there were none, and he discovered no bomb or anything resembling bomb-making materials.

After closing the closet door, he scanned the bedroom again. There was a bed, a single dresser, and an end table with a lamp next to the bed. He searched under the bed but found nothing. He then glanced at the ceiling; it was solid, with no opening visible. Campanella scratched his chin in unease and then turned his focus on the dresser.

Though it seemed unlikely a bomb could fit in such a small space, this was the only place left in the room he hadn't investigated. If it wasn't there, it could only mean the Jones must have hidden it in another room or part of the San Marco. He crossed his fingers and hoped this wasn't the case.

The cabinet had five drawers in all. The top two contained a combination of socks, underwear, ties, and belts, with the following two holding other garments, including work pants and undershirts. Before Campanella got to the last drawer, he glanced at the time. His watch read 20:32.

"Please be here," he said under his breath.

The dresser's bottom drawer was taller than the first four, and as he pulled on the handle, Campanella could tell something much heavier than clothes was inside. When the drawer was a third of the way open, he could see why. An explosive device filled the inner dimensions. He rubbed his hands up and down on his pants before pulling the drawer out until it was almost two-thirds open.

This position gave a clear view of a TNT-laced bomb with a timer wired to a fuse system. Campanella examined the arming device and soon determined that one flip of a toggle switch could activate the bomb. He considered taking the explosive device and disposing of it. But doing this would only alert Jones that an outsider was aware of the bomb and possibly the plot. That plan wouldn't work. No, he'd have to come up with something else.

Unlike the more complicated bombs Campanella had defused during his time in Iraq, this one only had three wires, and they were all black. If he cut the correct wire and hid the strands so they couldn't be seen, it might be enough of a delay to cause Jones to miss the window of Churchill's visit. Campanella rechecked the time. He was surprised to see fifteen minutes had passed since he squatted down, and it was approaching nine p.m.

Retrieving a small pair of wire cutters, he began following the leads from their various start and end locations. After determining what needed to be done, he was about to cut one of them when he felt the hair on the back of his neck bristle.

This astonishing sense of peril, an awareness intensified due to his surgeries, surged through his body. He stood and stepped over to the shadowy space next to the doorway. He waited and listened in a state of hyper-alertness. He could see most of the apartment from where he hid, but not all. He glanced at the dresser. The drawer was still open. Should he close it and come back? Or should he deal with whatever threat his senses were alerting him to and finish the job?

The decision was made for him when his internal alarm sounded once again. This time, he couldn't react fast enough as a massive fist slammed into the right side of his face. The strike spun him around and hurled him into the dresser he'd just been searching. The wooden bureau tilted precariously upon his impact, but he and the furniture stayed upright, if only momentarily.

Stunned and seeing stars, Campanella teetered and felt darkness filling his mind. And yet, even with this rushing sensation of unconsciousness, his survival instincts kicked in. He moved away from the dresser and raised his arms in a shielding posture. Blinking madly and shaking his head, the staggered American tried to regain clarity. That's when the second fist came flying his way.

Though he saw this assault coming, the punch still made it through his defenses and caught Campanella on the chin. The blow was another solid connection, and it sent him reeling backward. He crashed with all his weight into the furniture, and the dresser slammed back against the wall and to the ground, spilling much of the contents of the top two drawers.

At this point, a lesser man would have been down for the count, and Campanella's hulking assailant surely expected this to happen. But the attacking man's adversary was hardly ordinary.

Bruno continued throwing his huge bear-sized fists from every angle into every part of the American's torso and head. However, the fog from the earlier connection to Campanella's jaw had cleared enough that most of these punches were deftly blocked. After lengthy seconds, the barrage slowed as his attacker began to tire. This was when Bruno made the error he would have little time to regret.

Campanella saw the opening and threw his arms around him. The two men grappled like Greco-Roman wrestlers. They bounced off walls and furnishings, groping and grabbing each other, looking for any posture that would give them an edge.

Still in one another's grasp, they stumbled across the sitting room and spilled over the bulky cloth chair, smashing into the small writing desk. The dilapidated wooden structure exploded into a useless pile of splinters, but amazingly, the pair remained upright. Though Campanella was easily Bruno's better, the tight space and ill-placed furniture made it difficult for him to get the upper hand.

Suddenly, Bruno, desperate for some form of leverage, tried to squeeze the air from Campanella's lungs. This plan of attack was also a terrible mistake. Campanella reached up to the Italian's face and, using his thumbs, began to crush the big brute's eyes.

The Italian Bruno let out a terrifying scream, released his grip, and stumbled backward. He raised his hands and rubbed his eye sockets to alleviate the excruciating pain. This lowering of his guard was all Campanella needed. His punishing haymaker caught Bruno flush on the side of the face and sent him hurtling toward the doors leading to the balcony. The assassin crashed through the door, sending glass and wooden pieces flying.

On watch at the vacant building during this time, Salvatore stared in astonishment when he saw the man explode through the door. "My God! My God!" he gasped. "Everyone, come quick."

The anxious alarm brought all the partisans to the window, with every group member craning to see what Salvatore was gawking at. The opening was not large enough to afford a view, so Marco and Arturo frantically grabbed at a couple of the boards covering the windows. They pulled them down and away at the exact moment Campanella came storming out onto the balcony.

"Look! It's Joseph!" Berta cried.

Just then, Bruno regained his wits and saw Campanella racing at him. He put his head down, pushed off the balcony railing, and ran toward the American. They charged one another like two massive elk preparing to head-butt. But, right before the inevitable collision, Campanella ducked Bruno's outstretched arms, slid to the side, and kicked out his leg. This lightning-quick action tripped his attacker, and he flailed backward through the doorway, groping wildly at what was now thin air.

As Bruno tripped over Campanella's leg, the American went into a roll, bounced up to his feet, and spun around. He was about to race after the man, who was desperately trying to catch his balance when a movement out of the corner of his eye caught his attention. It caused him to take a quick but fateful glance.

He saw Jones rushing toward the inn. The man had noticed the commotion on his balcony and was running to investigate. When Campanella turned his head back to Bruno, the man was crashing into him at chest height. The Italian's bulk and momentum sent both men sailing backward. They hit the railing, flipped over the barrier, and plummeted toward the roadway some twenty-five feet below.

Campanella grabbed Bruno in a bear hug as they tumbled over the side and used his extraordinary strength advantage to maneuver his body so that when they impacted the ground, his weight would be on top of the other man.

This fact and the odd angle of the fall caused the Italian's head to hit the brick road first and split open, killing him instantly. Campanella, though not injured from the landing, had the wind knocked out of him. He rolled over, gasping as he desperately tried to refill his lungs with oxygen.

Jones had come to a screeching halt as he witnessed two men hurtling over the side of the balcony. He remained frozen in place as their bodies slammed onto the roadway.

"What the fuck?" Jones stammered. The area was dim and shadowy, but wasn't that Bruno and the American flying off the balcony of his room? He knew the men had to be hurt, or worse, but he also knew that going over to check on them was not a good idea. He couldn't afford to be involved in something that might affect the prime minister's assassination.

A small side street led to the San Marco's courtyard. Jones turned to go in that direction, but before he had taken two steps, an explosion of massive proportions erupted from the inn's second floor. He watched as the entire top half of the San Marco appeared to implode, sending deadly missiles of stone, brick, and wood, plus all manner of other contents, from the inn's upper rooms.

The hurtling debris assaulted the surrounding structures with catastrophic results, but the concussive shock wave caused by the explosion was equally as destructive as these flying fragments. This unseen force knocked Jones flat on his back and pummeled the building where the partisans hid, forcing the inhabitants to race for cover.

Large chunks of the ceiling rained down on the partisans while plastered walls buckled, cracked, and crumbled. The building shook and trembled but otherwise remained upright. After the dust settled, Santos called out to see if anyone had been injured and to determine what happened. Then, in a moment of instant awareness, he blurted – "JOSEPH!" Everyone dashed back toward the front to check on their leader.

Campanella, who hadn't fully regained his senses or breath from his balcony fall, was now covered by debris from the inn's destruction. He stayed conscious but knew he was cut and gashed in too many places to count. He felt blood trickling down his face and neck, and he couldn't move either of his hands to investigate how severe the wounds were. The wreckage from the inn had pinned his arms to his sides.

For several minutes, nothing happened. It was as if the world was standing still. There was no movement from any part of what was left of the San Marco nor from within the building which housed the partisans. Campanella lay on the ground, wondering if he would die under the massive pile of rubble. Had anyone seen him fall there?

At that moment, Paul Jones scrambled back to his feet. He had been far enough away to be free of injury. So, besides a ringing in his ears and his confusion about what had happened, Jones was unhurt. Reaching into his pocket, he pulled out his handgun. A flicker of movement to his right caught his eye, and he spun around with the gun raised. Two of his team emerged from the inn's courtyard, saw Jones in the street, and raced to see if he needed help.

****

"Gather your weapons," Salvatore said as he peered out of the broken window of their hideout, "Some of those men are still alive, including Jones. If Joseph is…well, no matter his condition, we must finish what we came to do! Paulo, you remain with Berta. Don't leave, and don't leave her side."

Those going outside retrieved their gear and headed for the street. As they rounded the corner of the building, the Englishman spotted them and reacted. Before the explosion, he'd planned to return to the San Marco, but things had changed. Without the bomb, all was lost. He needed to flee.

Turning to his comrades, Jones said, "Those men need to be eliminated. I'll head down that alley and come up from behind them. I don't care who those people are. Kill them all." Jones nodded and then sprinted off. The two thugs seemed shocked by his instruction but did as they were told. They got down in a crouching position with handguns drawn. Seconds later, two more assassins emerged from the courtyard and joined them.

Jones' four men had no idea who the advancing group was, but the strangers were armed and pointing their weapons at them, so they began firing. The distance between the two enemies prevented the assassin's handguns from being accurate. But even with this tactical disadvantage, a bullet sliced through Marco's thigh as he ran. The wound was more of a graze than a solid hit, and though Marco stutter-stepped, he didn't slow his assault.

With rifles and Campanella's automatic weapon, the partisans found cover and returned fire with a hail of bullets. The assassins were out-manned, out-gunned, and in the open. This formula soon resulted in their total annihilation, and as fast as the firefight started, it was over.

As they made their way to the unmoving corpses, nervous laughter could be heard. The partisans had done their job and hopefully foiled the assassin's grand plan. As Campanella had told them, though, the leader of this pack of jackals was not among the fallen.

CHAPTER 8

Jones fled down the alley to his left and then took a quick right to head south down the next street. He began running toward the building the partisans had been using when he saw two people emerge from a rear door. It was Paulo and Berta. Neither noticed the Brit as he ran down the dark passageway in their direction.

Without slowing, the Englishman came rushing out of the shadows and slammed his pistol butt end onto Paulo's forehead. The boy crumpled as if lightning had struck him. Berta whirled around at the commotion, and when she did, she came face to face with the assassin's leader. Before she could react, he pressed his gun hard into her stomach and put his finger to his lips. Berta didn't move or speak. She was too scared.

Jones grabbed her arm and spun her in the direction of the Villa. He jammed the weapon's barrel in her back and gave her a not-so-gentle push. Whispering in her ear, he warned, "If you scream or call out in any way, I will pull this trigger. Now get moving!"

****

Once the partisans made sure the assassins were dead, they ran over to where Campanella lay. Being as careful as possible, they began removing the debris. It took them almost ten minutes to remove the wreckage, but Campanella surprised them all by sitting upright after they did. He was tousled and bleeding from several wounds, but for the most part, he appeared undamaged.

"Oh, thank the lord," Santos said as he made the sign of the cross. "What in the name of all that is holy happened? One minute, we see you sail off the balcony wrapped up with this brute," he said while nodding at Bruno's body, "and after that, the entire building explodes."

"I'm not sure, exactly. While searching Jones' room, I found the bomb. But before I could disable it, this fellow attacked me. We fought, and the next thing I knew, I was on the ground trying to catch my breath.

Then, just as I began to recover – BOOM! Luckily, I got my face and some of my body under Bruno before the heavy stuff hit me. That may have saved me."

Looking up at the now destroyed inn, the frazzled man added, "I remember at one point during our fight where we knocked the dresser over containing the bomb. I can only guess that we must have triggered the timer and made the thing go off."

"It's amazing you weren't killed, truly amazing," Santos offered.

Campanella nodded his agreement and asked, "What about Jones? I saw him coming down the street before I went over the railing. Did you get him?"

The partisans stared at one another in confusion before glancing at the four dead men on the road. A limp and groggy Paulo came stumbling toward the group at that moment. He wobbled side to side and finally fell to his knees beside Campanella. The boy held the back of his head, which was gooey with blood. He felt dizzy and was almost incoherent as he tried to relate what had happened.

"Wait, you're not making any sense. Who took Berta?" Salvatore demanded.

"I…I don't know for sure. All I remember is when the shooting stopped, Berta and I looked out the window and saw everyone standing over the dead assassins. We thought the fighting was over and left the building to see if you were alright. The next thing I know, I wake up with my head bleeding, and Berta is gone. I promised I wouldn't leave her, and I didn't – not really."

"Jones," Campanella said grimly.

CHAPTER 9

"I won't tell you again. If you don't speed up, I will hurt you. And believe me, the pain I have in mind will be exquisite," Jones assured Berta as he prodded his captive toward the Villa Rivalta.

After the two arrived, they continued up the winding drive until they came to the same spot where she, Paulo, and Campanella had stopped only a few days earlier. Jones shoved Berta through a natural entry in the shrubs lining the driveway, allowing them access to a pathway parallel to the driveway. They followed the path until they reached a side delivery door.

"Move," Jones snarled as he jabbed the gun in Berta's back again.

"Stop doing that; you're hurting me," the girl protested as she blazed a glare of hate at the man.

"Shut up and move," Jones barked as he pushed Berta toward the door. The room they entered was a large storage pantry. Shelves of all sizes lined three walls, with the fourth wall fronted by a massive butcher-block table.

A wicker chair sat in the far right-hand corner, and Jones thrust the girl into it. "Sit down and shut up," he growled.

A man holding a wooden crate walked through a door to the Englishman's left. He stopped mid-stride when he saw Jones, and the men stared at each other for a long moment. Berta was unsure what was happening. The man who had just entered stood tall, well over six feet. He had slicked back salt and pepper hair with a pencil-thin mustache and a small patch of hair below his lower lip, and his pants and white shirt looked expensive and freshly pressed. Berta felt he had an aristocratic air about him.

"What are you doing here?" the man asked in a refined but heavy German accent.

"Franz, everything is totally screwed. Didn't you hear the explosion?" Jones said.

"What do you mean, everything is screwed? And no, I heard no explosion. And who the hell is she?" the man shot back as he lay the box on the butcher block table.

"The whole damned thing blew up. Most of my guys were killed or buried in the rubble. And this is the face of a person staring at me the last few days from a building across from the San Marco. Someone I believe might provide some answers for us."

Berta's face drained of all color. The man who had just entered walked up to where she sat.

"Who are you?" he abruptly inquired.

"None of your business," Berta snapped, sounding brave and defiant.

Without warning, the interrogator slapped Berta hard across the face with his hand. It happened so fast that she didn't have time to react or protect herself. Berta let out a yelp as she brought her hand to her face. Her eyes began to water with the slap sending stars exploding through her vision.

"What is your name? And before you answer, please know that the next time I strike, it won't be with an open hand," the man ordered.

Berta started to cry but managed to squeeze out, "Berta."

"Berta? Fine. See how easy that was and much less painful. Wouldn't you agree? Now, why were you watching this man?" he raised his fist to emphasize the importance of her response.

Berta's mind raced as she tried to come up with something logical other than the truth. She sat for a moment until the man took a menacing step closer.

"Okay, please don't hurt me," she pleaded through choking gasps. "I was hiding in that rundown place and…well, I'm not supposed to be there. I only glanced out the window for a few seconds to ensure no one noticed me as I left. I didn't know this man saw me, or I would never have returned."

The man glowered at Jones, who just stared back expressionless. He regarded Berta again and asked, "Who else was with you?"

Berta thought about saying she had been alone, but Paulo was with her behind the building moments before Jones had taken her. She hesitated briefly and then said meekly, "My boyfriend. It's why I was there. My father found out about us and forbade us from being together. I ran away, and we've been hiding there ever since. We only came out because of a terrible explosion across the street."

"Well, you should have listened to your father. I'm afraid your decision to run away will be rather costly." He turned to Jones and said, "Take her down to the boat house; I'll be along after I gather a few things we will need."

"What about my men and the bomb? They're all gone. We're finished. The job is over," Jones begged.

"We are not finished, you blithering English buffoon. We can get more men, and as for the bomb, I have always had another plan in case you and your morons weren't successful."

Jones clearly took offense at this man's choice of words but offered nothing in rebuttal. He feared this man, being a true coward at heart, so he took out his anger on the girl. The Englishman grabbed Berta by the arm, jerking her to her feet. "Come on," he said as he turned and yanked her, "you and I are going to enjoy getting to know one another! Well, at least I am."

****

The partisans raced toward the only sensible direction they thought Jones would take Berta – the Villa Rivalta. Campanella and Paulo trailed behind as their injuries prevented them from keeping pace. Paulo remained dizzy from the blow to his head, and Campanella's right leg had suffered a nasty gash from a piece of flying metal from the explosion. He had torn part of his shirt and wrapped the wound, but the injury was painful. The two hobbled in pursuit, with Campanella limping badly but still half-carrying the boy.

The partisans took fifteen minutes to arrive at the foot of the Villa's driveway, with Salvatore leading the way. As he did his best to catch his breath, he said through gasps, "There's no telling where they have her, so we must be careful. Arturo, you and Marco go up the left-hand side of the Villa.

If you see her, don't attempt to rescue her alone. Send someone back, and we will devise a plan to get her together. If you don't see her, keep going until you get to the back of the Villa. The rest of us will make our way down the right-hand side. If we spot her along the way, I will send someone to get you. If not, we'll continue to the end of the building. Once in those positions, we can decide how to go inside from there."

After checking their weapons, both groups headed off in their appointed directions. Salvatore scampered up the driveway until he saw an opening in the shrubs and darted in. His team followed the path running along the hedge line. When they reached a walkway leading to the front entryway, Salvatore advised Alberto to wait there for Campanella and Paulo. Alberto nodded and squatted behind a large arborvitae bush with his gun ready.

With the others following, Salvatore crept along until he arrived at a site where they could see the doorway Berta and Jones had entered earlier. They peered in through the upper glass panes but saw nothing. Salvatore signaled Pietro to place himself opposite the door and to wait.

Salvatore, Santos, and Aldo continued to the back of the Villa. Once in position, they looked to their left and spotted Arturo and Marco at the other end of the estate. When Arturo noticed Salvatore, he raised a finger to his lips. He lifted his pointer and index fingers to his eyes before pointing down to a wooden structure he believed to be a boathouse by the water's edge.

Salvatore dipped his head in understanding and pointed toward himself and his father, up to his eyes, and back to the small building. He then pointed back to Arturo and motioned for his group to investigate the Villa via one of the several doors between their two positions at the back of the house.

Salvatore turned to Aldo and whispered, "Go back to where Pietro is waiting. I want the two of you to go in through the side door. Be on the alert for the others as you search the rooms. Santos and I will make our way down to the boathouse. Aldo nodded, and he was off. Salvatore checked his weapon once more, as did his father. The two men regarded each other, and Santos tenderly touched his son's shoulder. He winked, and they headed toward the boathouse.

CHAPTER 10

"What are you going to do with me," Berta asked Jones as they entered the boathouse. At first, the Brit didn't answer. He just gave the girl a shove and closed the door behind them.

Looking Berta up and down, Jones sighed and said, "Well, I'm afraid you were in the wrong place at the wrong time."

"But I don't know anything, so you can let me go. You'll never see me again, and I promise I won't say anything to anyone," Berta begged as she sidled back and as far away from the man as she could.

The boathouse was tiny, at most ten feet deep by fifteen feet wide. There was a window in the back wall with a closed shutter covering it. A small gate leading to a rear dock area was in one corner, farthest from where Berta entered. On the opposite side, there was a cot with a soiled mattress and pillow on top.

Shelves lined the walls, and there was all manner of seafaring gear and fishing equipment on them. There were gaffes, reels, rods, and hooks. Most were in disrepair or rusty from lack of care and use, but two rods and reels looked new. A machete hung on a hook above a long butcher-block table like the one in the Villa's pantry. On the table lay a giant meat cleaver. The young woman was already scared, but the sight of these killing tools caused her legs to almost collapse.

Jones gave Berta a lecherous, leering gaze. He stepped toward her and said, "Pity, someone as beautiful as you…"

The door opened behind them, and the German from the Villa walked in carrying two rubber-coated aprons, several knives, a pair of wading boots, and a rope. Berta's stomach lurched at the realization of what the items might be for, and the feeling she was about to vomit began to overtake her.

Jones grimaced as he, too, predicted what might happen. After a moment, his grimace turned to a smile. Turning back to Berta, he barked, "Take your clothes off."

This single phrase instantly quelled Berta's sickness. Now, a new sensation took over – defiance. "I don't think so," she snarled as she glanced at the cleaver.

Jones lifted the gun and pointed it at her. "One way or another, your clothes are coming off. It's your choice, either alive with you taking them off or dead, and I'll take great pleasure in doing it. And before you even think about it, don't get any ideas about going for that cleaver. I'll shoot you dead before you reach the table."

"Maybe, but I'm not taking my clothes off, so go ahead and shoot," Berta dared as she looked over at the gate leading to the dock.

Jones smiled again as he saw her intent. The lecherous Englishman exhaled in resignation and sat his gun on the shelf to his right. He unbuttoned his shirtsleeves and rolled them up. In contrived acceptance, he sighed again, "I knew we were going to have fun, and won't it be exciting to have an audience?"

The other man rolled his eyes as he walked past Berta and over to the butcher block table. He laid the items he brought from the Villa on the wooden surface. Berta inched away from the tall, imposing man, inching closer to the dock stairs. She was about to dash to the gate and flee when she noticed a lock and chain securing it.

Jones moved toward her, but Berta caught his advance and shuffled back, going into the corner of the boathouse until she could go no further. She let out a yelp when she banged against the wall at her back. The Englishman laughed out loud. It was a sinister burst of delight.

"You're a sick fuck, you know that don't you?" Mueller scoffed at Jones. Jones grinned ear to ear like the cat that ate the canary. The other man shook his head. He wanted no part of this extracurricular activity and walked over to the door. "I'll be back in fifteen minutes – be done."

"Better make it thirty. This one's a bit feisty, I'm afraid," Jones answered. As he pounced on Berta and tore at her clothes, the other man casually walked to the door and grabbed the handle.

"What the…" Mueller fumed under his breath. He turned, looked at Jones, and said, "You idiot! Someone is sneaking along the path to the boathouse. You've been followed."

At this point, the would-be rapist had managed to wrangle Berta onto the cot while madly groping at her dress, trying to pull it up above her waist. Berta had never been a frail woman. Her life on the vineyard saw to that, and her recent trials had honed her strength. She fought him with all her ability, and though Jones was shocked at her feisty show of resistance, he finally managed to pin her arms to her sides.

Once he had her in submission, he snapped his head around and shouted in confusion, "What? Franz, I swear, I kept an eye out, and no one followed me."

Well, explain that to the armed men heading toward us right now."

Jones looked down at Berta with malice and desire. After a moment, his lips stretched stiffly back, and he said through gritted teeth, "I'm going to stand up now. I will shoot you if you yell, scream for help, or try to escape. Do you believe me?" Berta jerkily nodded. "Smart girl," Jones jeered as he slid off the disheveled girl and ran to the door. The two men stared toward the Villa, and Jones asked, "What are you talking about? Where?"

"There," Mueller urged as he pointed toward a row of trees lining the walkway. Salvatore and Santos were only twenty meters away. Mueller pulled a gun from his waistband and cocked it. Jones reached down at his pants and patted around his waist for his weapon. He suddenly remembered setting the pistol down before he assaulted the girl. He turned to retrieve it, but the gun was no longer on the shelf.

"Looking for this?" Berta asked. She stood in the middle of the room with Jones' gun pointed at his head. The girl's eyes were ablaze with fire and determination, and though disheveled from Jones' attack, she still conveyed an intense purpose.

Jones looked at the girl and then the gun. "I doubt you even know how to use that thing," he ridiculed.

"Try me," Berta taunted. While bearing the weapon in her right hand, she took her left hand and repositioned her dress. "And you, Mr. Hot Shot, whoever you are, drop your gun," she added while nodding at Mueller.

The German turned toward her. "I think not," he said, and as he did, he pushed Jones aside and fired his weapon. Berta knew what was coming, and she was ready. She fired her gun simultaneously and kept shooting. Two of her bullets slammed into Mueller, and she turned toward Jones and emptied the cartridge until her finger found no resistance in the trigger, and the gun only clicked harmlessly.

Both men collapsed to the floor as if their bones had liquified. Mueller went down first as one of the slugs from Berta had hit him square in the chest and exploded in and through his heart, killing him instantly.

Jones wasn't as lucky. Berta gazed down at him as he lay on the floor. Blood was oozing out of three holes in his body. One of the bullets had slammed into his left shoulder, one in his stomach, and one an inch above his groin.

"You were right, after all. This was fun," Berta said sarcastically. And then she dropped to the floor.

Chapter 11

Before the shots from the boathouse had finished echoing, each partisan was moving toward it. When the last of their group had reached the building's entryway, Salvatore was already heading out with his daughter in his arms.

The other men made a path as Berta's father dashed up the walk toward the Villa. Marco stared down at Berta as they passed. With terrified eyes, the stocky man stifled back a gasp as he noticed the large crimson stain on the left side of her dress.

Alberto, stationed by the Villa's front door as instructed, had seen Campanella and Paulo as they hobbled up the drive. From his hiding spot, he signaled to them and beckoned them over. They heard shots as he began a quick rundown of the team's original plan to find Berta.

They sprinted to the front door and, with guns drawn, burst through. Not seeing any resistance, they crossed the room toward a set of double doors to their right. As they went through those doors, Salvatore came rushing through a set of swinging doors from the back of the same room. He was carrying Berta, who appeared unresponsive.

Salvatore rushed past the concerned men as quickly as he could and conveyed his daughter to an oversized couch in the middle of the main salon. With the group of partisans looking on, Berta's father took a knife from his belt and carefully cut away the part of the dress where the blood had spread in a wide, sopping swath.

Once this part of the material had been removed, he discovered a gaping bullet hole about an inch below her left rib cage. Though blood continued seeping from this wound, it didn't seem to warrant the excessive amounts of blood on the dress.

To Campanella, the injury suggested there may be an exit wound on her back producing the excessive liquid. Salvatore looked up and understood the American's gaze. He gently turned his daughter on her side and saw where the bullet had passed through her body and out her back. This part of her dress was even more drenched with blood than the front.

At that moment, Alberto came rushing in from a side room with towels, water, and a first-aid box. "Here, I found this in a hallway closet," Aldo's son said as he handed the box to Santos.

Inside the box, Santos found bandages, gauze, and tape. He took the wad of gauze and began to clean the wounds. When finished, he had Salvatore apply pressure with two of the smaller towels while he reached into his bag and pulled out a small container of Sulfanilamide.

Santos' son removed the towel from Berta's stomach, and Santos poured the white powder on the bullet hole there. His granddaughter moaned but did not awaken. After the men dressed both wounds with antibiotics and bandages, they covered her with a blanket Sonny found in an upstairs bedroom.

During the next half hour, Santos recounted the recent events, at least to the point where they discovered Berta on the floor with two dead men lying nearby. "Even with all our efforts to keep her out of harm's way, things happened as the Journal said they would," Salvatore acknowledged at the end of the telling.

"Yes, it appears the past can't be rewritten," Campanella said matter-of-factly.

Santos caught his tone and was about to comment when Aldo asked, "What do we do now? Jones and a man we don't know are dead in the boathouse. Someone is bound to come to look for them, so we can't stay here."

"No," Campanella said bluntly.

"But what about Berta? We can't move her," Santos said.

"Here's what we have to do," Campanella said through a moan of pain. "I'm going to use Jones' car to take Berta and Paulo to an American hospital here in Naples. We'll have Paulo's head tended to, and Berta put into the hospital so they can tend to her wounds. I'll explain my version of what happened to the authorities stationed there and hope that everything will be well."

"Your version? What version is that?" Salvatore questioned.

"The one where two men kidnapped Berta, for reasons I won't need to clarify, and how Paulo and I followed them. A fight ensued. The two men knocked Paulo unconscious with a blow to the head. As I continued the fight, Berta managed to get one of her assailant's guns and shot the two, but not before one of them shot her. Paulo and Berta will not only be cared for, but they will be heroes. We'll all head home after Berta recovers in a few weeks."

"Which brings up another point..." Pietro chimed in, "...because as you tell it, the war continues here in Italy for many months in the north. This begs the question of when we will leave and how we can get to our homes."

All eyes were now on Campanella, who shook his head and said, "Well, that can't be easily answered. First, I think we should get Berta and Paulo to the hospital. Once we know they are being taken care of, I will explain what comes next..."

The End.…